The Redemption

LEGACY OF THE KING'S PIRATES | Book One

M. L. TYNDALL

BARBOUR
PUBLISHING

Published by Barbour Publishing, Inc., P.O. Box 719, Uhrichsville, Ohio 44683, www.barbourbooks.com

Our mission is to publish and distribute inspirational products offering exceptional value and biblical encouragement to the masses.

 Member of the
Evangelical Christian
Publishers Association

Printed in the United States of America.
5 4 3 2 1

*I dedicate this book to the only Father I have ever known
and the greatest Father in all of eternity:
the Father of all Fathers, my Lord and King, Jesus Christ.*

ACKNOWLEDGMENTS

So many people deserve my thanks for their support in the completion of this novel. I send my love to my family and friends who have always been there for me through all the trials and transitions of my life. Special thanks to my daughter, Crystal, who shares my love of pirates and was the only one willing to go see the movie, *Pirates of the Caribbean*, with me thirteen times. To my son, Josh, who models for me the heart of a true hero, and my husband, George, who although finds my idiosyncrasies and obsessions a bit odd, has always stood by me with his love and encouragement. To my mother—thanks for your endless love and faith in me. I believe you were more excited than I was when I learned *The Redemption* would be published.

Many thanks to my editors, Kathy Ide and Susan Lohrer, who without their gentle instruction and guidance, I could not have completed this novel. To my agent, Greg Johnson, who took a chance on an unknown author, and to everyone on the Barbour Publishing team who believed in my story.

And special thanks to all you who are taking the time to read my novel. I pray you enjoy reading it as much as I did writing it and that it richly blesses you.

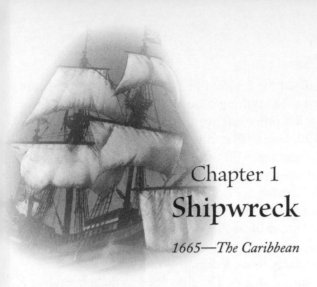

Chapter 1
Shipwreck

1665—The Caribbean

Charlisse bolted upright in bed, her heart pounding. The ship's tiny cabin rocked back and forth. She grabbed the bedpost to keep from being tossed onto the floor. Books flew off the shelves. A wooden chair tumbled clumsily across the room, crashing into the far wall. The ship bucked. She jolted off the bed, then plunged back onto the hard mattress, smashing her elbow into the bed frame. Pinching tremors shot up her arm. What was happening?

Charlisse tried to remember where she was. The merchant ship. She had bartered passage aboard from London to the Caribbean in search of her father—a man she had never met. He was the only real family she had left in the world. After spending the afternoon enjoying the fresh ocean breeze up on deck, she had come down to her cabin for a nap. In just a few short hours, the gentle rolling sea had transformed into a raging demon.

From outside the cabin, she heard a deafening roar—like a giant sea serpent—followed by a pounding on her window. She looked up at the round porthole. Fierce tentacles of water clawed to gain entrance.

Her body dove through the air. She landed on the wooden floor, the impact jarring her spine. A spike of pain shot up her back, piercing her head like the thrust of a sword. The cabin door swelled and groaned. Charlisse turned to see a flood of seawater burst through it and crash over her, propelling her toward the back of the room. Her head slammed against the wall. She gulped for breath and flung her arms through the turbulent water, searching for anything solid to cling to.

The ship lunged in the other direction, and the water gushed back out the door, carrying Charlisse with it. She grabbed the door frame. Her muscles strained to maintain a grip on the slippery wood, but the force of the torrent flung her out into the hallway.

She heard muffled screams up on deck. Fighting her way up the companionway stairs, she braced against the blasts of water that engulfed her. She popped her head above deck. A swirling tempest crashed over her, stealing her breath and crushing her against the railing. She opened her eyes, enduring the sting of saltwater, to see a deluge of rain so thick, it obscured everything into twisted, surreal shapes. The ship tilted to the left sending a cascade of water over its side. Broken riggings and sails, still attached to the mast, flung back and forth in the onslaught, threatening to knock overboard anyone who crossed their path. Black angry clouds growled and hurled bolts of lightning toward the ship.

This could not be the end of her life, not when she had finally gotten the courage to flee from the clutches of her depraved uncle. She could not die like this, not all alone, in a foreign sea, never knowing if she was ever loved—by anyone.

She saw the captain ahead of her as he clutched the quarterdeck railing. She wanted to reach him, to hear him say they would survive the storm, but dread of the tempest above gripped all her muscles and held them in place.

Another burst of wind and rain slapped her, stinging her face and shoving her down into the seawater that rose up the stairs. Drenched, she clambered upward again and stepped onto the slippery deck, deciding to brave the storm above rather than drown below in her cabin. A surging wave assaulted her and thrust her against the mainmast. She clung to it as the ship rolled to the right.

Sharp pebbles of rain pounded on her skin from every direction, carried on blasts of wind that pushed her one way and tugged her the other in a frenzied contest to dislodge her.

She made out the blurred shapes of men up in the top riggings, battling with the sails. Each heave of the ship tossed them about like paper dolls. Lightning cracked the stormy sky, illuminating them for a brief second before fading, leaving the disastrous scene imprinted on Charlisse's mind.

The black ocean swelled in a chaotic rage all around the ship, licking its lips in foamed peaks. An explosion of thunder blasted across the sky, shaking the ship from stem to stern. Each bone in Charlisse's body shuddered with the jolt.

The ship careened sharply to the right, riding on the swell of a monstrous wave. Her feet left the deck. Clutching the mast, she closed her eyes and clung to it with all her strength. The wood scraped her throbbing fingers as they slipped over the groaning pillar. Shouts echoed through the pounding rain, and she heard the stifled voice of Captain Hathaway in the distance. The ship righted itself, hovering in the air above the tempest, before it landed with a thud on the other side of the wave. Her feet pounded on the deck. The skin on her hands and arms burned raw with splinters from the mast.

She gasped and opened her eyes to see Captain Hathaway beside her. Fear etched the features of his old, weather-beaten face.

"Get below, Miss Bristol!" he shouted. " 'Tis not safe!"

No sooner had he spoken than the ship dove to the left. The captain disappeared into a blast of water that plunged over the deck. The flood punched Charlisse with the force of a cannon shot and muffled her scream, filling her mouth with the tangy taste of seawater.

She looked for the captain and was relieved to see him hanging on the side railing, shouting orders to the few crewmen who were still struggling to save the ship. One of the sailors scrambled up the ratlines, following his captain's orders. A wall of water struck him, tossing his body into the churning sea.

Charlisse closed her eyes. *We're all going to die.*

The roar of the storm suddenly dimmed. The tottering ship eased into a heaving roll. Charlisse popped her eyes open to see the waves no longer bursting over the deck. Wiping wet strands of tangled hair from her face, she glanced around the ship. She heard someone throwing up. Captain Hathaway bellowed orders that sent the remaining sailors scrambling across deck. *Is the storm over? Did we survive?* Charlisse dared not hope. Her eyes met the captain's. She smiled at him, hoping for reassurance, but he returned only a vacant stare before something drew his attention upward. His face took on a ghostly pallor.

Following his gaze, Charlisse saw a wall of black water towering over the ship. It pulled the sea from underneath them and rose like the wings of a dragon, white foam salivating on its forked tongue as it curled over the tiny vessel, ready to pounce. A fireball of terror stuck in her throat, preventing her from breathing. Trembling, she clutched the mast as tightly as she could.

The crew froze, staring at the monster. A few crossed themselves. The captain yelled, "Hold on!"

Then it hit.

The mountainous surge of water tossed Charlisse overboard and plunged her headfirst into the raging sea. Disoriented, she fought to find her bearings as she flailed in the cold, churning water. The salt stung her eyes, yet she saw nothing but darkness. Underneath the surface of the sea, the deafening sounds of the storm became a muted rhythm of swirling bubbles.

An eerie peacefulness engulfed her. Lured by its deception, she ceased struggling, wondering if it wasn't better to fade away into this serene underwater world. But then she remembered. She must find her father—to know if he loved her, wanted her. How could she die without ever knowing that at least one person in the world cared for her? A voice inside told her to hold on, not to give up yet. *God help me*, she prayed.

Her head popped above water. Instantly, chaos assailed her. Her lungs heaved for air between the waves that crashed over her head. The rolling tempest hurled her up and down. She felt nauseated. Her muscles ached. Seawater poured into her stomach. As the energy drained from her body, dread consumed her. She was going to sink to the bottom of the cold sea and die alone and unloved. No one would know what had happened to her, and no one would care.

Something hit her from behind. She turned to find a bulky slab of wood and grabbed it before it could drift away. With her last remaining strength, she crawled onto it and collapsed, breathless.

Lightning flashed, and she caught a glimpse of the ship several yards in the distance. It lay on its side, masts along with sails, sinking fast into the raging ocean. Several heads bobbed in the water. She heard periodic wails of the crew in between the howls of the storm.

She paddled in their direction, not wanting to die alone. But with every inch of progress, the storm tossed her farther away.

Tightening her grip on the wood, she felt helpless against the seething squall. Another large wave hit, carrying her upon its massive swell. From its crest, Charlisse saw the last remnant of the ship's white sails sink beneath the dark waters.

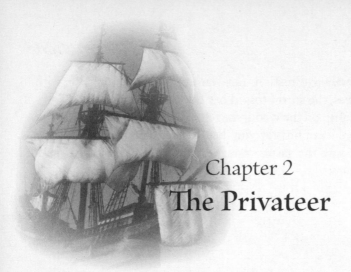

Chapter 2
The Privateer

Captain Edmund Merrick pressed the spyglass to his eye, steadying it against the rolling of the ship, and spotted a Spanish merchant vessel looming on the horizon. Sailing east from the port of Maracaibo on her way home to Spain, the ship undoubtedly held precious cargo. Unfortunately for her, she would never make it. He had hoped to find another ship today—one he had been tracking for months, but this Spanish conquest would surely bring enough treasure to satisfy the greedy appetites of his crew, as well as please the governor of Jamaica. Merrick had received a commission from Sir Thomas Moodyford in the name of King Charles II to "set upon by force of arms, and to take and apprehend upon the seas, or upon any river, or in any port or creek, the ships and goods of the king of Spain, or any of his subjects whatsoever."

Merrick smiled. He had gone from being a ruthless pirate one minute to being a soldier in His Majesty's service the next. He snapped the spyglass shut and barked orders to his crew. With additional sails hoisted and a slight course change to port, he knew the *Redemption* would overtake the slower trading ship. His crew strapped their pistols and cutlasses to leather belts and flung them over their shoulders and around their waists, in preparation for battle.

"They're signaling for a show of colors, Captain," the first mate shouted.

"Run up the Spanish flag," Merrick ordered, "but keep my ensign close at hand."

"Aye, aye, Captain."

"Prepare your weapons for battle, gentlemen." Merrick leaped down the quarterdeck stairs. "Clear the gun tackles and load the guns," he ordered the master gunner. "But don't run them out until my order."

Merrick scanned his raucous crew as they prepared for battle, salivating for the treasure that soon would be theirs. Never had he seen a more unsightly bunch of miscreants. Clothed in tattered, unmatched apparel "borrowed" from prior conquests, they strutted across the deck shouting obscenities toward their enemy. The stench of their unwashed bodies and foul breath wafted over Merrick as he stood before them. Despite their disorderly appearance, he knew if he didn't command their respect at all times, he would, one day, find a knife in his back.

"Take no life unless you have to," he commanded. "But make it quick and painless if you do. It's the treasure you're after."

He assigned ten men to remain above deck disguised as common fishermen and sent the rest scrambling down the main hatch, out of sight. Merrick slapped a large floppy hat over his blue bandanna and hid his pistols and cutlass under a long, black fishing coat. He hoped his trap would work. If need be, he could pursue and outrun the merchant vessel, but he much preferred a quick and easy target.

Standing on the main deck, Merrick leveled his spyglass on his prey as she came more sharply into view. Her crew sauntered about the deck, performing their duties, still unaware of the menace that was creeping up on her. A few more minutes and she would be within range of the *Redemption*'s cannons.

By his side stood Master Kent, his first mate, and Sloane, his quartermaster and old friend. Kent was the only pirate, other than Merrick, who had been graced with a formal education and who knew how to speak and dress in polite society. Merrick assumed the lad, who could be no more than nineteen or twenty, had been born to nobility, but Kent preferred to keep the details of his past to himself—a sentiment Merrick both understood and respected. Truth be told, the boy reminded Merrick of himself not ten years ago. Skilled in seamanship and able to command respect from the crew, Kent had earned his post as first mate.

The young lad glared at the merchant vessel, his eyes holding no fear, only an insatiable lust for blood and treasure that gave Merrick pause. He handed Kent the telescope, allowing him to peruse their enemy at close range. The boy stood near Merrick's height, a vigorous lad with curly brown hair and barely a whisker on his chin. His eyes twitched in excitement as he gazed on their victim. Giving the glass back to Merrick, he stood waiting for his command.

"Have the master gunner ready the gun crew," Merrick ordered, and the first mate spun on his heels and rushed down the companionway.

Merrick bowed his head and offered a quick prayer for the success of their mission and a minimal loss of life.

"I hope He heard ye," Sloane said.

"He always does, my friend." Merrick smiled. "But it's His will that will be done in the end."

Nodding at the quartermaster, he returned his gaze to the Spanish vessel. It was less than two hundred yards away, and the *Redemption* was flying down upon her, parting the calm sea with assurance.

Merrick slapped his hand on the railing and strutted across the deck. He ordered the gun crew to position a warning shot over the bow of the merchant ship, giving the Spaniards a chance to surrender without bloodshed. The master gunner ordered the crew to fire, and the shot let loose with a reverberating boom, shaking the ship to her keel and sending up a plume of gray smoke. It splashed, as intended, in the water on the starboard side of the merchant ship, and sent the crew of the Spanish vessel into a frenzied panic. Down came the red and white flag of Spain from the mainmast of the *Redemption*, and up went the Jolly Roger of Captain Edmund Merrick.

The remainder of the *Redemption*'s crew came up from under hatches, growling and shouting like a pack of hungry wolves bursting from a cage. The pirates on deck discarded their fishing garb and readied their weapons.

Would the vessel heave to and surrender? Or would she run? Merrick glared at the merchant ship through his spyglass as the distance between them lessened. Their intention soon became evident when they unfurled their sails, including topgallant and outer jib, and caught the wind in a billowing display of snowy canvas. Merrick cursed their captain under his breath. Why would he—outgunned, outnumbered, and heavier—choose a course of action that could only end in disaster?

Merrick shouted orders for his own sails to be spread with every inch of canvas to their yards. Upon catching the wind, the *Redemption* cut a clean white slice through the Caribbean waters in swift pursuit.

Time seemed to move in slow motion, heightening Merrick's senses. Every sound was magnified—the sea splashing against the hull, the jaunty snap of the wind in the sails, the shouts of excitement from the men readying themselves on deck, even his own breathing.

The larger merchant vessel could not outrun the pirate brigantine, and soon the ships sped side by side, not fifty yards between them. Captain Merrick fired a round toward their enemy that blasted through the midsection with a deafening roar, sending its yards and canvas crashing to the deck. Crippled, the Spanish vessel sat helpless in the water, awaiting her fate.

Merrick ordered Kent to furl top and main sails and ready the grappling hooks in preparation to board. The thrill of the impending combat sent a mixed shiver of excitement and tension through him. With the warm wind gusting through his long hair, his pistols strapped to his shoulder belt, and his cutlass in hand, he felt every bit the fierce warrior he used to be. No longer an outlaw pirate, he was now a privateer, commissioned by Britain, but, unbeknownst to most, he also had another agreement with the governor of Jamaica—to capture and bring to justice the most vicious pirates terrorizing the Caribbean. This arrangement appeased both Merrick's newfound faith in God and his hunger for freedom and adventure. The ship he'd been seeking as of late belonged to the first villain on the list—his ex-captain, a man whose cruelties had cost the lives of hundreds of innocent people.

As the pirate ship closed in, the desperate Spanish sailors fired off a volley of musket shot. The pirates scurried into position and returned fire. Kent approached Merrick. "Captain, shall I order the swivel guns to sweep their deck and put them in their place?" His face contorted in a mixture of rage and a thirst for blood that gave Merrick concern.

The captain shook his head. "That won't be necessary, Master Kent. The ship is plainly ours. There's no need for bloodshed." He eyed his first mate curiously. "See to it the men are ready with the grapnels. On my order, we'll spray musket shot to keep them at bay until we can heave the ships together."

Kent nodded, but his eyes burned with restrained defiance before he marched off to do his captain's bidding.

As the *Redemption* swept down upon its prey, the faces of the Spaniards contorted in terror. The pirates growled like animals, hurling obscenities in their direction. Yet the sailors stood their ground, rallied on by their courageous captain who stood on the foredeck, braying orders for them to take arms and position themselves for the inevitable boarding.

"FIRE!" Merrick bellowed. The air exploded with the crack of muskets and pistols and the thunderous shouts of the pirates as the *Redemption* came astern on the merchant vessel's starboard quarter. Smoke obscured Merrick's view and flooded his nose with the acrid sting of gunpowder.

Merrick ordered the throw of the grappling hooks. Six men swung the heavy irons above their heads before releasing them in unison. They flew through the air and landed with a clank, gouging the deck of the Spanish vessel. Then the lines were drawn taut, crashing the ships together with a thundering jolt.

The pirates drew their swords and scrambled over the bulwark of the captured merchant vessel like a flood of rats, with Merrick leading the way. Frantic shouting erupted, along with the clash of cutlasses, the blast of musket fire, and the agonizing screams of the injured. Yet the pirates continued their ruthless assault, fighting without rules of decency. Merrick had learned to accept their cruel form of battle, though his own skills had been sharpened under the expertise of the King's Navy where honor and decorum were highly esteemed.

The Spaniards fought with more tenacity than Merrick expected from common merchants, but they were clearly no match for such an unorthodox onslaught—in addition to being outnumbered five to one.

A loud shriek drew his attention behind him where he saw Kent in swordplay with a sailor who was on his knees, begging for mercy. The first mate raised his sword to strike the defenseless man.

Merrick charged over to stay his hand. "We do not kill uselessly!" he shouted, holding a fierce grip on Kent's wrist.

The first mate strained under his grasp. "But do we kill the useless?" Kent's hard look of disdain sent an icy shiver over Merrick. Releasing his hand with an angry toss, Merrick stood between the sailor and Kent. "No one is useless."

The first mate scowled, then shrugged his shoulders and strode away.

The Spanish captain called upon his men to stand down and the fighting ceased. Captain Merrick sheathed his sword, his breath coming in heavy gasps. His torn shirt revealed a bloody gash on his arm.

"Shanks, Royce, stay with me," Merrick ordered his men. "Jackson, get Brighton and see to the injured." Most of the pirates had already gone below deck to seek out the cargo. "The rest of you, search the ship and make sure there are no sailors hiding." Three of the men grabbed their pistols and headed down into the hold.

"Don't kill them!" Merrick shouted after them. "Bring them to me alive." With grunts of disappointment, the men disappeared below.

Merrick sauntered past the Spanish sailors, who had relinquished their weapons and were gathered in a small trembling group on the deck. He motioned their captain to step forward and spoke to him in fluent Castilian, informing him his crew would not be harmed. The man bowed, a wave of relief softening the fear that creased his face, and thanked Merrick for the assurance.

Masters in the art of pillage, the pirates scoured the ship as they searched for treasure in a much more orderly fashion than they did their fighting. The merchant sailors stood by watching as the thieves hoisted their precious cargo up from the hold and brought it on deck. Merrick realized why the merchant vessel's crew had been so bold as to attempt such a hopeless fight. The fortune stored below far exceeded his expectations: Spanish doubloons, pieces of eight, spices, silver, and pearls.

Yet Merrick cared nothing for the treasure—not since he had realized there was more to life than wealth. Turning his attentions to the wounded, he made sure they were attended to as quickly as possible. He searched for any of his own men in need of assistance, careful to avoid the slippery patches of blood splattered across the deck.

A solemn shape lay near the helm on the quarterdeck, a dark pool of blood staining the deck beneath him. Merrick's heart sank as he slowly turned the body over. It was Reeves, his bosun, a pistol shot through the head. The boy had been only fifteen. Merrick bowed his head and rubbed his eyes. Stomach convulsing, he said a prayer for the boy's family.

Chapter 3
Lost and Alone

The turbulent waves of the Caribbean Sea had subsided into a rhythmic swaying that lulled Charlisse into a much-needed sleep. Her knuckles, white from the intense grip she had maintained for hours, cramped as she loosened her hold on the bulky slab of wood. Nauseated, cold, and wet, not even the warm glow of the rising sun on her closed eyelids could dispel the gloom from her heart. She was afraid to open her eyes—afraid to find out she was all alone in the middle of a vast ocean. So she lay still, taking in the sounds and smells that told her what she feared was true.

Somehow she had survived the night. Was it good fortune, or the curse of a wrathful God? Her conscience determined it must be the latter since it would have been better to drown than to die slowly of thirst and exposure. Draped over the wood, too weary to move, she listened to the sounds around her—the lapping of the waves, the creaking of the wood beneath her, the distant chirping of birds. She sighed, giving in to the exhaustion and pain that consumed her body, and silently wished for death to come.

Wait a minute. Did I hear birds chirping? Sudden hope filled her. With great pain and exertion, she raised her head, scanned her surroundings, and discovered a speck of land in the distance to her left. It stood like an oasis in a desert, beckoning her. With renewed strength, she paddled toward it, using both hands and feet to move the slab of wood inch by inch across the blue expanse. After hours of struggle, aided by surf and waves, she finally crawled up on the shore and crumbled onto the sand.

She woke, disoriented, some time later and managed to sit up. Calm, crystal-blue waves caressed the shore and outlined ragged shapes in white foam on the glistening sand. Dark, fuming clouds retreated on the distant horizon, the only remnant of the terrible storm that had altered the course of her life so violently. It had done its damage, now was leaving, and seemed to be laughing at her on its departure.

She sat for quite a while, feeling numb. As the sun rose higher in the sky, the heat of its sharp rays jarred her from her state of shock. She tried to get up, but a wave of dizziness forced her back down to her knees. One more attempt, and she finally stood on wobbly legs.

Wreckage from the ship—a broken mast, pieces of a torn sail, a bucket—dotted the shore in both directions. Behind her the sand ended abruptly in a lush mass of tangled green, from which an orchestra of tropical birds performed. Each waft of the breeze carried upon it the sweet smell of flowers in bloom coupled with the earthy scent of moist vegetation.

Perhaps she was not alone. Maybe other survivors from the merchant ship had ended up on this island. With hopeful determination, she headed down the shoreline searching for any sign of human life, calling out greetings as she went. Her heart broke thinking that everyone else on the ship had perished, especially Captain Hathaway. He had been so caring and kind to her ever since she had first stepped aboard his merchant vessel, the *Calling*, in London. "Ye remind me o' my sweet daughter back home," he had said to her as they dined together one night. "And I'll not have any of the crew treating ye any different than as if ye were." He kept to his word. All of his sailors had behaved like gentlemen in her presence, and judging by their appearance, that had been no easy task. She had never known a man like Captain Hathaway—a man who had not wanted something from her other than friendship.

Hoping he had survived, she continued searching. The salt in her dress dried into a coarse grain that chafed her delicate skin, making every move forward an agonizing ordeal. As the afternoon progressed, the sand became a pile of sizzling pellets, and she had to keep to the water's edge to avoid burning her feet. Not accustomed to the hot, humid weather of the tropics, Charlisse stopped repeatedly to catch her breath and blot the perspiration from her brow with a torn piece of her dress. Yet she plodded onward through the endless sand and crashing waves for hours, stumbling over driftwood and seashells, only to find herself, after a long, tortuous afternoon, back on the very beach on which she had landed. Dropping to the sand, she burst into sobs. Hours passed and shadows slowly overtook the tiny island.

The half-moon scattered its light like shimmering diamonds across the black sea, illuminating clusters of tiny crabs that skittered to and fro over the sand. They approached Charlisse, but at the slightest move of her foot or a wave of her hand, they scurried off. She lay down in the sand and stared at the distant glowing orb, hoping the rhythmic sound of the waves would lull her to sleep, but restful slumber eluded her. Charlisse couldn't say whether it was the insects, the sand, or her thirst that kept her awake. Perhaps all three, plus the gnawing fear that she would soon be dead.

She had no fear of death itself—only the torturous journey she would have to endure before its peaceful repose overtook her. In the end, she would still be better off than if she had stayed in the comforts of London in her uncle's manor. She wondered what he would say if he knew she preferred starvation on a deserted island to living with him. She wished she had been there to see his face when he realized he no longer had her under his control.

Charlisse's thoughts drifted to happier memories of her youth when her mother had still been alive. She remembered the hours she'd passed in her mother's lap in front of a blazing fire, listening to story after story about her father. Her mother had described his character, his faithfulness and love, even his exploits at sea—which he had relayed to her during their courtship.

Charlisse would never forget the sparkle in her mother's eyes when she spoke of him, the laughter and the tears of joy that flowed down her sweet face.

In those cherished moments, Charlisse learned that her father was a merchant sailor, a captain, a man of good breeding and education. He couldn't be with them because he was working to provide a beautiful estate in the colonies for their family. Soon, her mother had told her, he would send for them. But three days after Charlisse turned eight, those dreams died and were buried along with her mother. No word ever came from her father. She was positive that if any letters had come, her uncle had destroyed them.

She smiled, envisioning what their first meeting would be like. His handsome face would light up at the sight of her, and he would fling his arms open wide. Charlisse would run into his strong embrace and sink against his chest. Tears of joy would stream down both their faces. Then he would tell her how he'd been searching for her for years, how he'd thought of nothing else, and how much he loved her—had always loved her. And she would finally be safe, be loved. And be home.

Behind her, strange scratching noises emanated from the forest. Curling into a ball, she hugged herself. Maybe it wouldn't be starvation that brought about her demise, but an attack by a ferocious animal or perhaps a poisonous snake, or maybe some giant sea creature would crawl up on shore and drag her back into the black ocean. She didn't want to die. Closing her eyes, she swallowed the burst of terror that rose to consume her. No. She must survive. Hugging herself more tightly, she strengthened her resolve and finally drifted off to sleep, dreaming of the father she never knew.

The squawking of a large bird with an odd pouch-shaped mouth startled Charlisse from her restless sleep. He stood less than ten feet from her, flapping his wings and making a hideous commotion. Apparently, he was as unhappy with her presence on the beach as she was at being there. She sat and waved her hands to scare him off, but he remained steadfast, staring at her with tiny black eyes. He pranced back and forth, like some vain courtier, stopping only to assail her with defiant shrieks. His resemblance to Milford, her cousin, brought a scowl to her lips. She had no more inclination to deal with this bird than she had with her pretentious relative. Rising precariously to her feet, she flapped her arms in the air, shouting at him until he waddled down the beach, scolding her as he went.

Her head pounded, her throat ached, and her legs and arms stung with small red bites. The sun was just rising over a calm, glassy sea. She licked her cracked lips at the sight of the saltwater, undrinkable though it was. She must find fresh water. Grabbing the empty bucket left from the ship's wreckage, she plunged into the tangled mass of green that bordered the beach.

Hours later, her feet throbbed, one of her toes bled, and red scratches covered her arms and face—scars from her battle against the vines and branches determined to guard their territory from all intruders. She defied them with a persistence brought on by excruciating thirst, plodding forward, her mind musing over the irony of her present circumstance compared to that of her past. Just three weeks before, she had left a life abundant in jewels, beautiful gowns, servants, food, and, yes, water.

Both the insects and shrubbery grew thicker with each step, and Charlisse felt as though she were being eaten alive. Would she ever emerge from this green nightmare? Or would she be sucked in and slowly devoured, leaving only a dry heap of bones for some unfortunate explorer to find? *Oh, God, help me find water.* Her prayer instantly reminded her of the last time she had called out to God, beneath the stormy waters of the sea, about to drown. Had He heard her then? She had survived, but for what purpose—only to die a more hideous death? No, perhaps she'd been spared so she could find her father. What was she saying? There was no God—at least none that cared about her.

She glanced around the forest, dabbing the perspiration on her forehead. The jungle teemed with life. Colorful birds chirped in a canopy of trees that reached for the sky like giant sentinels. A multitude of buzzing insects swarmed around her zipping in and out of the ferns and thick shrubs that held her captive.

Charlisse heard a familiar, bubbly sound. She turned in that direction and moved forward. *Could it be?* Thrusting branches aside, she emerged in a tiny clearing where a small creek, no wider than two feet, flowed from under a huge boulder and split a sparkling trail across the forest floor.

Dropping facedown, she brought handful after handful of the sweet nectar to her dry, parched mouth. Was there anything in the world that had ever tasted so wonderful? After splashing the cool water onto her face, she sat up refreshed, feeling the first glimmer of hope stir within her since she had landed on this wretched island.

The creek seemed to pour from within a huge boulder upstream, reminding her of a story she had heard from the Bible about people who were dying of thirst in a desert, and a man named Moses who prayed to God and struck a rock, from whence sprung a fountain of fresh water. She remembered her silent prayer from a few minutes ago but quickly shook it from her mind. *Pure coincidence.*

Charlisse dangled her sore feet in the invigorating water and splashed some of the precious liquid onto her skin and hair, trying to wash off the dirt and salt and soothe the itching insect bites. Her dress was filthy and torn, her petticoat in no better condition, and her long golden tresses— once the envy of London—were matted and encrusted with salt. But for now, her thirst was quenched, and that was all that mattered. She sat for hours, unwilling to leave her oasis, despite the rising heat and the increasing flood of insects.

The more she pondered her situation, the more fear squeezed her heart. She was alone on an uninhabited island in the middle of the Caribbean, with no reasonable chance of rescue. Charlisse Bristol, daughter of Lady Helena Bristol, granddaughter of Lord and Lady William Rochester of Hampstead, raised in the luxury of London nobility, yet for all her noble blood and courtly training, she had no idea how to survive on her own. Still, she felt no regret for leaving, and therefore resigned herself to accept whatever consequences fate had in store for her.

After filling the bucket, Charlisse struggled to her feet and plunged back into the tangled web of green, unwilling to give into her fears, unwilling to give up the hope that she would someday find her father.

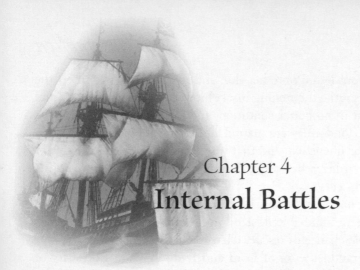

Chapter 4
Internal Battles

Exhausted, Merrick slumped into a chair in his cabin, allowing the ship's cook and doctor, Brighton, to patch up the sword wound on his arm. Oblivious to the pain, he was thankful to the Almighty that the wound was not deep. Others had not fared as well. He had lost one of his crew, and four Spaniards had died. The sight of blood and the smell of death lingered in his memory. It repulsed him.

Oh, how he had changed. There was a time, not long ago, when he had been as bloodthirsty a pirate as the rest of them. Death and torture were necessary means to an end, and that end was always the treasure and the power that came with it. *What was the value of a man's life, anyway?* he had once thought. Most were filled with pain and suffering. Why, he was actually doing them a favor by setting them free of the burden of living.

But now, he knew the value of a man's soul, made in the image of his Creator, and killing did not come easily for him, even for the sake of his country.

"Boy, we gave't to them Spaniard cockerels, eh, Cap'n?" Brighton exclaimed, wrapping the wound. "They sure were fooled by yer fishermen trick." After ripping the bandage with his teeth, he tied the final knot, causing Merrick to wince. "Sorry, Cap'n."

Merrick flexed his arm as Brighton packed his supplies into a canvas bag. "Thank you, Brighton. Did you see to the other wounded?"

"Aye, aye, Cap'n. Just like you said, them first, then you." As he left, Sloane entered with a tray of hot tea, followed closely by Master Kent.

The sounds coming from the deck told Merrick the pirates were already celebrating their victory. The first mate reeked of rum and blood.

"The loot is stored below, Captain, and the prisoners are in the hold," Kent announced. "What course should I set?"

Merrick glanced out the window and saw the flaming remains of the merchant vessel they had blasted with cannon fire after relieving it of all goods and people. "Turn her ten degrees to starboard, south by southwest. We'll find a nice little island for our new friends to inhabit." He gave a playful grin.

Kent returned his smile with an "Aye, aye, Captain" before rejoining the revelry upstairs.

Sloane set down the tray and poured the tea. "We made a good haul this time, Cap'n. Gold and silver worth more'n ten thousand pieces of eight, bushels of pearls from the Rio de la Hacha, not t' mention spices, coffee, gunpowder, and tobacco. The best loot I seen since Cap'n Morgan's raid on Gran Granada."

Merrick rose and walked to a mahogany armoire to get a clean shirt. He sighed heavily. "I grow weary of this meaningless hunt for treasure."

"Aye, I know ye's got a much bigger prey in mind these days, but ye's still got the crew to be thinkin' of," Sloane said. "How about a shot of rum with this tea, Cap'n?"

Merrick turned and gave a sly grin. "You know me well, my friend." He hesitated, and then indicated a small amount with his fingers. "Just a little."

The rum went down with a warmth that soothed every nerve in his body. It was a familiar and dangerous seduction, one he had fallen prey to on more than one occasion. But by the grace of God and the strength of his own will, he knew his limitations, so when Sloane offered him more, he politely declined.

"Ye've changed a lot, if I might say so," Sloane commented, "an' fer the better, says I."

"Really? I wonder." Merrick sat and laid his head back on the chair. "I used to be able to handle all this killing."

"And ye think it better to have no feelin's on it at all? To not let it bother ye? Now ye have a conscience, Cap'n, and that be a good thing, to be sure."

"Maybe, but it doesn't make my job easier."

"Would ye rather be the way ye were before? Not carin' who ye be killin'? Why, ye were as ruthless and devilish as the rest o' them blokes out there. Listen to them now, gettin' drunk and carryin' on like a bunch o' animals." Raucous laughter, loud boasting, and the crash of broken glass drifted down to the cabin. "And ye was a lot meaner, too, if I might say so."

Sloane sat on a nearby chest and took a swig of rum, then corked the bottle and laid it aside. He was a middle-aged man, short and thick and well muscled. He had been a sailor all his life and a pirate only recently. The years at sea had cracked his face like a worn piece of driftwood.

"Now that you're a godly man," he continued, "ye make a much better cap'n." He hesitated. "And friend, too, I might add."

Merrick smiled at his quartermaster. "You've been a good friend, too, Sloane." Rising, he put a match to the lantern swaying overhead. The flickering light dispelled the gathering dusk and cast drifting shadows across the wooden floorboards. "Well, at least the crew will be happy for a while when they get their portion of the loot." He gave a halfhearted smile.

"Aye, Cap'n, ye needn't be worryin' about them. Ye've well earned their respect, at least the lot o' them. Ye're as stern as needs be when the occasion calls fer it, and ye're fair to all. Ye ain't no coward, neither, and ye fight right alongside them. An' ye won them all a good amount of treasure." He swiped the sweat from his brow. "I don't hear much complainin' from them."

Merrick sipped his tea. "Maybe you're right. But you know as well as I, they can turn on you quicker than the strike of a snake." He walked over to peer out the window. "I wonder sometimes why I signed up to captain this crew of cutthroats." He chuckled. "I always have to keep one eye on them, one eye on the Spanish, and another eye open while I sleep should either of them sneak up on me." He turned and crossed his arms over his chest.

"Aye, Cap'n, ye wouldn't be havin' it any other way, and ye know it. What else would ye be doin'? Wearin' lace and prancin' around London, sword-playin' with royal brats and being at the whim of the earl?" Sloane lifted his eyebrows and got up to retrieve the tea tray.

"Your blatant soliloquy has sufficed to remind me why I am indeed on this ship." Merrick smirked. "In fact, why I am indeed anywhere but back in London with my father. Thank you. It does make me wonder what I will do when England is no longer unhappy with Spain."

"Well, that's most likely a ways off. And ye'll think o' somethin' when the time comes."

Merrick nodded. "For now, at least the plunder keeps me afloat until I can catch that worthless cutthroat and bring him to justice before he can slaughter any more innocent people."

"Aye, that it does. Don't worry, Cap'n, ye'll be crossin' paths with him soon." Sloane lifted the tray and headed toward the door. "Anything else I can get for ye?"

"No thanks, Sloane. I'm going to get some rest."

Merrick sprawled on his feather bed, hoping the exhaustion of the day would overcome the restless thoughts in his mind and pull him into a deep slumber. But visions of Reeves's pallid face lying in his own blood—a gaping hole in his head—would not escape him. Rising, he paced the cabin and grabbed the bottle of rum. He uncorked it and smelled the pungent aroma. Taking in a deep breath, he swirled the golden liquid around in the bottle.

"No!" he shouted, slamming it down on his desk. "Please, Lord, give me strength."

During the next three weeks, Charlisse traveled twice around the island's perimeter and found two different types of fruit—one, an egg-shaped fruit filled with sweet white pulp and the other, an oval fruit filled with tart flesh. Since she had not died after eating them for several days, she assumed they were not poisonous, although she began to think death would bring a welcome change. She gathered palm fronds and created a small bed up in a tree near the beach where she had arrived, high above the crabs and other crawling creatures. Other than her daily trips for water, she spent most of her time there.

She tore up her once-beautiful gown and used the bodice as a washrag, the sleeves to tie up her hair, and her skirt as a blanket at night when a chill overtook the island. Clothed in only her petticoat and undergarments, she had abandoned all modesty in the unlikelihood of ever seeing another human being. Even though she tried to maintain proper hygiene, an odor of perspiration and filth radiated from her body, and she sorely missed her toilette back home.

One afternoon, a fierce rainstorm passed through, stirring up the waves and flashing lightning across the darkened sky, bringing with it terrifying memories of the storm she had endured at sea. A loud rumble of thunder followed. It began low and then cracked open into a reverberating boom that shook the tiny island in a deafening blast. Charlisse imagined it was the angry shout of God, bellowing at her for all the wrongs she had committed. She shouted back at Him, shaking her fist in the air, no longer caring what His wrath would bring.

Aside from these occasional downpours, time passed in endless boredom. An agonizing loneliness invaded her soul. Her only companion was the bird who had woken her on her first morning here. He followed her almost everywhere she went, squawking at her. It seemed he was scolding her for some infraction she had committed. She named him Jack after one of the servants in her uncle's manor house who always griped about everything. The bird's attitude did not discourage her, however, from talking to him at great length about her life and how miserable she was, and how fitting it was that she should die alone on an island talking to a complaining bird.

Longing to know the love of a father—her father—was the hope that kept her going from day to day. But soon three weeks melted into four, then five, and time seemed to drag on into eternity. Charlisse felt as though the last remaining pieces of her mind were drifting out to sea with each morning tide. Each night, she had harrowing dreams. Memories of her past swirled together like one gigantic nightmare with no beginning or end. She decided she must be dying, and dying slowly, because her entire life appeared before her eyes, not in one big flash, but in jumbled chunks of mixed reflections, allowing her to agonize over every detail.

A bright light reflecting off the gold crucifix that hung around her uncle's neck shone in her eyes, waking her. He stared down at her, his baggy eyes filled with desire. Then his countenance changed, his smile transformed into a look of indignation. His angry voice yelled, "Your father is dead, you insubordinate child! And he is not coming back." His face grew red, his cold eyes flashing with fury. Then his voice softened into a snake's hiss. He grinned wickedly. "God is your father now, and He has put you in my charge." He leaned closer. She cringed in the dark.

Suddenly, the vision changed. She heard her mother crying, and she saw a young Charlisse running down the hall trying to find her. "Mother, Mother!" The hall grew longer with each stride. Charlisse couldn't reach her no matter how fast she ran. "Mother!" she screamed in desperation, but her mother's crying faded into the empty halls until it was gone, the sweet sound of her mother's voice snuffed out forever. The silence was deafening.

Charlisse sat up with a start. Forgetting where she was, she lost her balance and fell from her perch. Thankfully, a large branch below halted her fall. Bruised and scratched, she scrambled back into her makeshift bed. Darkness surrounded her along with the all-too-familiar sounds of the crashing surf. She lay back down and cried. *Oh, God, please rescue me from this place.*

Chapter 5
The Encounter

The morning trade winds carried fresh scents of the sea and the sweet spring tropics. Captain Merrick stood at the main deck railing, sipping his tea and thanking God for another day of glorious freedom roaming the crystalline Caribbean waters. He had found a small island in the shipping lanes, where his crew loaded the prisoners from the merchant vessel onto a longboat and rowed them ashore. It wouldn't be long before the Spaniards were rescued.

Merrick had seen enough death for a lifetime. He only hoped his mercy wouldn't weaken him in the eyes of his crew. So far, none of them had dared challenge him on anything of importance—partly from fear, he imagined, since it was obvious to all that his skill as a swordsman far surpassed their own.

His eyes scanned the horizon, looking for an uncharted group of islands he had once seen this way in passing. The *Redemption* needed to be careened, and he must find a safe place in which to do it, preferably a hidden harbor. Having the ship grounded and tipped to have its hull scraped of weeds and barnacles put the pirates in a precarious position should an enemy happen upon them. Nonetheless, it had to be done every few months or the wood would rot through, and the ship would lose considerable speed—a highly unfavorable condition in the trade of piracy.

The pirates were just beginning to lumber about the deck, where several of them had passed out during the festivities the night before. The few alert enough to climb the ratlines were assisting with the sailing of the ship. Most, however, would spend the day lying about in the sun, drinking more rum to ward off their pounding headaches.

The atmosphere aboard a pirate ship always amazed Merrick. Unlike His Majesty's Royal Navy, discipline and order were strongly lacking among a crew of pirates. The men took their shifts randomly, working out schedules among themselves. Although skirmishes broke out now and then, most of the pirates were able to resolve things on their own. Votes were taken on major decisions, including which ships to attack and which to leave lie, but in the heat of battle, Merrick was in supreme command.

He ran his ship a bit more ironhandedly than other pirate captains did. The articles he made his crew sign—which included the exact percentage each man would receive of the treasure captured—demanded stricter rules of decorum and propriety than normally seen among pirate crews. For instance, random and senseless killing was prohibited, as was the ravaging of innocent women found on any of the ships or ports they attacked. The pirates who chose to crew his ship were obligated to sign his articles. Although some did so begrudgingly, they still complied, most likely because Captain Merrick's skills in procuring vast amounts of treasure were well known throughout the Spanish Main.

Finally, he spotted the island he searched for. "Thirty degrees to starboard, Mr. Kent," Merrick ordered, looking for an easy inlet. The first mate ordered the helmsman as directed, and the sails shifted in the wind with a billowing snap.

Sloane came up beside him. "That be the island ye were thinkin' of, Cap'n?"

Merrick nodded, folding up his telescope. "Yes, I think it'll do quite nicely." He walked down the steps, Sloane by his side. "Wake the men, and get the ropes ready. We're going ashore." He smiled at his friend. "We could all use some rest on dry land, eh?"

"Aye, aye, Cap'n." Sloane took off to do his commander's bidding.

Merrick gazed at the emerald green oasis coming into view. As beautiful and enticing as it appeared, a sense of foreboding overcame him—a feeling he had only had once before, when he had stumbled, drunk and half dead, into a small church in Port Royal. His life changed dramatically for the better after that event. What did the Lord have planned for him on this tiny island?

"Stop your squawking!" Charlisse screamed, bolting upright in her make-shift bed ten feet above the jungle floor. A wave of dizziness flooded her. "That stupid, indignant bird." She plopped back down and threw what was left of her filthy gown over her head. "What is he yelling about now?"

With her energy depleted and no more edible fruit on the island, she remained in her tree, making only occasional trips for water. Her limbs felt like anchors, and it took every ounce of strength to lift them. When she did, her head pounded and her breath came in short gasps. The sweltering heat of the tropics consumed her, burning away, bit by bit, her will to go on.

Each night she prayed for death to come, and each morning, as the sun's brilliant rays stabbed her eyes, she cursed God for prolonging the agony of her life. She no longer had the energy to even swat the insects away, and the torment of their bites and stings, and the incessant itching, was even worse than the burning of her empty stomach. Her hope of being rescued and finding her father had been consumed by weeks of suffering and loneliness until she'd forgotten what it felt like to hope for anything, save an end to her misery.

Now, just when she thought her existence could deteriorate no further, Jack was at the foot of her tree, flapping his wings and shrieking, demanding her attention for reasons beyond her understanding.

When it became apparent he would not allow her to die in peace, she decided to make a trip to the creek for some water to quench the burning thirst in her throat. Whether or not she had enough energy left to make the journey, she didn't know, and didn't care.

Holding onto a nearby vine, she tried to jump down to the branch below, but her head grew light, her knees grew weak, and the forest whirled around her in blurred green shades. The vine broke, and she fell, missing the branch, and landed on another one farther down. Cursing, she tried to right herself, but her foot slipped again, and she toppled to the ground, twisting her ankle with the impact of the landing. A shard of pain shot up her leg.

Jack squawked off toward the ocean, ruffling his feathers. Ignoring him, she grabbed her bucket and limped down the now-familiar jungle trail.

An hour later, she emerged from the green thicket with half a bucket of water and several fresh scrapes on her arms and legs. Mechanically, she put one foot in front of the other, favoring the injured ankle, which was now noticeably swollen. She wondered if she had already died and this was her own personal hell. Was she destined to wander about on this desolate speck of perdition for all eternity, enduring scorching temperatures that never cooled, swarms of bloodthirsty insects that never relented, and a hunger and thirst that were never satisfied? *What did I do to deserve this?*

As she approached her tree, Jack screeched—this time it was a frightful scream that chilled her to the bone. Upon coming into view of the shoreline, she saw two men, unshaven, dirty, and armed with pistols and cutlasses. She instantly dove under the cover of the jungle foliage, her heart beating wildly. She had never expected to see another human being, and the shock of it sent her emotions whirling. Was it possible she could be rescued? Could God have taken pity on her after all? As she watched, one of the men held Jack's beak while the other twisted the poor bird's neck. Jack went limp.

Charlisse dropped to the ground, tipping the bucket and spilling the precious liquid. She put her hands to her mouth to keep from screaming and crouched there, unable to move.

One of them swung poor Jack over his shoulder, and they both laughed as they headed up the beach toward an outcropping.

Even after they walked out of sight, Charlisse remained fixed to her spot, unable to move, terrified and nauseated. Several minutes passed as the sounds of her world returned to normal—the lapping waves, the chirping of the myriad colorful birds, the buzzing of insects. But there was no Jack. Those gruesome men had killed him.

Wiping the beads of perspiration from her forehead, she tried to think. The hope that had sprouted within her only moments ago when she first spotted the men now shriveled and died. Where had they come from? How many were there? Did they have a ship, or were they stranded here like she was? A sliver of smoke ascended from beyond the small peninsula. Their camp was close—close enough that, she decided, she could sneak over and take a peek. She climbed back into her tree and waited for nightfall.

The rest of the day dragged on endlessly as the temperature soared higher in her vermin-infested bed. She tried to sleep, but her nerves were strung tight. Sounds of male laughter and occasional musket shots pierced the noises of the jungle.

Finally, the sun touched the western horizon, taking with it its blistering heat. A slight breeze fluttered the leaves. It would be dark soon. Charlisse arose, throat parched, wishing she had not spilled the water from her bucket.

When complete darkness had overtaken the island, she climbed down from her tree, making sure her grip on each branch was secure before moving to the next. Her ankle throbbed in time with the pounding of her heart. At the bottom, she held her hands out in front of her in the darkness and took a few tentative steps. As her eyes adjusted to the night, she quickened her pace, wondering from which direction she should approach the camp. She stubbed her toe against a rock, tripped, and let out a loud groan, hands flying to her mouth. Had they heard her? Fortunately, the ocean waves had picked up in ferocity, and their crashing on the shore drowned out any other sounds, even the humming of the insects. But a full moon was also rising, illuminating the landscape, forcing Charlisse to stick to dense forest and avoid open spaces.

She had never ventured out much after dark, due mostly to her fears—fear of the unknown, fear of the unseen, fear of vicious night creatures conjured in her imagination. But tonight the vicious night creatures were real, and she was heading straight toward them.

As she neared the men's camp, the noise of revelry grew—laughter, curses, shouts, the crackle of a huge fire. A pistol shot thundered through the night sky. Charlisse jumped. Wavering in her resolve, she stood motionless. Perhaps it would be better to retreat quietly and die alone in her tree. These men did not sound friendly. Yet curiosity drove her forward, along with a resurging hope that somehow she might be delivered from this hellish island.

Crouching behind a bush, she made out the shapes of men sitting on the beach. She crawled as close as she dared to the edge of the jungle, her heart pounding so furiously, she feared it would betray her presence. Even in the cool night air, perspiration moistened her body, pulling her petticoat in a tight embrace. Something crawled onto her hand. She shook it off without making a sound. Had she become so accustomed to the heat and monstrous insects that they no longer bothered her?

So many men! Forty at least. But were there others she could not see? Perhaps they were skulking about the jungle behind her. Turning her head, she listened for any unusual movement before returning her attention to the camp. The men sprawled around the fire, passing jugs back and forth while chomping on some kind of meat.

Food. The smell of it was intoxicating! Her mouth watered, and she wondered where her body found the moisture. She shook uncontrollably, whether from hunger or fear, she didn't know.

Some of the men stood and pushed each other in heated arguments. Others staggered around in the sand, cursing. The massive, dark shape of a grounded ship loomed offshore, tipped in the shallow water and tied with ropes to sturdy trees that lined the beach. The ship was a welcome sight, but from the looks of her crew, it might as well be full of holes for all the good it would do Charlisse.

Several minutes passed. As she watched the men, she realized what they were. Many a story had made its way back to England about the bands of sea-roving thieves that haunted these waters—violent, depraved ruffians who attacked ships without provocation and ravished innocent women. They were pirates.

Charlisse decided to return to her tree, better to die a painful death alone than at the hands of these savages. She turned to leave, but the smell of roasting meat drew her back, giving her hunger more strength than her fears.

The laughter and shouting soon died as the pirates, overcome with rum, began to pass out in the sand. If she waited long enough, she might be able to enter their camp unnoticed. Cowering behind the bushes, not ten yards from the fire, she waited for the remaining men to drive themselves into an unconscious stupor.

Finally the camp was silent. Yet she did not move. Arrested by terror, she remained in place, her stomach cramping in ravenous expectation. The crackling of the fire subsided. The flames reduced to glowing embers, casting ghostly shadows on the tree trunks that surrounded the camp. All she heard was the splashing and churning of waves as they climbed onto shore, spewing their moonlit foam as far as they could before retreating.

From her hidden shelter, she looked down and selected a round stone the size of her palm. She held it in her hand, assessing its weight, then tested her ankle for a possible flight. Standing, she cast the stone into the middle of the camp and waited, breathless, ready to flee should the pirates awake. No one stirred.

Nauseated and dizzy, she crept from her hiding place. Her legs shaking, she moved forward, keeping a watchful eye on everything around her. Each noise seemed amplified, especially her footsteps—sounding more like an elephant stomping over loose shale, than a thin, frightened girl creeping across the sand. Still, no one stirred.

As she came closer, she heard the men snoring and grunting. She stood in the midst of them, her eyes fixated on one thing—the black pot that sat near the fire. She stepped cautiously over the sleeping forms, careful not to touch any part of them.

A loud thump and a groan sounded from her right. She froze, barely breathing, then slowly turned toward the noise. A jug of rum lay on its side, gulping its contents onto the sand next to the twitching form of a burly pirate muttering in his sleep. She closed her eyes, fighting a wave of dizziness, and stood still for a minute. Her mind engaged in an intense debate with her stomach whether to turn and run as fast as she could, or to keep going and satisfy the needs of her flesh. Her stomach won, and she continued onward.

When she came to the fire, she stooped and reached inside the black kettle. Something rustled behind her. Fingers poised over the chunk of meat in the still-warm pot, she froze. Waited. Heard nothing but the snoring pirates and the crashing surf. Gingerly, she closed her hand around the food.

"Well, well," a deep, sardonic voice said, "do we have a little thief in our midst?"

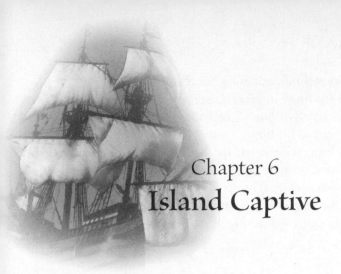

Chapter 6
Island Captive

Charlisse looked up into the piercing, dark gaze of the most fearsomely handsome man she had ever seen. He towered over her, the breadth of his shoulders hinting at a powerful chest and arms hidden beneath his baggy white shirt. He wore dark breeches tucked into black boots that climbed to his knees. Two leather belts, one strapped to his shoulder and the other around his waist, held pistols, one large knife, and a cutlass. A stormy blue scarf covered the top of his head, under which a mass of jet-black hair fell in disarray to his shoulders. His lips parted in a crooked and playful smile as his penetrating stare dove deep into her soul. The warm chunk of meat slid from Charlisse's shaking hand and landed in the sand by the stranger's feet.

Merrick had noticed the girl's presence as soon as she entered the camp. With his head lying on a fallen log, he'd watched her from under his hat. She looked harmless enough, but his curiosity piqued on two accounts—where on God's green earth could she have come from, and why would any woman take such a risk? As she crept toward the pot of meat near the fire, he realized she was after the food, and he decided to have a bit of fun with her.

Now she stood shaking before him, a ragged, pathetic thing covered with filth and bug bites. Her hair was a tangled mess intertwined with twigs, grass, and dirt. Her feet were bare and bleeding, and she wore the remnants of a white petticoat, now soiled and torn. Slowly she raised her face to his, the moonlight illuminating her features.

Merrick lifted his brow in pleasant surprise. "Alas, what rare beauty hides beneath this ragged disguise?" he quoted from a poem he had read recently. A smile touched his lips.

She stared at him, wide-eyed, for a second before narrowing her glance. In a quick burst of energy that belied her condition, she dashed off toward the jungle. Merrick caught up to her in seconds and clamped his arm around her waist. She struggled in his grasp like a wild animal. Then suddenly, her body sagged against his.

Charlisse heard male voices—at first faint and muffled, then growing stronger, then fading away. An irritating buzzing rang in her head, and a pulsating heat enveloped her. She felt as if she were being roasted alive.

Something cool touched her forehead.

"Wonder where she came from, Cap'n?" A gruff voice said. The coolness migrated to her neck. "Pretty young thing. Looks like she's been here awhile, poor girl."

Charlisse tried to open her eyes, but they felt as though they had been pasted shut. She managed to pry her lids apart and was confronted by a vicious-looking man with long brown hair, an earring, and a patch over one eye. Startled, she gasped and struggled to sit up.

"Whoa, little one." Strong hands forced her back down. "I think she's comin' to, Cap'n."

Charlisse rubbed her aching head. Above, palm fronds fluttered like feathers in the breeze, providing shade from the searing sun that sat high upon its throne in the cerulean sky. She heard sounds of the surf and the chirping of birds, but it all seemed like a hazy dream. A man knelt beside her. She remembered those dark, intriguing eyes from the night before. *Was it last night? How long have I been unconscious?*

"Can you eat?" he asked gently.

"What?" Charlisse tried again to get up.

He propped blankets behind her and nudged her back down. "You have a fever, miss." Turning around, he called for someone to bring soup.

Everything spun. She glanced through her lashes at the man beside her. A striking man with a firm jaw and eyes the color of ebony. A brace of pistols crossed his chest and a cutlass hung at his side.

The man with the eye patch laid his hand on her forehead. "She be in the thick of it, Cap'n, but I don't think it'll kill 'er."

"This is Brighton, our ship's doctor," the dark-haired man reassured her, "and I'm Captain Merrick."

The soup arrived, carried by a short, stout man with shaggy gray hair that sprouted from his head and chin. He smiled, revealing two gaping holes on his bottom row of teeth, and handed the bowl to Brighton.

Charlisse gazed at the three filthy-looking brutes who attended her and knew her situation was extremely perilous, no matter how courteously they behaved at the moment. Visions of Jack flung over the pirate's shoulder, limp and quiet, passed through her mind. She shuddered. Closing her eyes, she wished for death and whispered, "Pirates."

One of them chuckled at her declaration, and suddenly strong arms supported her back.

"Try to eat something," a deep voice said.

The broth smelled delicious. The bowl touched her lips, and she took a sip, allowing the warm liquid to slide down her parched throat. Another sip and she forced her eyes open. The captain crouched only inches away, supporting her back. His warm, musky scent drifted around her. She felt his moist breath on her skin.

"Jus' a wee bit more, miss," the doctor said, tipping the bowl.

After gulping down her last swallow, Charlisse felt strong arms lay her back down. She looked up into the captain's deep, dark eyes. He was saying something about sleeping and getting well and that she was safe, but she couldn't quite make it all out. She was sure she must be dreaming anyway.

Images like the scattered pieces of an incomplete puzzle drifted through her mind—the bright stars of the night sky, the cool ocean breezes, someone covering her, the heat of the day, the scorching sun flickering in her eyes through the palm fronds overhead, the sound of laughter, shouting, a bird squawking.

Brief memories of being fed more soup, of male voices around her, and muscular arms supporting her, flickered through her thoughts. One minute she burned up with fever, trails of perspiration trickling down her face and neck, the next minute she woke, shivering uncontrollably.

Sometimes her mind drifted from her present agony, venturing to a dark place where painful memories lurked, waiting to torment her. But she did not allow them dominion over her for long. She clawed her way back to semiconsciousness, preferring her present suffering to the agony of being trapped forever in her past.

Captain Merrick supervised the careening of the ship, doing his best to speed up the process. His men toiled, bare-chested and sweating in the blistering sun, scraping and burning the weeds and barnacles that had deposited themselves on the *Redemption*'s keel. They were nearly done and were now patching places where the wood had begun to rot.

"Prepare the pitch, Jackson," he commanded.

"Yes, sir," the bulky man's deep voice resounded as he marched off to obey his captain's orders. Jackson, the ship's master gunner, stood a head above Merrick, his black skin glistening with sweat in the blazing sun. His shaved head resembled a cannon ball, except for the three gleaming, gold rings that dangled from one ear. Merrick had rescued him from slavery aboard a Spanish merchant ship a year ago and offered him his freedom and a pirate's life.

Once the ship was ready, Merrick would put the girl on board, where he would have a better chance of protecting her. The woman added an unwanted responsibility to his already arduous tasks as captain. He saw the way the men looked at her, despite her disheveled and sickly appearance. He knew that with a little rum and an opportunity, they wouldn't think twice about taking advantage of a young, sick girl who could not defend herself, even though they had signed Merrick's articles to the contrary.

The girl's fever had broken early that morning, and she slept peacefully now. She had been anything but peaceful during the past few days. At the height of her fever, she had screamed out in anger, pleading for help, terror distorting her comely features.

Something terrible had happened to this girl. What, he could not imagine, nor how she came to be alone on this island. One thing was certain, a young, fragile thing like her did not belong in the middle of the Caribbean, especially not with a band of ruffian pirates. He must take her to the nearest civilized town, away from his men—and away from him.

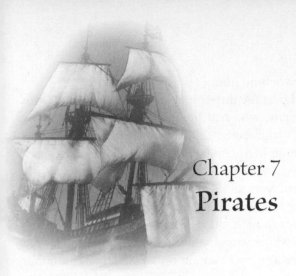

Chapter 7
Pirates

Charlisse regained consciousness long before she opened her eyes. Lying motionless, she listened as she tried to piece together the events up until now. As her memory returned, so did her fear, striking like a sharp knife in her heart. Shouts, curses, and the crackle of a fire filtered to her ears, and she knew she had not been dreaming. She had been captured by pirates.

Opening her eyes to tiny slits, she peeked through thick lashes to see men moving in the distance. Another stood about five yards away, with his back to her. She rose to her elbows, straining her aching muscles. Her world tilted slightly. None of the pirates looked her way. Their ship lingered just offshore, tipped on its side, tied to several trees by thick ropes strung from its mast and hull.

Charlisse realized this might be her best chance to escape—before anyone knew she was awake. She could dash into the forest, and by the time they realized she was gone, maybe they wouldn't have the energy or desire to find her.

She struggled to sit up, but her head pounded, and her arms shook beneath her. Collapsing down onto the blanket, she huffed. The nearest pirate turned and grinned, scratching his gray beard. She recognized him as the man who'd brought her the soup. "Cap'n!" he yelled.

Several of the men turned her way and gawked. A tall man in a billowing white shirt—the captain—headed toward her.

"I take it you're feeling better?" Merrick raised a brow and knelt beside her. The doctor approached behind him.

Charlisse's gaze drifted over the three pirates: the doctor, the one with the eye patch; the older pirate, who had brought her the soup; and the captain, who, though still a frightening sight, wore clean, stylish clothes and carried himself with the air of a gentleman, quite in contrast to his two friends. His bold perusal frayed her already tattered nerves. Nonetheless, she determined to return his stare with all the confidence she could muster.

"I demand you let me go at once," she said with a raw, cracked voice that left her intended impact somewhat lacking in authority.

Merrick smiled. "And where would you be going, young miss?" He waved his hand at the lush scenery. "You are on an island, and a rather small one at that."

Charlisse blew out a sigh. "I assure you, sir, that fact has not escaped my attention."

The pirates exchanged chuckles.

"Am I free to go," she asked, "or am I your prisoner?" Charlisse looked at the captain, trying to keep her gaze steady and not allow the cringing fear that was rising within her to surface.

"May I remind you, miss"—the captain's mouth curved in a faint smile—" 'tis you who wandered into our camp, not the other way around."

"What do you intend to do with me?" she whispered, starting to tremble.

"Don't worry. We mean you no harm," the captain said, his voice mellow and reassuring.

She didn't believe him, not for a moment.

"I'll go get ye some more soup," the older pirate announced, getting up.

Brighton touched her forehead. "Fever's gone, Cap'n. She just be needin' rest now."

Overcome by familiar feelings of helplessness, tears welled behind Charlisse's eyes. She forced them back with effort gained from years of practice, far back into a deep, dark place—a locked room reserved for all her unshed tears.

Noises behind the captain caught her attention. A small group of pirates approached, headed by a young man wearing taffeta breeches, silk stockings, and a rich crimson damask waistcoat. His elegant apparel and cultivated demeanor seemed ill-suited for the company he kept. A grotesque and filthy band of men sauntered behind him, leering at her as they drew near. Charlisse's heart grew faint at the sight of them.

"Captain, aren't you going to introduce us to the lady?" the leader asked, flashing dark eyes and an icy smile.

"Sleep," the captain told her curtly. "We'll talk later." He stood to intercept the advancing men, saying something to them she could not hear. With grunts and curses, the band of rogues scurried away, but their elegant leader continued to argue with Merrick. Finally, he, too, turned and stomped away.

Charlisse wondered why the captain had kept his crew from her. Perhaps he was waiting for her full recovery—or maybe he intended her for himself. She allowed for no other possibilities, for that would be a fool's optimism, and she was not a fool.

The gray-haired pirate returned with food, and Charlisse ate as much as her shrunken stomach could tolerate. For the first time in many days, the gnawing ache of hunger ceased. She knew her strength would soon return. When it did, she would formulate a plan of escape.

The pirate captain avoided Charlisse for the rest of that day. She spent her time resting as much as she could and eating whatever the man—whose name, she discovered, was Sloane—offered her. By midday of the following day, she felt much better, her strength almost completely restored. But her fear had not subsided. In fact it had only intensified as her peril became clearer.

Still clothed in a ragged petticoat, she became increasingly uneasy and self-conscious at the bawdy looks shot her way from the pirate camp not more than ten yards from where she lay. As the work on the ship neared completion, the large brigantine was brought upright and anchored off-shore, and without anything further to do, the pirates sauntered aimlessly about camp and spent most of their time drinking rum.

Charlisse had no idea what her course of action should be—no brilliant escape plan had formed in her mind. Sloane, who had apparently been assigned the troublesome duty of guarding and tending her, was as amiable as she supposed any pirate could be. Yet she became increasingly anxious as time passed, wishing that fate would simply proceed with whatever hideous plan it had devised for her.

The glaring sun aimed its golden rays between the gaps of swaying palm fronds above her, casting patches of light that danced across her petticoat. Momentarily mesmerized by their exotic ballet, Charlisse stared at them, unable to think clearly. She looked at the pirates that milled about the camp. A few glanced her way. Averting her eyes, she gazed at the soothing, familiar sight of the turquoise waves that caressed the tawny shore, hoping to find solace there.

She felt a fleeting spark of hope—one she dared not cling to—brought on by the surprising civility of the captain. All too often, however, she had discovered kindness was only a mask under which people hid selfish, evil motives. How could that not be true in this case, with a man who made piracy his profession?

She felt his piercing stare upon her even before she looked up, and when she did, her gaze locked with his. Even though he stood on the other side of camp, she felt as if he were reading her every thought. Another pirate called him and he turned away, leaving Charlisse flustered. Was it only fear or something else that caused this whirlwind of emotions within her?

She tried to get up, but her limbs shook. After several seconds of intense straining, she managed to balance on wobbly legs. It felt good to be on her feet again—to regain some small measure of control. All eyes shifted in her direction, and Sloane appeared instantly at her side.

"Where be ye goin', miss?" he asked.

"What does it matter?" she snapped. "I can't escape you and your fiendish friends." She slapped sand from her petticoat and glared at Sloane, who stood, silently regarding her. A breeze picked up, fluttering through her hair. The spicy sting of rain filled her nostrils even though the sky was clear. She sighed, giving him her best pleading look. "I need to take a short walk."

"It be best if ye stay close to the cap'n, miss."

"Really? Why is that?"

Sloane darted an apprehensive look toward the camp. "I don't mean to be worryin' ye none, miss, but some of the other men ain't as chivalrous as the cap'n, if ye know what I mean."

"Chivalrous, you say?" She smirked, glancing at the captain who was again glaring at her from across the camp. She held her hand out to

Sloane. "Might you escort me to the water's edge, sir?"

Sloane chuckled. "Not too many ladies have called me *sir* before." He hesitated, grinning at her, his face reddening. After glancing back at Merrick—who nodded—Sloane offered her his arm.

The sparkling water was an artistic blend of turquoise and jade green. Its waves glittered in the sunlight like precious jewels before disappearing on the shore, dissipating into a million shimmering pieces of white crystal. Palm fronds danced gleefully in the wind, rejoicing in the magnificent view nature had given them.

Charlisse dipped a foot into the warm saltwater. A myriad of colorful fish darted to and fro among the coral reefs, and she watched them with the curiosity of a child seeing something extraordinary for the first time. Envying their carefree life, she wished more than anything that she could transform into one and swim away. . .away from the pirates, away from her life, away from her past.

She waded out to her knees, holding up her petticoat, and splashed the warm saltwater onto her arms and face. With her eyes closed and the warmth of the sun and waves massaging her tense muscles, she dreamed she was happy and safe—if only for a moment. But the sounds of the pirate camp broke her trance, and she knew that happiness was only a fleeting dream, not something to ever be realized, at least not by her.

The sky darkened, the wind picked up, and soon heavy droplets of rain pounded on her. She remained in the water, allowing the warm rain to wash away the grime and dirt of the past month. She remained until her hair was dripping and little rivulets of water ran down her body. She remained even as the waves grew larger and threatened to pull her out to sea. She remained because she didn't want to return and face the horrors waiting for her. But the only thing in front of her was the raging ocean, and she knew that horror all too well.

She turned toward Sloane, who looked like an overweight drowning rat, and saw the captain standing on shore beside him, watching her. He grinned from under his hat. Charlisse splashed through the surf toward them, trying her best to avoid the incoming waves that crashed against her back.

When she reached the shore, the captain handed her a brown tunic. Charlisse grabbed it, but he did not let go. His playful glance skimmed over her and a smile lifted one corner of his mouth.

Charlisse yanked the tunic from his grasp. "You cad!" she exclaimed, holding it up to her chest.

"At your service, milady." He tipped his hat, bowed gracefully, and strode off.

"So this is your chivalrous captain?" she huffed, quickly donning the oversized tunic.

Sloane scratched his head. "Well, miss, he did get ye the shirt, eh?"

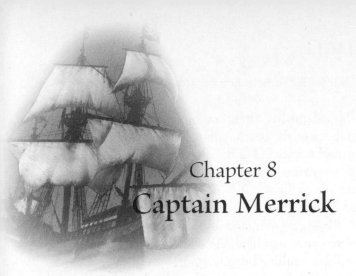

Chapter 8
Captain Merrick

The rain soon stopped, and Charlisse spent the afternoon sitting under the palm trees, examining her captors with a mixture of interest and trepidation. Most of them busied themselves hoisting barrels, crates, and furniture into cockboats, which were then rowed out to the ship.

Back and forth they went, returning all the ship's supplies in preparation for what Charlisse assumed to be its imminent departure. She gulped and grabbed a strand of her hair—still wet from the ocean—twisting it between her fingers. *What will they do with me?* They had fed her and nursed her back to health, but for what purpose? Would they take her with them, or leave her here to die alone? Now that she was nearly well, maybe they intended to satisfy themselves with her before they sailed away.

She thought of her father. As her strength returned, her quest to find him resurfaced with renewed fervor. Her only hope of achieving her goal seemed now to be in the hands of these pirates and their enigmatic captain.

She had never seen such men. Some walked around bare-chested, their sweat glistening in the hot afternoon sun; some clothed themselves in silks, taffetas, and velvet in a mismatched array that was obnoxious to her fashion sensibilities; some had long shaggy hair, while others were bald; some were thin, some stout. Most were dirty both in appearance and in the vulgarity that proceeded from their mouths. One man—the one they called the doctor—had only one eye. Another man was missing a leg below the knee, but with the help of a cane, he moved around as well as any of the others.

The man who caught her attention, however, was the captain. She watched him stride about the beach, talking with the men, helping them load supplies onto the cockboats. He carried himself with the easy assurance of a man of power—a natural leader who had obviously earned the respect of his men. Pirate or not, he was a most handsome man. She felt drawn to him and hated herself for it. This silly attraction could only be due to insanity brought on by weeks of hunger and loneliness, coupled with a fever that had plainly eaten away half her brain. For according to profession and appearance, he could be nothing but a scoundrel, a thief, and a rogue.

Darkness dropped its shroud over the tiny island. Though her day had not been strenuous, exhaustion weighed upon her. After a meal of dried beef and biscuits, Charlisse sank to her blankets, but found her slumber hounded by familiar nightmares that tormented her by night and haunted her by day.

Merrick lay by the fire, desperately seeking rest before the dawn of a new day, a day that would bring an abundance of work and new challenges as they sailed out from this island haven. The pirates had retired from their drinking unusually early. Most were already asleep. Merrick, envious of their peace, could not find a way to join them. It was the girl. He could not get her out of his mind.

In the past few days, she had blossomed before his eyes, regaining her health and beauty with each passing minute. He cursed himself for behaving like a lecherous cur that afternoon. When he'd seen her standing there, dripping wet and looking so alluring, he'd wanted nothing more than to take her in his arms. To have slipped back, if only for a moment, into his old salacious self was discouraging, and it made him wish all the more for the moment of their departure. Then he could deposit her in some civilized port, where she would be safe, away from him, and away from his unruly crew.

Merrick sighed. There was more to this girl than just a comely face. She had a strength in her. He saw it in her eyes—a courage and fortitude that could not be hidden behind her timid exterior.

He prayed silently, thanking the Lord for all his blessings and asking for strength and wisdom.

Charlisse sensed someone staring at her, even in her half-conscious state—even in the darkness that still held the island in slumber. The thick tropical clouds that meandered across the starry sky allowed only choice beams of a bright moon to filter down between them. A chill ran down her spine and she sat up, peering into the blackness. She saw the shadowy outline of the captain.

"What do you want?" she demanded, holding the blanket up to her chest.

Merrick remained in the shadows, silent, examining her.

Finally he spoke. "You have nightmares in your sleep." His voice was deep and calm.

"And what concern is that to you?"

He shifted in the sand, hesitating. "I'm wondering," he said, "what circumstances brought you to this island alone."

She sighed, remembering the shipwreck, the terror of her ordeal of the past month, the starvation, the loneliness, the yearning for a death that never came.

Now, captured by pirates—rumored to be men without morals or decency. And this man, their captain, sitting before her now, what did he want? What sort of slippery charade was he playing?

"It should make no difference to you, sir," she said.

"Why must you be so difficult, miss? It makes a great deal of difference to me, since you have put me in the rather precarious position of defending your honor."

Charlisse grabbed a lock of her hair. "It is neither my desire nor my request that you defend my honor, or anything else of mine. In fact, I can only assume I am your prisoner, a captured spoil, a prize of your trade, if you will." She studied him, but he did not flinch, made no comment.

The wind picked up, and a burst of moist tropical air blew over her, softening her mood. She reconsidered her harsh tone. Despite his chosen profession—and the degradation that went with it—he had saved her life and hadn't allowed his men to ravish her. Yet.

"However, sir," she added more softly, "I am thankful for your care."

"See, that wasn't so hard," he taunted.

"What?"

"Being courteous."

Charlisse gazed out into the night, anywhere but at his handsome face. The moonlight sparkled into silvery foam on the waves as they crashed ashore, the sound so familiar to her now that it was almost soothing. The fire had nearly died down in the middle of the camp and the pirates' revelry with it, bringing an ill-suited, peaceful mood over the whole scene, except for the dangerous man beside her. She turned to face him.

"I booked passage on a merchant ship from London to Port Royal," she conceded. "We went down in a storm, and somehow I ended up here alone." She thought of Captain Hathaway. "I don't know what happened to the rest of the crew."

"How long have you been here?"

"I'm not sure." She shook her head. "Four or five weeks, perhaps. I lost track of everything after awhile. I thought I was going to die."

Merrick glanced out at the ocean and then over to the dark forest beyond the beach. A sliver of moonlight escaped the clouds and lined the planes of his face. "You must have been horrified, a lady all alone in such a frightening place."

It was a strange thing for a pirate to say. Why would he care how she felt? He had called her a lady. She had been raised as one, to be sure, but had never really felt the part. "Who says I'm a lady?" she retorted. The words were out before she realized it might be more advantageous to assume the role among these men.

Charlisse saw the captain's eyes widen and one eyebrow lift.

"You hold yourself as a lady, miss. It's obvious from your speech and your mannerisms," he said, "but if you wish me not to treat you as a lady, I'd be happy to oblige." A ruthless smile curved upon his lips.

Ignoring his barb, she let the silence hang between them, confused at his wavering moods—one minute kind, the next threatening.

"What was your business in Port Royal, if I may ask? It's unusual for a lady to be traveling alone."

"You may ask," she replied curtly. "But it's my turn to ask a question of you."

"Very well."

"What do you intend to do with me, Captain? I know who you are and what you do. I've heard the stories—"

"You've heard stories about me?" he interrupted with a snicker. "I'm flattered."

"Not about you, specifically, Captain. . .Merrick, is it?—"

He nodded. "At your service, milady."

"—but about pirates in general."

"Well then, maybe you should tell me what I should do with you." A smirk lighted upon his face. "Since you've heard the *stories* that I obviously have not."

Charlisse searched his eyes. A soft sea breeze blew in from the ocean, lifting his hair. It was as black as the night and as wild as the man who wore it.

Why was he being so obstinate. But what did she expect from a pirate, or from any man? Hadn't her uncle done the same thing?

His voice suddenly softened. "May I ask your name, milady?"

She hesitated, unsure. "Charlisse Bristol."

"Charlisse. . ." He nodded. "It has a beautiful sound to it."

A cloud passed overhead, consuming him once again in shadow, and she wondered at the sudden sense of loss she felt. No longer able to see his eyes, she looked away.

He stood. She flinched. "Have no fear. I'm simply moving myself to a more respectable distance, for I do perceive I'm not only keeping you from your sleep, but causing you some distress, as well." He bowed. "Please rest, you'll need it for the trip tomorrow."

"Trip? What trip?" There was an edge of fear in her voice.

"We're to set sail tomorrow," he announced.

"Where to?" she asked anxiously. Then the significance of his words sank in. "I can't go on a pirate ship!"

"I'm sorry, milady, but it's the only ship I have, so you'll have to make do, and as far as where we are going, rest assured, I will drop you off at your port of choice—Port Royal, wasn't it?—as soon as possible. Your presence is as much a burden to me as mine undoubtedly is to you."

Chapter 9
Aboard
the Redemption

Charlisse entered the captain's cabin, sinking her bare toes into the soft fibers of a Persian rug. Sloane followed close behind. The cabin carried a dark and mysterious atmosphere and smelled of spices and wood. The décor was masculine and harsh, yet elegant and intriguing, like its master. The small room was eloquently decorated, indicating a taste for the trappings of nobility, which seemed at odds with its owner. A grand mahogany desk stood to one side, covered with maps and books in disarray. Brass candlesticks, silver trinkets, and a small gold chest filled with glowing pearls also sat haphazardly upon it.

A bookcase made up one wall, filled with all manner of scholarly books. Next to it rested a beautifully crafted armoire. A small bed, framed in carved oak, filled the left corner beside a large stained-glass window that showered myriad delicate colors across the oak floor. A teakwood trunk lay open next to the bed, overflowing with vests and doublets, black suits, and fine ruffled Holland shirts.

Exhausted, Charlisse plopped into one of two cushioned leather chairs.

"Cap'n says you best stay here, miss, for yer own protection," Sloane said. "I'll bring ye some tea after we set sail." He closed the sturdy oak door with a thud.

Charlisse snuggled into the soft leather, enjoying the feel of a chair beneath her again. She sighed. She had simply gone from one prison to another—from the deserted island to a cage with four walls. At this point, she had no idea which one she preferred, although at least this prison moved and could possibly take her to Port Royal. No matter what she faced along the way, she must survive—if only to look into her father's eyes just once.

Scanning the room for a weapon, her eyes landed on a leather-bound book on the desk. *A Bible?* She got up to examine it. Indeed, it was a Bible. Puzzled, she picked it up and shuffled through the pages. A pirate and a man of faith—the two did not seem to coincide. Thoughts of her uncle instantly flooded her mind: a bishop in the Church of England with flowing robes and golden crucifix—a perfect picture of sacred piety—yet inside a twisted, enraged man. Why, even thousands of miles away, could she not forget him and the horror he had inflicted on her? "Hypocrites, all of them," she muttered, tossing the book back on the desk.

Shouts from above filtered to her ears, along with the snap of the sails as they caught the wind. The ship heaved, and she grabbed the desk to keep from falling.

Fear gripped her soul—fear of once again being completely dependent upon the mercies of a man. She sat on a cushioned ledge by the window and peered out on the retreating island. Trembling, she cursed herself for her weakness.

She must have eventually dozed off, for a quiet tapping on the door woke her, and Sloane entered with a tray of tea.

"Here ye go, miss, some nice hot tea an' biscuits fer ye." He placed the tray on a small table by the bed and stood, waiting. She gave him a blank stare, then continued to gaze out the window.

"Come on, now, miss. Ye need to be eatin' somethin'." He poured some tea into a cup. "I know yer skeered."

The savory scent of the biscuits drifted around her, tickling her nose, alluring her with their sweet warmth. Her mouth watered. Finally, she gave in, grabbed a biscuit, and sat in a chair. The dough was soft and caressed her mouth with a buttery flavor. She couldn't remember the last time she had eaten anything this delicious.

"How did you become a pirate, Sloane?" she asked. "You don't seem to fit in with the rest of these scoundrels."

He gave a hearty chuckle. "Well, miss, I thank ye for that," he said, shuffling his feet. "I used to be a sailor." He looked at her with a sideways glance and a gleam in his eye. "A respectable one, that is. Didn't know me mother or father. An orphan I was, wanderin' the streets of Aruba till I snuck aboard a merchant vessel anchored near the island. Well, instead o' throwin' me off, the captain, a fair man, kep' me on and made me his cabin boy. As I grew bigger an' stronger, he taught me the ways o' the sea, an' I became a midshipman." Sloane smiled. "He was a good man—a finer captain could n'er be found. He was the only father I ever knew."

Charlisse sipped her tea, intrigued by the story. "What happened to him?"

"Ah, he retired, miss. Went back to England, he did, an' I got work on another merchant vessel after that." Sloane scratched his thick beard and shifted uncomfortably. The cutlass strapped to his hip reminded Charlisse that he was just as dangerous as the rest of them, no matter how friendly he seemed.

"And how did you come to sail with Captain Merrick?"

A smile crossed his lips. He sat down and took a biscuit. "Well, that be a story, for sure, miss. You see, I worked my way up to first mate. We was sailin' on a merchant ship when we was attacked by pirates."

"Merrick?"

He nodded, took a bite, and chewed. "He took our ship without a shot and gave us all the option of dyin' or signin' pirate articles an' joinin' him." He chuckled, crumbs flying from his mouth. "It weren't much a choice, if ye ask me."

Charlisse frowned. "How long ago was that?"

Sloane scratched his head under the purple headscarf he wore, staring out the window. "It's been nigh on three years, I figure." He shoved the rest of the biscuit in his mouth and grabbed another.

"And do you enjoy being a pirate, Mr. Sloane?"

"It's not what ye be thinkin', miss. The pirate life is free and wild and plenty more lucrative then bein' a merchant sailor, says I. But," he added, "I would only sail as a pirate under Merrick's flag."

"You do seem to admire him."

"He's a good man. Ye'll see, miss." He stood. "But now I have to be getting' back to me duties." He grinned then left, locking the door behind him.

Charlisse paced the cabin floor, jiggling the lock on the door more than once, and wondering where she would go even if she found herself unfettered. Sifting through the papers and charts on the desk, she searched for a knife, a pistol, or even a letter opener—anything she could defend herself with. She opened drawers, examined every book on the shelves, and finally sat, exasperated, on the ledge by the window, distressed at the horrible twist fate had thrown at her. Glancing out the window, she admired the sunset as it spilled across the horizon in an artist's display of oranges, reds, and purples, slowly drawing all traces of blue from the ocean, leaving only black in its place. It chilled her to think that the most beautiful, glorious things in the world—like the ocean or the sky—could also be the most deadly.

The door suddenly opened, startling her, and in walked Merrick, filling the room with his presence.

"A gentleman should knock before entering a lady's room," she blurted, immediately regretting the arrogance of her assumption.

"Well." He cocked one eyebrow at her. "That would imply I'm a gentleman and you are a lady. Neither of us has conceded to either title as of yet." He slammed the door, pulled off his waistcoat, and threw it across a chair. "Besides," he added, "this is the captain's cabin, not a lady's room."

He stood staring at her, his dark eyes at first harsh, but slowly softening. He sighed, then removed his brace of pistols and placed them on the desk, leaving his cutlass hanging at his side.

Charlisse watched his broad back as he fumbled with something on the desk. Her eyes moved to the pistols he had laid there. Tension formed knots in her stomach as she waited, wondering, dreading his next move.

"I've arranged for a bath and some proper clothes for you," he said without turning.

"I don't want them," she replied curtly.

He faced her, his lips curving in a smile. "Take them or not, that is up to you, Lady Bristol. But I don't recommend you remain so. . .sparsely dressed"—he gestured toward her apparel—"with fifty disreputable men on board."

A blush warmed Charlisse's face, and she turned away quickly, hoping he hadn't seen. A knock on the door brought a welcome interruption.

"Enter," Merrick said.

"Here ye go, Cap'n." Sloane walked in, carrying a large tub. A beautiful green dress and a towel were flung over his shoulder. Another man followed with two steaming jugs. Sloane set the tub down on the floor, and the other man filled it with the heated water, sending Charlisse a sly glance from time to time.

"Thank you, Sloane, Royce. That'll be all." The two men backed out of the cabin, leaving them alone once again. "You have twenty minutes before I return. It's your choice what to do with it." Merrick headed out the door. "I'll be right outside," he added before leaving the room.

Charlisse couldn't figure out if the captain was being thoughtful and kind or just cleaning her up to satisfy his ribald whims. She hesitated, unsure what to do. The warm water looked inviting, and she felt horribly filthy.

She crept over to the tub and climbed in. With one eye constantly on the door and a towel nearby to cover herself with, she scrubbed the dirt from one section of her body at a time, cleansing the fading insect bites, soothing her dry, sun-baked skin, and rinsing the saltwater from her hair.

Growing worried about the time, she dried herself and quickly donned the dress, a beautiful jade green with lace at the collar and sleeves, a tight-fitting waist, and long, flowing silk skirt. For the first time in a month, she felt clean and refreshed, almost like a lady.

She looked around for a mirror, and her gaze landed on Merrick's pistols lying on the table. How could she have forgotten about them? She glanced at the door, hesitated, then hurried and grabbed one. It was heavier than she expected. *Now what should I do with it?* The bed. She could stuff it under a pillow until she needed it.

The door creaked. She swung around, holding the pistol behind her back as the captain entered.

His eyebrows shot up, at her appearance or the fact that she had done his bidding she couldn't tell.

"Much better," he commented.

"I hope you know, sir, I have no intention of becoming another trinket with which you adorn your cabin," she shot back at him.

"I fear, milady, this will be a very long trip if you insist on being so contrary." His dark eyes glinted with humor. "Especially since we will be sharing such close quarters together."

Charlisse glanced at the small bed behind her, feeling a pounding dread pulsate through her veins. She turned back around. "I beg your pardon. Sharing quarters?"

He sauntered toward her, his boots echoing ominously on the wood floor. "This is the captain's cabin, and I am the captain. Surely you don't suggest I sleep with the crew?" A hint of a smile played on his lips, and Charlisse wasn't sure if he was serious or simply continuing to find enjoyment in her discomfort.

"I don't care where you sleep, as long as it's not here." Her tone was defiant, but her cracked voice betrayed her fear.

The closer he came, the more she shook. He had removed the scarf tied about his head. His black hair was pulled back, revealing his handsome features. Dark stubble covered his chin and the muscles beneath his tight-fitting shirt twitched as he approached. He loomed over her by at least a foot.

"Stay away," she warned him, backing up slowly. She ran into the bedpost and could go no farther.

The mocking grin remained on his face.

Charlisse's fingers ached under the weight of the pistol. It began to slip in her sweaty hands. With a burst of desperate courage, she flung it out in front of her and pointed it straight at Merrick. The pistol shook uncontrollably.

"I *will* shoot you!"

Merrick crossed his arms over his chest, his smile broadening. "Is that so?" Nodding at the pistol, he added, "You might want to load it first."

Charlisse stared at the gun then back at him. Was he lying? How could she tell? She had no idea how to use one of these hideous things. His eyes gave away no fear, only glittered with their usual cocky arrogance. The gun wavered in her shaking hands.

With lightning speed, Merrick grabbed it out of her grasp. Gasping, Charlisse glared up at him, defeated.

Slumping down on the bed, she awaited her fate.

Head down, she heard him chuckling as he returned the pistol to its brace. "I suggest you not kill the only man on board this ship who is protecting you."

Tears welled up in her eyes, but she fought them back and lifted her chin, unwilling to show any sign of weakness. "And who, sir, will protect me from you?"

His wanton gaze covered her from head to toe. An uncomfortable silence stretched between them. Self-conscious under his scrutiny, Charlisse dropped her eyes.

"That will have to be God," Merrick said.

She looked up at him. "Then I fear my situation is hopeless."

Merrick shot up an eyebrow. "You have no faith in God, milady?"

She sighed. "He gave up on me a long time ago."

"Perhaps it is the other way around." He flung the brace of pistols over his shoulder and walked toward the door. "I will have your dinner sent to you. I don't make a habit of dining with someone who has held a pistol at me." He smiled. "At least not the same day." He opened the door.

"Captain?"

He stopped in the hallway and turned to face her. "Yes?"

"Was the pistol loaded?"

"I always keep my pistols loaded, milady." Amusement twinkled in his eyes before he shut and locked the door.

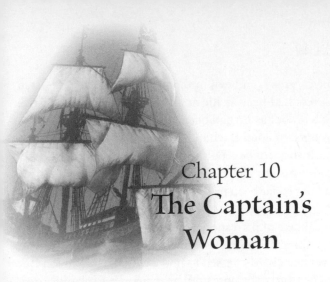

Chapter 10
The Captain's Woman

Merrick leaned against the main deck railing, allowing the warm night breeze to soothe both his temper and the unfamiliar feelings stirring within him. With his belly full and a shot of rum to top it off, he'd thought he could easily forget the infuriating girl that resided in his cabin and focus on more important things. But visions of her kept floating into his mind—the way her curves filled out the green silk dress she wore, the golden curls that cascaded over her shoulder, her full pink lips always in a pout, and those soft blue eyes that could turn to ice in a flash.

He had not had a woman grace his cabin for a long time, and never had a true lady entered there. What was he to do with her until he could get her safely to Port Royal? She presented a challenge indeed. With each passing day, as her health improved, she became more beautiful. How was he going to keep his crew from such a lovely treasure? He sighed, shaking his head. It wasn't only the crew he didn't trust, but himself, as well.

Not that he was the vile rogue he once had been. Two years ago, he had given his life to Christ—the best decision he had ever made. Now he had purpose and meaning, a relationship with the God of the universe who loved him, and more joy and peace than he'd thought possible. Yet his past often crept up to haunt him.

It was one thing for God to fish him out of the mud in which he had been wallowing for so many years, and quite another to complete the long and laboriously painful task of cleaning him—of turning a heart

57

blackened by selfishness, greed, and evil into one that was pure. He often wondered if any progress had been made at all or whether he was just as bad a student in God's school as he had been at Oxford.

There were moments, of course, when he surprised himself, when he would commit an unselfish act or be repulsed by some activity he previously enjoyed. But here stood this fair, delicate flower within his grasp and free for his taking. He had not so far been tested with so delicious a temptation as Charlisse.

Women were a weakness of his, especially the beautiful ones. They had always been mere playthings to him—existing solely for his enjoyment, and he'd certainly never been hard-pressed to find a willing companion But now he had vowed to the Lord to be pure until he married—a relatively easy promise to keep up to this point. How quickly his resolve had changed.

There was more to this lady than her exquisite beauty, however—something that roused more than his physical passion. She was courageous. Not many would have dared to hold a pistol so blazingly at him, man or woman. He chuckled, remembering her expression when he snatched it so easily from her grasp. She had spirit and strength. He admired that.

Merrick sighed, looking out at the moon sitting above the horizon, waning just like his resolve. *Oh, Lord,* he silently prayed, *You said in Your Word, You would never leave me nor forsake me, that You give strength to the weak. I trust You in this. Please give me the strength to become the man You want me to be.*

The sea plunged and bucked in the night like the wild passions raging within him, but the stars above were clear and bright like the Lord's truth and love. Perhaps He was saying to Merrick, *I understand what you're going through, and I will guide you; I will be with you.* Merrick stared at the expanse of sea he would have to cross hand in hand with temptation. He hoped the Lord's strength would be enough—for he knew his own would not be.

A circle of light, muted in a pleasant blend of colors, danced back and forth across Charlisse's eyes, keeping rhythm with the rolling of the ship. Under closed lids, she examined the floating glow with curious regard as she slowly regained awareness. A few minutes passed before she remembered where she was.

Bolting upright in bed, she glanced around the cabin. Captain Merrick sat at his desk, reading the Bible, his head bowed in deep thought—or was it prayer?

After a moment, he slowly closed the holy book. "Sleep well?"

"How long have you been in here?" she demanded, furious at herself for sleeping so soundly.

"All night," he replied, getting up from the desk.

Where was the usual smirk? He seemed to be in a somber mood this morning. Or perhaps he was just tired.

Merrick picked up a pile of blankets from the floor next to his desk and placed them on his chair.

"Did you sleep in here with me?"

His piercing gaze fixed on her, both brows raised. "Yes, I did. And I assure you, milady, it was in your best interest."

"I beg your pardon! What of my reputation?"

Merrick gave her a sideways glance and strapped on his knife belt and baldric. Slinging his brace of pistols around his neck, he replied, "My sincere apologies, milady, but my interest lies more in your safety than your reputation, which at the present time, we have yet to determine."

Fully armed, he stared at her with a wild look in his eyes, and Charlisse didn't doubt for one minute that he was a dangerous man. She felt her face flush.

"I'll see about your breakfast." He put on his hat, tipped it at her, and left.

Charlisse fell back onto the soft bed, her blood boiling. Who was this man? Was he gentleman or scoundrel? His mannerisms and the way he had treated her so far indicated he was a man of honor. But the way he looked at her with those dark, sensual eyes that lured her into their depths implied he was nothing more than what he appeared to be—a pirate, a thief, and a villain. She wondered how long before they reached Port Royal and she could be free from his irksome company.

Port Royal. Perhaps her father was there now, waiting for her. Had he received the letter announcing her arrival? Had he received any of her correspondence of the past twelve years? No reply had ever come—none that she knew about. But then any mail she received was first inspected by her uncle, whose hatred for her father was exceeded only by his hatred for her mother—his own flesh and blood.

Her mother's death twelve years ago marked the end of Charlisse's childhood and the hopes and dreams that went with it. Charlisse's mother had died of a broken heart, the product of years of endless grieving for the loss of the man she loved and the shattered hopes of promises left unfulfilled. Yet from the stories her mother had told her, Charlisse knew her father had loved them both. When her mother, Helena, had told him she was with child, she'd said he'd been so overcome with joy that he'd stayed up all night, holding her and singing to her. The next day he'd gone through the town and handed out gifts to everyone in celebration of becoming a father. How could a man like that have abandoned them? Charlisse would not believe it.

Port Royal was the address of her mother's last correspondence with her father, and although it seemed a foolish girl's dream to find him, Charlisse would fight to fulfill that dream at all costs.

If her father could not be found or, God forbid, was dead, she would be alone in the world, and if that were the case, it would have been better if she had drowned in the shipwreck along with the crew.

The morning hours dragged on. Charlisse paced in the small cabin until she thought she would go crazy. With her health almost fully restored and her nerves on end, she felt like a little ship mouse caught in a trap—a deadly one—and her instincts to flee were rising at full force.

The rhythmic creaking of the wooden floorboards with the movement of the ship added to her irritation, along with the heat and humidity that rose by the minute. The tiny room was unbearably stifling. She needed air. When would they arrive at Port Royal? She couldn't stand the waiting—the endless waiting for whatever vicious plan fate had determined for her.

When Sloane arrived with lunch, she begged him to ask the captain to allow her to come on deck for a short while. He left shaking his head, telling her not to get her hopes up, but surprisingly, when the pirate returned, he had a smile on his face.

"Cap'n says it be all right fer a few minutes, but I have to escort ye."

"I suppose he wasn't too happy about it," Charlisse said.

"That be true, miss." He led her down the companionway and up the stairs to the main deck.

The Caribbean breeze, although warm and humid, splashed across her face and neck like a cool gust of winter chill. Taking a deep breath of it, she closed her eyes as it filtered down her dress and caressed her warm skin. It smelled of salt and fish and a hint of sweet tropical flowers.

If she allowed herself to dream, she could imagine for a moment— a precious, fleeting moment—that she was safely aboard her father's merchant ship, that she had found him and he loved her.

When she opened her eyes, she saw only the leering gaze of a few pirates, working in the shrouds, who had stopped what they were doing to stare at her.

"Back to work, you jackals," bellowed a deep voice from above her.

Grumbling, the pirates returned to their duties. Charlisse's eyes found Merrick standing gallantly on the quarterdeck, hands on his hips, face like stone, shirt and hair blowing in the wind. Their gazes locked for a moment before he turned away. She had meant to at least nod at him in appreciation for allowing her on deck, but his fierce demeanor dissuaded her.

"What puts the captain in such a foul mood?" she asked Sloane as they approached the railing.

"Naw, miss, he's not in a foul mood." He looked down, frowning. "He just gets a bit harsh now an' then. The nature of his command, ye know."

"Or his personality."

"Naw, miss, ye be misjudgin' him, methinks."

Charlisse examined Sloane's weathered face. His eyes squinted in the bright sunlight, but she could find no insincerity in them. Burly and stout, he reminded Charlisse of Captain Hathaway. Scratching his coarse gray beard, he pointed to something out in the water.

"Look there, miss."

Her eyes followed his hand to find a group of large, glistening creatures jumping in the waves only a few yards from the ship.

"Oh, how wonderful," she exclaimed, leaning farther over the rail for a better look. "Are they dolphins? I've never seen them before."

"Yes, miss. Beautiful animals they are, and friendly, too."

The dolphins skipped in and out of the water, keeping pace with the ship. "What are they doing?"

"I don't knows much about them, miss, but I'd say they was escortin' us to Port Royal, wouldn't ye?"

Charlisse chuckled. "Yes, it does seem so." It felt good to laugh.

She glanced over the exquisite scene. No land was in sight, just the vast, blue ocean, calm and deep, extending as far as she could see, its waves twinkling in the sunlight. Small, dark clouds gathered on the eastern horizon. The thought of another storm sent a spike of unease through her.

She noticed movement behind her and turned to see several more men. Some loitered in a group by the foredeck stairs, passing a bottle among themselves, others had started a game of cards, and two of them were mopping the deck. A vile and frightening group, they were armed with all manner of swords, knives, and pistols. Most were young—under thirty, she'd guess—and they looked at her as if they hadn't seen a woman in a very long time. She shivered.

One man, who leaned arrogantly against the railing across the deck, kept staring at her. When their eyes met, his mouth curved in a smile. He took off his hat and bowed. Charlisse quickly turned around to face the sea.

"Don't be worryin' about none o' them, miss," Sloane said. "They's under strict orders by the cap'n to not be touchin' ye."

"Is that so?" Charlisse felt her stomach clench, but offered Sloane a half smile. "How does he manage that?"

"By claimin' ye fer hisself, miss."

"Claiming me?" Her lips tightened. "Am I merely property to be claimed on some pirate's whim?" Charlisse felt her face growing flush. *The outright audacity*, she thought. She belonged to no man—not anymore—and never would again.

Sloane glanced at Merrick up on the quarterdeck, where he stood examining a chart that was lain out before him. "Well, miss, he tells them ye are his, if ye know what I mean. They know better than to touch the cap'n's woman." He gave her a sly look.

Something hard in her began to soften. The sensation felt both awkward and vulnerable. She didn't like it. As if reading her thoughts, Sloane added, "Don't ye worry, miss. The cap'n's will is stronger than most."

As the afternoon waned, the clouds blackened overhead, swarming over the ship like vultures, obscuring the sunlight, and riding on a wind that swept Charlisse's long, golden hair behind her. The dolphins left, taking their playful mood with them. Perhaps it was an omen of bad of things to come. Sadness overtook her.

Attributing Sloane's comment to his overrated opinion of his captain, Charlisse ignored it.

"Tell me more about the captain, Sloane."

He grinned. "With smilin' pleasure, miss, ye see—"

"May I interrupt?" The voice was dark and silky.

Charlisse turned to see the pirate who had bowed to her so courteously from across the deck. His face was as smooth as his voice, and his smile nearly as charming as his manner. He wore brown knee breeches and silk stockings, a shirt trimmed in lace under a doublet of violet taffeta. His dark, curly brown hair fell to his shoulders in a fashionable style. Young, tall, and well-built, he stood with a confidence Charlisse found strangely reassuring.

Sloane frowned and did not make the expected introduction.

The pirate took off his hat and bowed. "I don't think we've been formally introduced, milady. I'm Kent Frederick Carlton."

"How do you do, Mr. Carlton." Charlisse nodded, surprised to find so eloquent a man on board a pirate ship.

"And you are?" He held out his hand.

She offered him hers. "Charlisse Bristol."

His lips touched her hand and lingered there too long. A grin spread over his face.

"I trust you have been treated well thus far, milady." He shifted his eyes, nodding to where Merrick stood. A look of apprehension crossed his gaze.

Sloane cleared his throat.

"As well as can be expected, I suppose." Charlisse swerved her gaze to Merrick then back to Kent. "How kind of you to inquire." She smiled. Hope flickered within her. Perhaps she had found an ally on board this ship of miscreants.

Stepping closer, Kent leaned toward her. A heated wave flowed over her as she stared into his dark brown eyes. "If you are in need of anything, please call upon me." He winked, and Charlisse's breath quickened.

"Ah, by thunder." Sloane snorted. "That'll about do it, Master Kent." He stepped between them.

"I was only being polite." He donned his hat, still smiling. "Surely

I'm allowed to speak to the lady."

Sloane stood his ground, his right hand inching toward his cutlass. "Cap'n's orders. No one's to be botherin' her."

Kent's gaze shifted to Charlisse, who had backed against the railing. "Was I bothering you, miss?"

"Not at all."

A movement behind him caught her attention. Following her gaze, Kent turned to watch Merrick descending the quarterdeck steps, anger lining his expression. For a moment, the dashing pirate paused, his lips twitching beneath his thin mustache. Then he stepped back.

"Until later, milady." He bowed once again.

Sloane let out a sigh.

Kent focused his dark, beady eyes on his captain as he strode by. The two men's gazes locked; then the captain turned to Sloane. "Take her below," he ordered. Without a glance at Charlisse, he returned to his charts.

Down in the cabin, Charlisse questioned Sloane about Kent.

"He be the first mate. Good sailor. Better at swordplay than any I seen in a while. I'm glad he didn't draw his sword." He grinned at her and then added in a capricious voice, "Bit of a jackanapes, if ye ask me."

"I thought he was rather charming."

Sloane wrinkled his brow. "Looks can be deceivin', miss." He headed for the door. "Ye just be stayin' put."

A gust of wind whipped up his charts, and Merrick glanced at the approaching storm—just a summer squall, nothing to worry about. Rolling up his scrolls, he issued an order to furl the topsails.

Merrick knew it was a bad idea to allow the girl on deck. It was a bad idea to have a woman on board in the first place. She was an uncontrollable distraction that only caused dissention among the men. He recalled the sight of her leaning on the rail, her waist-length golden curls blowing in the wind, the sound of her feminine, childlike laugher as she watched the dolphins. He could hardly keep his eyes off her. How could he captain a ship and keep his men in line with this exquisite beauty flashing before their eyes like a sparkling diamond within reach, yet untouchable?

Kent. The boy reminded him of himself not long ago—hotheaded, lecherous, and arrogant. If anyone was a threat to Merrick on this ship, if anyone would dare challenge his authority, it was Master Kent. He knew this because Merrick had done precisely that, nigh three years ago, on another ship, to his own captain.

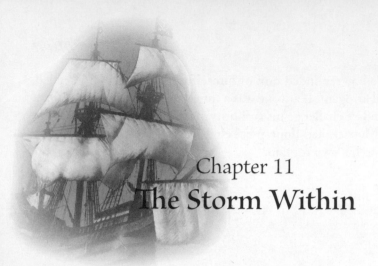

Chapter 11
The Storm Within

The rain came down in torrents, pounding mercilessly on the window of the cabin, trying to reach in and grab Charlisse and plunge her into the sea once again. With each crashing wave, the ship swayed feverishly. Charlisse clung to her bed, sick to her stomach—not sure whether her sudden illness was caused by the rolling of the ship or her nerves.

A flash of lightning streaked the darkened sky, followed by an enormous boom that rumbled through the ship, testing each timber and bolt with its fury.

The cabin door opened, and she looked up to see Merrick removing his hat. Water poured from its brim onto the floor.

He looked at her. "It's a summer rain, milady. It should be over soon."

"We will not go down?"

A smile curved his lips. "One never knows with these summer squalls." He took off his drenched waistcoat and threw it onto a chair.

An awkward silence filled the room.

When she saw the lift of his eyebrow, she knew he was teasing her.

She turned her back to him and asked, "When will we get to Port Royal?"

Removing his baldric and cutlass, he sank into one of the leather chairs that faced her. He shook his wet hair and combed it back with his hand before fixing her with an intense gaze.

Charlisse shifted her eyes away from his, uncomfortable under his scrutiny.

"About two days," he finally answered her.

She nodded, looking back out the window. Another burst of thunder blasted across the sky.

She jumped.

"I assure you, milady, you are quite safe."

She shot him a fierce look. "Am I?" When he said nothing, she added, "Perhaps from the storm, at least."

The swaying lanterns cast eerie shadows across the room.

Merrick got up and poured rum into a dirty glass. His expression was grim. That observation brought her no comfort.

She heard a tapping on the door, and Sloane entered, carrying a tray on which sat a steaming pot of tea, three cups, and some biscuits. "Jus' some dried beef an' old biscuits tonight, I'm afraid, due to the storm." He set it down and looked from Merrick to Charlisse.

With a jerk of his head, Merrick downed his rum. "Sit, eat with us," he insisted.

"Why, thank ye, Cap'n. Don't mind if I do." Sloane offered a biscuit to Charlisse and plopped into a chair beside Merrick, who had returned to his.

She shook her head. The ship continued its chaotic rolling, and she wondered how anyone could eat anything at all. Yet the two pirates consumed biscuits as if they were sitting at a picnic on dry land.

Another clap of thunder bellowed. Charlisse sprang off the bed and began pacing, her silk skirt swooshing with each step. She felt flushed and dizzy and had a hard time keeping her footing. When she reached the desk, the ship made a sudden lurch to the port side and she almost fell.

"You'll get used to it after a while," Merrick said, chuckling. "Maybe you should seat yourself." He pointed to the bed.

"No, thank you. I need to walk."

"Some tea might settle yer belly some," Sloane offered.

After several minutes of trying to keep her balance on the heaving ship, Charlisse had a horrifying vision of herself sprawled out on the floor in front of these two men. She sat on the edge of the bed, accepting the cup from Sloane's outstretched hand.

The warm tea soothed her throat. She hoped she would keep it down.

Leaning back in the leather chair, Merrick propped his feet on the table, while Sloane continued to devour biscuits. Charlisse could see where the old sailor got his corpulent figure.

"So, Miss Bristol, what draws you to Port Royal?" Merrick asked her in the most congenial tone she had heard come out of him yet.

She hesitated, wondering whether he was searching for information, or just passing idle moments. "My father is there." Before the words left her lips, it occurred to her that claiming to have a strong, protective father waiting for her in Port Royal may keep this pirate captain at bay.

"Ah, yer father," Sloane exclaimed. "That be good, miss."

"Is he awaiting your arrival?" Merrick asked, sounding suspicious.

"Of course he is. And if I am delayed," she added for good measure, "I assure you, he will spare no expense to search for me and exact revenge on those who kept me from him."

"Is that so?" Merrick smirked. "Then I expect he's out looking for you now since your arrival has already been delayed by a shipwreck?"

Ignoring him, she played with a lock of hair that had fallen in her lap, wishing she had pins with which to put it up properly.

"What does your father do?"

She fixed him with a cold eye. "He's a merchant sailor, if you must know, based in Port Royal. He sent for me to come and live with him."

"Hmm."

"You don't believe me?"

"What does it matter?"

"I believe ye, miss," Sloane said between bites.

Merrick gave his friend a kick on the leg. "You'd believe her if she said she was the queen of England, you gullible old fool."

Sloane grinned and offered Charlisse more tea.

She declined, her stomach still uneasy.

"You're from London, then?" Merrick continued his questioning.

"Yes."

"Where in London?"

She searched the captain's face. He lips wore nothing but the insolent smirk that frequently played there. "Hampstead."

Merrick took a sip of tea. "Yes, I know the area."

"What of it?"

"You come from a noble family," he stated.

Charlisse said nothing.

"Fine gowns, jewels, balls to attend, the best tutors?"

Charlisse lifted her chin. "So?"

Merrick sighed, his brow furrowing.

"Something troubles you, Captain?"

He took a bite of beef and lay back in his chair, his gaze never leaving her. "So you left the comforts of home, bartered passage on a lowly merchant vessel, without benefit of escort, and embarked on the dangerous crossing from England all by yourself?" Merrick glared at her, raising a brow.

"That I did. And I don't see how it is any business of yours." She met his stare defiantly, but saw skepticism behind his eyes. What would he do when he discovered she quite possibly had no sheltering father waiting for her in Port Royal? Every ounce of her being hoped that she did. It could be true, after all, but this pirate was not dull of wit.

" 'Tis mighty dangerous to be travelin' alone, miss," Sloane added. "Especially a lady as young as yerself." He stuffed the remainder of the dried beef into his mouth.

"With that I will agree." Merrick set down his tea. "Whatever the reason, you have my utmost regard for attempting such a precarious journey. I know of no other lady who would have been so brave and so resourceful."

The esteem in his gaze and sincerity in his tone unnerved Charlisse. She shifted on the bed. "What do you mean 'whatever the reason'? I told you my reason."

"Do you know what I think?" Merrick leaned forward and placed his elbows on his knees, looking at her with those imperious eyes.

Unable to hold his gaze, Charlisse looked down.

"I think you're running away from something."

She looked up, gathering her resolve. "Your opinions are of no interest to me, Captain."

Merrick leaned back, a faint smirk on his mouth.

"If you must know, my mother died," she said, her voice shaky. *Well, it was true, though it happened twelve years ago.* "And as I have said, my father sent for me."

"He sent for you but provided no means for you to get there, nor a proper escort for your protection?"

"Do you dare insult the honor and intentions of my father, sir?" Charlisse's eyes narrowed. Her stomach clenched and made a gurgling sound she feared would give away her nervousness.

"I beg your pardon, milady." Merrick bowed his head slightly. "My deepest apologies. That was not my intention. I was only inferring that if you were my daughter, I would not let such a precious and valuable creature travel these dangerous waters alone."

"I assure you, sir, I can take care of myself," she snapped, not missing his compliment.

"Indeed, so you have shown."

Charlisse sighed and looked toward the window. The rain had stopped, but a sudden chill came over her. She rubbed her arms. Was this the price of her passage to Port Royal, to endure these probing and insulting questions? She had never met such a pompous and infuriating man. It was as if he could see right through every lie she uttered, only to toss each one back in her face. Yet, if these childish banters were the only cost of the voyage, she resolved herself to endure them. She feared, however, she would pay a much higher price before reaching her destination. From the corner of her eye she caught the sultry glare of the captain still upon her, causing a shudder to traverse her spine at the thought of becoming his unwilling mistress.

Sloane lay back in his chair, grinning, hands folded over his full stomach, and watched them.

Charlisse turned back to find Merrick's gaze covering her. A few strands of wet hair had fallen into his face. He reached up to scratch the stubble on his chin.

"You have no other family?"

"None that I trust." Tears burned behind Charlisse's eyes, but she forced them back.

"Never fear, milady." Merrick regarded her with concern. "We shall get you safely to Port Royal."

Sloane inched to the edge of his seat in an effort to rise. " 'Tis a brave thing ye be doin'." He stood and grabbed the tray. "Now I have to be goin'."

Merrick nodded. "I'll be up in a minute."

With Sloane's departure, the mood in the room changed to one of tense apprehension. Did the captain have this effect on every woman who found herself alone with him?

He was still seated, perusing her. A grin twisted his mouth.

"I perceive you are enjoying yourself at my expense," Charlisse stated, still rubbing her arms from the cold that had crept into the room.

Merrick stood and headed toward the armoire. "I am enjoying myself. I'll admit to that." He retrieved a blanket.

Charlisse's stomach dropped. She watched him, her pulse quickening.

"But I could be enjoying myself much more." He grinned wolfishly and walked toward her.

Wide-eyed, she backed away from him. With each thud of his boots on the wooden floor, her heart sank a little lower and her nerves clenched a little tighter. Memories of a horrid past rose to torment her.

He sat next to her on the bed. Meeting his gaze steadfastly, she willed herself to show none of the fear that pulsed through her body. The sharp look in his eyes softened. His hair was the color of ebony. Still damp, it touched the collar of his white shirt. He smelled of rain and musk.

He reached up and swung the blanket around her shoulders. Its warmth brought instant relief from the cold and momentarily allayed her fears.

Charlisse felt a rush of heat flood through her that both terrified and confused her. Why was she feeling this way? This was certainly not the behavior of a lady. A true lady should not feel desire—especially not for such a rogue. Shame swept through her. Her uncle had been right about her. Clearing her throat, she shifted back on the bed, avoiding his gaze—and those penetrating dark eyes.

He raised his hand. She flinched, looking up. He hesitated, searching her eyes. He reached up again, more slowly this time, and caressed her cheek, moving a strand of her hair aside.

Bewildered by his tenderness, Charlisse turned her face away. "How did you become a pirate?" she asked, hoping to distract him—and herself.

For a moment, all was silent. She felt his gaze scour over her. Then he chuckled. " 'Tis a long story. But, I daresay, we may have more in common than you would think, for I, too, left my home and all I knew to come to these adventurous waters, though for different reasons, I assure you. You came to find your father. I came to lose mine."

He looked away and Charlisse stared at him, watching his jaw flex. He ran a hand through his hair and returned his gaze to hers, and for the first time since she'd met him, no haughty sneer shielded his features.

Reaching up, he pulled the blanket tighter around her shoulders.

The familiar action sent Charlisse's heart racing. "You do not intend to harm me." Her words were more a statement than a question.

Merrick grinned. "You never fail to surprise me. Such boldness from so young a lady." Regard shown in his eyes. He shook his head. "Quite the contrary, I assure you."

A flicker of gentleness passed across his expression. Hope sprouted within Charlisse but was instantly crushed as his perusal of her grew more intense. His steely façade gained dominance once more. Charlisse sensed a battle brewing behind his eyes.

He reached up to touch her again, then dropped his hand and turned away. Bolting from the bed, he buckled on his baldric and cutlass, grabbed his coat and hat, and slammed out the door without saying a word.

Several hours later, Charlisse heard him return. Sleep had not come to her, no matter how hard she tried. The storm had finally subsided and a deadly silence had overtaken the ship. It only added to her frayed nerves.

She heard him removing his boots, coat, and weapons. Peeking from underneath her blanket, she saw him standing in the darkness, a shadowy outline, barely discernable. His presence filled the room, like a panther ready to strike. He stood silently for several minutes before he finally lay down on the floor.

Charlisse remained rigid as she waited for the sound of his deep breathing, assuring her he was fast asleep.

"Wherefore let him that thinketh he standeth take heed lest he fall. There hath no temptation taken you but such as is common to man: but God is faithful, who will not suffer you to be tempted above that ye are able; but will with the temptation also make a way to escape, that ye may be able to bear it."

Merrick closed the Bible and prayed silently. *You are faithful, Lord. I believe Your word and put my trust in You. Rid me of my evil thoughts and ways, and create in me a new heart. Make me a man of honor and integrity as I serve you, my King.*

Looking up, he saw the angel sleeping in his bed. She did look like an angel, especially when she was asleep—and her mouth was shut. She intrigued him: but why? What was it about her that allured him? Surely it wasn't just her beauty and refinement. He had met many such ladies before and found most of them tiresome and unambiguous. Charlisse was hardly that. She was unpredictable and mysterious: terrified, yet more courageous than any woman he had met; vulnerable, yet defiant and independent; extremely feminine, yet with a man's strength of mind and will; cautious and distrustful, but with a hint of concealed trust and reliance.

Where other women swooned under his attention, she resisted his charms, not offering him the slightest flirtatious glance. Maybe that was it. His pride was bruised. Finally, a woman who did not crave his affections, and he couldn't stand it.

He got up from his desk and strapped on his weapons. The noise stirred her from her sleep, and her eyes opened—those ocean-blue eyes. She made no comment, merely watched him.

"What, no complaint about me sleeping here with you?"

She sat, pulling the quilt up to her chin and propping herself up with pillows. "Would it do me any good?"

He smiled, buckling his baldric and grabbing his boarding ax and knives. "Tell me your father's name."

"Why?" Charlisse rubbed her eyes.

Waking up from her slumber, she seemed so childlike, but even in her sleepy state, she had a petulance that pricked his pride. "Maybe I can help you find him." His dark brows lifted. "Why must you be so mistrusting?"

Charlisse stared at him with narrowing eyes. She finally conceded, "Edward Terrance Bristol."

Merrick stopped short, and his face turned white. *Edward Terrance Bristol.* The name hung in the room like a dank vapor.

"You know him?" Charlisse's face brightened.

"No." Merrick shook his head, a chill coursing through him. "That's impossible. I must be thinking of someone else. I don't know any Edward Bristol."

"Sail ho!" a voice boomed from above deck.

Tying his pirate's scarf around his head, he turned away. He grabbed his hat and walked out the door, unable to look at her pleading eyes.

Chapter 12
The Trap

Merrick strode onto the main deck. The *Redemption* had entered a morning fog that hovered upon the sea like a bird of prey, creating a ghostly silence as the ship glided through the calm water.

Edward Terrance Bristol. Just hearing that name spoken out loud set every nerve ablaze. Surely, he had misunderstood her. The Edward Bristol he knew could not possibly be her father. The Edward Bristol he knew was a wicked pirate who'd been terrorizing the Caribbean with his cruelties for years—the same man Merrick had been hunting these past months, the same man he intended to bring to justice for his murderous atrocities. Rubbing his pounding temples, Merrick shook his head. Impossible. But how many Edward Terrance Bristols could there be? He looked off into the horizon and up at the man in the crow's nest.

"What say you, Royce?" he bellowed.

"Sail ho," he repeated. "Two points off the starboard side."

Leaping to the foredeck, Merrick joined Kent, who had already positioned his telescope in that direction.

"Sleep well?" Kent teased.

Ignoring the taunting remark, Merrick snatched the spyglass out of Kent's hands. Charlisse was not a topic of discussion, especially with this young firebrand. "What do you see?"

"I can't quite make her out, a small merchant vessel, perhaps. She drifts in and out of the fog."

Merrick positioned the scope, holding it steady. The gray mist presented a blank canvas, peaceful and unnervingly quiet. After a few minutes, a dark brown hull slowly formed, appearing for a second before being swallowed in the haze again. A few more minutes and it materialized once more, staying longer this time, affording him a better look. Straining his eyes, he scanned for the familiar markings that would tell him this was the ship he searched for. But he found none. Perhaps it was for the better. This was not the time for a battle with a vicious pirate, not with a lady on board. The sooner he could remove her from his ship, the sooner he could resume his hunt for this wicked murderer.

Closing the glass with a snap, he handed it back to Kent and stared off into the fog. "Stay away from her," he ordered, knowing Kent would understand to whom he referred.

Kent was silent beside him, but Merrick felt the tension between them rise. He fixed his eyes upon him.

"Of course, Captain." His hand slowly moved to the hilt of his cutlass. He met Merrick's intense gaze with his own.

"Do not defy me, Master Kent. You will regret it."

Merrick stood firmly, not releasing the lock his eyes had on Kent's. The chill of the fog crept into his bones. He could hear the first mate's hurried breathing and see the conflicting thoughts pass behind those beady brown eyes.

The rhythmic lapping of the waves against the bow as the ship cut through the water created an eerie sound in the otherwise tense silence.

Kent slowly released his grip on his cutlass and looked away. "What about the ship, Captain?"

Merrick shook his head. "We leave her be. Something's not right. I feel it."

"But she's within our grasp."

"We have more than enough to trade at Port Royal." Merrick started down the steps. "She doesn't look big enough to be worth our time."

"She'd be an easy target. We'd be foolish not to take her." Kent's voice was filled with lingering contempt as he followed his captain.

Merrick continued walking.

"Let's put it to vote then," Kent protested.

Merrick sighed. Kent was right. As stated in the articles the crew had signed, the pursuit and acquisition of all targets was to be decided by majority, a normal procedure aboard most pirate vessels. Merrick had no choice. And he was sure he knew which way his greedy crew would vote.

After gathering the pirates, Merrick explained the situation, and by a showing of hands and a chorus of *ayes*, his prediction was confirmed. They would pursue and capture this easy prize.

The fog slowly dissipated and the trade winds picked up, affording the *Redemption*—with her yards full and her canvas billowing—a speedy course toward her intended prey.

Excitement charged through the crew as they armed themselves. Some clambered into the shrouds while others hung on the bulwarks, longing for the ship to come closer into view. The gun crew gathered below, anxiously awaiting orders to fire their deadly missiles.

Kent and Sloane joined Merrick on the main deck. He extended the spyglass once again.

"What be wrong, Cap'n?" Sloane asked.

"Something seems amiss," Merrick mumbled. "Surely they have spotted us by now." He narrowed his eyes, peering through the glass. "Yet they sail on as if we were not here."

"May I?" Kent asked, hand outstretched.

Merrick gave him the telescope.

Seconds passed before he folded it and said with a sly smile, "Perhaps they are just too stupid or too consumed with drink."

"Cap'n," interrupted a strong voice.

Merrick turned. Jackson, his master gunner, came up behind him, his ebony muscles bulging. The three gold earrings hooked in his right ear glittered in the sun. He was a frightening figure alone, but armed with pistols, a boarding ax, and a knife as long as his arm, his appearance was more than enough to send terror through any enemy.

"Yes, Jackson?"

"The guns be run out an' loaded."

Merrick nodded, turning back toward the merchant vessel. He felt a shiver of trepidation rush down his back. "Hard to starboard, Master Kent. Bring her around for our guns to bear, but keep a quick pace with her."

Kent nodded and headed off.

"Jackson, fire one warning shot over her bow on my order."

"Aye, aye, Cap'n," the huge man replied. He turned and left.

"What 'bout the girl?"

Merrick looked at Sloane. "Keep her in the cabin. She'll be under your charge. Do you mind?" He patted the sailor's back with a grin.

"Me? Why would I be mindin' sittin' with a pretty girl when I could be up here fightin' an' hollerin' with a bunch of ugly, sweaty men?" Sloane chuckled.

"Why, indeed?"

Merrick watched as the pirate turned and headed down the companion-way stairs. He prayed the crew of the merchant vessel would surrender quickly and without bloodshed, for he had no desire for Charlisse to witness any bloody carnage that would surely sever her already frazzled nerves.

Kent approached and stood waiting further orders. The captain gave the nod, and the first mate bellowed down the companionway for Jackson to fire. The warning shot served its purpose. The merchant vessel slowed its course and raised a flag of truce.

Never in his career had Merrick seen any ship give up so easily. He eyed them cautiously as the *Redemption* approached on the ship's larboard side.

The sharp rays of the rising sun had scattered nearly all the fog, and the temperature had risen rapidly. Even so, Merrick felt a chill he could not shake.

His pirates, preparing to board, began shouting insidious curses at their enemy to frighten them. If they could force them to surrender without a shot, it would keep the ships from being damaged and prevent loss of life.

Merrick studied the faces of the merchant ship's crew. No fear registered on their expressions—none. They all stood there quietly, hands in the air.

Something was terribly wrong.

"Sail ho," an agitated voice shouted from above him.

Merrick turned just in time to see a jet of gray smoke coming from a massive ship that emerged from the fog behind them. A second later, the boom of a cannon sounded, and a spray of water splashed the hull not two feet off their stern.

Merrick bellowed a string of orders, instantly shifting his attention from the small merchant vessel to the looming giant that was attacking from behind them. His crew, at first stunned into silence, quickly recovered and scrambled across the deck, obeying his commands.

"All hands on deck," he roared. "Unfurl the topsails. Set the stuns sails and the outer jib. Helmsman, hard aport." He hoped the turn would give the approaching ship a smaller target for her guns. The *Redemption* picked up speed.

Men raced up into the shrouds to give the sails every inch of canvas they had as they turned toward the wind.

Pistol shots rang through the air, whizzing by his head. Merrick turned to see the sailors on the merchant vessel firing upon his men. Puffs of smoke filled the air. The stench of gunpowder stung his nose. Someone screeched behind him, and he turned to see Hawthorn, one of his youngest men, fall to the deck, clutching his shoulder.

Plucking a pistol from its brace, Merrick scanned the deck of the merchant vessel, and upon seeing the sailor whose smoking gun was still aimed at the *Redemption*, he fired. The man hit the deck, holding his leg. His wide-eyed friends grabbed him and leapt down the hatch in a frenzy. By now, the merchant ship was out of range. Merrick returned his pistol to its brace, cursing himself for being such a fool.

Brighton knelt by Hawthorn, pressing a cloth to his wound. "Take him below," Merrick ordered, flinging himself up the ratlines to the main cross trees. He braced himself, holding the telescope steady as the ship sliced through the water.

The ship that had fired on them was a galleon. The gold and scarlet banner of Castile flapped tauntingly from her main mast. She turned starboard, presenting her guns.

Merrick lowered his glass and looked about. The *Redemption* had every inch of canvas stretched to her yards. Checking the direction of the breeze, he ordered a ten-degree turn to larboard. The ship turned, and the *Redemption*'s sails caught the wind with a jaunty snap. Soon they would be flying through the Caribbean at top speed. But would it be fast enough to outrun the Spanish vessel?

Another cloud of smoke spewed from the galleon, followed by a thunderous boom. Merrick barely had time to warn his crew before the shot tore through the tip of the mainsail.

Chapter 13
The Chase

The blast sent a violent jolt through the cabin, toppling Charlisse to the floor.

"Are ye a'right, miss?" Sloane rushed to her side, a look of concern on his face.

Charlisse heard the pounding footsteps of the pirates as they rushed back and forth, shouting things that were so vile and perverse, she shivered in disgust. Something terrible was happening.

Taking Sloane's outstretched hand, she stood, bracing herself against the rocking of the ship. A sudden crack filled the air, and a loud boom reverberated through the hull, sending her to the window in panic. A large plume of gray smoke obscured her view. *It must be from our cannons.* It had never occurred to her that they would do any pirating while on their way to Port Royal, but why not, if the opportunity presented itself? They were pirates, after all.

Her eyes darted to Sloane's. "What was that? Did we fire on someone?" She swallowed nervously.

"Naw, miss. There's naught to concern ye. I'm sure Cap'n's got it all under control." He glanced toward the door with an apprehensive look. "But I'll jus' go see for meself."

He patted her hand and turned, but Charlisse wouldn't let go. She didn't want to be alone. She didn't want to be trapped, not knowing what was happening. She didn't want to sink again into the Caribbean waters—or worse, be blasted into tiny bits! Her mouth went dry and her tongue wouldn't move, and though she tried to beg him to stay, no sound passed through her lips.

"I be right back," Sloane said, prying his hand from hers.

After he left, Charlisse waited two minutes that seemed like two hours before deciding she would rather tempt her fate above deck than in the cabin, trapped like some bird in a cage.

She made her way through the companionway and reached the main deck, spotting Captain Merrick up on the foredeck near the bow, feet spread apart, telescope aimed past the stern. Sloane stood by his side.

Charlisse crept to the side rail and peered over to see the source of their excitement. A large ship pursued them. A Spanish flag flew from beneath the crucifix at the head of its mainmast.

As she watched, a jet of charred smoke burst from its dark hull. Seconds later, she heard the thunder of the cannon. She froze, realizing they had been fired upon.

The shot just missed the starboard side of the *Redemption*, plunging into the ocean not two yards off the hull of the ship. It sent a spray of saltwater over the railing, drenching Charlisse. She jumped backward, lost her footing on the slippery wood, and plopped to the deck.

Chuckles erupted from all around her.

A strong arm grabbed her by the waist, lifting her to her feet, and she looked up to see Merrick's half smile. "I thought I told you to stay below." His voice was stern but carried a bit of humor as he held her tightly against him. His arms were warm and strong.

"I can't stay down there not knowing what's happening." She gave him a pleading look. "If I'm to face death, I wish it to find me staring squarely back upon it, not hiding from it beneath a pillow."

His hair was pulled back, but one strand had come loose and was blowing in the wind, tickling her face.

"Well, I can't have you up here distracting everyone," he said, still not relinquishing his hold on her. "Including me." He glanced at Kent, who had climbed up onto the crosstrees for a better look at their adversary. "What say you, Kent?"

"They're coming straight for us now, full speed," he yelled. The first mate slid down the backstay, landed on his feet next to them, and gave Charlisse a wink.

Merrick hesitated then took Charlisse by the hand up the foredeck steps. He led her to the foremast. "Hold on to this and stay here," he ordered before turning his attention back to the galleon.

Sloane returned with a chart and compass. Several minutes passed as the captain studied the maps, periodically glancing at the sun and the compass. "Turn her fifteen degrees to port, Master Kent."

"Fifteen to port," Kent bellowed across the deck to the helmsman as he headed down the stairs, directing other men to task.

The *Redemption* flew through the water with everything she had, all sails full, plunging into the waves and sending the spray back over the deck in sparkling showers.

The water sprinkled Charlisse's face and neck, the wind blew her long hair behind her, and the ship lunged beneath her. She felt a rush of exhilaration she had never known before. Despite the frightening circumstances, she felt alive for the first time.

She looked at the captain. His brows furrowed over a thoughtful gaze.

"Why do you run?" Charlisse asked. "Why not fight?" Not that she wanted a battle, but she was curious why a pirate would let such a handsome prize slip through his hands.

Merrick glanced up at her. "Because, milady, the only way to take down a galleon of Spain is by trickery. They have forty guns to our twelve and double our men."

"Will they fire on us again?"

"No, we are out of their range," he answered, "for the time being."

"But didn't they already hit us?"

"Just a flesh wound." Merrick looked up from his chart, folded it, and handed it to Sloane. "Check on Hawthorn and report back to me."

"Aye, Cap'n."

Merrick glanced at the mainsail. His eyes darkened. Two pirates worked on it with cord and needle.

"What are they doing?" Charlisse asked, her gaze following Merrick's.

"Repairing the tear to prevent the split from widening."

"If they can't, won't that affect our speed?"

"Possibly." Merrick's gaze became troubled as he looked at the galleon racing behind them. "Don't worry, miss. Freshly careened, the *Redemption* can easily pull eleven knots—maybe nine or ten without damage. The galleon at top speed can only achieve eight."

The captain faced into the wind. Charlisse watched his back from where she clung to the foremast. Who was this man? Pirate? Gentleman? Commander? Man of faith? He both confused and intrigued her. And that frightened her the most. He was unpredictable, and unpredictable men were dangerous, untrustworthy.

He stood there undaunted, shirt billowing in the wind, arms crossed over his chest as though he commanded the world—unconcerned that a Spanish warship pursued him.

He turned suddenly and caught her staring at him. Their eyes locked for an intense second. A hint of a smile formed on his lips.

Sloane jumped up the steps. "Hawthorn be okay, Cap'n," he announced. "Shot went clean through him."

Merrick nodded and turned back around. He commanded his men with efficiency and authority, sending them up and down the shrouds to adjust the sails for maximum wind.

Merrick's eyes narrowed as he glanced at the oncoming threat. Charlisse saw that the galleon had gained on them. She kept her fears to herself, not wanting to give Merrick cause to send her back to that stifling cabin.

The sight of the Spanish ship closing in on the *Redemption* clenched her heart in fear. Visions of being sunk to the bottom of the Caribbean flooded her thoughts, or worse yet, of becoming a Spanish prisoner, a victim of the hideous and vicious tortures the Spaniards inflicted on those whose religious views differed from their own.

Merrick was looking through his telescope off the front of the ship when Kent approached. He lowered the glass and tapped it into his hand, a look of apprehension marring his features.

"Captain, they're coming up on our starboard quarter, bearing their guns, and almost within range."

Merrick nodded, his gaze resting on the galleon, still a mile astern, but slowly gaining. Nothing in his expression betrayed any fear.

Master Kent darted anxious glances at the Spanish ship. He cleared his throat. "Any further orders?"

The terror in his voice sent a flutter through Charlisse's stomach. Her legs ached from standing on the rocking ship. She leaned back on the mast.

Merrick pointed off the bow of the ship. "Do you see those islands?"

Kent narrowed his eyes, following the indication of his captain's hand, and after a few moments, his troubled gaze melted into one of enthusiasm. "Yes, I do," he said with interest. He paused before adding, "Ah, Captain. I see your plan now, and a. . ."

Overhearing only part of the conversation and curious to see what Merrick was pointing at, Charlisse stepped toward the bow. Kent turned and held out his hand to help her. Receiving it, she allowed him to guide her to the railing. Then shielding her eyes from the sun, she saw the little cluster of islands to which the men were referring.

"I don't understand," she said.

"Well, miss—" Kent began, his voice oozing charm.

"That will be all, Kent," Merrick interrupted. "Prepare the men to furl top- and mainsails at my command."

The first mate hesitated, staring into Charlisse's eyes with a look of understanding. His curly brown hair blew freely in the breeze from under his black headscarf. His dark brown eyes, narrow as a hawk's, roved over her. She returned his smile.

"Yes, Captain," he sneered, without breaking the lock he had on her eyes. Then he turned and strode away.

"We are shallow on the draft, milady." Merrick watched his first mate leave with a troubled look in his eye.

"And what does that mean?"

"It means the *Redemption* can go much closer to those islands than our Spanish friends can." His voice held a tone of mischief.

She turned from him and looked out toward the islands. Several minutes passed. She felt his gaze still upon her. He took a step closer to her, brushing his arm against hers.

"Thank you for allowing me to stay on deck, Captain. I hope I haven't been too much trouble."

The corner of his mouth lifted in amusement. "The only trouble you have caused is the distraction due to your beauty." His hand covered hers on the rail. She felt her cheeks redden. Yet she did not remove her hand from the warmth and strength of his. It was more comforting than she cared to admit.

When Sloane approached, she jerked her hand away.

They were nearly upon the islands. Merrick bellowed orders, sending hands up the shrouds to lower the topsails and topgallants.

"Why are you slowing the ship?" Charlisse asked.

"The islands have cays and reefs surrounding them that must be carefully navigated. I cannot approach at full speed."

"Won't the galleon catch up to us then?"

"Let's pray they do not, milady." Lifting one eyebrow, he added, "Oh, I forgot, you don't believe in God."

Charlisse cast him a sideways glance.

"I need to take over the helm for a time." He bowed. "Stay here with Sloane. You'll be safe." He tipped his hat and left, shouting orders for two of the pirates to man the stern chasers.

She watched him take over the wheel on the quarterdeck and felt suddenly alone. His flatteries both delighted and frightened her. But perhaps that was all they were—just vain flatteries, without any real depth of feeling.

The Spanish warship swiftly descended on them. Charlisse felt as though the *Redemption* were a mouse scrambling for a tiny hole while a large cat—with much bigger claws—chased in fast pursuit.

She glanced at the captain standing at the helm and saw only dauntless assurance in his manner, but that did nothing to allay her fears.

Merrick focused on the delicate navigation. Even so, he could not get the woman out of his mind. He remembered her standing at the bow of the ship, the mist glittering on her hair and sparkling like diamonds on her skin. He knew she was frightened. Yet she stood on the forecastle deck, her head lifted high, facing her fate with more tenacity than most men he'd known. Most of the ladies of his prior acquaintance would be cowering below, crying on their beds. He admired the strength in her, and with that admiration came an overwhelming desire to protect her—something he had never felt for any woman before.

The sound of cannon fire jolted him from his thoughts. The Spaniards, no doubt aware of his plan, were making one last attempt to hit the *Redemption* as the distance between them closed. The shot missed their larboard quarter by just three yards—bathing them with saltwater before plunging to the bottom of the sea.

Captain Merrick immediately answered their fire with the rapid spit of chasers on his stern. If he could just hold them off for a few more minutes, the *Redemption* would be safe.

Chapter 14
The Challenge

Captain Merrick stood at the main deck railing and squinted his eyes at the setting sun. The *Redemption* gently bobbed in the shallow waters among the cluster of islands, safe for the moment behind the natural barriers of reef and cay.

Sloane handed the telescope back to him. "Looks to me, Cap'n, the galleon's anchored herself as close to the islands as her keel will take her. But thanks be to God, we be out of her gun range, eh?"

Merrick took a look, as well. "Yes, indeed." He nodded, lowering the glass. "It appears they hope to wait us out." He sighed. "I've neither mind nor inclination to sit idly by while our food and water—already in short supply—dwindle away."

Kent joined the two men. The sun dragged its last rays of daylight down below the horizon, leaving behind fuzzy images that grew dimmer in the twilight. Soon they would see nothing save what the tiny crescent moon allowed them.

"Surely we can escape them in the darkness," Kent said.

Merrick shook his head. "I cannot navigate through these reefs and cays without the light. It would be suicide."

A few pirates gathered behind them.

Sloane shifted his stance. "Then they've got us trapped here, eh?"

Growls sounded behind Merrick. He turned around.

"So, Cap'n's got us caught like a fish in a net," exclaimed one of the pirates, looking around at his fellow mates. "Told ye he was as soft as the underbelly of an eel. We shoulda stood our ground and fought them Spanish jackanapes, says I." He spat on the deck near Merrick's boots. Grunts of approval followed.

"Har, I be agreein'," added Royce. He hunched forward, his profile that of a hungry raven eyeing a promising morsel. "Now all's we can do is sit an' wait till we either starve to death or make a run fer it, an' they pluck us out o' the water and send us to the Spanish dungeons."

Sloane jumped in front of his captain, hand on the hilt of his cutlass. "Listen to me, ye young jackals," he growled. "Cap'n's ne'er done ye wrong. He'll be gettin' us out o' this fer sure. Ye all be as squawky as nervous hens."

Stepping forward, Merrick laid a hand on his friend's shoulder. His firm gaze landed on each of the pirates in turn. They were a dangerous and fickle band of men, but he knew how to handle them. The dark figure slithering up on his left was another story.

Kent squirmed past Merrick to stand in front of the pirates, a leering look of anticipation on his face. "Looks like the men have lost faith in you, sir." He smirked. "Perhaps they're in need of a better captain." He looked around at his companions with cool assurance. "I would have fought the galleon and defeated the Spaniards, not run away like a coward."

"Aye, aye," several pirates agreed.

The rambunctious mob were grunting their approval of Kent's declaration when Jackson appeared behind them, a head taller than most, and parted the crowd. He reached Merrick and turned to face the men. Silence descended upon the mob. The ex-slave rarely spoke, but when he did, he was worth hearing.

He crossed his arms and stood firmly. "Cap'n's done naught to make ye turn on 'im. We'd be at the bottom of the sea right now if Master Kent was the cap'n." His voice boomed across the deck. "I stand wit' the cap'n."

"Cowards come in all sizes." Kent's eyes glinted with humor as he glanced across the pirates, who chuckled in response.

"That'll be quite enough, Master Kent." Merrick stepped forward, his gaze drifting over the entire group. "You men know fair well that only by trickery, deceit, or surprise can a ship our size hope to obtain victory over a galleon. I have proven that to you on more than one occasion." He looked each of them in the eye with such piercing dominance that some dropped their gazes. "That was not the case today. If any of you scurrilous scalawags think you could have done better, then egad, you are more fools than I gave you credit for." He glared at his first mate. "But I'll not defend myself to the likes of you, Kent. If you're up to it, then challenge me fair and square and be done with it. I grow tired of your whining."

In the long, silent pause, the pirates looked toward Kent.

"As you wish, Captain." Kent's lips twisted in a crooked smile. He bowed gracefully and drew his cutlass, a look of grim determination on his face.

Charlisse had gone below as soon as she knew they were safely within the haven of the islands. With the torturous heat, the struggle to remain standing on the heaving ship, and the excitement of the chase, she felt exhausted.

She lay down on the soft feather bed that smelled like Captain Merrick and breathed in the musky scent. A smile came to her lips before she realized it, and she bolted upright, alarmed at the unfamiliar emotions that swept over her.

Rubbing her fingers where his warm hand had clasped, she remembered the way his nearness brought every cell in her body to life, waking each one from a deep, long sleep.

What was happening to her? Was she nothing more than the trollop her uncle had always told her she was? Was she so wanton, so lacking in self-control, that she succumbed to any man graced with looks and charm, regardless of the degradation of his character?

Falling back on the bed, Charlisse's thoughts drifted to another man: Richard Farrow, son of the Earl Winston Farrow, the only other man—from a past deprived of such acquaintances—who had evoked similar feelings. She had just turned sixteen when she met him. Although her uncle had kept her away from most formal occasions, she had convinced him to let her attend a ball thrown by the Duke and Duchess of Galchester.

Weeks in advance, she'd chosen her dress: a sapphire satin gown trimmed with cream lace and lined with pearls—the most exquisite garment she had ever seen. On the night of the ball, she pinned up her hair with pearl combs inlaid with rubies, allowing a few delicate golden curls to gracefully touch her shoulders. She had never felt more beautiful.

She'd spotted Richard as soon as she entered the ballroom on her uncle's arm. He was the most handsome and eligible man in London circles, top of his class at Oxford, trained in the art of war at the military academy, and heir to the Farrow fortune, which encompassed quite a substantial estate.

He stood across the candlelit room in his military dress. She had seen him on several different occasions, and a graceful bow or nod to her each time indicated he had seen her, as well. Now, under his eloquent perusal, she felt a blush rise to her cheeks.

Fortunately, her uncle had been whisked away by a man wishing to talk to him on some important matter, leaving Charlisse uncharacteristically alone.

Richard walked up to her and bowed. "I don't believe I've had the pleasure, Lady Bristol." He held out his hand. "Richard Farrow, at your service." He smiled and took her hand, kissing it gently.

Charlisse noticed several of the other young ladies across the room glaring at her behind outspread fans.

She curtsied politely, giving Richard a tremulous smile. "It is a great pleasure to meet you, Lord Farrow."

He smiled, flashing exquisite white teeth under a black mustache. His eyes were as blue as hers and full of life. His hair, chestnut brown and wavy, was pulled back revealing a strong, handsome face. Not releasing her hand, he placed it under his elbow and drew her out onto the dance floor, where a minuet was playing. "Wherever does your uncle keep you, Miss Bristol? I must admit, I search for you most ardently at these drab events, but this is the first time in many months I've had the pleasure of gazing upon your beauty."

Charlisse smiled politely, not sure how to answer. "My uncle keeps me under his watchful eye, I'm afraid, milord."

Richard took her hand and swirled her over the floor as if they were floating on a cloud. Young Lord Farrow was apparently as good at dancing as he was at everything else. "What a pity. The very room lights up in your presence."

For the first time in her life, Charlisse felt cherished—like a princess. Those few minutes with Richard gliding gracefully across the room—the envy of all those around them—were the best moments of her life.

But like all fairy tales, this one came to an abrupt end. From the corner of her eye, Charlisse saw the red, angry face of her uncle as he approached through the crowd. He grabbed her arm and yanked her away from Richard, hauling her out the door under the curious glares of the nobility.

Charlisse glanced back at Richard, who stood forlornly, a look of shock on his handsome face.

Back at home, her uncle threw her into her room. Piece by piece, he ripped off her beautiful dress, until the floor around her was littered with azure satin. "I should have known not to leave you alone. You are a whore just like your mother. How could you let that man touch you?"

Once he had stripped her bare, he glared at her as he always did, and as always, staring at her unclad body incensed him further. He opened the drawer of her walnut credenza and grabbed the familiar whip. Forcing her down to her knees beside her bed in repentance, he beat her across the back. "Everyone at the ball will know you for the tramp that you are. Is that what you want?"

The whip was small, but its sting was not. With each strike, Charlisse leaned over her bed in agony, feeling the burn of the leather as it shredded her delicate skin. She did not scream. She would not give her uncle that satisfaction. But she could not stop the flood of tears that sprinkled onto her bedspread and soaked into the fabric leaving stains of painful memories. What had she done to deserve such repeated beatings? Was she a harlot like he said? Had her mother truly been a tramp?

After the whipping, under her uncle's direction, she climbed into a hot bath, where he applied a hard bristle brush to her skin. He scrubbed until she was red and raw, quoting passages from the Bible about sexual immorality, lust, and impurity. He said he was washing away her sin and shame. Afterward, he locked her in her room and left her there alone for days. This ritual was repeated with more frequency and fury as she grew older.

That was the first and last ball she ever attended. A year later, she heard Richard Farrow had married a young lady from Yorkshire. She never saw him again.

Angry shouts rescued Charlisse from the morbid thoughts of her past. After rising from the bed, she crept cautiously up the companionway to see what trouble was brewing aboard this pirate ship.

As she neared the main deck, she heard the deep, commanding voice of the captain issue a challenge, but she was unable to see him through the group of pirates who cluttered the deck.

She heard the scraping of a sword against its scabbard. The horde of men parted, backing away from some perceived threat. Instantly, Charlisse saw Merrick, his dark eyes smoldering like coals, facing Kent who held the tip of his sword at his captain's heart.

"Are you sure you want to do this, mate?" Merrick asked.

"Afraid you'll lose the ship to me?" Kent flashed an arrogant smile. Something in the way he was standing, fidgeting back and forth, with a tight grip on the hilt of his cutlass, gave Charlisse the impression he was more frightened than he let on.

Merrick stood with calm assurance, sizing up his challenger.

With lightning speed, the captain drew his cutlass. He whipped it against Kent's blade with a loud clank, sending the first mate tumbling backward.

Recovering quickly, he lunged back at his opponent.

The pirates shouted and howled as the two battled in skillful swordplay. But it wasn't just play. Theirs was a deadly game. The thought that Merrick might lose the battle sent an uneasy chill down Charlisse's spine. She hadn't forgotten his strange reaction to the mention of her father's name. He had heard of her father before, she was sure of it. If Merrick were to die tonight, she would never know what he knew. Perhaps he could lead her to her father.

Hilt to hilt they fought with strength and speed. The clanging of their swords echoed through the thick, moist night. Kent rushed Merrick. The captain cleared the foredeck railing with a graceful leap, barely evading a deadly thrust. Frustrated, Kent stormed up the steps and charged his captain, slashing his sword before him. Blow after blow, he pushed Merrick back. He lunged, and the tip of his blade sliced through Merrick's shirt, leaving a trail of blood that glistened black in the moonlight.

Kent grinned. "I'm too fast for you, eh?" he said, panting.

"Come and see." Merrick motioned with his fingers for Kent to come closer.

The pirates shouted and placed bets, each for his chosen victor. Charlisse felt sick watching their greed and callous disregard for their captain and first mate. One of them would most likely die tonight.

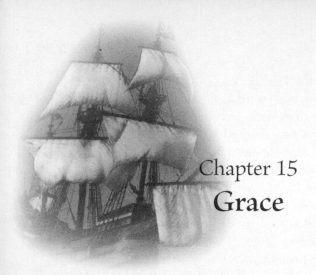

Chapter 15
Grace

Charlisse watched as Kent slashed his cutlass once again toward Merrick. The captain sidestepped, bringing his blade in from one direction then quickly shifting to another. With a swift flick of his sword, he snapped the cutlass from Kent's hand, sending it clattering to the deck. Merrick lowered his sword, taking a step toward his opponent. Kent drew a knife and lunged at his captain. Charlisse's heart leapt to her throat. She gasped.

Merrick arched to the side, and the knife stabbed only air. Kent drew back for another deadly thrust, but before he could plant the blade, Merrick pounded the knife from the first mate's grip with the hilt of his cutlass. The knife joined Kent's sword on the deck with a clank that echoed over the ship. Chest heaving, Merrick positioned the tip of his blade at Kent's heart.

Kent stood, breathless and wide-eyed. The two men stared at each other. The crew began chanting, "Kill 'im, kill 'im, kill 'im," the intensity of their voices rising with each utterance.

The sharp point of Merrick's cutlass brought forth a rivulet of crimson, staining the first mate's shirt. "Seems your friends have turned on you," Merrick said, fixing Kent with a hard gaze.

Kent swallowed nervously. His eyes silently pleaded with Merrick. His upper lip twitched, but he did not beg for quarter.

Moments passed as the chanting continued. Merrick yelled for Sloane and Jackson. "Take him below and lock him up," he ordered.

Jackson seized Kent, nearly lifting him off his feet and led him away.

Merrick lowered his blade.

The chanting ceased and the pirates, muttering in disgust, quickly divvied up their winnings.

From the foredeck railing, Merrick glared down on his traitorous crew. "Anyone else wish to challenge my authority as captain?"

Charlisse shrank against the companionway railing, lest he see her.

"You, Maynerd? Royce?" He pointed his cutlass at the two men who stood in front of the pack.

The pirates averted their gazes and shook their heads. "No, Cap'n."

"Then get back to work, you worthless pack of mutinous rats." His fierce tone sent the pirates scrambling across the deck. Merrick sheathed his cutlass and wiped the sweat from his brow.

Charlisse slipped back down to the cabin, breathing a sigh of relief at the outcome of the battle, convincing herself her feelings of joy stemmed from purely selfish reasons concerning her own safety and finding her father. Merrick was obviously the lesser of two evils when compared with Kent, but that did nothing to allay her fear of him. Having now been a witness of his severity toward his crew—not that it wasn't richly deserved—she realized he was not a man to contend with.

Moments later, the cabin's oak door slammed open, and Captain Merrick stormed into the room. He threw his baldric and pistols down onto a chair without a glance at Charlisse. Hands on the edge of his desk, he leaned forward, his damp, black hair falling in strings over his face.

Brighton crept in behind him, carrying a small satchel. Alarm tightening his features, he glanced at Charlisse, who sat frozen on the bed. "Um. . .um, Cap'n?"

Merrick whirled around. "Get out!" he yelled, his dark eyes flashing.

"But ye be hurt."

"And *ye be* taking sides against me on my own ship!"

Brighton hesitated, studying the red stain so stark against the white of Merrick's shirt.

Merrick took a step toward him. "Get out, or I'll have you thrown overboard with a cannonball strapped to your boots." The ship's doctor darted from the room, crashing into Sloane, who was just coming through the door.

Shaking his head, Sloane came in, and closed the door behind him.

He cautiously eyed Merrick. The captain ran his hand through his slick hair, and his gaze met Charlisse's as if he'd just noticed her. The ferocity in his eyes frightened her.

Grabbing the bottle of rum, he took a heavy swig and wiped his mouth on his sleeve. Fury faded from his countenance.

"That cuckoldy scamp be locked up below, Cap'n," Sloane said.

Merrick nodded, taking another swig before slamming the bottle down on his desk and finding a seat in one of the leather chairs.

"You're hurt." Charlisse nodded toward his shirt.

Merrick looked at her, a trace of curiosity in his eyes. "It's nothing, just a scratch," he said, examining the wound.

Sloane got up. "Take off yer shirt." He collected the bottle of rum and removed his violet scarf, releasing his mop of frizzy, gray hair.

Merrick lifted one eyebrow.

"Just do it, ye stubborn carp."

Merrick sighed and pulled his shirt over his head.

"What happened?" Charlisse feigned ignorance. She had seen the fight, true enough, but she still had no idea what had started it.

"I'll tell ye wha' happened, miss," Sloane said. "That young cocky jackanapes thought he'd be takin' over this ship from the cap'n. Down to the devil with him!"

He dribbled some rum onto his scarf. "So he gave his challenge. The cap'n an' him fought, an' the cap'n won, as ye can see."

An angry red slash angled across Merrick's thickly muscled chest from his left shoulder to his arm. He winced when Sloane applied the rum. The muscles in his arms flexed, still bulging from the fight.

"That's a waste of good rum, my friend." He gave Sloane a pained grin.

"Why would Kent do such a thing?" Charlisse looked at the wall, the bed, the desk—anything but the broad expanse of Merrick's chest. Yet her gaze kept seeking him. What was wrong with her?

"That rogue has wanted to take over this ship since he came aboard," Merrick said. "He's young, hot-tempered, and arrogant. When mixed with education and training, as in his case, those qualities foster a volatile combination."

"A bit like ye are, if I may say so." Sloane chuckled, but seeing Merrick's sour expression, added, "Or *were*."

Merrick's frown faded. "Yes, I suppose you may say so."

Sloane dabbed the rum-soaked scarf onto Merrick's wound again, pressing where the cut was deepest. Merrick flinched and grabbed his friend's hand. "That'll do. Enough of your doting."

Sloane pulled away in a huff. "You'll be needin' a bandage."

Merrick gave him a dismissive wave, then turned to Charlisse. "Frankly, I'm surprised Master Kent took this long, especially with you aboard, milady."

Charlisse wasn't sure what he meant. With every one of Kent's gestures and glances, he had appeared to be quite civil. Still, she realized her predicament on this ship could be much worse without the captain. "I'm glad you won."

"I'm overwhelmed by your concern," Merrick said, his eyes flickering with humor as he laid his hand on his heart. "At least I merit a position slightly above a cutthroat like Kent."

"Not far above, I assure you." Charlisse tossed her chin in the air.

Merrick lifted one brow. "I can certainly make arrangements for you to spend some time alone with Master Kent down in the hold. Perhaps, afterward, your opinion of me would change."

Charlisse snorted and grabbed a lock of her hair. "I consider you no less the rogue than he is. The only difference is that he hides his villainy behind a façade of gentlemanly behavior, while you make no pretense at such civility."

Sloane chuckled.

Merrick glared at his friend. "Go get Jackson. We need to plan our next move."

"Aye, aye, Cap'n." Sloane returned the rum bottle to the table and headed out the door. "An' I be getting' ye a bandage, too," he said before closing it.

Charlisse faced Merrick, wondering whether she should have been so rude. When would she learn to control her tongue? The last thing she wanted to do was ignite the captain's rage. Besides, she must find out what he knew about her father. If she angered and insulted him, why would he tell her anything? A trickle of blood escaped his wound. She wanted to wipe it. She wanted to tell him that she couldn't get him out of her head.

Instead, she sat silently, barely breathing, while his gaze took her in with those intense eyes that always seemed to be reading her every thought. They were mesmerizing, and she knew without a doubt that if she looked into them too deeply or for too long, she would be forever under their spell.

How could she, a supposed lady, find this pirate, this knave, so appealing? It made no sense, and she attributed it to an unchaste flaw in her character—one her uncle had assured her she had. Impure tendencies or not, she would not give in to the debased feelings that consumed her when he was near.

"What will you do now?" she asked.

"First, I intend to get us out of this trap." He stood and walked over, then dropped to the bed beside her.

Her heart fluttered. *Must he sit so close to me?* "But what of the crew?" she asked, scooting away, trying to mask her inner turmoil behind a composed voice.

A grin appeared on his lips. "What of them?"

She could smell the rum on his breath—or was it from Sloane's doctoring? "Will they follow your command?"

"For the time being," he answered. "Until the next time a challenge is made, which I hope I have pushed further into the future by my victory today."

He touched his wound and winced, then looked up at her again.

He was so close that she could feel the heat from his body.

"A captain grows stronger each time he quells an attempted mutiny," he said. "He gains the respect and fear of his crew, making it harder for the next to challenge him. The only thing is"—he hesitated, looking toward the door—"not killing Kent may have put me in a weaker position with the men."

"Kill him? After the battle was over? Why?"

"He challenged me." He shrugged. "It's the code we pirates live by."

She turned away, disgusted. "Why didn't you?"

"It's not the code I live by anymore," he said. "Besides, he reminds me of someone I knew once. If there was hope for that man, there could be hope yet for Kent."

Charlisse saw sincerity in his eyes. Was the man he spoke of himself?

He raised and lowered his arm, stretching it, and his wound began to bleed.

Instinctively, she retrieved the discarded shirt from his chair and pressed it over his cut. His hand rose to cover hers, and she immediately regretted her action. Their eyes met once again. She felt her heart jump and her stomach clench. His other hand stroked her cheek. Burning waves radiated through her.

Slowly, he leaned closer, his mouth inches from hers.

Charlisse jumped off the bed and stepped back.

One black eyebrow raised, he said, "I wasn't going to bite you."

Charlisse fidgeted and paced to the other side of the cabin, catching her breath. She had to divert his attention. Perhaps this was a good time to ask him about her father. She turned and curved her lips in the most alluring smile she could effect, feeling foolish. "This morning, when I said my father's name," she stuttered, "you seemed to know him." Her father. Maybe if she had known the love of a true father, she wouldn't be so easily taken in by the charms of this pirate.

Examining her, Merrick tossed the bloody shirt to the floor. "It can't be the same man."

"But wh—"

The door swung open and in stomped Jackson and Sloane.

Merrick greeted them and all three men surrounded the captain's desk, where he began relaying his plan of escape.

Charlisse retreated to her spot by the window and gazed out over the black sea, feeling frustration bubble up inside her. Merrick knew something about her father, yet every time she mentioned his name, the captain avoided her questions.

After an hour of discussion, Merrick rolled up his charts. He slapped Jackson on the back. "Post a night watch just in case our Spanish friends decide to pay us a visit." The large man nodded and marched from the room. Sloane remained next to the desk.

Merrick donned a clean shirt and strapped on his weapons.

"You're to take the galleon tonight?" Charlisse asked.

"No, milady." Merrick grinned mischievously. "But we will prepare a surprise for her in the morning." He tied his hair back and fitted on his scarf. "Sloane will watch over you until I return."

He winked at her, put on his hat, and left before Charlisse could protest.

Charlisse turned to Sloane. "I'm sorry you are always left with the task of being my nursemaid."

"Ah, don't be worryin' yer pretty little head 'bout that, miss," he said, making himself comfortable in one of the chairs. "I be gettin' too old fer this pirate stuff anyways."

Charlisse moved to the bed. "Do you know a man named Edward Terrance Bristol?"

Sloane laid his head back and closed his eyes, but a stern expression crossed his features. "Now, ye best be gettin' some sleep. 'Twill be a long one tomorrow."

"Why is that?"

"Tomorrow we take a Spanish galleon."

Chapter 16
The Kiss

When Sloane began to snore, Charlisse laid her head on the pillow and tried to rest, but sleep did not come easily. An eerie silence crept over the ship as it sat passively in the shallows of the islands. Maybe it was the rhythmic movement of the sea that she missed—the way the ship creaked and moaned in exuberant song as it sailed along. But tonight, the *Redemption* slept soundly—not even the usual revelry of the pirates shattered its peaceful repose. It was unnerving.

Charlisse got up and paced the tiny cabin. She ran her fingers over the books lining the shelves, shaking her head at the exquisite collection of fine literature—so at odds with the character of a pirate captain. Perhaps she could find something among his things that would help her understand him—his weaknesses, strengths, what mattered to him. Avoiding the bottles of rum, she picked up a gold figurine of a soldier, examined the workmanship, and then tried on a silver ring embedded with rubies that lay next to it. It was too big for her small fingers. She admired the brass candlesticks, the fine silver chalice. Lifting a velvet bag, she sifted through its glimmering contents—rubies, sapphires, and emeralds. Lustrous pearls glowed from within a small silver chest, threatening to overflow onto the captain's desk. Shuffling through the charts tossed about haphazardly, she spotted the open Bible. What attracted Merrick to this ancient book? Her uncle had told her it was the Word of God, but was it? Was anything he had told her true? She turned to walk away, but wait. Maybe this was Merrick's weakness—this God of his. She sat down, only willing to read the page Merrick had open.

And we know that all things work together for good to them that love God, to them who are the called according to his purpose.

Sloane muttered in his sleep and turned in the chair. Charlisse skipped down a few lines.

What shall we then say to these things? If God be for us, who can be against us? He that spared not his own Son, but delivered him up for us all, how shall he not with him also freely give us all things? Who shall lay any thing to the charge of God's elect? It is God that justifieth. Who is he that condemneth? It is Christ that died, yea rather, that is risen again, who is even at the right hand of God, who also maketh intercession for us. Who shall separate us from the love of Christ? shall tribulation, or distress, or persecution, or famine, or nakedness, or peril, or sword? As it is written, For thy sake we are killed all the day long; we are accounted as sheep for the slaughter. Nay, in all these things we are more than conquerors through him that loved us. For I am persuaded, that neither death, nor life, nor angels, nor principalities, nor powers, nor things present, nor things to come, nor height, nor depth, nor any other creature, shall be able to separate us from the love of God, which is in Christ Jesus our Lord.

The love of God. Where had God been when her uncle had beaten her, whipped her, lusted after her, and berated her with insults? She slammed the book shut and stood, even more restless than before.

What attracted a man like Merrick to the idea of a loving God who gave His life for him? He seemed too strong a man to be in need of anyone or anything, especially an elusive God, who for all she could tell had abandoned the creation He insisted He loved so much.

Hours later, as Charlisse lay on the bed, floating in and out of consciousness, she heard Merrick return and Sloane leave. When the captain finally settled on the floor, something in her relaxed, and she drifted to sleep.

The squawking of birds filled her ears—at first soft and distant, then growing louder, jarring her from her sleep. For a brief moment, she thought she was back on the deserted island again, and a shard of terror ran down her spine. Darting up, she rubbed her eyes. The morning sun was just filtering through the stained-glass window. She saw the sleeping form of Captain Merrick on the hard floor. Despite the intense pressure and responsibility that coursed through his daily life, he slept peacefully. She envied him.

He stirred, opened his eyes, and slowly propped himself on his elbows. When he caught her gaze upon him, a smile curved his lips—that sultry smile that could melt her heart if she let it.

Turning aside, Charlisse fumbled with her hair, pushing the wayward golden curls from her face, keeping one strand between her fingers.

"You always play with your hair when you're nervous." His deep voice broke the silence.

She darted him a quick glance. "I'm not nervous."

"Hmm." He jumped to his feet, rubbed his neck, and moved his injured shoulder back and forth. "It will be a busy day, milady." He looked at her. "I hope it will not be a deadly one, but it would be in your best interest to stay in my cabin."

"I will not be locked up in here like some pirate's booty along with your other plunder."

Merrick chuckled. "Is that so? Well, by all means, milady, come above. I could use someone to man the swivel guns."

She thrust her chin in the air. "Are you going to take the galleon?"

"That's my plan, yes."

"Will you kill the Spaniards?"

He stopped short and looked at her solemnly. "That is not my intention." He took off his shirt and tossed it in the corner. "Yet sometimes killing is unavoidable." He opened his armoire and grabbed a clean shirt, his thickly corded muscles gliding across his back as he moved. "The galleon is a worthy prize, and I have others to answer to besides myself."

"Who? Your disloyal crew, who turn on you at the slightest opportunity?"

"Harrumph," Merrick let out, exasperation showing on his face. "They have a part in my decisions, to be sure." He sat in his chair and pulled on his tall, black boots. "There are things you don't understand, miss."

"Oh, I understand perfectly well," she said, getting up. "I understand that the pull of greed can be stronger than the sanctity of human life."

"Then you don't know me very well."

"I know you're a pirate. That is all I need to know." Charlisse strode to the window and peeked out.

At his silence, a twinge of regret pinched her heart. Had she been too harsh? So far, he had done nothing to harm her, and the mercy he extended to Kent last night revealed an inner core of decency. But maybe it was all an act—a pretense of civility to gain her trust, to get her to lower her defenses so he could lure her into his web. How could there be a good-hearted pirate?

She rubbed her eyes, still swollen with sleep. But she did know one thing. This pirate captain was a volatile man—in more ways than one.

Seeing him open his Bible, she added in an insolent tone, "There is much about greed in there. Perhaps you should read those verses."

He looked up and cocked one eyebrow. "Now you are an expert on the Word of God? I thought you didn't believe in Him."

Huffing, she turned her gaze back out the window. She watched the palm trees that swayed in the distance, the tumultuous feelings in her heart as fickle as the palm fronds vacillating in the morning breeze. The new wave of emotions that flowed through her made no sense, and she decided, once again, they were not to be trusted.

The sun broke above the trees of the little island and sent its brilliant rays like a fan over the shoreline, setting aglow the rippling waves and crystallizing the grains of sand. The scene reminded her of the other little island where she had spent the last month, and where she would probably have died if not for this pirate with her now.

She turned to face him. He finished reading, stood, and strapped on his weapons. After tying his hair back, he gazed at her, uncertainty wrinkling his brow. Silence stretched between them. Charlisse realized he faced great peril today, possibly even his own death. Her insides quivered at the thought. He must have seen the concern in her eyes for he smiled and sauntered over to her.

He stood so close, his scent showered over her in waves of musk and salt. "Never fear, milady. I'll be quite all right."

"Why should I care?" Charlisse snorted and snapped her gaze away.

He put his finger under her chin and lifted her face to his. Her body tensed and her heart quickened, but she stared up into his dark eyes, determined not to reveal her writhing emotions within.

"A kiss for a soldier about to go off to battle?" A faint smirk alighted on his lips.

"I should think not. How dare you suggest such a—"

Merrick started to turn away. Clutching his arms, Charlisse swerved him back around and drove her lips onto his. He responded immediately, encircling her in his arms

Pinpricks of excitement showered over her. Something within her melted, and she lost all resolve. She closed her eyes, enjoying the warmth and vigor of his lips as they hungrily sought hers, the musky smell of his skin, the scratch of his stubble against her cheek.

He released her, a wicked grin on his face. Stepping back, he gave her a gracious bow, grabbed his hat, and left the room without a word.

Charlisse stood stunned, feeling as though she would melt into the floor. She touched her lips, still experiencing the tingles that rippled through her—unknown feelings, exciting and powerful.

She liked them.

Sitting on the bed, she clung to the post, ashamed, embarrassed, and beginning to believe that her uncle's accusations had been true all along. How could she have thrown herself at Merrick so easily? *How weak I am!*

The passions that had consumed her slowly faded, and a firm determination sprouted in their place.

This must never happen again.

She must stay away from Captain Edmund Merrick.

Chapter 17
The Galleon

Loud voices above Charlisse and the gentle forward heave of the ship stirred her from her thoughts. She rushed to the window, anxious to resume the journey to Port Royal, but distressed for the galleon's fate. Not that she harbored any fondness for the Spanish, but she certainly wished them no harm—especially not at the hands of this merciless band of scoundrels.

It occurred to her that she had an unwarranted confidence in Merrick's abilities to capture the galleon. With the taste of his lips still on hers, she lay back on the bed, feeling helpless in many ways—helpless to stop the carnage, helpless to make her way to Port Royal and find her father, and helpless under the spell Merrick had cast upon her. Helplessness had been an all-too-familiar guest in her heart for too many years—the kind of guest who always dropped in, made himself right at home, and stayed long past his welcome. It was time to throw him out, if only she had the strength to do so.

On deck, with assurances from Jackson that the *Santo Domingo*—for that was the name engraved on the galleon's hull—was sufficiently disabled, Captain Merrick navigated the *Redemption* back out through the outlying reefs.

The men responded to his commands as if there had been no attempted mutiny the night before, and Jackson took over his new post as first mate with enthusiasm. He and a small group of men had sneaked over in one of the cockboats—under cover of night—and had entwined twenty feet of cable chain about the galleon's rudder. The Spanish warship would have no steering capabilities whatsoever.

Even amidst the excitement, Merrick could not shake thoughts of the lady below. Why had she kissed him? Not that he was complaining, but her sudden affection baffled him in light of her rude and often impertinent behavior. Her lips had been soft and warm. He'd felt them quiver at first, but when she finally succumbed to him, he could feel the passion within her climbing to join his. The kiss became the sweetest of his life, and that was no small thing, considering the numerous kisses he had enjoyed.

"Cap'n, the galleon unfurls her sails," Jackson yelled from the shrouds, bringing Merrick's attention back to the task at hand.

The Spanish warship, alerted to their presence, was attempting to catch enough wind to turn and bear her guns on the gaining pirates.

Merrick held the glass to his eye and could hardly contain a chuckle as he beheld first the confusion, then the fear on the soldiers' faces when they realized their rudder was disabled, leaving them to drift at the mercy of the morning breeze. They rapidly approached the shoals that surrounded the islands and quickly furled their sails again and dropped anchor.

That was exactly what Merrick had expected. He stood by the rail of the quarterdeck, at the head of the companionway and shouted for the master gunner to ready the gun crew and load and run out the guns.

With careful maneuvering, Merrick positioned the *Redemption* fifty yards aft of the Spaniards on the windward side, offering the galleon a view of the pirate ship's six gaping mouths itching to spit out their fiery missiles. He leveled his telescope, hoping to see the banner of Castile descend and a flag of truce take its place.

Instead, demi-chasers from the galleon's stern pelted the deck of the *Redemption*, sending his crew ducking and cursing under a hard rain of deadly shot.

"Fire!" Merrick bellowed, and the *Redemption*'s broadside boomed, shaking the ship to its keel. Thick white smoke temporarily clouded his view. When it dissipated, he saw the blackened holes left by their round shots in the hull of the galleon—one below the waterline on the larboard quarter and the others smashing her bulwarks at the waist.

Merrick held the glass to his eye, trying to assess his enemy's mood. Were they going to surrender, or was the commander too full of stubborn pride to relinquish so soon?

Sloane came and stood beside him, while another pirate yelled from the railing, "Blast 'em, Cap'n, blast 'em! What are ye waitin' fer?"

Merrick lowered his glass. A Spanish galleon was no small prize, but to take her he must avoid boarding her in hand-to-hand combat, for his fifty men would be no match for the two hundred aboard the galleon. He must cripple her first to the point where the Spaniards believed they would sink, but not enough to plunge her into the Caribbean's depths before his crew could get on board and relieve them of their treasure.

Although the ship was bilging fast and listing heavily to larboard, there were still no signs of surrender.

Merrick slapped the glass shut and ordered the ship to come about. "Helm, hard aport!"

With straining cordage and creaking blocks, the *Redemption* swung slowly around, close-hauled, bearing its larboard gun ports ominously at the galleon. She emptied them in a thunderous volley that hammered its larboard side. The ship listed under the impact, putting it out of position for any return fire.

When the smoke cleared, Merrick brought the *Redemption* even closer. He followed up with bar shot that slashed through the galleon's rigging and tore into the mainmast. His crew, upon his order, swept the weather deck with swivel guns and musket fire from the tops. Merrick hoped this final onslaught would dissuade the Spanish captain of any further attempts at resistance, and thus any additional loss of life.

With each thunderous blast of the cannons, Charlisse felt as though her slender body would explode. She barely had time to recover from the last one when the *Redemption* made a swift turn to one side, tossing her across the small cabin.

The pirates bellowed. Musket and pistol shots cracked the air. In the distance, she heard an agonized scream.

Creeping up the companionway, she slunk up on deck and crouched behind the mainmast, scanning the scene before her.

The galleon was ten yards off their starboard side. Several charred and smoking holes lined her hull. The mainmast had cracked like a tree split with an ax and had toppled seaward, taking its sails with it and dropping its ratlines and cords in a tangled web. Black smoke poured from the hatch on the waist. The once-mighty galleon leaned heavily and was bilging fast.

The distraught Spanish soldiers in their black corselets and high-crested helmets scrambled across the deck on the orders of their commander, whom Charlisse could see standing on the poop deck, his black periwig blowing in the wind as he gazed at the oncoming enemy.

The pirates chanted, "Death, death, death, death. . . ," as they waved their fists and weapons in the air. An ominous chill sped down Charlisse's spine.

She saw Merrick standing on the foredeck, looking like the pirate captain he was—one hand on the hilt of his cutlass, the other on his hip, calmly awaiting the outcome of their assault. A slow grin appeared on his lips when he saw the red and gold banner of Castile lowered, then quickly replaced by a white flag of truce.

The pirates shouted in victory. Merrick spouted orders that brought the *Redemption* alongside the galleon to grapple her in a wood-crunching thud.

The faces of the Spanish soldiers paled as they backed away from the mass of pirates who now spilled over the bulwark. Like a horde of hungry wolves wearing hideous grins, they collected the muskets, pistols, knifes, and scabbards the Spaniards had tossed to the deck in surrender.

Charlisse stood frozen in her spot behind the mainmast. If the pirates were going to torture and brutalize their prisoners—like so many stories she had heard—she would witness it for herself and learn just what type of men they really were, along with the captain who led them.

Those piercing black eyes met hers as he strutted down the forecastle steps. His brow lifted momentarily, and he gave a quick nod to Sloane then tilted his head in her direction.

Donning his captain's hat and his waistcoat of black taffeta with silver lace, Merrick stood steadfastly awaiting the arrival of the captain of the *Santo Domingo*, who was being escorted aboard the *Redemption*.

The commander of the galleon halted before Merrick, his face flushed and swollen—from anger or embarrassment, it was hard to tell. He stared into the captain's eyes with an impudence that seemed to exude from his pores. He bowed and announced his name: Admiral Don Francisco de Espinosa.

With a sweep of his plumed hat, Captain Merrick bowed and spoke in fluent Castilian. An astonished look crossed the admiral's face.

Sloane joined Charlisse. She asked him if he understood what they were saying.

"Bits an' pieces, miss, my Spanish's worse than my English." He chuckled and listened. "I think he's sayin' somethin' like, we won't be hurtin' them none."

The wave of relief alighting first on the admiral's face, then passing over his crew, was evidence that Sloane had understood correctly.

Merrick ordered the galleon's longboats lowered and filled with the disarmed Spaniards, who sped for the nearby islands before the pirates could have a change of heart.

The admiral, however, remained aboard the *Redemption,* standing next to Merrick as he watched every article of value being expertly ravaged from his ship, the hull of which sank lower with each passing minute. Despite his defeat, the admiral wore a look of insolence. He turned to Captain Merrick, now speaking English. "A fine act of military seamanship, Captain. Quite unexpected from. . ." He hesitated, his voice tinged with fury.

"From a pirate?" Merrick's mouth curved in a grin. "I assure you we are not all unlettered brutes."

The admiral grunted.

"Your trap was well executed, Admiral," Merrick repaid the compliment. "But for next time, a bit of advice, if I may? Make sure the animal you lure is less cunning and less ferocious than you are, especially when you carry such treasure." He nodded toward a broken chest of jewels being hefted over the bulwarks by six of his men. Several small holes allowed precious stones to spill from its sides onto the deck. Two pirates scampered after it, greedily snatching up the fallen gems, laughing as they went.

A red flush rose over the admiral's face. Beads of sweat formed on his brow where protruding veins pulsed.

"I've not had the pleasure or your acquaintance, sir?" he said in an insidious tone.

"Captain Edmund Merrick, of the pirate ship *Redemption*." Merrick offered a mocking bow. "A ship you would do well to avoid in the future, Admiral," he added with a malicious gleam in his eye.

The admiral's mouth compressed into a thin, angry line as he watched the last vestiges of wealth being stripped from his ship.

Charlisse beheld the proceedings with great interest. None of the Spanish soldiers had been tortured, maimed, or killed, and the treasure—more than she had ever laid eyes on—had been relieved from the galleon in a most orderly fashion. She watched Merrick oversee it all with commanding authority while he conversed politely with the admiral he had defeated.

When the pillaging was complete and the ship nearly sunk, the admiral, much to his obvious chagrin, was sent ashore to join his crew, with the assurances of Captain Merrick that word would be sent to Hispaniola of their whereabouts.

Two pirates, who had been found locked up in the hold of the galleon, stood before their new captain, giddy at their sudden turn of good fortune. They readily accepted the duties Merrick assigned to them.

The captain gave the command to weigh anchor and unfurl the sails. With canvas spread to the favoring breeze, the *Redemption* set out to sea again, riding lower in the water, her hold bulging with treasure.

Charlisse, escorted by Sloane, went to the side railing to watch the remains of the galleon slip into the sea. Merrick approached her, resting his hand possessively on her lower back. She jumped under his touch and a warmth rose to her face. She dared not face him.

"Watch," Merrick said, pointing toward the galleon. "You might enjoy this."

Charlisse followed his finger and looked at the abandoned warship, its drooping sails still flapping in the wind, nearly half its hull underwater. For a few moments, it sat motionless. Then a deafening roar echoed through the air, shaking the *Redemption*. The galleon ignited in a colossal burst of orange and yellow that sent pieces of wood and canvas flying high into the cloudless sky. The ship split in two. Within minutes, it disappeared in the jade green waters of the Caribbean.

"What caused that?" Charlisse asked. "I heard no cannon blast."

"Naw, miss." Sloane eyed her with glee. "We set her powder kegs to go off afore we left."

"Now, milady, if you don't mind going below?" Merrick asked with more politeness than usual. "The men are well into their drink for such an early hour and a bit more rambunctious than would allow for your safe presence among them."

Charlisse had noticed the glances filtering her way, but she made no attempt to leave. Instead, she lifted her eyes to meet the captain's in a valiant stare. "Are we back on course for Port Royal?"

"Yes, milady, about a day's journey from here." His voice was stiff and formal, but his eyes held a mischievous glint.

She glanced at his lips, remembering their kiss, and a shimmer passed through her. Embarrassed, she averted her gaze, hoping he hadn't noticed, but when their eyes met again, his playful grin revealed that he had. *He knows the effect he has on me.* What other things would he dare attempt now that he was under the assumption she held affection toward him?

Fighting to regain control, she shot her gaze back to his, determined that he would not cause her to falter in her purpose, either by his steamy regard or the flutters his presence sent through her body.

"Milady?" He gave her a questioning nod toward the companionway stairs.

Sloane started walking and turned toward Charlisse. "I'll escort ye below, miss."

"No, thank you, Mr. Sloane," she said, without releasing her lock on Merrick's eyes. "I can take care of myself."

A chuckle escaped the captain's lips. "Very well, as you wish." He bowed. "Milady." Then turning, "Come along, Sloane."

"But, Cap'n," Sloane protested, casting an uneasy glance at Charlisse.

"Sloane." Merrick's voice was stern.

Grumbling, the old pirate turned and followed his captain below.

Charlisse glanced across the deck. Groups of pirates huddled together passing around bottles of rum, snickering among themselves. An occasional glance shot her way, but she remained steadfast. Ignoring them, she turned, clutched the railing, and looked out over the sea. Merrick had left her at the mercy of these salacious brutes. But wasn't that what she had asked for?

"Hey, sweetheart, are ye all alone?" A gruff voice jeered behind her.

"Where's yer lover boy?" another man said.

Alarm pricked at every nerve. Her fingers hurt from the intense grip she maintained on the railing. If she went below, she would be admitting her weakness—admitting she needed the captain. The turquoise sea was calm, inviting. She thought of jumping in, of escaping both the pirates and her helplessness. But she had been in that ocean before, and it was no more merciful than the God Merrick worshipped.

"How's about a littl' rum, darlin'?" The gruff voice was louder now, closer, and she heard the ominous thump of heavy boots striking the wooden deck. They were headed her way.

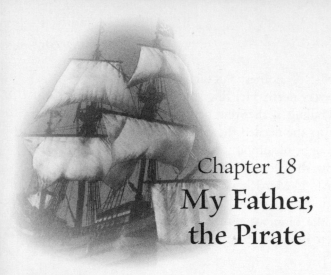

Chapter 18
My Father,
the Pirate

Releasing her grip on the rail, Charlisse spun around. At least ten pirates skulked toward her with rum dripping off their chins and lascivious smirks on their lips. Flashing her gaze at the stairs, she dashed toward them and flung herself down, missing the last two steps and landing with a thud. She barely heard the growls of the pirates over the beating of her heart. Springing to her feet, she barreled into the captain's cabin.

Merrick looked up from his desk, lips lifted in sarcasm. "What took you so long?"

Charlisse huffed and limped to the bed, rubbing her thigh. She would not play this game with him. Plopping down, she folded her arms across her chest and gazed toward the window. She heard Merrick's chair scrape the floor.

"I won't be gone long, milady. I caution you to remain in my cabin, but since you can take such good care of yourself, please do not feel as though you are my prisoner. Wander about the ship any time you like."

Charlisse glared at him, narrowing her eyes. She wanted to wipe that smile off his haughty lips.

He winked at her and closed the door. She could hear him chuckle as he left.

Charlisse, exhausted from the excitement of the morning—plus a lack of rest from the night before—drifted off to sleep on the captain's soft feather bed.

Merrick had been right about the pirates' mood. They'd been loud when she fell asleep and even louder now as she awoke. Their fiendish howling echoed through the ship as though they were a pack of wolves wailing at the moon on a lonely night. She heard music accompanied by the clang of swords and enough swearing to make a hardened sailor blush.

Casting an anxious glance at the door, she hoped Merrick was keeping a strict vigil over his men and that he had not joined in the drunken revelry. The thought set her nerves on edge. No matter how distrustful she was of him, he was her only protection aboard this ship. Yet, under the numbing effects of alcohol, any restraint he held on his passions would be easily loosed, especially in light of their recent kiss.

The door burst open and in bounded Sloane and the captain. Charlisse jumped at the sudden intrusion, feeling her heart leap into her throat.

"I just be sayin', Cap'n, that some of the men are asking fer ye to send him down to Davy Jones's locker. They says it's only fair after what he done."

Merrick took off his hat and scarf, tossed them onto the desk, and turned to face his friend. "Everyone deserves a second chance. Where would I be without second chances, eh?"

Charlisse breathed a sigh of relief as she realized neither one of them had been drinking.

Sloane remained standing near the open door. " 'Tis true, Cap'n, but he be nothin' like you, says I. His is the cold heart of a cruel villain. Ye can see it in his eyes. Besides, ye don't want to appear weak in front of the crew."

"The Good Book says"—Merrick argued, pointing to the Bible on his desk—"to forgive and to love your enemies, does it not?"

"Har, but it don't say to be lettin' people stab ye in the back more than once."

"No, I believe it says to let them do it seventy times seven." Merrick smiled. "Don't worry, my friend. I can handle Kent. Once ashore at Port Royal, he won't bother us anymore." His abrupt tone put an end to the conversation.

"Aye, Cap'n," Sloane said begrudgingly. He glanced at Charlisse.

"Miss, I be gettin' some food for ye. Be right back." He left, slamming the door behind him.

Charlisse sat on the bed, trying to mask the twirling emotions that consumed her in Merrick's presence. "What of Master Kent?"

"The crew wants him tortured and killed. It's the pirate way," he stated. "But as you know, I have no intention of complying with their wishes. Kent is a wild, impetuous boy, but I perceive he may have learned his lesson this time." He leaned back against his desk and faced her, arms folded over his chest. "He reminds me a little of myself not long ago, and I would be in a far worse place today if someone had not taken a chance on me."

"Indeed? And what place, pray tell, could be worse than captaining a crew of pirates?" Charlisse straightened her back. "The few times I've spoken with Master Kent, I've found him to be no more wild or impetuous than you are. In fact, he's been quite charming."

Merrick glared at her. A wild, unnerving look crossed his eyes. "Perhaps you are not as good a judge of character as you may think." Rising, he took a step toward her. The tip of his cutlass scraped over the wood of the desk behind him, giving Charlisse a start.

Her pulse rose. She looked away and grabbed a lock of her hair, twisting it between her fingers. He was nearly beside her when Sloane knocked and barreled in with a tray of food.

"Here ye go, some warm food fer a change." He placed the tray on the table and plopped into one of the leather chairs, glancing back and forth between Merrick and Charlisse. "Did I interrupt somethin'?"

Merrick smirked at Charlisse. "Nothing that can't be continued later."

The three of them sat to enjoy a meal of beef soup, biscuits, salted pork, and tea. Charlisse ate until she could eat no more. With the threat of the galleon behind them and the prospect of arriving in Port Royal tomorrow, her spirits were higher than they'd been since before the shipwreck. If she could just survive one more night with this pirate captain then this torturous journey would come to an end. She would find her father and live happily in his protective, loving care.

The conversation flowed between Sloane and Merrick. Charlisse listened with interest, intrigued by every word—so unlike the conversations she was used to in London. These men spoke of sword fights, sea battles, wind and weather, mutinies, treasure, and exotic ports. Everything about them was different—their lifestyle, dress, mannerisms, and culture. She had once thought such people existed only in storybooks, but here they were, sitting right beside her. Certainly she would enjoy the drama more if she weren't part of the terrifying plot.

The glittering colors of the stained-glass window dulled as the sun set on the Caribbean, and the *Redemption* was soon shrouded in darkness. The blacker the night sky became outside, the louder the sounds of revelry grew.

Sloane and the captain each slapped down a shot of rum before the old pirate left, tray in hand, to check on things above deck.

Charlisse found herself alone with Merrick again. She determined to keep the conversation light and avoid contact with him.

"So, tomorrow we shall arrive in Port Royal?" she said with a shaky voice.

"Yes, as I have said." Merrick sprawled in one of the leather chairs facing her, a look of complacency on his face.

"What is your business there?" Charlisse inquired.

"Pirate business." He smiled, continuing to penetrate her with his dark gaze.

She sighed, fidgeting on the bed. "Since you have been there before, perhaps you could tell me where I might begin the search for my father."

Merrick's smile faded and he closed his eyes.

Charlisse huffed. "Won't you please tell me what you know about him?" she pleaded.

He moved to the edge of his seat, looking at her sternly. "I don't know your father. I only know the name, and it can't be the same man."

"How many Edward Torrance Bristols can there be in the Caribbean?"

Merrick got up and poured himself another glass of rum, downed it with a quick tip of his head, and glanced back at her. Pain and unease burned in his gaze.

"There are only a few people who know him by that name. I'm one of them."

Charlisse waited.

"Others know him as Edward the Terror." He paused.

"The terror? What are you saying?" She felt her whole body tense.

"That he's a pirate, a blackguard."

Charlisse's heart sank. *It can't be true.* "My father is not a pirate," she stormed. "He's a merchant sailor. My mother has letters." She felt suddenly dizzy.

"I'm afraid it's true," Merrick added gently, turning to face her.

"No. You have been misinformed." She jumped off the bed. "My mother would never have married a pirate! Who told you this?"

Merrick pushed his hand through his hair. "He was my captain."

"You sailed with my father?"

Merrick nodded. "If he's the same man."

Her father was real—not some elusive dream she had been chasing for years. Perhaps he was a pirate, but if he was, did that make him wicked? Captain Merrick was proof that kindness could dwell in a pirate's heart.

"What type of man is he?" she asked.

Merrick rubbed his eyes and turned away. "Let's just say he did not come by his name 'The Terror' by chance."

Charlisse paced in front of the bed, the floorboards creaking loudly, echoing the state of her emotions. "You're lying. He's a good man. He loved my mother, and he loves me. I read his letters. He was planning to bring us to the colonies to be with him." She grabbed the bedpost and leaned her head against it.

"Milady," Merrick said, "the man I know is anything but a kind, caring family man. He is vicious and cruel, one of the most ruthless pirates on the Spanish Main."

She shook her head, unable to stop the tears that trickled down her cheeks. "Why are you lying to me?" Yet even as she said it, she could think of no reason for him to lie.

Merrick walked over and grabbed her shoulders. "Please sit down and let me explain."

She jerked herself from his grasp and turned away. "You don't want me to find my father, do you?" Her voice carried an edge of cynicism. "You want to keep me right here with you. That's it, isn't it?"

"If I wanted to do that, it would be an easy thing to accomplish, milady, since you are already here in my cabin and completely at my mercy. Why play games?"

There was a long pause. Charlisse stared out the window.

"I was your father's first mate on his ship, the *Nightmare*, for two years," Merrick continued. "The things I saw—the things he did to the crews we captured—I dare not repeat. He thought nothing of torturing the innocent victims who happened to find themselves in his path. He raped and beat women. He tied many of his own crew to the anchor of the ship and dragged them on the bottom of the ocean for nothing more than a mere disagreement."

A shudder ran through Charlisse. She continued staring out the darkened window, trying to stifle the sobs that rose in her throat.

"Because of his cruelty I gathered the crew and took over his ship."

She swerved and gave him a look of fearful disdain.

Merrick shook his head. "I left him on an uninhabited island."

"To die?"

"For God to decide."

"And what did your God decide?" she asked sarcastically, afraid to know the answer. Had she come all this way just to find her father was a pirate? And dead?

"He's not just my God, but everyone's." Merrick regarded her with tenderness.

Charlisse stomped her foot. "Answer my question. If my father is dead, I will never worship this God of yours."

"Never fear, your father survived, for I have heard he is in command of another ship."

"Then I shall find him at Port Royal," she announced, thrusting her chin in the air. "Pirate or no pirate, terror or no terror." Her eyes burned with unbidden tears. "He loved my mother, and he will love me."

Merrick ambled toward her. "I beg you, milady, do not. He will not welcome you as you wish."

"How do you know?" A tear escaped her right eye.

He reached up to wipe the wayward tear, but she stepped out of his reach, rage rising within her.

"I shall find my father and he will want me, you'll see. He's not what you say he is. He cannot be," she snapped, backing away.

Merrick stared at her, squinting in an intense, piercing gaze. His face reddened. "Then perhaps I *will* keep you for myself. To protect you from your own foolishness. The idea of having you near is not without appeal."

Charlisse backed into the edge of the bed and sat, shaking with fury and shock, tears pouring down her cheeks. Merrick marched toward her, grabbed her by the shoulders, and forced her to look at him. His hair fell around his face, and his eyes were ablaze. "If that's the only way I can keep you from throwing yourself into the clutches of a madman, I vow I will do it."

Charlisse trembled, realizing she had pushed this pirate too far. Why had she behaved so rashly? All she had to do was wait one more night, but instead she had provoked his wrath. Now, would he ever set her free?

Merrick grunted and jerked away. Stomping over to his desk, he grabbed a bottle of rum, and left, slamming the door behind him.

Charlisse fell in a heap on the bed and sobbed uncontrollably.

It had been a long time since Merrick had felt this enraged. Not even Kent's challenge had evoked such overwhelming emotion. Marching down the companionway and up the stairs, stepping over two inebriated men along the way, he headed toward the bow of the ship, where he plopped down on the poop deck.

Edward the Terror. Of all the women in the Caribbean, he had to cross paths with the daughter of Edward the Terror, and not only cross paths but bring her aboard his ship. Edward was the one man he hated most in the world and the one man whom Merrick would do anything to capture or kill, whichever came first. Could she really be his daughter? She was nothing like him. He chuckled at the irony.

The moon was a sliver in the night sky, like a sly grin, mocking him. Lifting his bottle, he offered it a toast and took a long swig. Then, swinging his feet over the bow, he watched the mighty ship split the savage sea into two streams of turbulent white.

The ocean was calm tonight. Merrick took in a deep breath of her salty scent, looking off into the distance where the waves glistened like liquid silver in the moonlight. Beyond, they faded into a darkness so intense it was as if the ocean fell from the face of the earth. No wonder people used to believe the world was flat.

He took another swig of rum and wiped the back of his hand across his face. On a night when he should be celebrating his victory over a

Spanish galleon, he found himself frustrated and furious, and over what? A woman—a foolish girl with foolish dreams. Why did she affect him so? He should just let her go her own way when they reached Port Royal—set her free and be done with her. If she wanted to go looking for a man who would reject her and break her heart what business was it of his? Besides, he should not get involved with her if she was truly Edward's daughter. No one, especially not some senseless girl, would stop him from his mission—his God-given mission to rid the Caribbean of the brutal atrocities committed by depraved men. Edward the Terror was the first and the worst scoundrel on his list, and the world would be a better place without him.

He could not bear the thought of what that villain would do to his own daughter. Perhaps Merrick should keep Charlisse prisoner after all. He smiled as the rum began to take effect, warming his body and allowing sensuous thoughts to drift through his mind. He shook his head, ashamed. "Lord, help me," he whispered into the evening breeze. He knew he should pray more. But tonight, he also knew he intended to drink more, and the two did not seem to mix.

Several hours passed, and Charlisse, with no more tears to shed, lay in bed, eyes swollen, unable to sleep. She left the lamps lit in case the captain returned. If he was going to attack her, she wanted to be prepared for his advance. She had come to realize that in addition to all his other alarming qualities, he was a man with a quick temper and a propensity for drink. From her experiences with her uncle, she knew that was an explosive combination.

She felt all hope draining from her and a numbness creeping in to take its place. She lay there wide-eyed, staring at the door, musing over the night's events and the shocking news of her father. How could she believe what Merrick said? Yet why would he lie? If he wanted to keep her with him, he would not hide behind some false sense of chivalry and solicitude.

Yet she had no one in this world except her father, and therefore no recourse but to refuse to accept Merrick's words. After all, there were the letters. She had read them, and they were filled with longing and love and

M. L. TYNDALL

tender words, words that gave her hope and a belief that no matter what kind of person he had become, her father would love her.

The door creaked open. Charlisse darted up, ready to defend herself against the captain's temper. But the face appearing from behind the heavy slab of oak caused her to release a sigh of relief. It was Kent. His initial smile twisted into a malicious grin, however, as he closed the door behind him, looking like the cat that had just cornered a mouse.

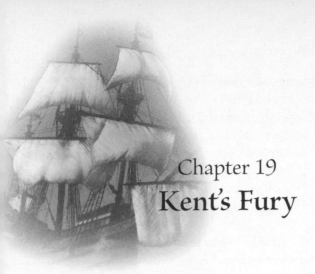

Chapter 19
Kent's Fury

Kent bowed graciously. "Milady."

"Oh, Master Kent." Charlisse wiped the tears from her face and patted her hair in place. She rushed toward him, casting an anxious glance at the door. "How did you get out of the hold?"

Kent fingered his mustache, his eyes alight with mischief. "The captain released me." He lifted his brows. "I suppose he saw the error of his ways."

His eyes scoured over her hungrily. Charlisse felt a twinge of apprehension, but wouldn't let it squelch the hope that had sprung within her upon his entrance. Here was a true gentleman. Should Merrick not reconsider his stance, perhaps Kent could help her escape when they got to Port Royal.

Charlisse spun around, wringing her hands. "I'm afraid the captain is a bit angry with me. He frightens me."

Boots thumped on the wooden floor, and two strong hands clutched her shoulders. "Indeed he can be quite a brute as you have no doubt witnessed. Quite a savage, if you ask me. Why, you wouldn't believe the number of women he's enslaved in this cabin over the years. Ah, the atrocities."

Alarm spiked through Charlisse, sending her heart into a rapid beat. Somehow she could not believe that, not of the captain, not after the respectful way in which he'd treated her.

Kent leaned down. The scent of rum and leather assailed her. "That is why I am here—to treat you in the manner a true lady deserves." His warm breath washed over her neck.

Jerking from his grasp, Charlisse whirled around and stepped back. A lewd desire burned in his eyes that she'd not noticed before. "Perhaps you should leave. Merrick said he was returning shortly."

"Is that so?" He approached her, hand on his chin, staring off into space. "Hmm. . ." His eyes came alert. "I believe you are mistaken. I have just seen him, quite inebriated, I might add, up on the poop deck, singing into a bottle of rum."

Charlisse's eyes widened. She began to tremble.

"Surely he has passed out by now," Kent said, waving a jeweled hand in the air. "So unlike our pious captain, don't you think?"

Charlisse scooted back to the bed.

Kent's dark eyes smoldered with desire as he perused her. His broad chest heaved, and his muscled arms twitched near the cutlass hanging at his side. Charlisse felt her insides crumble with fear as he moved toward her.

"I will cry for help," she shouted, jumping off the other side of the bed and backing up against the window.

"Go ahead, milady. No one will hear you. Everyone on this ship has passed out. Even your friend Sloane is fast asleep."

He pounced on her. Charlisse screamed. He covered her mouth and dragged her toward the door. She groaned and grunted, making as much noise as she could from under his heavy hand crushing her lips. Still no one came.

She felt his skin between her teeth and bit down. Kent jerked back. He laid a violent backhand against her cheek, sending her flying to the floor. "I'll teach you to bite me, wench!"

The sting from his slap radiated in burning waves across her face. She laid staring at the floorboards, panting, a thousand terrifying thoughts passing through her mind.

He yanked her to her feet again—sending an excruciating stab of pain through her shoulder—and dragged her to the desk. Grabbing one of Merrick's scarves, he stuffed it into her mouth and tied it behind her head. She struggled against his forceful grip, but he was too strong. Swinging her up over his shoulder, he headed out the door and down the stairs.

They passed several sleeping pirates. Charlisse squealed, grunted, and groaned, but they did not even stir. *Where is Merrick? Where is Sloane? This can't be happening.*

At the bottom of the stairs, Kent carried her down a narrow aisle. He arrived at a closed door, kicked it open, dropped her onto a pile of lumpy burlap sacks, and slammed the door behind him.

"Hmm, you were more trouble than I expected," he said, loosing the gorget at his throat. He began to unbutton his doublet.

Charlisse's eyes darted around, looking for anything she could use to defend herself. Only crates, drums, and sacks filled the tiny room, and they were no match for Kent's weapons. Pulling the scarf from her mouth, she screamed.

Kent smiled, wearing a look of victorious arrogance. "They won't hear you down here." He threw his pistols onto a crate, and they clanked against the wood, out of Charlisse's reach. "In fact, soon you will be screaming with delight, I assure you."

He slunk toward her. Charlisse backed away. How familiar this feeling was. How many times had she felt cornered, trapped like a fish in a net, weak and defenseless? How many times had she been unable to control what was happening to her, unable to hide, unable to even turn off the feelings of horror that overtook her?

Kent drew his knife and leaned over her.

"Please don't," she implored in a last-ditch effort to appeal to any core of decency in him. But his eyes were cold and intent. No sympathy lingered in their depths.

A malicious grin spread over his face. "Maybe I can't have the captain's ship just yet, but I can have his woman." He hefted his knife and, starting at the collar, sliced her dress down the front.

Charlisse thrashed beneath him, kicking and clawing. She pounded him with her fists. But he only laughed at her efforts. In the commotion the knife cut her skin, bringing forth a trickle of blood that stained her bodice.

"Now look what you've done," Kent said, his lecherous smile fading.

Grabbing her by the remnants of her dress, he lifted her and ripped it from her body, leaving her clad in only her torn petticoat. He pushed her down and climbed on top of her, pinning her arms to the floor with his weight. His rum-drenched breath fanned over her face. His eyes were filled with rage.

Charlisse couldn't move. She was going to be ravished, and there was nothing to be done about it—no one here to rescue her, no one who even knew where she was, except perhaps God, if He existed. She remembered all the times she had cried out to Him in desperation during the past months. Somehow, she had survived every one of those treacherous episodes. Had He answered her prayers? "God, help me," she whispered.

Suddenly, a blast exploded in the room. The door burst open, slamming against the wall. Charlisse, her back pressed against the splintered floorboards, heard and felt the vibrations of heavy boots coming her way. She saw the terror on Kent's face as he was lifted off her and thrown backward. He hit the wall with a thud. Even before he reached the floor, Merrick was on him, holding him against the wall by the sheer force of his wrath.

Charlisse sat up and covered herself with the remnants of her dress.

Merrick threw Kent across the room, sending him tumbling over a crate. Kent stumbled to his feet and frantically swung his gaze, evidently searching for his knife, which had flown from his grasp when Merrick grabbed him. He whipped out his boarding ax and barreled toward Merrick with the fury of a wild animal.

The captain drew his cutlass to stop the oncoming blow and sliced Kent's hand. The ax flew through the air. Weaponless and in a frenzied rush, Kent slammed his shoulder into Merrick's body, and the two careened against the far wall. Merrick's cutlass fell from his grasp and clattered across the floor.

Kent pummeled Merrick in the stomach. He landed a good blow across his face. The captain doubled over.

Terror rose in Charlisse, clambering its icy claws up her throat. *Get up, Merrick! Get up! Please don't leave me alone with him!*

The first mate stood over him, panting and gloating over his success. He raised his hands to land a fatal blow upon Merrick's back. The captain, in a new burst of rage, sprang up and struck Kent hard across the jaw. His head swerved around under the blow, spurting out a circle of blood.

Merrick backed him against a tall stack of crates. He clutched the first mate's shirt and thrashed his head over and over against the hard wood.

"I didn't do anything to her," Kent yelled.

Sloane burst into the room, a look of horror on his face. Merrick continued pounding Kent, holding him upright against the crates, but Sloane made no move to stop him. Kent's body now flopped lifelessly with each thrust. She had to do something. No matter what kind of monster Kent was, she could not watch him be battered to death.

Charlisse slid from the corner and grabbed one of Kent's pistols still lying on the crate where he had deposited them. Dropping her torn dress, she lifted the cold, heavy weapon and pointed it at the ceiling. She turned her head, closed her eyes, and squeezed the trigger. Nothing happened. The pounding continued, and Kent's moans grew softer. She shook the pistol and tried again. This time it exploded with a loud crack and a burst of flame that threw her body backward. The weapon flew from her hands and landed with a clank, still smoking. The sharp smell of gunpowder filled the tiny room.

Both the captain and Sloane swerved around ready to face a new opponent. Sloane had his hand on the hilt of his cutlass, ready to draw, but stopped when he saw Charlisse. She retrieved her dress then stood trembling.

Kent slid to the floor. Merrick stood panting, his gaze moving from Charlisse to Sloane and back again.

"How did he escape?" Sloane asked.

Merrick shook his head and took a step back. "Don't know," he huffed. "Take him and lock him up. Post a guard this time."

Nodding, Sloane hoisted up the battered Kent and helped the man stagger from the room.

Captain Merrick turned, his gaze taking in Charlisse where she now stood in the shadows against the far wall. He rushed over. "Are you hurt?" He reached for her, but she flinched from his touch.

Charlisse could not stop her body from trembling. She had so resigned herself to the inevitable fate of Kent's violation that even when Merrick tossed his body from her, her mind could not accept her deliverance. Too many times had she cried out to God for help and too often been disappointed. Now, surely she must be dreaming.

Her champion stood before her, but she could only see in his eyes the unrestrained rage that had almost killed Kent. It did nothing to comfort her.

He was still breathing hard, sweat glistening in beads on his chest, visible through his torn shirt. Fury shouted from his eyes. Every muscle strained taut, ready to strike at any moment.

Merrick took a deep breath and pushed his hair back from his face. He held out his hand again. "I won't hurt you. You have my word."

Charlisse hesitated, searching his eyes, wanting to trust, needing his comfort and protection more than anything, but still so unsure. Holding her torn dress up to her chin, she shivered, feeling her legs begin to give way.

Merrick's eyes, normally full of haughty sarcasm, now carried a warmth she had not seen before. Was it genuine? He moved toward her.

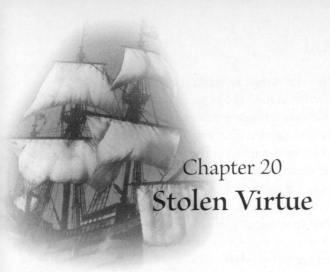

Chapter 20
Stolen Virtue

Charlisse flew into Merrick's arms. Tears flowed down her cheeks, and the tight knot within her released its hold on her emotions.

"Shh. You're all right now." Merrick rubbed her back, engulfing her in his strong embrace. "I'm sorry," he said softly.

Charlisse tried to tell him it wasn't his fault, but the words would not come. All she could do was lean her head on his chest and sob, letting out all the tension and terror of the night into the warmth of his strong arms.

Merrick lifted her chin and wiped the hair from her eyes. "Let's get you back to the cabin."

When they pulled apart, there was a bloodstain on Merrick's shirt. He looked at Charlisse with alarm. "You're hurt?"

"It's nothing." She backed away, clutching her gown to her throat.

He glanced around the room, walked to one of the crates, and pried it open with his knife. Pulling out a beautifully sewn red-and-brown quilt, he handed it to her. "Wrap yourself in this." He turned his back.

Tossing her tattered gown aside, Charlisse enfolded herself as modestly as she could in the blanket and came up beside Merrick. He wore a brooding expression on his face. Turning, he swept her up in his arms and carried her to his cabin.

"I need to find you some proper clothes," Merrick said, laying her gently on the bed, "and some salve for your wound." He held her hand, giving it a gentle squeeze. When he turned to leave, she would not let go.

"Please don't leave me alone," she pleaded, her face moist and red.

He looked into her eyes. He saw a vulnerability in their depths that he had never seen before. She needed him. For once, she was willing to admit it. His heart warmed at the thought. "Of course."

After closing the door, he moved one of his chairs closer to the bed and sat down. He held her outstretched hand and brought it to his lips, then gently caressed her arm. She tensed at first, but after a few minutes, her taut nerves seemed to unwind. Her skin was so soft. Merrick felt his pulse rise.

Anger and shame burned in Merrick's soul. His fury was not directed toward Kent anymore. He realized the boy would probably never change. His fury was now with himself. He had left Charlisse alone, defenseless, while he was off overindulging in rum—something he had not done in years. There was no excuse for it. *Have I really changed? Or am I the same reckless cad I always was?*

It was one thing to allow his wicked temperament to bring trouble into his own life, but quite another to hurt someone else in the process, someone who depended on him for protection. How could he ask her to forgive him? How could he ever forgive himself? And not just for what had happened with Kent, but for the thoughts that now sped across his mind like burning arrows. Every fiber of his being yearned for her with a searing passion he was not sure he could control. Every fiber of his being yearned to touch her, to hold her. He prayed silently for strength, shifting his position, and shaking the thoughts from his mind.

"I shouldn't have left you alone," he admitted. "I shouldn't have been drinking."

"There's no way you could have known." She glanced up at him, her blue eyes still brimming with tears. "You saved my honor, and quite possibly my life. How can I blame you?"

"Then," Merrick began uneasily, "he did not violate you?" He slid his hand down her arm, remembering when he had burst into the room and seen Kent on top of her. He had never felt such rage. And when he saw the condition of her dress he had realized that maybe he was too late.

She shook her head.

"Thank God." He sighed.

"A few more minutes, though. . ."

He wiped a tear from her eye. "Let's have no more talk of it."

At a quiet knock on the door, Merrick bolted from the bed. He grabbed one of his pistols and shoved it into the top of his breeches. With the recent mutiny, Kent's attack on Charlisse, and the inebriated condition of the crew, he wasn't taking any chances. He opened the door slowly, then breathed a sigh of relief when he saw Sloane's cheerful face.

The old pirate handed him his cutlass. "Thought ye might be needin' this, eh?"

Merrick took it, remembering now that he had left it in the storage room, not caring about anything but Charlisse after the battle had concluded.

In his other hand, Sloane carried a tray. "Some tea for the miss, to calm her nerves a bit?"

Merrick motioned him to enter. "What would I do without you, my old friend?"

"Har, methinks ye'd be in sore shape." Sloane chuckled, nodding at Charlisse as he set the tray down. "Some chamomile tea for ye, miss. I bin savin' it for a proper moment, an' this seems as good as any."

Charlisse sat up, wrapping the blanket more tightly around her. "Sloane, you are an angel," she managed to stutter.

He poured the steaming liquid into one of the cups and handed it to her.

"Are ye all right?"

She nodded, taking the cup with shaking hands, nearly spilling the hot tea over its brim.

"That cuckoldy jackanapes! Why, I'd send his innards flyin' off the bow of this ship if I could."

Sloane turned to Merrick, flashing stern eyes of condemnation. The captain solemnly returned his stare, knowing full well he alone was to blame for the atrocities of the evening.

Grabbing a bottle of rum, Sloane poured a splash into Charlisse's tea before she could protest. "It'll help calm yer nerves."

Taking a sip, she coughed then thanked him.

"Well, I best be lettin' ye get some sleep." Sloane patted Charlisse on the shoulder. "Ye'll feel much better in the morn, ye'll see." He headed out the door, turning to face Merrick before closing it. He tipped his head toward Charlisse. "Is she hurt?"

The captain shook his head, and Sloane let out a sigh.

"Kent?" Merrick whispered.

"All locked up, Cap'n, an' I set Shanks on guard. He ain't goin' nowheres." He gave Merrick a furtive glance, scratched his thick beard, and left.

The captain closed the door and slowly turned to face Charlisse.

She sipped her tea. He thought he saw her shoulders drop slightly. Perhaps the warmth of the rum was beginning to soothe her frayed nerves.

"Sloane is a good man," she said, her voice shaky.

"I know." Merrick approached her.

"I can't say I've ever met a kinder gentleman."

Merrick chuckled, looking at the tangled mass of golden curls that fell over Charlisse's back. Unable to keep his hands away, he reached up to touch them. "I daresay poor Sloane has never been called a *gentleman* before. I think he would find it amusing to hear you say so."

As he moved aside the fair strands, he noticed a series of narrow pink marks on her back. From her struggle with Kent? Alarm shot through him. "What are these?"

"What?"

"These marks on your back."

Charlisse shot up, dropping her tea. The cup shattered on the wooden floor. Squeezing the blanket to her chest, she stared at the broken china, then at Merrick. "They are nothing." She knelt to pick up the cup but swooned and nearly fell.

Merrick stooped beside her and lifted her to the bed again. "I'll get it."

Trembling, Charlisse clung to the bedpost as if it were her only friend. She began to cry.

Realizing they were scars and not fresh wounds he said, "Who did this to you?" He bent to pick up the pieces of china. He deposited them on the table and sat down next to her, reaching for her hand. She pulled away. He sighed, got up, and walked to the desk, combing his hand through his hair.

"It was my uncle," she said in a shaky voice.

Merrick turned, leaned back on the desk, and looked at her.

Charlisse fidgeted with her hair. "He was my ward after my mother died."

"I'm sorry for your loss. How old were you when you lost her?"

"Eight."

Merrick waited for her to continue, hoping she would, but not wanting to cause further distress. She seemed suddenly small and frail, so unlike the bold, defiant lady she usually pretended to be.

The lantern light glowed over her shoulders, sparkling in the highlights of her hair as it cascaded down in a mass of tangled curls. She looked up at him then averted her eyes, holding the blanket even more tightly around her.

"My uncle whipped me for the first time when I was thirteen," she said softly.

Merrick's heart squeezed tight. He sat on the chair facing the bed. "Why?"

Still avoiding his gaze, she replied, "I wasn't sure at first. I thought I must have done something terribly wrong, but I could not imagine what it was." Charlisse stared at him, tears overflowing upon her cheeks. "He said I was just like my mother—a whore."

Merrick clamped shut his jaw.

"He told me he would purify me." She hesitated, speaking between sobs. "He would purge the sin and filthiness out of me."

Merrick wanted to take her in his arms and comfort her, but he waited, anger churning inside him. "What would make him think such a thing?"

Charlisse shook her head. "I don't know. There were never opportunities for me to behave with impropriety. I was kept under lock and key, forbidden to even have friends." She dabbed at her tears with a corner of the blanket.

"You were never courted?"

Charlisse laughed. "Courted? I was not allowed to talk to a boy my own age. Only once did I ever dance with one, and for that I paid dearly."

Merrick tried to fathom a childhood of such abuse, but he could not. His own youth had certainly not been filled with love and pleasant memories, but compared with what she was describing, it had been paradise. "What—" He stopped, trying to form the words and stared down at the cracks in the floorboards beneath his boots. He wanted to help her—to take away her pain, but he didn't know how. "What did he. . . how. . . ?" He looked up at her.

Tears spilled over their lashed brim and trickled down her cheeks, leaving trails of sorrow behind. She did not meet his gaze. "He would disrobe me. Then. . ." She hesitated, swallowing. "He would recite to me scriptures from the Bible about chastity, purity, and immorality."

Merrick was beginning to get the picture, and it was making him sick.

"Then he beat me with a whip—as penance for my sinful nature and to purge the wickedness from my soul."

"Charlisse." Merrick studied her face, but she did not return his gaze, still hanging her head low. "You were without clothing during this whole ordeal?"

Charlisse nodded, sniffing.

"Who is this uncle of yours?"

"Richard Hemming, the Bishop of Loxford."

Merrick stood up, sending his cup crashing to the floor. "A man of the church? A bishop?"

Rage bubbled inside him. How could anyone hurt this sweet, innocent girl? Visions of her small body cowering under the pelting blows of a man—her own uncle, someone who called himself a representative of God—flooded his thoughts. Bile rose in Merrick's throat. "How many times did he do this?"

"Many times," she answered. "More often toward the end."

"The end?"

"Before I ran away to find my father."

Merrick paced, his heavy boots pounding the floor.

"So you understand now?" she asked.

"What?" Merrick swerved to face her.

"Why Kent. . .why he—"

A dart of shock sped through Merrick. "Do you think what he did was your fault?"

Charlisse's moist eyes widened. "My uncle said men are attracted to women of low morals."

"Men are attracted to women, period." He grabbed Charlisse's hand. She closed her eyes, leaning on the bedpost.

"Look at me," he demanded, squeezing her hand.

Finally, she opened her teary eyes.

"None of what has happened to you is any fault of yours—not what your uncle did, nor what Kent did. Do you understand?"

She stared at him blankly.

"Your uncle was a sick man. He carries the fault for his actions, and he will have to give an account to God for them. And Kent is just a wicked knave who forced himself on you merely because you are a beautiful woman and because he wants anything he believes is mine."

Charlisse's glistening gaze swung back and forth between his eyes, as if she were searching for sincerity in them.

"If I may be so bold," Merrick said with a somber look, "it is my suspicion that your uncle was dealing with a lustful attraction to his niece. Unable to control it, he blamed you for it. He disrobed you for his own pleasure, and when it aroused him, he beat you. Don't you see? He was the one filled with wickedness and filthiness, not you."

"What of my mother?"

"I don't know your mother. But I do know you, and you have proven your character beyond reproach."

Charlisse's brow creased. "But I'm. . ." She looked at him, puzzled. "But it's in my nature to. . ."

"No. If you were a woman of loose morals, why have you been able to resist my considerable charms?" With raised brow, he offered her a mischievous grin.

One side of Charlisse's lips upturned in a half smile while she stifled a sob. "Your words are sweet to my ears." She took an unsteady breath. "I long for them to be true."

"Then believe they are." Merrick surrounded her with his arms and pulled her close to him, feeling her resolve melt as she leaned against his chest. "I know men like your uncle. They are cowards, preying on the innocent under the guise of religious piety. They make me sick. And it sickens me even more to hear how your uncle abused such a young, innocent girl." He lifted her face. "Shake it from your mind. You are as much a lady now as you always have been." He kissed her forehead.

Merrick inched his chair next to the bed and sat watching Charlisse until she fell asleep. Still shaky from her ordeal, she didn't seem to mind his close proximity, and he welcomed the change.

After he heard her breathing deepen and saw her body relax, he rose and retreated to his hard wood floor. It would be impossible for him to get any sleep with Charlisse so near. There was too much of the old Merrick left in him.

Quietly, he repented his overindulgence in rum, his temper, and his selfishness when he left Charlisse defenseless against Kent. There were probably a number of other infractions and failures, but he couldn't remember them all and instead appealed to the mercy and forgiveness of his loving Savior. He thanked God for the strength and grace He had bestowed on him to handle all the challenges of the day. In particular, self-control. What a wretch he was for even entertaining such desires, especially after what she had been through. He shook his head, ashamed. Difficult as it had been at first to restrain himself when she so willingly fell into his arms, after he had heard the story of her horrendous past, something changed within him, and he no longer had to battle so vehemently against his raging passions. With each tear that slid down her creamy cheeks, his heart ached even more.

A strong desire to protect her from the advances of any man surged within him. She had suffered too much to be thrown once again into the lion's den, and this time with the most ferocious of all beasts—her own father. How could she endure the attacks of another man she should be able to trust above all others? It would destroy her. No, Merrick must protect her at all costs. And not only protect, he must help heal her wounds by leading her to the only One who could show her that she was worth dying for—the One who had created her and who loved her beyond measure. It would certainly aid that cause if Merrick treated her more like the lady she was and less like some tempting morsel served on the plate of his sensual appetite. With this new resolve firmly in place, he quickly fell asleep.

Nightmares invaded Charlisse's fitful sleep like enemy troops trying to regain lost territory. They swept down on her unawares with an arsenal of weapons against which she had no defense: arrows of impurity, pistol shots of shame, swords of disgrace, and most of all, cannonballs of unworthiness. The figures that wielded them were dark, slimy creatures without faces.

Leading their charge was her uncle, in his brown robe, gold crucifix beaming from his breast. He rode a black horse whose nostrils spurted blood with each blast of air.

She bowed to the ground in humiliation, baring her back to the onslaught of vile weapons. Slash after slash they tore her flesh, leaving their marks of reproach upon her—a stigma for all to see. She was a marked woman, unchaste and contemptible.

Falling to the ground in a crumbled heap, she sobbed.

The roaring of the army slowly dissipated, leaving only the sound of her weeping and the wrenching of her heart as it broke in two.

Someone smoothed ointment on her wounds. The moment the gentle hand applied the salve, the pain disappeared.

A sweet fragrance filled the air, and a light—a soothing light—shone upon her. She turned around slowly. A man stood beside her, dressed in a white robe. He smiled, and she heard Him say, "You are clean now, beloved."

Chapter 21
Beginnings

Merrick rose early, his body sore from the fight with Kent. After lighting a candle, he spent some time reading the Bible and conversing with his Father, getting direction and guidance for the new day. When he was done, he sat beside the bed and protectively watched the angel sleeping there. At least she had been able to get some rest after last night's trauma.

Her back was to him. As the light filtered in through the window, she stirred. The delicate curls of her hair flowed over the pillow like gentle waves across a white beach. Seeing the pink scars on her bare skin, he cringed in anger as her story came rushing back to him.

Startled, she sprang up and turned to face him. The morning chill alerted her to the blanket slipping down, and horrified, she grabbed the wayward cloth and clutched it to her neck. She hoped Merrick hadn't noticed, but she could tell from his mischievous smile that he had. A scorching heat rose within her, making its way up onto her face.

"A gentleman would not stare at a lady while she sleeps."

His mouth curved in a roguish grin. "Indeed."

Charlisse clutched the quilt and gave him a cold stare, amazed at his audacity. A moment passed in which his grin faded and a spark of remorse crossed his eyes.

"My apologies, milady." He nodded. "I perceive I have caused you some discomfort. Let us begin again, shall we? Perhaps my behavior of last night will help to improve your opinion of me?"

Charlisse examined his eyes and found a playfulness in them. He raked his hand through his black hair. At least two days' stubble covered his chin and neck, and his torn white shirt was bloodstained—evidence of his fight for her virtue. His intense gaze contained an odd mixture of admiration, protectiveness, and desire. No one had ever looked at her that way before.

"Yes, your behavior was quite noble," she admitted.

"Let's not be so formal. Did we not pass the outer bounds of mere acquaintanceship last night and become close friends, if not more?" There was a devilish twinkle in his eye. "Or must I start over with you at the dawn of each new day?"

"We will be friends," she conceded. "And, my friend, I would greatly appreciate some decent clothing." Charlisse thought she saw a flicker of disappointment in his eyes. Her heart fluttered, remembering the tender moments they had spent together the night before. Was it the rum Sloane had slipped into her tea that made her disclose so many intimate details of her life to this pirate? And what about those moments resting in his arms? Was that the way a lady behaved? A flood of heat again consumed her. She had allowed him too many liberties.

Merrick stood and approached her. "I will accept your offer of friendship and consider it a great privilege, but my heart hopes for much more." She looked up at him. Upon seeing the sincerity in his eyes, she looked away, feeling suddenly vulnerable.

Merrick sat and took her hand in his, his expression staid. "You shared your heart with me last night, and I hold that in precious confidence. Please also know that I meant everything I said about the circumstances of your upbringing and the purity of your character." He squeezed her hand. "I hope you will give it some consideration and allow your heart to heal from such a hellish beginning." He paused, then added, "Appeal to God, our Father, for He can heal even the most hardened and damaged souls."

Tears welled in Charlisse's eyes at the mention of her torturous past. She had never revealed—physically or emotionally—to anyone what she had revealed to this pirate, this rogue. Shame bubbled up in her like a burning fountain. She cursed herself inwardly for being so weak and foolish. Yet here Merrick stood, offering her his comfort. He had taken advantage of neither her nor her tender emotions. A tear escaped its lashed boundary and slid down her cheek, and Merrick gently wiped it away. He leaned down and kissed her hand. Charlisse felt her resolve weaken. Could this man be genuine in his concern for her? Smiling, he stood. "Now I shall see about proper attire for you." Strapping on his weapons, he turned and walked out the door, offering her a wink before slamming it shut.

The room was so empty after he left. *What is happening to me? Am I falling in love with this pirate? Or are my emotions simply surging from the trauma surrounding me?*

Shaking her head, she sank back, her mind unwilling to accept what her heart told her was true. It was just silly, girlish emotions—a crazy infatuation brought on by his kindness and protection. Since she had never known a real gentleman's affection, how would she know if this was love or just a passing fancy?

She sighed and crossed her arms in front of her. Right now she needed to focus on finding her father. He was all that was important. Today they would arrive in Port Royal. The thought of finally meeting him sent ripples of excitement through her soul. Yet Merrick's words of warning also echoed in her mind. Her father couldn't be who Merrick said he was. He just couldn't. She decided to put it out of her mind.

She didn't see the captain for several hours. Sloane had brought her a dress, a few pins he had found for her hair, a tub of water for washing, and some breakfast, which she hardly ate—her stomach still uneasy from last night's ordeal.

The dress was a beautiful sapphire blue chiffon over a velvet bodice and skirt, with embroidered lace at the collar and sleeves. She wondered about the poor woman who had owned it prior to her—before being *relieved* of it by these pirates.

After washing and dressing, she combed through her tangled hair and pinned it in a loose bun of cascading curls. Then she examined herself in the tiny mirror next to the armoire until she was pleased with her appearance—telling herself it was for her father alone that she concerned herself so.

In the early afternoon, after Sloane reassured her that Kent was locked up and well guarded, she ventured up on deck where only a few pirates loitered in the sun. Most of them were still below, recovering from their excessive drinking.

The strong trade winds filled every inch of the sails, sending the *Redemption* on a rapid course through the turquoise water and leaving a trail of white foam as evidence of its grand passing. Charlisse clung to the side rail, closing her eyes, feeling the sun cover her in a mantle of warmth while the wind caressed her skin and danced playfully through her wayward curls. She was growing fond of sailing, the exhilaration of it, the freedom, with the world—or at least the seas—as her home: no barriers, no restrictions, each day bringing a new adventure. She could easily see its attraction for a man like Merrick.

Strong arms reached from behind her, encircling her waist possessively, and she felt the captain's warm breath on her neck even before he spoke. "You look lovely."

Charlisse jumped, unaccustomed to a man's gentle touch, but soon each taut nerve melted beneath his warm embrace. She turned her face, feeling his stubble on her cheek, and looked up into his dark eyes.

"We'll be in Port Royal in about an hour," he said.

For some reason, the announcement did not bring her as much joy as she'd expected. Suddenly, all she wanted was to continue sailing aboard this mighty ship, feeling the wind caress her, the spray of the sea shower her face, and Merrick's strong arms around her. But of course, that was not possible, nor even rational. She had not come to the Caribbean and suffered all that she had just to be swept away by some God-fearing pirate—no matter how handsome or chivalrous he was. He was a fantasy, a dream that could end only in tragedy. With great effort, she shifted her thoughts back to reality. "What happens then?"

"I have some business to attend to, but I'll be leaving you with a very reliable acquaintance of mine until I can rejoin you."

Charlisse shook her head. "You will do no such thing." She jerked from his grasp and stepped aside.

"And then, milady," he continued, "we shall see about your father."

Charlisse smiled and turned to face him. "You will help me?"

Merrick narrowed his eyes at the horizon. "I will find him, yes," he said, his face stern. "Besides," he added with a smile, "I can't have you running around unescorted in Port Royal, now, can I?"

Charlisse studied the depths of his dark brown eyes. The wind tossed his black hair behind him in wild abandon. A hint of a grin played on his handsome lips, and a foreign feeling came over her. It was a feeling of being taken care of, of someone watching out for her, loving her.

A mixture of emotions swirled within her—fear, uncertainty, hope, and joy bundled together in a chaotic wrestling match. She glanced away, unable to handle the fervor of his gaze. He stepped closer. Turning her face with his finger, he lifted her chin, and his lips found hers.

A gruff snort sounded from their left. Charlisse sprang back from Merrick. Sloane stood next to them, wearing a wide grin that revealed his missing teeth.

"Sorry to be interruptin', Cap'n, but here be the charts ye requested." He handed Merrick some scrolls, but the captain's eyes never left Charlisse's.

She felt a blush rise on her face and quickly excused herself to go below.

Sloane watched her leave and turned to the captain, a look of suspicion in his eyes. "Are ye sure ye be knowin' what yer doin?"

Merrick shook his head. "No."

"Don't git me wrong, I like her. She's smart and kind and a mite pretty, too, says I. But she also be young and innocent, and now looks like she be trustin' you." He paused, lifting his eyebrows patronizingly at Merrick. "*Should* she be trustin' you?"

Merrick smiled at his friend and gave him an acknowledging nod. Sloane had witnessed Merrick's prior treatment of women, before he had met the Lord, and it had been anything but honorable. *Am I truly different now?*

Lost in his thoughts, Merrick headed up the forecastle steps. When it came to Charlisse, he wasn't sure what he was thinking or feeling. Ever since he first laid eyes on her, on that deserted island, his heart had been a jumbled mess. He was drawn to her from the very beginning, longing to protect her, to care for her, to know everything about her. But was it only her beauty that attracted him? *No, it was much more than that.* He loved every minute he spent with her, even when she was cold and her tongue vicious.

Now when he touched her, she no longer withdrew; when he kissed her, she responded. This new yielding was awakening every sense in his body and soul. Yet, the more territory he gained, the more he wanted. Could he trust himself with her?

How could he entertain such thoughts? She was so vulnerable now with everything that had recently happened and her future yet so unclear. *Does she even care for me? Or am I simply the first man who has been kind to her?* There were so many things in her life that needed to be dealt with before she added a lovesick pirate to the picture. Was he being fair to her, or was he thinking only of himself? Was he thinking at all? He thanked God they were arriving in Port Royal today for he wasn't entirely sure he could withstand another night alone with her.

One thing was certain. Charlisse must not be allowed to find her father. He would not lose anyone else he cared for to that madman. If that beast was at Port Royal, Merrick must capture him and bring him to Governor Moodyford before Charlisse could find him. If she later discovered what Merrick had done and hated him for it, so be it. He was willing to take that chance. The thought of losing her caused a throb of anguish in his heart, but he had no choice. Edward must be stopped before he incited another slaughter like the one at the Arawak village.

As he stood on the foredeck staring at the sparkling sea, the saltwater sprinkling his face, he closed his eyes and said a silent prayer for wisdom, for guidance, and for the tender girl the Lord had put into his care.

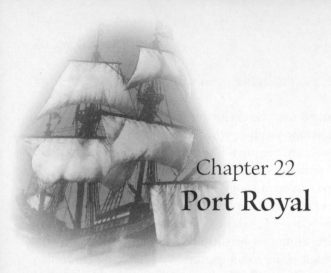

Chapter 22
Port Royal

Cannon fire erupted from the hull of the *Redemption*, shaking the ship through its waist. In sturdy reply, the mighty guns of Fort Charles sent off a volley of round shot, hurling the twelve-pound balls of iron harmlessly into the blue waters of Kingston Bay. The arrival of the pirate ship had been announced, and a flurry of activity sprouted on the docks.

It was a grand event when a ship arrived, especially a pirate ship, bringing with it lonely men who had treasures to trade and pieces of eight to spend. Shopkeepers and tavern owners, as well as prostitutes, salivated for the wealth so freely spent by these rakish men. Kegs of Kill Devil rum were rolled out into the street while vendors and doxies displayed their wares.

Charlisse stood by Captain Merrick's side as he issued orders to lower tacks and sheets, put the helm down, and release the anchor. A crackle of excitement charged through the ship. The pirates readied themselves to go ashore, licking their lips in anticipation of the pleasures that awaited them.

Crates of ill-gotten plunder were hoisted on deck and loaded into cockboats to be sent ashore. There they would be sold for gold and silver coins, which would then be divided among the crew, according to predetermined articles of piracy signed by all who sailed under Captain Merrick.

Charlisse could hardly believe she had finally made it to Port Royal. To her left, the huge stone towers of Fort Charles loomed like giant sentinels guarding the bay. Massive cannons thrust their muzzles through the crenels of the battlement. At a distance, she could see the burst of activity at the docks awaiting their arrival and the shops and taverns that lined the narrow streets of the city.

Other ships floated idly in the bay, and Charlisse wondered if one of them belonged to her father. Renewed hope sprang in her heart. She glanced at Merrick. The warmth in his returned gaze penetrated her soul, and a sudden sadness overcame her. Was her adventure aboard the *Redemption* at an end?

He squeezed her hand and instructed her to stay on the ship with Sloane while he went ashore and handled the exchange of monies.

"When you bring all this treasure to shore, won't they know you're a pirate and have you arrested?" Charlisse asked.

Merrick chuckled. "Sorry to disappoint you, milady, if all this time you have been under the impression that I am a scandalous rogue. In fact, I have a commission from the governor of Jamaica to attack and plunder any Spanish vessel sailing these waters."

Charlisse looked at him, lifting her brows. "So you're not a pirate?"

A devilish sparkle shone in his eye. "Well, let's just say I'm a legal pirate." He tipped his hat, then turned and strode away.

Some time later, as promised, Merrick returned and assisted Charlisse into one of the cockboats where Sloane and two other men waited. Shielding her eyes from the sun that retreated on the horizon, she glanced back at the magnificent ship as they set off for shore. Black cannon heads protruded from the hull. Two wooden masts towered like sentries against the purple and red hues of the evening sky, exquisitely flayed with ratlines, shrouds, and furled, sleeping canvas. The word *Redemption* was carved and painted black on the crimson bow.

An unexpected sorrow weighed on her heart, for she didn't know if she would ever board the mighty ship again. Her gaze lowered and met Merrick's as he sat across from her. Understanding passed between them in the moments their eyes locked. Charlisse looked away, wondering if she had lost her senses. Only days ago, she would have done anything to escape the clutches of this pirate captain. Now, after the terrifying voyage, the battle with the Spanish galleon, and even Kent's attack, she found no joy at the prospect of being free of Merrick.

What spell had he cast upon her? Or was she so starved for love that she flung her heart, without reservation, to whomever would have it? She glanced at him as he eyed the approaching shore. His firm jaw set toward the wind, he sat with the assurance of a commander. He had proven himself a gentleman, but he was still a man, and therefore not to be trusted. A father's love—the love of family—was the only kind of love on which she could depend. Claws of dread etched up her spine as she remembered Merrick's insistent declaration of her father's debased character. She would find her father and prove to Merrick he was wrong about him—that Edward was not a cruel pirate, but the loving, generous man her mother had described. She'd read the affectionate letters he'd sent home, and they were not from the hand of a pirate.

He'd loved her and her mother. If only she could be with him, could prove to Merrick that he was wrong, that Edward the Terror was some other miscreant. She must focus all her attentions on finding her father and make every effort to squelch the consuming infatuation running rampant over her emotions.

Upon reaching the dock, the captain placed her hand on his arm. "Stay close to me."

Sloane came up beside them. "I done what ye asked, Cap'n, though ye know how I feels about it." The sailor cast an apprehensive look toward Charlisse then back at Merrick.

"Thank you, Sloane."

An uneasiness gripped Charlisse. "Pray tell, what did you do, Mr. Sloane?"

Sloane's jittery gaze swerved to his captain.

"I had him release Kent." Merrick faced Charlisse. "I will not suffer his presence on board my ship any longer, and I cannot bring charges against him for an act that most of the men in this town have committed." He sighed. "In any case, I have washed my hands of him."

Charlisse scanned the crowd around her, unnerved by the news that the hound who assaulted her roamed free.

Merrick patted her hand. "You have nothing to fear from him anymore, I assure you."

Sloane removed his hat and executed an ungainly bow. "It's bin a pleasure, miss."

"You're not coming with us?" Charlisse looked up at the old man of whom she had grown quite fond in the past few days.

"Naw, miss." Sloane smiled, fidgeting with his hat.

"Sloane has some celebrating to do," Merrick interjected.

"But I hope to be seein' ye agin, miss, real soon."

"So do I, Mr. Sloane." Charlisse stood on her tiptoes and gave him a kiss on his cheek.

Sloane's grin widened, and his weathered face turned a deep shade of red before he turned and plodded off.

"Do you make it a habit, milady, of kissing every pirate you meet?" Merrick teased her as he escorted her down the street.

Charlisse smiled.

The streets of Port Royal bustled with commotion. African slaves as well as half-castes and Caribs poured from the taverns at their owners' bidding to serve the newly arrived clientele. The smells of roasted pig and stewed turtle floated in the evening breeze, prompting a rumble from Charlisse's empty stomach.

Pirates, adventurers, and merchants from all over the Spanish Main were already partaking of rum from the barrels parked in the dirt streets in front of overcrowded taverns. Singing and laughter blared from within the raucous public houses.

Merrick, with a protective grip on Charlisse's arm, walked calmly and authoritatively down the main street.

Eyes wide, she watched the scantily clad women call lustfully to their would-be lovers who passed by, seducing them with buxom breasts and bare legs, offering suggestions that both appalled and nauseated Charlisse.

As they walked along, several men called Merrick's name, inviting him to join them, and it made Charlisse wonder, once again, just what type of man he was.

He turned down a street that led inland. Men standing in front of taverns and boardinghouses perused her with lustful eyes, but made no comment or movement in her direction. Charlisse felt her heartbeat quicken. She clung tightly to Merrick's arm.

Vulgar shouts, obscenities, and daring challenges poured into the streets along with the metallic clank of clashing swords. A musket shot split the evening air with a loud crack, and Charlisse jumped. Merrick patted her hand reassuringly and smiled, his black hair blowing in the evening breeze.

As they passed by one particularly loud tavern, a woman slithered up to Merrick. She wore a tight-fitting indigo peasant dress, from which her voluptuous figure abounded. Her heavily painted face made it difficult to tell whether she was attractive or not, but her piercing gaze took in Charlisse like a hawk after its prey.

"Merrick, where have you been?" Her voice was as sultry and slick as a polished sword. She rubbed against him.

Slowing his pace, he gently pushed her away as two more doxies, hanging from balconies that overlooked the street, called out his name affectionately and waved.

For the first time since Charlisse had met Merrick, he looked flustered. Conflicting thoughts flooded her mind. How did these unscrupulous women know him so well? Was his piety just an act to win her heart? She yanked her arm from his grasp.

The painted woman continued to pursue him.

"Martha." Merrick stopped and turned to her, grabbing Charlisse's arm once more. "Forgive me, but I am otherwise engaged." He looked up and tipped his hat at the women on the balcony, who continued to coo his name.

Charlisse tugged her arm, trying to wrench it from his grasp.

"So I see," the woman hissed, looking Charlisse up and down.

"In fact, I'm afraid my attentions are *permanently* occupied elsewhere," he added. "Martha, I wish you the best." He bowed slightly, offering her a polite grin, then continued on his way, pulling Charlisse with him.

"You'll change your mind, Merrick," the harlot called after him. "I know you. You'll git tired of that fancy prude, and you'll want a real woman. When you do, I'll be here."

They walked on in silence. Charlisse continued trying to tug her arm from his. "Don't let me keep you from your friends," she muttered.

A crooked smile played on the captain's lips. He glanced at her. "I do believe you are jealous." He laughed.

"You flatter yourself, Captain. I am not jealous. I'm simply implying that you no longer need keep up a pious façade on my account." And she meant it. Now that the truth was out, she felt appeased in her resistance of his charms and her assessment of his honor. She was only another conquest to him—but this sortie was one in which he would not be victorious.

Merrick continued walking, wearing a playful smirk.

As shops and taverns gave way to small houses and stables, the noise of revelry fell behind them.

"Where are we going?" Charlisse snapped, further angered at his silence. She sensed his gaze upon her, but did not look up.

"Right up ahead. We are almost there."

Charlisse stared into the deepening twilight and saw a small church made of stone, with a wooden door and a tall steeple that housed a bell. Light from a lantern that hung by the door spilled over carefully tended flowers on either side of the stone pathway.

"I'm not going to a church." She resumed her struggle to be free.

He led her to the side of the building, tenderly backed her against the stone wall, and placed both hands on her shoulders. His gaze was unyielding.

"It's not the type of church you're used to. Reverend Buchan is a good friend of mine." He paused, examining her.

She turned her head to the left and saw a small cottage nestled against a grassy hill behind the church. Warm light streamed from windows, and wisps of smoke drifted up from a stone chimney on the roof.

"You're going to leave me with a clergyman?" Her voice cracked.

"I trust Thomas. He's a good man—a true man of God. Not like your uncle. He will take good care of you until I return."

"Where are you going?"

"I have some business to attend to."

"Oh, I know what business you mean." She snickered, eyes narrowing.

She tried to move aside, but Merrick pulled her back, amusement flickering in his smile. "No, you don't. It's not what you're thinking." Charlisse wrestled from his embrace. Releasing her, he walked away.

"I thought I heard someone out here," a mildly accented male voice bellowed from the opened cottage door. "Merrick, is that you?" The silhouette of a tall, thin man stood in the warm lamplight spilling from the room.

"Thomas." Merrick approached him and gave him a hearty embrace. "It's been awhile, my friend."

As they greeted each other, the reverend looked over and saw Charlisse creeping out from the shadows. "And who is this fair maiden you bring with you, Captain?" Without waiting for a reply, he escorted her inside. "You shouldn't be out here in the dark. Merrick, where are your manners?" Grinning, he leaned toward Charlisse. "He still has a bit of pirate in him, I would say."

Several candles and oil lamps created a comforting warmth in the humble two-room cottage. The tall man, who still had his hand on her arm, led Charlisse to a wooden rocking chair next to a warm potbellied stove. He wore dark brown breeches, boots, and a farmer's tunic and belt. A cluster of thick blond hair crowned his head, and his blue eyes sparkled with clarity and kindness.

There was nothing in his demeanor or his dress that indicated he was a man of the cloth, at least not one that Charlisse had ever seen. That brought her some measure of comfort.

"May I introduce you." Merrick pointed at her. "Lady Charlisse Bristol of London, this is Reverend Thomas Buchan. Reverend Buchan, Lady Bristol."

The reverend approached her and kissed her hand. "My pleasure, miss."

"Lady Bristol," Merrick continued, "was the victim of a shipwreck that left her stranded on an island. My crew and I found her there while careening my ship." He sat down on a worn brown couch centered in the room.

Reverend Buchan cast her a look of concern. "How terrifying for you, miss," he said then added, smiling, "on both accounts." He glanced back at Merrick, eyebrows lifted. "What mischief have you been up to, my reformed pirate?" He slapped the captain on the back and sat down next to him. "What brings you here?"

"The lady searches for her father, and I have promised to assist her." The last phrase he said loudly with his gaze locked upon Charlisse. She forced an angry smile in return. "I would ask you to keep her in your charge for a few hours while I attend to some business."

Thomas agreed wholeheartedly and promptly got up to serve them tea and biscuits. While they were enjoying the refreshments, Merrick, at the reverend's request, briefly described his exploits of the past few months. The two of them laughed and joked like old friends.

Sitting back, Charlisse pondered her next move. Why did she always allow herself to be under the authority of men's decisions? Neither Merrick nor the reverend could keep her here against her will. Yet the captain had said he would help her find her father. Could she trust him to keep his word? She had no idea where to start looking for Edward. At least Merrick knew this port and its people. Terror gripped her as scenes from their quick jaunt through Port Royal flashed through her mind. Most certainly it would not be safe for her to wander around unescorted. She needed Merrick, and there wasn't much she could do about it.

"How have your studies been going as of late?" The reverend's voice drew Charlisse's attention back to the conversation.

"Very well. Excellent, as a matter of fact." Merrick nodded and took a bite of a biscuit. He chewed for a minute then swallowed. "His Word gives me great strength and wisdom."

"Ah yes, there is power in the Bible."

Merrick glanced at Charlisse. "And I have needed it."

Smiling, the reverend leaned back in his rickety chair. The wood creaked in complaint. "And your prayers?"

Merrick set his cup down. "Difficult, I'm afraid." He raked his hair, but then his eyes brightened. "But always answered in extraordinary ways."

Charlisse listened to this last topic with a great deal of curiosity, not that Christianity meant anything to her personally. Why would such a strong man—a man who could command the respect of a devious crew, a man with such unorthodox tendencies as piracy and drink—find comfort in an invisible God?

"It warms my heart to hear it." Reverend Buchan pounded his fist on the arm of the chair and stood, making his way toward Charlisse. Grabbing a rag, he picked up the pot of tea and offered her some more.

Charlisse held out her cup. "Yes, thank you." She examined him as he poured the tea, noting his calm, happy demeanor, the twinkle in his eyes—he was nothing at all like her uncle.

"And what of you, miss? Shipwrecked? How horrifying for you." He set the pot down on the stove. "You are searching for your father? Was he on the ship, as well?"

Charlisse darted a quick glance at Merrick. "No. He lives here at

Port Royal." She sipped her tea. "My mother died, and he's all the family I have left."

The reverend took Charlisse's empty hand in his and gazed at her. "I'm so sorry. There's nothing worse than losing someone you love." A sheen of moisture glistened in his eyes. He squeezed her hand. His rough, warm skin was somehow comforting.

Charlisse set her cup down and returned his gaze, trying to mask her confusion at his concern and quell the tears that rose to her own eyes.

"You have been through quite a lot for such a young lady," Reverend Buchan said, offering her a warm smile as he turned to face Merrick.

The captain scooted off the couch and approached her. He bowed. "I will return as soon as I can.

Charlisse stood, eyeing him with suspicion. "Then you will help me find my father?"

"As I have said." He nodded, grabbed his hat and walked out the door.

The muggy, night air surrounded Merrick.

He turned to face the reverend. "Take good care of her, Thomas."

"Of course." Thomas shut the door and came in step beside his friend. "Who is she really?" He cast the captain an inquisitive glance.

"The daughter of Edward Bristol."

The reverend stopped walking, a look of astonishment on his face.

"Or so she claims," Merrick added. "It's what I intend to find out."

"Tonight?"

Merrick nodded. "I saw Edward's ship at bay. I know where he might be."

"Where's that?"

"At his favorite haunt, of course."

"Are you sure you want to confront him there?" Thomas's brows wrinkled together. "He won't be alone."

"I have no choice." Merrick glanced back at the cottage. "She's desperate to find him, and unless I lock her in the hold of my ship—which may still be an option," Merrick said with a slight grin, "I fear I may not be able to stop her from venturing out tomorrow, with or without an escort, to seek him."

The reverend folded his arms across his chest. "You risk much for the lady."

"I can take care of myself." Merrick patted the hilt of his cutlass. "And I won't be alone. A few of my men will be with me."

The warm night air was filled with the trill of crickets as their evening chorus wafted upon the strong breeze coming off the sea. Normally a soothing sound, tonight it grated on Merrick's nerves.

The reverend looked at him. "You love her, don't you?"

Merrick's brows lifted, and his gaze shifted to the window of the cottage, hoping for a glimpse of Charlisse. "Is it that obvious?"

"I know you like a son, Merrick. I can see it in your eyes."

"She's like no other lady I've known—so unpredictable. She has my head forever in a spin. I never know what she's thinking."

Thomas grinned. "But if you capture her father and have him hanged—as has been your plan for this past year—she may never forgive you."

"Don't you think I realize that?" Merrick turned and stepped away, staring off into the darkness. "It's all I've been thinking about for the past few days."

Silence stretched between them. A gust of wind struck the palm tree overhead, sending its fronds fluttering like giddy children in the warm breeze, mocking Merrick's predicament.

Thomas shuffled his feet in the sand. "What will you do, then?"

Merrick raked his hair and turned around. "Pray, Thomas. Pray that Edward has changed—that he is not the vicious monster he was a year ago. If I see any remorse in him at all, I may stay my hand—for Charlisse's sake."

"And if not?"

"He must be stopped." Merrick sighed and gave Thomas a troubled look. "You know as well as I do what he did to the Arawak village."

Thomas nodded, concern creasing his face. "I know they were your friends."

"And they suffered dearly for that friendship." Merrick shifted his gaze away, feeling the burn of hatred bubbling in his soul.

"Do you still believe he butchered them simply because they knew you?"

"Why else, Thomas? They had nothing he wanted."

Thick clouds crawled in overhead, obscuring the moonlight. Merrick turned to leave.

"God be with you." Thomas placed his hand on the captain's shoulder.

"Let's pray so." Merrick sighed. "For I dare not face Edward the Terror without Him."

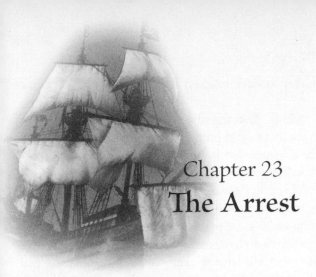

Chapter 23
The Arrest

Merrick rounded a corner and entered a dark alleyway. Up ahead, the shadowy outlines of three men huddled together around the post of a lamp-lit porch. As he approached, their postures straightened. Merrick continued walking. Sloane fell in beside him while the other men followed.

"He's there, Cap'n."

Merrick nodded.

"Are ye sure ye be knowin' what yer doin'?" Sloane asked.

Merrick glanced at his friend.

Sloane scratched his thick beard. "I mean, the Dead Reckoning? Methinks Edward may be havin' lots of friends at that vermin-infested tavern."

"And enemies, too, knowing him."

Merrick marched on, picking up the pace. They turned onto a wider road, lit at intervals by oil lamps sitting atop wooden posts—casting eerie silhouettes over the closed shops lining the street. "Don't worry, I know Edward. His pride will forbid him to fight without honor in front of so many witnesses. If fate thrusts it upon me, and I must challenge him, he'll have to adhere to the rules of a fair duel."

"And ye think ye can take 'im?"

The corner of Merrick's mouth curved upward. "Of course. Where's your faith, man?"

Sloane chuckled. "In yer abilities, to be sure, Cap'n, but not in yer ruthlessness."

The sounds of drunken revelry reached Merrick's ears. Only a few more blocks.

"I made a pledge to God to bring the odious mongrel to justice," Merrick said, "and as much as I would prefer to run him through with my sword and be done with it, I intend to honor my promise."

Of course, exactly how he was going to perform such a feat, he hadn't a clue. Somehow, he must capture Edward and deliver him to the governor without any of his crew protesting. What Merrick needed was a miracle, and it just so happened he knew someone in that business.

Was it possible Edward had changed? Merrick had every reason to believe people, even the most vile and wicked, could give up their evil ways, but deep inside he doubted Edward ever would, and if he hadn't changed, Merrick must never allow him to meet Charlisse.

Merrick signaled as the Dead Reckoning came into view and the four men stopped. He rechecked his weapons—the knife strapped to his thigh, the other one on his belt, the two pistols on his baldric, and his cutlass secured in its scabbard. Taking a deep breath, he prayed he wouldn't need them tonight.

Turning, he nodded at Jackson and Brighton behind him. "No one makes a move save on my command."

"Aye, aye, Cap'n."

Merrick swerved his gaze to Sloane. A determined, approving look passed between them before he set his face staunchly toward the Dead Reckoning and marched onward.

It was a large building as taverns went, hammered together from the wooden planks of aged old ships—pirate ships that had long since died and given up their worn and crusty parts for new iniquitous purposes. The rotting, salt-encrusted wood gave the place a feeling of foreboding, of death and decay and wickedness. Parts of a mainmast formed the posts on the front porch, and a rusty anchor guarded the captain's door that served as an entrance. It now stood open, spilling out the overflow of debased humanity. Through the windows, Merrick saw shadowy figures flowing like the waves of a tempestuous sea. Hideous screams and curses shot through the humid air.

Draped over the railings on the top and bottom floors, like colorful rugs set out to dry, were street harlots, displaying themselves in unabashed exposure, luring men to trade their fortunes for the passing pleasures they offered.

Two of them slinked up to Merrick, smiling and whispering pleasurable suggestions. Tipping his hat in their direction, he brazenly took the steps up to the front door, amazed that their seductions held no attraction for him anymore. Instead, he felt pity and sorrow, and a deep sense of remorse for having ever partaken of their defiled fruit.

Captain Merrick stopped, took a deep breath and said a silent prayer before pushing his way through the drunken mob that cluttered the doorway. Sloane, Brighton, and Jackson followed at his heels. Instantly, Merrick was assailed with the mixed stench of tobacco, body order, stale rum, and urine, and he nearly choked at the wave of torrid memories these scents evoked in him. Not much had changed since he had made this squalid tavern his haunt not two years past. How astounding that a place he had once considered a second home could send such waves of repulsion through him.

The same bar he remembered—made up of the bulwark of a ship—stood in the center of the room where libations poured freely for all who had the coin to pay, lubricating the tongues and inebriating the minds of those who gulped down the vile liquids.

Tables of all shapes and sizes, made from the capstans of ships, filled the bulk of the room. A mass of human forms, male and female, sprawled across them, spilling onto the stools and crates surrounding them.

Toward the back, on the left, were doors leading to other rooms and a stairway, littered with harlots enticing their victims to the rooms above.

Candlelit chandeliers and oil lanterns hung from the rafters, showering a ghostly gloom over the whole wretched scene.

Merrick took a step forward, prying his foot from the sticky floor splattered with vomit and bird droppings. A sailor bumped into him, mumbled, and then fell against Sloane. The old pirate pushed him aside, cursing, and the man lunged out the door, holding his hand to his mouth.

Merrick maintained a calm air of authority as he scanned the room looking for the familiar face of Edward the Terror. His men came up beside him.

He took another confident step forward, and several pairs of eyes shifted his way. "Why 'tis Cap'n Merrick," one stocky man yelled.

"Aye," a lanky lad bellowed. "Come join us fer a drink, Cap'n." Barely able to stand, he pointed toward Merrick with his sloshing mug of ale as he clung to the back of a chair. Four grisly looking men played cards on the table beside him amidst fly-infested food and spilt drink that dripped onto the floor.

"Captain." A stylishly dressed man on his right nodded as he passed.

Merrick squinted through the smoke-filled tavern, ignoring the greetings tossed his way, and searched the darkened corners where Edward usually hid—like the rat he was. Then he saw him in the left rear corner, the ominous light of a dim lantern revealing his debased features.

At the sound of boots approaching, Edward looked up, and a sinister smile crept over his lips. His expression did not carry a trace of the surprise Merrick had expected. To Merrick's astonishment also, a familiar face appeared next to Edward's, the arrogant leer of Master Kent, whom Merrick had released in good faith not three hours earlier.

The demeanor of his former first mate, which had been humble and apologetic when Merrick had last seen him, now carried an abrasive insolence as he leaned back in his chair, arms folded across his chest.

"Curse me mother's grave, if it don't be Captain Merrick," Edward said with a jeering smile and eyes smoldering in hatred. "I see ye've brought yer littl' minions with ye." He nodded toward the three men behind Merrick. "Take a seat, have a drink. Tell me what mischief ye've been up to since ye stole me ship and left me to die on that godforsaken spit of land."

He poured rum into a mug and motioned Merrick to join him. Two men emerged from the shadows and took their places on either side of Edward.

Alarms sounded within Merrick as his gaze passed from the two men to Kent and back to Edward.

They had been expecting him.

"I have since come to regret my folly," Merrick said, offering a contemptuous bow. "I should have strapped a cannon ball to your legs instead and thrown you off the plank for the sharks to feast on your ornery carcass."

Edward's face reddened, and the veins in his neck bulged. He shoved to his feet, toppling his chair behind him. One of his men brashly drew his sword.

Merrick fixed the man with a cold stare and gestured for him to sheath his weapon. "I have come neither to drink nor to fight."

"Aye, I heard ye found religion." Edward cackled and those around him joined in. "No longer a partaker of the evil vices of rum or the brutal pleasure of a good fight, *Captain*?" he said, spitting in contempt on the table. "Lost your stomach for it?"

Edward the Terror was indeed an imposing man, tall and brawny, thick and strong as a bull. A long braid of gray hair ran down his back, matched by a scraggly beard that framed his thick ruddy face. He wore a captain's hat decorated with a plume of ostrich feathers, proudly displayed as a symbol of his self-imposed status. Fully armed and brazen, he had the air of a commander and the arrogance of a man who had not lost many battles. He took a swig of rum, piercing his enemy with icy blue eyes—eyes the same color as Charlisse's.

Flashing images bombarded Merrick's mind—headless, battered bodies; ravished, naked women whose insides had been torn asunder; lifeless, tiny children who died clinging to what was left of their parents; the smoking, blackened remains of a village that was once full of life and laughter. Merrick felt his insides ignite, burning away all decency, like the fires that had destroyed the Arawak town.

"But I heard ye have not given up women." His enemy's voice broke Merrick's trance. "Kent has informed me of the rare young flower ye've been plucking aboard yer ship."

An uneasy hush fell on the usually boisterous crowd.

"You did know Master Kent here is me nephew, didn't you?" Edward's eyebrows lifted. He slammed his mug onto the table, splashing the liquor over its brim. He strutted over to where Merrick stood.

Jackson made a move forward, but Merrick held up his hand.

"Humph." Edward scowled at Jackson before returning his gaze to Merrick. "I sent him to yer ship to be a spy, and ye obligingly made him yer first mate. I thank ye for that." A low rumble of laughter passed over the crowded room.

Merrick remained stoic, taking in this new bit of information. He thrashed it about with the myriad of exchanges that had occurred between him and Kent. Now things began to make sense. He silently cursed himself.

"What would you say if I told you I made the acquaintance of a girl who claims to be your daughter?" Merrick knew full well the answer he would receive. But for Charlisse's sake, he must know with all certainty before he made his next move. Perhaps he was wrong. Would the news of a daughter find its way to any deep hidden tenderness left in Edward's soul? Or would not even this happy discovery be able to penetrate the outer crust of his heart, a heart thickened by hatred and brutal acts of violence?

"I would say she's one of many fortunate offspring I have sired all over the Caribbean!" The room again broke into laughter. Edward glanced around, glowing under the attention.

Merrick fingered the hilt of his cutlass and stared at his enemy with cold contempt. Sloane nudged him from behind, and Merrick could sense the tension in his friend winding up like a taut bow ready to fire its deadly weapon.

Edward stood, legs spread apart, with arms folded over his barrel-like chest. He cocked his head. "What would this girl want with me?" he asked.

"Only to know her father."

Edward tugged at his beard and looked around the room wearing a cocky grin. "Bring the lass to me, then. If she's pretty enough, I'll have no trouble complying with her wishes."

The room exploded with howls. Merrick's temper rose like a bubbling pool of lava.

Edward continued chuckling.

"Why ye swaggering dawcock!" Sloane bellowed, lunging forward.

Even the man's own flesh and blood was not sacred to him. Merrick could endure insults to himself, but he would not have this licentious villain talk about Charlisse as if she were a cheap strumpet. Merrick halted his friend's advance and instead, pulled his own hand back and hardfisted Edward in the jaw, sending the powerful man tumbling backwards into the arms of two of his crew.

"I see the years have only further added to the darkness in your soul." With difficulty Merrick contained himself from beating the man senseless. Edward staggered back to his feet, rubbing his chin.

The mob roared. Kent jumped up, swaying and muttering something unintelligible. He pointed his pistol at Merrick.

Jackson and Brighton drew their weapons. The crowd backed up.

Merrick cast his former first mate a cursory glance. "Beware, Kent. Twice we have fought, and twice I have bested you. If you make it a third time, it may be your last."

"Sit down, boy!" Edward bellowed. "I can fight me own battles." He pushed his nephew aside, jaw flexing with irritation.

Kent's eyes flashed. For a moment, he looked as though he would point his pistol at Edward. Then, lowering it, he staggered back to his chair.

"This matter will be resolved quicker than the pious captain here thinks," Edward roared. He drew his sword in a flash of glinting steel and held the tip to Merrick's throat.

The room burst into cheers as the reckless band of men called out of their bets, loyalties aside.

From behind him, Merrick heard three pistols cock. Two of Edward's men drew their swords.

Merrick did not flinch. He stared defiantly into Edward's eyes. Within the depths of them, something sinister cooked. Edward had an unusual confidence facing a battle with a man who had bested him on more than one occasion. Merrick knew his ex-captain. His pride would not risk an embarrassing defeat in front of so many witnesses. Something was amiss. A shudder of foreboding hit every nerve.

"Come now, gentlemen, lower your weapons. This is between Edward and me, eh, Edward?" Merrick glared at his enemy.

"If that's the way ye wants it, so be it." Edward nodded at his men, and they sheathed their swords. Merrick heard his own men return their pistols to their braces.

The point of Edward's sword pierced Merrick's skin. He lifted an eyebrow. "I do recall defeating you once at this game, sir. Do you intend a repeat performance in front of your friends?"

The obstinate pirate narrowed his eyes into tiny slits of burning coals.

Images of the Arawak people—Merrick's friends—flew through his mind. The compassionate face of Caonabo, their *cacique,* or chief, smiled at him with gleaming teeth so bright against the brown of his skin and eyes that always overflowed with kindness. Merrick could almost hear his laugh, the one that sprang from deep within his belly. Merrick shook his head, remembering what had been left of Caonabo's body when he found him sprawled across the bloody beach—a product of Edward the Terror's violent rampage.

The seconds passed in slow motion. The crowd screamed, calling for a fight—demanding one, in fact, now that they had invested their coins.

Merrick didn't hear them. The insidious clamor faded into the background. All he could see were Edward's fiery eyes and the trickle of sweat that formed on his brow. It sat there momentarily, glistening in the lantern light, before making its way slowly down toward his gray eyebrows.

Merrick tore his cutlass from its scabbard, clashed it against Edward's, first on one side and again on the other. The beefy man stumbled and tried to recover his balance, but his blade flew from his grasp and clanged to the stone floor.

Merrick now pressed the tip of his cutlass to Edward's throat, his lips pursed into a thin line of determination. The throbbing of his heart followed the heat of his anger up his neck and into his head until it clouded his thoughts with nothing but revenge. His hand shook. His body trembled, ready to explode. He wanted to thrust Edward through. He wanted it more than anything in the world.

"Do it, ye carp," Edward demanded. "End me worthless life."

Merrick tightened his muscle for the final plunge, but as he stared into Edward's blue eyes, he saw a vision of Charlisse. He hesitated. Sloane reached from behind him and stayed his arm.

Merrick lowered his sword.

Grumbles of disappointment cracked across the room like the roar of thunder, but just like thunder, the rumbling drifted away, leaving in its wake a deadly silence. The look of surprised relief on Edward's face gave way to an evil grin. Merrick heard the thump of heavy boots behind him.

"Captain Merrick," a commanding voice said.

The cocking of several pistols echoed through the room. "Captain Edmund Merrick," the voice boomed again. "Drop your sword, sir."

Every instinct screamed for Merrick to slice the evil smirk from Edward's face. But he didn't. He released his weapon with a clatter to the floor and turned to face the source of the intrusion.

The barrels of six pistols greeted him from behind a British officer in full uniform, who presented an open document. Sloane, Brighton, and Jackson jumped in front of their captain, hands on the hilts of their cutlasses.

"Tell your men to back off, Captain," the officer ordered, "or I'll have you shot where you stand."

Merrick nodded toward his crew. "Do as he says." They lowered their hands.

The pirates grumbled.

The man lifted his document and peered at the parchment.

"On order of Thomas Moodyford, his majesty's governor of the Isle of Jamaica, said privateer, Captain Edmund Merrick, shall be seized and placed under arrest immediately on this day, the first of July in our Lord's year sixteen hundred and sixty-five, having been accused and with much evidence therein, of the crime of piracy, having performed diverse robberies on the high seas in the West Indies, and in particular done great damage to the merchants of Great Britain, having broken signed articles with said governor to act as privateer only against the Spanish forces in the West Indies."

The pirates erupted into a haggle of shouts and curses.

"There'll be no trouble here, or I'll send the whole lot of you to the gallows!" the officer bellowed over the din.

"On what evidence do you so accuse me?" Merrick asked.

"On the evidence found on your ship, the *Redemption*," he replied. "That is your ship, Captain?"

Merrick nodded. "It is, sir, but what evidence do you speak of?"

Kent snickered in the corner.

The officer nodded to two of his men, and they grabbed Merrick, rapidly disarming him. "You can take that up with the governor."

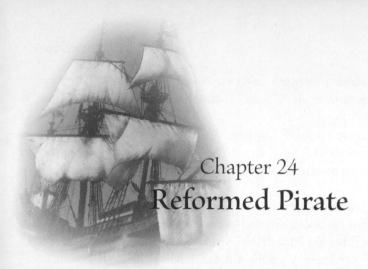

Chapter 24
Reformed Pirate

It's getting late, don't you think, Reverend?" Charlisse stood by the window of the cottage, peering out into the murky shadows. She grabbed a wayward curl that had escaped from her bun and twisted it around her finger. She had spent the past three hours sitting by the warm stove, drinking tea and listening to Reverend Buchan talk about his adventures in the American British Colonies.

His stories fascinated her, and the more he spoke, the more she grew fond of him. Sparkles of inner joy radiated from his eyes and the comforting peace that flowed all around him put her immediately at ease. She felt as if she'd known him all her life.

"I wouldn't be worrying, miss. Merrick can take care of himself." A look of anxiety passed over his face before his peaceful countenance returned. He fidgeted in his seat and offered her more tea.

Charlisse wondered when the good reverend would begin his God-given duty of redeeming her degenerate soul. Surely Merrick had told him when they had been whispering out in front of the cottage that she had lost her faith. By now, the reverend must have devised some tactic to persuade her of the error of her ways and compel her to repent of her sins and return to the church. But she was ready for him. She would inform him just what the Church of England had done for her, or rather *to* her, and all under the godly authority of the bishop, her loving uncle.

She declined the tea. "My concern is not for Captain Merrick, I assure you. My only desire is that he return to help me find my father."

Charlisse walked back and sat down next to the reverend. She would admit to needing the help of men for now, but she did not need the help of a God who had abandoned her long ago. "How did you come to know Merrick?"

He smiled. "Well, that's a most interesting story." He leaned back in his chair, folding his hands over his stomach. "I had been settled here only about six months—sent by the Lord to start a church and spread the good news amidst this crowd of scandalous heathens before they took over the whole island." He chuckled. "It was late one night, and I heard noises in the sanctuary. You see, I didn't have this cottage back then. I lived in an upper room in the church itself. So, when I heard the noises, I crept downstairs to see who it was. I was a bit frightened because as you have seen, the island's inhabitants are not the most. . .respectable citizens."

Charlisse smiled.

"As my eyes grew accustomed to the darkness, whom did I find curled up on one of the pews but Captain Edmund Merrick, drunk and bleeding from several sword wounds and a musket shot to his shoulder."

Charlisse's breath caught in her throat.

"Then I heard British troops marching in the street," the reverend continued, "and as I looked down at the poor man, who was barely breathing, a pair of pleading eyes took hold of my conscience. I could not allow them to find him, at least not then. So I hid him in my room, tended to his wounds, and kept the royal authorities at bay for the next few months until he recovered."

"And you became good friends?"

Reverend Buchan nodded. "Yes, almost like father and son." He smiled and got up to put another log into the stove. "You see, Merrick, like most young men of position and privilege, lacked nothing as a child, yet as he progressed into manhood, found none of it satisfying. He had everything the world considers necessary for success: power, title, fortune, good looks. . . ." He glanced toward Charlisse, flashing a sly grin. "As well you know," he added.

She looked down momentarily, feeling a blush warm her face.

"A superior education," he continued, "and every opportunity for achievement and prosperity." He closed the stove door. "But he was not happy, not fulfilled, empty inside. So casting it all away," the reverend said, waving his hand in the air, "leaving everything he knew, he headed out on his own adventure in search of purpose and meaning. He had not found it within the confines of civilized society, so he sought it outside those barriers, in the lawlessness and debauchery of a class of people who followed no rules but the lusts of their own flesh."

He sat back down and took a sip of tea. "What I found, huddled on my church pew, was the outcome of such a quest. And though he had been quite a successful pirate and had made a well-known and much-feared name for himself on the Caribbean, he was even more miserable than he had been before: so hopeless that no amount of drinking or—pardon my crudeness—philandering could fill the aching hole in his spirit. Though he did try." He chuckled. "He did try."

Charlisse flinched, remembering the woman who had slithered up to Merrick earlier that evening. The thought of her, or any woman, with him gave Charlisse a sick, painful feeling in her stomach that was disconcerting. She pushed the unfamiliar feelings aside.

"You speak of Merrick's position and fortune. He never spoke to me of his family back in England. Who are they?"

"Ah." Reverend Buchan's eyebrows rose. He got up from his chair. "So he didn't mention his family to you. Well, no wonder." He walked to the window, gazing into the darkness. He seemed troubled, and Charlisse wondered if it was Merrick's long absence that made him uneasy.

"All his life, he's been known only by his family—his name," the reverend said. "I don't suppose he wants to live in that shadow anymore."

"So he had a noble upbringing?"

"Yes, the finest, I assure you." He turned to face her, crossing his arms over his chest. "Have you heard of Edward Hyde?" he asked.

"Of course, who hasn't?"

Reverend Buchan remained quiet, a coy smile playing on his lips.

Charlisse waited for him to respond, the growing silence sparking her curiosity. "No," she finally said, widening her eyes. "Earl Edward Hyde is Merrick's father?"

Reverend Buchan nodded. "His real name is Edmund Merrick Hyde."

Charlisse glanced down, gathering her thoughts. She didn't know much about the earl except that he had followed Charles II into exile and then became one of his chief advisors. He was appointed Earl of Clarendon upon Charles's reinstatement to the throne in 1660. If Merrick was his son, then he was a very important and powerful man. Suddenly, his mannerisms, his education, his skill with a sword, and his *arrogance* all made sense.

"Edward Hyde pushed Merrick to excel in everything he did," Reverend Buchan continued. "He sent him to the best schools, provided the best military training, introduced him to the most powerful and influential nobles in London—including the king himself. But he confined Merrick to a rigid, regimented lifestyle, told him what to do, where to go, who to talk to, and even what to eat." The reverend shook his head. "There was no love, no fatherly affection or approval, and Merrick's spirit soon withered under such strict control."

"I cannot see him in such an environment." Charlisse sighed, still finding it hard to believe.

"No, neither could he. He hated the confines of London nobility, the pretensions of society, and the decadence. He even became disillusioned with the Church of England, which seemed more preoccupied with power, wealth, and politics than with the feeding of the poor and hungry and the spreading of the gospel." The reverend walked back to the stove and held his hands out to it. He looked at Charlisse. "So he turned his back on God, on country, and on his family, and sailed to the Caribbean," he said, lips curving into a smile, "where he used his intelligence and skill to become one of the most revered pirates on the Spanish Main."

Charlisse sat back, musing over the tale—like one she'd heard in a storybook—the rich, young prince changing his identity and leaving all he had to become a commoner. True, Merrick was no real prince, but with Edward Hyde as his father, he was as close to one as a man could get. And this story took a fascinating turn, for not only had the prince become a commoner, but a thief, a villain, and a pirate!

Charlisse, too, had left a life of wealth and comfort—granted, for completely different reasons—but she could understand how someone could reach a point where all the money, power, and position in the world could not overcome the pain and emptiness in one's soul.

She looked up at the reverend who was still standing by the stove.

"Merrick is no longer the brutal pirate you described. Were you the one who changed him?"

The reverend glanced at her, a twinkle in his eyes. "Me?" He chuckled, shaking his head. "No, I have no power to change anyone, miss. It is Merrick's relationship with God, through his Son, Jesus, that has changed him."

Charlisse fixed him with a cold eye. "I know all about God," she sneered, "and my associations with Him have caused me nothing but grief."

"Is that so? Begging your pardon, miss, I would seriously question whether your association with God was with the loving God of the Bible, or with the impersonal, institutionalized god of organized religion. The latter I have no doubt disappointed you."

"What is the difference? Isn't there only one God?"

"Yes, to be sure. One God, and one way to approach Him—through Christ, His Son." Excitement sparked across his face. "It's possible that you know *of* God but that you do not truly *know* Him."

"With all due respect, Reverend, isn't God supposed to communicate with us, guide and teach us through His representatives here on earth?" The reverend began to answer, but Charlisse continued, her face hot with emotion. "Well, I had an encounter with one of your God's representatives, and if he is anything like God, I'm quite content to remain on my own."

"Indeed." The reverend wore look of genuine concern. "Tell me more."

Charlisse took in Reverend Buchan with a scrutinizing eye. Was his apparent regard for her real? Or was he like so many other "men of God" she had met, pulling her into his trap by feigning concern, only to pounce on her after she had bared her soul. She didn't trust him, no matter how genuine he seemed. "My uncle is the Bishop of Loxford," she began, her voice quivering. "Have you heard of him?"

"Why yes, Bishop Hemming. I know of him—by reputation only."

"Well, then you know he is highly revered and respected in the Church of England, governing over one of the richest dioceses in the country." She sighed, looking away, feeling a spirit of despondency overshadow her.

She opened her mouth to continue but shut it suddenly. Moments passed. She fought the tears pooling in her eyes. "Well, no matter," she whispered, resigned. "If he was God's representative and God allowed him to do what he did, then I want no part of your God."

The reverend sat, silently looking down at the floor, his hands folded in front of him.

Charlisse wondered if her words hadn't been too harsh. *Had she insulted him? Or perhaps made him angry?* The silence grew uncomfortable, and she stirred in her seat. His eyes were closed, and his lips moved slightly. When he looked up at Charlisse, his expression reflected a compassionate regard.

"I am truly sorry for what your uncle or anyone else has done to you in the name of God. I don't know what you have gone through, but I can see it must have been something horrendous to have evoked such an ardent response—at even the mention of your uncle's name. I have no explanation except to say that your uncle and others like him cannot be truly men of God. They are counterfeits, seeking only wealth, power, and pleasure. They prey on innocents in the name of the Lord, but they do not know, nor do they serve, the one true and living God." He hesitated.

Charlisse felt his gaze upon her, but she did not look up.

"As to why our good Lord allows things like this to happen, I can only say that undeserved, unfortunate, and often painful events happen to good people for reasons only God knows, and those reasons are always for the ultimate good—though it is difficult to fathom at the time."

Charlisse got up and paced across the room. "I cannot accept that. I do not believe that if there is a God who loves His creation, He would allow such horrible things to happen. Where was He when I was alone and oppressed? Where was He when I cried out to Him in the night?"

"He was right there with you, crying alongside you."

"Hmm." Charlisse peered through the window into the darkness, a thick blackness that matched the anger and bitterness in her soul. She didn't want to think about this right now. She only wanted to think about one thing. Finding her father.

"So am I to believe that *God* transformed Merriok from a scandalous, bloodthirsty pirate into a moral, kindhearted gentleman?" Sarcasm dripped from her voice.

"Yes, absolutely!" Reverend Buchan's face lit up. "You see, that's the power of the cross. No power on earth can truly change the nature of man, except Jesus. As soon as Merrick believed and accepted the sacrifice of Christ, the Spirit of the living God came and dwelt in him, transforming him into the man God intended him to be. It's a relationship, not a set of rituals and rules."

Charlisse had never heard anyone speak of God like this before, not in all her uncle's eloquent speeches, nor all the hundreds of sermons she had heard at church. "You're not from the Anglican church, are you?"

"No, miss, I'm a Presbyterian," he said proudly. "We believe in this." He walked over and held up a big black book, which Charlisse recognized as a Bible—the same type Merrick had in his cabin.

The reverend made it sound as though God wanted an intimate relationship with His children—that He wanted to work individually in their lives to make them better people. It was so unlike the cold, ominous, foreboding God about whom she had been taught all her life.

She had not known Merrick before his transformation, but she could not deny that he was now a man of integrity and kindness.

She glanced over her shoulder at the reverend, whose eyes were still upon her in expectation. He was also unlike any man of God she had known. A genuine love emanated from him, so much so, that it shone through his eyes as if his very spirit were overflowing with it.

A pounding on the door startled her from her thoughts. "Merrick!" she cried. She rushed to open it. The reverend jumped in front of her, motioning her to be quiet.

He glanced around the room, flung open a cabinet, and grabbed a shovel. Holding it above his head, he crept toward the door. The pounding resumed, sending pulsating echoes through the room.

"Rev, let me in!" a hoarse whisper sounded from outside.

Cracking the door, the reverend peered out and lowered the pot just as Sloane burst into the room.

"The cap'n's been arrested!" he said, eyes blazing.

Charlisse's heart skipped a beat.

"They're goin' to hang him." Sloane added, still breathing hard. "At Execution Dock."

Chapter 25
The Prison

W hen?" Charlisse demanded. "When are they going to hang him?"

"Don't rightly know, miss," Sloane spat between breaths. "More 'n likely not till next Friday. Fridays are hangin' days here in Port Royal."

"Who arrested him?" the reverend asked.

"The gov'nor. He was chained and taken away by a band o' British troops not an hour ago."

The reverend peered into the darkness before shutting the door. "Have a seat, Mr. Sloane." He gestured toward a chair. "Let's calm down and hear the whole story."

"There be nothin' to tell, Reverend." Sloane remained standing. "The cap'n got in a bit o' a brawl with Edward the Terror down at the Dead Reckoning." He cast an apprehensive glance at Charlisse.

"My father?"

"Aye, miss."

Charlisse clenched her jaw and shouted, "He knew where my father was, and he didn't tell me!"

The reverend took a step toward her. "It was for your protection, Miss Bristol."

Charlisse swerved to face him. "You knew about this, too? Is there no trustworthy man to be found anywhere?"

"Naw, miss. Ye be misunderstandin', methinks."

"Then please do explain, Mr. Sloane. The suspense overwhelms me."

Heat rose up her neck. "Better yet, I shall go see for myself." She started for the door. "Is my father still at this place—what did you call it—the Dead Reckoning?"

"Aye, miss, but I wouldn't be goin' down there if I was you."

The reverend grabbed her arm. "Miss Bristol."

Charlisse tugged against his grasp. Turning, she saw the calm determination on his face. "You can't keep me here." Tears burned in her eyes. Her father was right down the street. Shock and fury and fear combined in a tremble that overtook her.

"Let's sit and hear what happened first," the reverend said, tilting his head toward a chair. "I will not keep you here if you truly wish to go. All I ask is that you hear what Mr. Sloane has to say."

Charlisse stared into the reverend's eyes. Not a trace of anger or insincerity lurked in their depths. She shifted her glance to Sloane.

"Please, miss. Ye needs to hear this." Concern touched his weathered features.

Her resolve weakened. "As you wish." She allowed the reverend to lead her to a chair and was thankful for the repose it brought to her wobbly legs when she sat.

The reverend nodded at Sloane. The old pirate shifted his feet and glanced at Charlisse. "Miss, the cap'n wanted to see for hisself if yer father had changed. He didn't want ye to meet up wi' him if he were still the varmint he always were."

"But why didn't he tell me what he was doing?"

"'Cause he knows ye would've wanted to come along, miss." Sympathy softened his scratchy voice, and she realized that he was right.

Charlisse nodded.

"By the powers, if ole Edward was a better man, Merrick was not goin' to capture him like he planned."

"Capture him?" Charlisse jumped to her feet. "What are you saying?"

Sloane and the reverend exchanged glances.

The reverend motioned Charlisse to sit. "Merrick's history with your father goes way back."

"Yes, I know. He told me he sailed under my father's command."

"Well, thar's more to it than that, miss," Sloane piped up. "But it don't make no difference now. Merrick was willin' to forego all his schemes against Edward fer yer sake, that was if there were any spark of decency found in 'im."

"How noble," Charlisse spat.

Sloane took a seat and scratched his beard. "Har, it was noble. Ye don't understand. The cap'n put hisself in grave danger by confrontin' Edward at the Dead Reckonin'. But he knew he had to do it, seein' as ye would go lookin' fer him in the mornin'. It woulda been far better to grab Edward durin' the day when he would be sleepin' off the night's drink, don't ye see?"

Charlisse stared into Sloane's eyes. She saw only kindness there. Her glance shifted to the reverend, who stood, arms crossed over his chest, returning her gaze. When she had thought Merrick was out chasing women, he had gone instead to confront her father. There was bad blood between them, that was sure. Had he truly put himself in harm's way for her sake?

"What happened?" she asked.

"Methinks Edward and Kent—"

"Kent? He was there?"

"Aye, he was, miss." Sloane nodded. "Methinks they were expectin' Merrick and set a trap fer 'im."

Charlisse shook her head and began pacing the tiny room.

"On what charge did they arrest him?" The reverend inquired.

"Not rightly sure, Rev." Sloane wiped the sweat from his brow and fidgeted. "From what I heard, they say he was piratin' on British ships, which I know ain't true, 'cause I've bin with him for near three years now, and after he signed them articles with the gov'nor, he ain't attacked nothin' but the Spanish."

The reverend tugged his ear. "What evidence do they have?"

"I dunno, Rev." Sloane shook his head. "I came here as soon as I saw where they took him."

"Well, I'm sure it's all just a misunderstanding," the reverend said in a voice that betrayed his apprehension.

Charlisse's thoughts swam in a pool of confusion, trying to stay afloat above the murky waters of doubt and betrayal. She didn't know who or what to believe. Was her father the raffish vermin everyone said he was, or was he the kind, loving man her mother had adored? Why did Merrick hate him so much? What had happened between them? Or was Merrick just trying to keep her for himself? No, she didn't believe that anymore. Panic shot through her at the thought of him dangling from a hangman's noose like a common pirate.

"Reverend, we must go to him." Charlisse turned, grabbed her cloak, and headed toward the door. "Sloane, show me where the jail is."

"That's not possible, Miss Bristol," the reverend said, gently grabbing her arm. "They do not allow visitors after dark. We must wait until morning."

Charlisse stared at him for a moment, then sighed and trudged back to her seat.

The reverend offered Sloane some tea and biscuits, which he readily accepted.

As she watched him devour his evening snack, Charlisse wondered how he could eat with such a crisis afoot. She grew queasy just watching him. Merrick was in jail, and her father was so near she could feel him. Yet she felt powerless to do anything for either of them.

Charlisse accepted another cup of tea from the reverend and forced a smile, trying to hide the conflicting feelings that tormented her. It was going to be a long night.

The morning sunlight sparkled on the ripples of Kingston Bay, creating a glimmering aura that brought an undeserved beauty to a town still simmering in a drunken stupor. The reverend's carriage rumbled along the deserted streets, the *clip-clop* of the horse's hooves echoing through the alleyways.

Charlisse had spent a restless night, fitfully tossing on the reverend's cot in the back room, while he and Sloane slept on couches in the front salon. The thought of Merrick alone in a cold prison cell upset her more than she could have dreamed possible. Even more distressing was the news that her father had put him there.

She looked out over the quiet streets. He was right here, in Port Royal—the man who had loved her mother, the man whom her mother had loved more than her own life. She was so close to him now, she could sense his presence.

Staring into the empty windows of the taverns and boardinghouses that lined the street, she wondered if he was in one of them. Or perhaps—the thought occurred as she glanced out over the bay—he was on his ship. Several rocked idly in the calm waters, and she allowed her gaze to wander over each one, trying to guess which of them might possibly be his.

She spotted the *Redemption*, and a twinge of pain struck her heart. The mighty ship seemed empty as she bobbed forlornly, waiting for her master to return.

The reverend snapped the reins lightly to spur the horses onward as they came upon the harbor docks. While half the city slept well into the morning, the hardy dockworkers and shipmen were already receiving the cargo from a new arrival. Bells chimed and merchants unloaded their goods from cockboats gliding to the quay. Slaves carried heavy loads on their backs and heads. The smells of fish, sweat, and saltwater swept over Charlisse. A couple of seamen looked up and took off their hats, nodding politely to her as the carriage passed.

Beyond the docks, they ascended a shallow incline and passed several tall, whitewashed stone buildings that bordered a narrow street. The day grew warm, and the sapphire blue chiffon dress Charlisse still wore clung uncomfortably to her skin. She grabbed the fan the reverend had given her and fluttered it about her face, trying to alleviate the heat as well as calm the nervous tension that was forming in the pit of her stomach. It did nothing, however, to assist either cause, and she dropped it to her lap in frustration. She had so many questions about her father that only Merrick could answer. The carriage jolted forward, and Charlisse shifted her thoughts to Sloane, wondering what progress he was making. Much to the reverend's apparent dismay, he had headed off shortly after dawn to gather as many men as he could who were still loyal to Merrick—should more drastic measures be required to release him from prison. She shivered at the violence and possible loss of life those *drastic measures* would entail.

They rounded a corner and the iron gate of Fort Charles loomed before them, jarring Charlisse from her thoughts. The British soldiers who stood guard smiled at the reverend and waved them through without question.

Beyond the entrance, a courtyard stretched in a spacious circle surrounded by thick walls of stone. To the left, gun turrets rose menacingly into the blue sky, pointing their thirty cannons out over the bay, defending the harbor from enemies and pirates alike. Gray brick structures lined the inner walls in a semicircle with the exception of three tall white buildings with pointed brown roofs that stood off to their right.

British officers in crisp red and white uniforms marched in formation across the dry grounds, the stark landscape relieved only by occasional green bushes that grew in circular planters. The reverend pulled up next to one of the white buildings and assisted Charlisse from the carriage.

A surprising wave of cool air flowed over Charlisse as she and the reverend entered the building. She squinted, adjusting her eyes to the dim lighting. A man in a lieutenant's uniform sat behind a desk, his head bowed over a mass of parchments. A bench stretched next to the door, and a narrow table, layered with books, stood to one side. On the wall to the left hung a painting of a British regiment clustered around a cannon. Their commander perched haughtily on his white stallion behind the action, wafts of frosty air bursting from his horse's nostrils. On the wall behind where the man worked, hung four large muskets on hooks, one on top of the other.

"Have a seat; I'll be with you momentarily." The man gestured toward the wooden bench without looking up.

The reverend and Charlisse remained standing. The officer busied himself with the chaotic pile of papers scattered across his wooden desk, stopping only to dip his pen into a bottle of ink and scratch something across one of the documents before shifting his attention to the next.

After several minutes, he sighed and lifted his head. Recognition flickered in his eyes when he saw the reverend. His gaze moved to Charlisse and immediately he stood and bowed, buttoning his red waistcoat and running his hands through his hair.

"So, Reverend, which of the prisoners have you come to save from the gates of hell today?" His gaze scanned Charlisse. "I see you have brought an angel to assist you."

"May I introduce Miss Charlisse Bristol, visiting from London."

"My pleasure, miss." The lieutenant took her hand and kissed it.

Charlisse nodded politely.

"I have not come to save any from eternal doom," the reverend said, "but to save one innocent man from false imprisonment."

"Indeed." The officer cocked his head. "And who might that be?"

"Edmund Merrick. He was brought in last night."

One of the two doors opened behind him, and another soldier entered. He stood at attention briefly, gave a brisk salute, and handed the lieutenant more documents. Without looking at the papers, he sighed and tossed them onto his desk.

At one time, the lieutenant must have been handsome, but now the scourge of hard work and time had left deep impressions in his face, and although only about forty, he carried himself like a man weary from life. His periwig lay haphazardly on a chair, and for an officer of the crown, his uniform was unusually slovenly.

"Who did you say?" he asked again.

"Edmund Merrick," the reverend and Charlisse said in unison.

The lieutenant shuffled through a pile of papers on his right and finally pulled one out. "Ah yes, the pirate."

"He's not a pirate," Charlisse stated.

"Begging your pardon, miss, but that's what it says here." The lieutenant glanced again at the document. "Got the governor's signature and everything."

"Well, the governor is mistaken," Charlisse said, feeling the reverend's light touch on her arm.

The man's eyebrows shot up.

"What she means," the reverend interjected in a calm voice, "is that we have reason to believe there may be falsified evidence in this case. What do we need to do to have the charges against Merrick revisited?"

"You'd have to go to the governor himself," the officer replied, tossing the paper down and sitting back in his chair. "This particular arrest came directly from His Lordship."

The reverend looked down, folding his hands in front of him. Charlisse fidgeted at his side, wondering why he didn't do something.

"May we at least view the evidence presented against Captain Merrick?" the reverend asked.

The lieutenant shook his head. "Not unless you are his relation."

"May we see him?" Charlisse took an anxious step forward, wearing her sweetest smile.

The officer's gaze scoured over them, his eyes shifting back and forth between theirs. "You can see him, Reverend, but not the lady. It wouldn't be safe for her in the prison."

"No, please, Lieutenant. I must see him," Charlisse said, hoping her desperation was not evident in her voice. She could not fathom being so close to Merrick and not being able to see him—if only to find out the truth of what had happened with her father, of course. "Please," she pleaded. "Surely you and your men are capable of protecting one woman?" She gave him a coy glance.

The man stood, clearing his throat. "Yes, quite so, miss. We are more than capable, of course, but I'm afraid you would find the prison most offensive to your delicate nature."

"Make an exception for the lady," the reverend said, "as a favor to me, Lieutenant."

The soldier paused, gazing first at Charlisse and then at the reverend. Charlisse saw the stern resolve melt from his eyes.

"As you wish. But one of my men will accompany you both." He nodded at the man who still stood at attention beside him.

"Absolutely." The reverend smiled, squeezing Charlisse's hand.

The dark corridor smelled of mold and decay that seemed to seep from the stone walls like beads of sweat on a condemned man. Torch held high, the soldier assigned to accompany them led the way through a bolted door and down a stairway. Charlisse heard a scream in the distance. The putrid stench of urine, sweat, and disease assailed her. Holding a handkerchief to her nose, she clutched the reverend's hand for support as they reached the bottom of the stairs and began walking down a long aisle.

The first few cells appeared empty, but then prisoners began to scramble forward, shaking the iron bars that held them in and grinning maliciously at the passing party.

Charlisse did her best to hide behind the reverend, but did not manage to escape the attention of some of the inmates who flooded her with vile and perverse entreaties. The largest cockroach she had ever seen scampered boldly on the floor in front of them, barely avoiding her right shoe. Charlisse shrieked. The reverend patted her hand. They proceeded around a corner and down another row of cells until the guard stopped abruptly.

At first, Charlisse couldn't see anything in the dim light. Then something stirred in the shadows that covered the back half of the cage, and out sauntered Merrick. By the swagger in his step, the lift of his chin, and the imposing look in his eyes, Charlisse would've thought he marched across the deck of his ship issuing commands, instead of across a tiny, dank cell awaiting his trial. "Should have known it was you causing all that commotion." His lips curved in a smile.

Seeing him behind bars, Charlisse's heart sank. What would happen if they could not procure his release? As he faced her now, the thought of losing him caused waves of dread to spiral through her. His dark eyes regarded her with such tenderness, and she realized for the first time how much she'd come to depend on him.

Abandoning all pretense, Charlisse rushed up to him, pushing her hands through the bars into his. He lifted them to his lips. "Miss me?"

His dark brown eyes examined her, filling her with all the love and longing they contained, overflowing like a well that was too full to hold the consuming feelings within. The warm touch of his strong hand, his musky smell, the spark of playfulness in his eyes, all brought the fears of her sleepless night back. A tear escaped her eye and slid down her cheek.

He reached through the bar and gently wiped it away, his expression softening. "It will be all right, sweetheart," he assured her. Charlisse smiled at the endearment, temporarily forgetting her desire to question Merrick about her father.

Merrick's glance landed on the reverend, who stood off to the side. "My friend," he greeted him.

The reverend approached. "Haven't we done this before?"

Merrick chuckled, nodding. "Yes, indeed." He clutched his friend's hand. "You see, my dear," he said to Charlisse, "nothing to worry about. This is not so uncommon an occurrence. And as before, the good Lord will deliver me, eh, Reverend?"

"Let us pray so, my friend. Do tell us, Merrick, what happened, and what we can do to assist you."

Merrick flashed an uneasy look at Charlisse. He began to pace, raking his hand through his hair. He wore only a white shirt, black cotton breeches, and calf-high boots. Yet even stripped of his weapons, he exuded fierceness. Turning, he looked at them both and sighed, glancing at the guard who stood some distance away. "I saw your father," he said, looking at Charlisse.

"I know. Sloane told us."

"And you didn't question me on our encounter immediately?" Merrick gave her a perplexed look.

Charlisse shook her head, unable to explain why she hadn't, even to herself. "Sloane said you went to capture my father. Is that true?"

Merrick stared at her for a moment, then turned away. "Yes."

Charlisse grabbed the bars. "But why? You knew he was my father."

A shudder rippled across Merrick's back before he turned to face her. Rage boiled in his eyes. "You don't know him." He shook his head. "I had to stop him."

"From what?"

Merrick glanced at the reverend then back at Charlisse. "From murdering more innocent people like he did at the Arawak village."

"What are you talking about?" Charlisse felt her eyes fill with tears. She loosened her painful grip on the bars.

"It doesn't matter." Merrick approached her, the anger gone from his eyes. "If he had just shown me one ounce of decency, I intended to let him go—for your sake, milady."

He held out his hand, but Charlisse backed away.

Clutching the bars, Merrick shook them, his face reddening, before he turned away.

The reverend stepped forward. "Merrick, what can we do to help you?"

"I believe Edward and Kent placed evidence on board the *Redemption*."

"What sort of evidence?" the reverend asked.

"I'm not sure." Merrick shook his head and paced across his cell. "Most likely articles looted from a missing British vessel that could be uniquely identified with that ship—a ship I can only assume to have been a victim of your father's." His gaze landed on Charlisse.

"But how would they have gotten on the *Redemption*?" Charlisse asked, wiping tears from her eyes. She wanted to believe him, even if it meant her father was a pirate, but she knew Merrick kept his ship well guarded.

"It had to be Kent." Merrick approached the bars. "He's the only one who had access. I also discovered something else."

"What?"

"Kent is your father's nephew."

Charlisse clapped her hand to her mouth. *My cousin?* That unscrupulous, scandalous vermin was related to her? The monster who had attacked her was her cousin? "How did you find out?"

"Edward told me. Kent was there at the Dead Reckoning with your father. He was planted on my ship as a spy all this time, and I didn't know it. I trusted that little jackanapes."

Charlisse began to tremble, and Merrick grabbed her hands through the bars. "I'm sorry."

She looked up at him, tears welling in her eyes. "Am I to find all my relations are pirates and villains?" she half laughed, half cried.

He kissed her hands. "Perhaps, but it makes no difference to me, and it shouldn't to you, either."

Charlisse gazed into his eyes and found nothing but warmth and concern in them. She loved him. She knew it now. When or how it had happened, she had no idea, but she knew she did not want to live without him. How cruel were the thorns of fate to pierce her heart with love for a man who wanted her father dead.

The reverend cleared his throat and drew closer. "What can we do, Merrick? How can we prove your innocence?"

Merrick sighed, shaking his head. "We need proof that whatever they found on my ship was planted."

"Surely your crew will speak up for you," the reverend interjected. "They can testify that you have not attacked British ships."

"No doubt, yes, most will, but who's to believe them? They are only pirates, after all." Merrick ran his hand through his hair. "No, we need someone who knows what Edward and Kent did, someone credible, who holds neither affection nor fear toward either of them. Surely they have many enemies here in Port Royal."

"Time's up," the guard shouted from behind them, giving Charlisse a start.

She cast Merrick a troubled look.

"Sloane will know what to do," Merrick quickly said. He grabbed her hands. "Under no circumstances are you to approach your father or Kent, do you understand?"

Charlisse stood staring at him, not willing to make that promise.

"Do you understand me?" Merrick said forcefully.

The guard approached.

Merrick turned toward the reverend. "Thomas, please take care of her. I put her in your charge."

"Absolutely," the reverend said. "And don't worry. We will do all that we can. God is with you, Merrick. Remember that."

"I do, Thomas, I do, and thank you." Merrick took Charlisse's hands one more time and brought them to his lips.

"I can't leave you here," she sobbed, her eyes burning with emotion.

"Don't worry, I've been in far worse situations."

"Come on, miss." The guard reached out to grab her, but Merrick stared at him with such ferocity that he hesitated, then let his hand drop. Quickly, the reverend intervened and clasped Charlisse's arm, pulling her from Merrick.

She clung to Merrick's hand as long as she could before she was forced to let go. The reverend led her away, but her gaze never left Merrick's. His reassuring wink was the last thing she saw before the closing prison doors took him from her sight.

As the sound of their footsteps faded into the distance, the gloom and chill of his prison once again engulfed him. Merrick pounded the iron bars in frustration before falling to his knees and bowing his head before the only Person who could truly deliver him.

Chapter 26

The Battle between Good and Evil

The next few days passed in a blur of mindless activities and endless hours. Charlisse did her best to keep her hopes up and not succumb to the discouragement and fear that were eating away at her heart. With Merrick in prison—his fate yet unknown—and her father somewhere in Port Royal, conflicting emotions and desires assailed her. Her father's proximity tugged at her heart. Like the grapnels of a ship, it wrenched at the distance between them, dragging her closer and closer. But when their ships collided, would she find him to be the vicious pirate everyone said he was, seeking only what he could get from her without offering any love in return? And what of Merrick? Thoughts of him locked in that dank cell clenched at her soul and consumed her like a fire that burned but was never quenched. What should she do?

Disaster had always been at the helm of her ship, driving her resolutely from one tragedy to another. Whenever she began to see a glimpse of sunlight on the horizon, he would steer her back into another deadly storm of misery and calamity. On occasion, she would try to wrestle the helm from him—to regain control of her ship and her destiny—but he was always too strong. Exhausted, she would simply give up and resign herself to his every whim.

Why should this time be different from all the others? Why, when she had found love, hope, and a chance for happiness within her grasp, would she expect it not to fade into the darkened horizon with all her other dreams?

Yet, there was a sense of anticipation surrounding Reverend Thomas. With every passing minute, she was more and more grateful for his presence. He always had a word of encouragement and cheer, no matter how dire the circumstances, and he always gave credit to God. In fact, it astounded her that he spoke to the Almighty as if he knew Him personally—as if the Creator of the universe was actually walking along beside him.

Somehow, just knowing the reverend had the ear of God gave Charlisse hope. That and the knowledge that Sloane and Jackson worked day and night in an effort to secure their captain's release. While Jackson took command of the *Redemption*, protecting it from any attempted mutiny, Sloane had assembled a few loyal crewmen to search for any witness who would be willing to testify on Merrick's behalf.

Yet after two days of befriending at least half of the scurrilous mob that frequented the taverns of Port Royal—and forfeiting many pieces of eight toward beverages in the hopes of loosening their tongues—they discovered that not one of them was willing to risk the vicious wrath of Edward the Terror.

"Don't go bein' discouraged, miss," Sloane said, after giving his daily report of the prior night's activities to the reverend and Charlisse.

Charlisse stood in the reverend's parlor, wringing her hands. "But no one saw anything or knows anyone who did?"

"Not that they'll be sayin' in front of a court, miss." Sloane fingered his hat, shifting his feet back and forth.

The reverend lay his hand on Charlisse's shoulder. "Don't worry. They haven't talked to everyone in town yet, have you, Mr. Sloane?"

"No, not at all, Reverend." Sloane produced a forced grin.

"And while they continue their search for a witness, I've arranged an audience with the governor day after next."

"But what will we tell him? We have no proof." Charlisse paced, twirling a lock of her hair between her fingers.

"We will appeal to his sense of reason, to his knowledge of Merrick's character. We will simply tell him the truth."

"And he's just going to let Merrick go on our word?" Charlisse sneered.

"Miracles happen every day, Miss Bristol."

"Not to me."

"Perhaps it's time for one then." The reverend cast her a playful smile. It did nothing to uplift her spirits.

Sloane took a seat, his sword clanking against the table leg. His red-streaked eyes drooped and his shoulders hung lower than usual. Most likely he had been up most of the night endangering his life on the streets of Port Royal in an effort to save his captain.

Abandoning her nervous pacing, Charlisse alighted in her usual chair by the stove. "What is the Arawak village?" she asked, catching the immediate attention of both men.

The reverend topped off Sloane's tea. The two men exchanged a glance.

Charlisse waited, wondering at the odd look that had passed between them. "Merrick spoke of an Arawak village when I saw him last," she said. "It has something to do with my father."

The reverend spoke first. "The Arawak are a people indigenous to the Caribbean. They are all but gone now. Only a few tribes exist in remote locations."

"What happened to them?" Charlisse asked.

Reverend Thomas took a seat at the table with Sloane. "Spanish slave raids nearly wiped them out during the past century."

"How awful." The idea of treating people like animals simply because they came from a different culture, or their skin was a different shade, or they were considered subhuman in some way abhorred her. "But what do they have to do with my father?"

"The Arawak are a good people, miss," Sloane said. "The cap'n happened upon one of their villages in Cuba when we was searchin' for a place to careen our ship." He took a sip of his tea and returned his glance to Charlisse. "They befriended us, fed us, and allowed the whole crew to stay wi' them as long as we liked." He nodded. "Good people, kind an' gentle. Merrick took a real likin' to their chief—Caonabo, I think 'is name was."

The reverend stood and walked to the window, shifting his feet uncomfortably as he gazed outside.

"Well, ye see, miss, every time the ship be needin' careenin' the cap'n took us to their village." Sloane smiled. "We spent many a happy day there.

Aye, them was the days, to be sure."

"What happened?" Charlisse asked tentatively, dreading his answer. The reverend glanced over his shoulder at Sloane.

"Well, miss, turns out yer father—" Sloane coughed. "I mean Edward. He musta found out how much Merrick liked the Arawak, 'cause the next time we landed on their shore, we found 'em all killed."

Charlisse gasped.

"Not just killed, if ye know what I mean, but slaughtered, torn t' pieces, real brutal-like."

Charlisse rose to her feet, trembling. "And you think my father did this?" she asked with angry skepticism.

"We know he did, miss. He left the cap'n a note describin' all he done and why."

Her head swimming, Charlisse sat down, unable to comprehend not only this barbarous act, but that it was her father who had performed it. "Why?" She looked up at Sloane. His eyes swam in moisture. He looked away, coughing.

"Fer revenge. Fer Merrick takin o'er 'is ship and leavin' him to die on that island, 'tis all."

"It can't be true." Charlisse buried her face in her hands.

"But it is true," the reverend finally said. She heard him approach. "Now you understand why Merrick believed it was his duty to capture Edward and bring him to justice." He knelt beside her and took her hands. Charlisse lifted her head to meet his gaze. "That is, until he met you and found out Edward is your father. Oh, what a quandary love placed upon him."

"Love?"

The reverend gave her a sideways glance and stood. "Surely you know his feelings for you by now."

She shook her head. Right now, she didn't know anything. Nauseated, she excused herself to go outside for some fresh air. Her world was falling apart as it had so many times before. Her father was a pirate. Not just any pirate, but an evil, heartless savage. How could she be the offspring of a man who could commit such ruthless acts? What did that make her? All her life, how she had longed for her father's love—cried out for him in the night when she was beaten and alone. But now those hopes were crushed in the face of a brutality she could not fathom. To make matters worse, it seemed her father had conspired to have the man she loved. . . *The man she loved? Was that true?* Reaching up, she rubbed her forehead, unable to deny the intense feelings growing within her. She pictured Merrick in that prison cell. Even there, though he quite possibly faced death, his concern had been for her, not for himself.

But he was not dead yet. She would not resign herself to this twist of fate. The urge to fight rose within her. This time she had something to fight for—an amazing man who had shown her what love was for the first time in her life. Maybe Merrick's love would fill that aching hole in her heart that she had thought only a father's affections could satisfy. Maybe she had no need of a father who would only bring her more pain. Perhaps God—if there was a God—had led her to Merrick. He was her hope. He was what she had been searching for. After a few minutes Sloane came out, tipped his hat at her, and left.

In the evening, as was his custom, the reverend sat back in his rocking chair, pipe in one hand, his Bible in the other, and read a passage aloud. This particular night, he read from the Gospel of Matthew. They had just finished dinner. Charlisse had assisted with the cleanup and now sat on the couch sipping tea, wondering what Merrick had to eat, if anything. She didn't mind the Bible reading. The reverend's voice was soothing, and the passages he read were somehow comforting. In fact, on this fourth night in his company, she found herself looking forward to it.

"Ask, and it shall be given you; seek, and ye shall find; knock, and it shall be opened unto you: For every one that asketh receiveth; and he that seeketh findeth; and to him that knocketh it shall be opened. Or what man is there of you, whom if his son ask bread, will he give him a stone? Or if he ask a fish, will he give him a serpent? If ye then, being evil, know how to give good gifts unto your children, how much more shall your Father which is in heaven give good things to them that ask him? Therefore all things whatsoever ye would that men should do to you, do ye even so to them: for this is the law and the prophets.

"Enter ye in at the strait gate: for wide is the gate, and broad is the way, that leadeth to destruction, and many there be which go in thereat: Because strait is the gate, and narrow is the way, which leadeth unto life, and few there be that find it."

The reverend stopped, took a couple of puffs from his pipe, and stared into the room as if deep in thought.

"Is that really from the Bible?" Charlisse asked.

He looked over at her. "Absolutely. Why?"

"I've never heard it before. It makes God sound like He really cares for us, like a father would his children." She looked away from the reverend's compassionate gaze. "Like He wants to give us good things."

"And why not? We are His children."

"I don't know. I never thought of God that way."

"Maybe you should start." He smiled.

A few moments of silence passed before Charlisse looked up at the reverend again. "What is this strait gate and narrow way of which it speaks?"

"That's simple. The strait gate and narrow way is Jesus. He's the only way to God and the only way to life, here on earth and in eternity. Here's another. I'm sure you've heard this one."

"For God so loved the world, that he gave his only begotten Son, that whosoever believeth on him should not perish, but have everlasting life."

Charlisse nodded. "Yes, I am familiar with that scripture. And I do believe, but I don't feel any differently. God doesn't seem to care about me."

"But it's more than just a belief, you see. Faith without works is dead. You must do something. You must receive Him, have a relationship with Him. You must follow Him." The reverend moved to the edge of his chair, his pipe forgotten on its tray nearby. He paused as if he were about to say something, then folded his hands and looked down.

Is he praying? Charlisse felt a warm flutter in the core of her being—there one second and fading the next. Shrugging it off, she asked the reverend, "You have that relationship with Him?"

He looked up and nodded.

She cast him a mocking glance. "Then maybe you can ask Him why He allowed Merrick to be arrested?"

"That's not for us to know. But we could pray for Merrick, if you'd like."

"Oh, I don't pray." Charlisse shook her head.

"You don't have to do anything. Just bow your head and agree in your heart with what I am saying."

Charlisse eyed him with suspicion. She felt she was being trapped into something, but for Merrick's sake, she conceded.

The reverend lowered his head. "Our Father," he began, "we thank You for Your manifold blessings: for our food, our warm home, and all Your provision. We thank You for the gift of Your Son, through whom we receive Your grace and eternal life. We thank You that You love us enough that all we have to do is ask You for something, and You long to give it."

Uncontrollable tears filled Charlisse's eyes accompanied by a strange warmth that welled up inside her.

The reverend continued, "We come before You now with just such a request. Our friend, and Your son, Edmund Merrick has been falsely imprisoned. We lift him up before You and ask, Lord, for Your blessing on him, for Your protection over him, for Your comforting presence to be with him. We pray, Father, for his release from prison, and for Your will in this situation for all involved. In the name of Your Son, Jesus Christ, we pray, amen."

Charlisse quickly wiped her eyes and looked up. "Thank you."

He nodded. "It will be all right."

"I wish I could believe that."

"The Lord works in mysterious ways, miss. Perhaps He will use Sloane to find the evidence needed to clear Merrick's name." He picked up his pipe and tapped it. "And we have yet to appeal to the governor. There are still things we can do. Have faith."

Charlisse sat back in her chair. *Yes, there are still things I can do.*

Nothing else was said that evening. Charlisse pondered all the reverend had told her. For some reason she could not stop tears from pooling in her eyes. Assuming it to be nothing more than the outcome of an emotionally exhausting day, she excused herself early and retired to the back room. She tried to sleep, but as on many nights before, she was unable to find the dark, comforting repose of deep slumber.

Strange feelings tormented her. It was more than her anxiety for Merrick, her longing for her father, or her fear of the future. Some unseen force tugged at her, beckoning her with a soft gentle whisper.

When she finally did fall asleep, it was only to have her mind invaded with terrifying images from her past. She tossed fitfully on the tiny cot as a darkness invaded her soul, bringing with it visions of her uncle, his brown robe, the large crucifix that always hung from his neck, mocking her with its brilliance. It was a symbol of life and hope to so many, but to her it meant only terror and disgrace. The beatings, the shame of her nakedness, the insidious name-calling, the days spent locked alone in her tiny room—memories that haunted her restless slumber.

During the day, she could somehow push them back to a dark place in her mind where they did not taunt her. There cowering in the shadows, like demons afraid of brightness that might expose them for what they were, they hid, waiting until all shreds of light illuminating her mind faded into shadows.

Then they crawled out on all fours, scattering like insects to every corner of her thoughts, tormenting her over and over again. *God doesn't love you, you little whore.* She heard her uncle's booming voice echoing through the cold hallways of his manor. His eyes, so clear to her now, drooping, wrinkled, and bloodshot: wicked eyes, oscillating between hatred and what she now realized was lust. Other than to whip her, he had never touched her, but he had done more damage with his words—and with his evil glare—than any physical contact could have.

She was naked, curled in the corner of her dark room, the shadowy form of her uncle slowly descending upon her. Suddenly, a door opened where a door had not been before. A waterfall of bright light poured from it, saturating the entire room with its brilliance and warmth.

Her uncle, furious at the intrusion, roared and sprang to shut the door, but with all his efforts, he was not able to budge it.

The light from the door slowly molded into the figure of a man, sending her uncle scurrying for the darkest corner of the room. Charlisse was not afraid. She rose and slowly walked toward the door. The man held out his hands to her. His radiance showered her with peace and love.

"Caw. Caw. Caw." The hideous sound jerked Charlisse from her dream, and she jumped from her bed, panting. A large, ugly, black crow stared at her from her window ledge.

"Caw. Caw. Caw." The bird glared at her with tiny beady eyes that squinted in wicked delight.

"Shoo, get out of here!" she yelled, but the crow remained steadfast, like an omen of evil, wings spread, hovering in the window, blocking out the lustrous dawn of the new day.

The reverend barreled through the door, a look of concern on his face. He glanced from Charlisse to the crow and took another step forward. The crow bellowed one more "Caw" before it turned and flew away.

Charlisse grabbed a blanket and covered her nightgown.

"Sorry for the intrusion, miss," the reverend said. "When I heard you scream, I thought someone was in here." His blond hair stuck out in every direction.

Charlisse glanced at the open window, trying to shake the eerie feeling that something—or someone—*had* been in there. Why had the crow fled so rapidly when the reverend entered? She looked up at him.

"You look tired," he remarked, his eyes still puffy from sleep.

"I don't sleep well," Charlisse admitted. "But thank you for coming to my aid."

The reverend stood for a moment, looking perplexed. He rubbed his eyes. "Well, I'm making breakfast," he stuttered, turning to leave. "It's Sunday, you know—church today. I'm having one of the ladies who attend church bring you some fresh clothes."

It was a beautiful day, warm and sunny, and as promised, one of the reverend's parishioners brought over two simple, but attractive, dresses for Charlisse. After bathing, dressing, and pinning her curls up in a loose bun, she felt refreshed, but could not shake from her thoughts the strange dreams that had tormented her sleep.

The Sunday service in no way resembled the ceremonies she was used to in England. To her surprise, the small chapel filled up near to overflowing with families with small children, single people—mostly men—and even some Negro slaves. Most of the men owned sugar plantations, she was told, but a few had reputable businesses in town.

After a few hymns—which everyone sang with extreme enthusiasm—the reverend delivered his sermon. Charlisse had never heard anyone talk about God the way the reverend did. His words mesmerized her. Like sharp arrows, they pierced through the casing of her heart, leaving her extremely uncomfortable. Shifting in her seat, she couldn't wait for the service to end.

Afterward, the reverend's time was taken up with greeting his parishioners and various other duties, and Charlisse, not in the mood for small talk, excused herself to the cottage, where she spent the remainder of the afternoon.

Restless, she paced her tiny room, unable to sit still. Her thoughts kept drifting to Merrick, wondering how he was, wondering what would become of him. *And what of her father? Should she go looking for him? What would she find when she found him?* She hated the waiting. It was driving her mad. Everything was so uncertain. She felt like a ship tossed about at sea without a rudder. It had been two days since she had seen Merrick. Tomorrow, the reverend promised, they would visit him after their appointment with the governor. It was the only thing that kept her sane.

By the time the reverend returned and Sloane appeared for his evening report, Charlisse felt as though she were standing on a towering cliff, ready to topple over the edge.

Sloane shook his head. "Still can't find any one willin' to stand up against Edward."

Charlisse sank onto the couch and wept. No amount of consolation by either of the two men could comfort her. It wasn't just Merrick. It was her father, her uncle, the shipwreck, the pirates, and her whole miserable past. Everything was mixing into one big pot of sludge, and it was about to boil over. She must do something. This time, she would not allow fate to swallow her blossoming hope into the abyss of despair, not when love had finally taken residence in her heart. Tomorrow she would plead Merrick's case to the governor, but if her petitions fell on deaf ears, she would have to take matters into her own hands.

Chapter 27
The Redemption

Captain Merrick sat on the cold floor of his dark cell. It had been four days—at his best calculation—since he had been thrown down into this pit, and with nothing to do but ponder his fate, the time had dragged on like an eternity. He had grown tired of counting the cockroaches that scuttled across the dirty stones and was now doing something more productive. He was bringing to memory verses from the Bible.

The only relief in his gloom had been seeing Charlisse, but that was a few days ago, and her absence brought an aching fear to his soul. With her father and Kent prowling Port Royal, wreaking their wicked plans, Charlisse was not safe.

He could think of nothing worse than the loss of his freedom—his control. It was one of the main reasons he had forsaken home and fortune back in London. There had been nothing in his life that was not under the strict scrutiny of his powerful father. He could do nothing, go nowhere, make no plans that weren't under the severest regulation. Now he was in a different kind of cell, not the bondage of conventional society, nor the restrictions of religious dogma, nor even the unyielding requirements of position and power. Yet these iron bars and stone walls were equally confining.

Not too long ago, he would have been enraged at his unjust imprisonment, hating those who had lied to put him in this cell, bent on vengeance.

Instead of hatred, he felt nothing but pity for Edward and Kent. They were miserable, lonely men who would do anything to satisfy greed and lust that would forever be insatiable. It was a life he had gladly forsaken when he became a follower of Christ.

In the place of revenge, however, he felt an intense fury at being confined—of having no control, completely unable to act. He stood and paced his cage with the frenzy of a wild animal. Did he fear death? Did he fear the gallows? Not nearly as much as he feared being helpless. *Lord, what are You trying to show me?* he silently asked, looking up to heaven. Thomas always said when troubles abounded, God was either trying to teach him something or change his direction.

Merrick leaned against the iron bars that confined him, their icy rods imprinting chords of dread down the muscles of his back. A rat scampered across his cell. It stopped, stood on its hind legs, and wrinkled its nose at Merrick. Gray-haired and corpulent, it reminded him of Edward, and Merrick sprang toward it, hoping to squash it under his boot. Squealing, the rodent scampered off and darted through a crack in the wall. Merrick chased it and kicked the hole through which it escaped. "Not this time, old man," he said. "But soon, very soon."

He stomped back to the bars and leaned his head against them. He would bring that murdering mongrel to justice. And he would no longer let his feelings for Charlisse interfere with his goal. Surely, she would understand now that she had seen her father's true nature. But regardless of whether she did, her relation to Edward gave Merrick even more reason to lock up the man. Her longing for a father would bring only disaster if she found him. What a fool he had been to think that a monster like Edward could ever change.

Charlisse was out there with Edward and Kent, protected only by a clergyman. What would happen should their paths cross? Would Kent finish the job he had started and then pass her off to her father as a spoil of war?

Merrick shook the bars with a fury that sent flakes of rust swirling down on him like angry insects. He had to get out of here! *How can I protect her, Lord? How can I capture Edward? How can I serve You from within this prison?* He released the bars with one last thrust and paced to the stone wall, raking his hand through his hair. Slamming his fist into the wall, he felt his wrath bubble over. *Just get me out of here, Lord, so I can help her!* He felt ashamed of his anger and mistrust of God, but still he could not find the strength to stifle them. He offered a quick prayer for Charlisse, hoping God would answer it, despite his own failings.

Charlisse's sleep was even more fitful than the night before and held her captive to the flighty and dismal thoughts that invaded her mind. She floated in a slumber too shallow to invite nightmares. Yet even so, the terrifying sensation of standing on a high precipice lingered in her soul. It was as if someone—or something—was trying to push her over the edge, and deep down she knew if it succeeded, she would be lost forever.

Her thoughts shifted to the man in her dream who stood in the doorway of light—so full of love and peace and warmth. He beckoned her, calling to her in a gentle, quiet voice. Who was he? And what did he want? Maybe she was going mad.

Charlisse tossed aside the tangled blankets and sat up on the cot, her body moist with perspiration. An eerie silence crept in the night air. Not even the crickets dared to chirp outside her window.

With a handkerchief, she dabbed at the moisture on her neck and slid off the bed. Her long, white nightgown clung to her as she walked toward the window for some fresh air, trying to relieve the conflicting thoughts that tore at her soul. A wave of unusually frigid air poured over her damp gown. She shivered.

The moonlight, which had filtered into her room only moments earlier, dissipated behind a mass of dark clouds. Waves of fear gripped her. Once more a crow landed heavily on the window ledge. Charlisse bounced back, startled. He let out a hideous "Caw!" and stared at her with an intensity that sent a shiver of alarm down her spine. His beady red eyes glowed in the dark.

An overwhelming sense of evil permeated the room. Like a dark fog, it crept over the window ledge, down the wall, and across the wooden floor until it surrounded Charlisse's bare feet. Inch by inch, it ascended her legs.

She could hear her own heart beating. *Tha-thump, tha-thump, tha-thump.* Her breath came in frosty clouds. *Why is it so cold?*

The crow let out another ear-shattering "Caw." This time, it sounded almost human. The feathered beast examined her. His hooked beak spread in a wicked grin.

The fog had reached her knees. She could no longer feel her legs beneath its advance. If she didn't stop it, she knew it would swallow her whole.

Frozen in terror, she clasped her hands together and did the only thing she could think to do. She looked up to heaven and prayed. "God, if You are there and You care about me, please. . .please," she stuttered, not knowing what to ask, hesitating, feeling foolish. "Please, I need You."

Suddenly, the dark clouds that were holding captive the rays of a full moon sped aside, allowing a flood of light to enter the room.

The crow glared at Charlisse with a frightening intensity. Cocking his head back and forth, he seemed to be pondering some new and unexpected development.

He let out one last angry "Caw" and promptly flew away.

As soon as he was gone, the fog of evil foreboding retreated, slowly slithered out behind him, until it too disappeared out the window.

An incredible sense of peace and joy swept into the room, riding on the beams of moonlight that now showered over Charlisse like tiny dancing angels. Uncontrollable tears streamed down her cheeks.

She fell to her knees. A sense of shame overcame her, an unworthiness, a filthiness. She bowed her head, sobbing, unable to face the penetrating purity of the light.

A finger underneath her chin slowly lifted her head. When she opened her eyes, there was no one there, only an overwhelming sense of love that poured into her, filling her up and bubbling over until she could do nothing but smile.

A giggle escaped her mouth and then another and another, and she felt as though she were a little girl sitting in her father's warm, protective lap while he tickled her affectionately.

She sat like this, basking in the shower of love for what seemed only minutes. But when the moonlight was transcended by the glow of dawn, she realized it had been hours.

She stood and ran to the window to greet the new day with an anticipation she had never felt before. Birds of every color flitted between kapok trees and palms. Beautiful hibiscus flowers and orchids in full bloom offered their sweet nectar to hummingbirds that hovered over them, fanning them with wings too angelic to see. A small, chubby green and yellow bird with a red beak landed on a branch near the window and proceeded to sing her the most beautiful song she had ever heard.

Throwing on her robe, she ran out into the main room of the cottage to start some tea and wait for the reverend to awaken, but he was already up, Bible in his lap, smiling at her when she entered the room. She ran and knelt beside him. They exchanged a knowing glance.

"Did you not sleep, Reverend?"

A smile lit up his eyes. "Sometimes the Lord calls me to prayer instead of sleep. Last night was such a night."

"Prayer? For what?"

"For you."

Charlisse could not imagine anyone caring enough to sacrifice sleep to pray for her, especially someone she hardly knew. Eyes wide, she looked at the reverend. "Reverend, something happened to me last night." She told him the story, unable to stop her tears as she relayed the details of her experience. All the while, the reverend listened with great interest, a knowing smile steady on his face.

"Reverend, what happened to me?" she asked.

"Isn't it obvious? You called upon God, and He answered you." He gave her hand a squeeze and grinned. "All He asks is that we seek Him with all our hearts, and when we do, He can't help but respond."

"So that presence I felt, that love and joy, was God?"

"Yes, it was His Holy Spirit. It was Jesus, our Lord showing you how much He loves you."

Charlisse looked away, excitement erupting within her. "So He's real? He exists!"

The reverend smiled.

"And He loves *me*?"

The reverend nodded with enthusiasm. "Do you want to become one of His children?"

Charlisse gazed at the reverend, searching his eyes for any speck of doubt or betrayal. But she found only sincerity and love in their depths. He believed in this God. He had sacrificed everything to follow Him.

Could Charlisse do any less? How could she deny God's existence—as well as His love for her—after He had revealed Himself to her in such a tender way last night? A warm fluttering grew within her. "I do," she said.

There in a tiny cottage on the outskirts of one of the most wicked cities in the Caribbean, thousands of miles from the only home she'd known, Charlisse prayed to her new Father in heaven, giving her life to Him.

Afterward, she lifted her face, dried her eyes, and gave the reverend such a warm embrace that he chuckled with delight. Although none of her problems were gone, and her situation was the same, she no longer felt the weight of frustration, fear, and helplessness that had recently plagued her every thought. They had been replaced with hope and an assurance of love she had never dreamed of before, from a God who cared for her beyond her understanding.

Charlisse, however, did not have time to bask in her newfound joy. After finishing her breakfast, she quickly got dressed, and set out with the reverend to make their appointment with Governor Moodyford. Now she would see what miracles God could perform, for it would take a miracle, indeed, to get Merrick released from prison. She thought of her father— the man who had put him there. With the power of God on her side, perhaps even Edward's hardened heart would melt, and she would have the loving reunion with her father she always dreamed of.

Chapter 28
Hope
without Hope

The humidity and heat climbed with the relentless passage of the sun in the cloudless sky as Charlisse and the reverend traveled down Fisher's Row in their horse-drawn buggy. The governor's residence, otherwise known as King's House, was located near the batteries that protected the entrance to the harbor. Taking in a deep breath of sea air, Charlisse believed with all her heart that everything was going to be fine now—that Governor Moodyford would see the sense of their arguments, release Merrick, and the illustrious captain would be home in time for supper. With God on her side, what other possible outcome could there be? Nothing but cheerful anticipation bounded from her soul—so very different from yesterday's hopelessness.

In fact, everything today was more beautiful, more glorious than she ever remembered. The warm breeze blew a few wayward curls loose from her bun. She smiled as they tickled her neck. Had the sky always been this incredible shade of cerulean blue? Palm fronds danced in the trade winds, giggling with delight as she passed by.

An old sea-turtler had just rowed his boat ashore loaded with turtles. From under his floppy brown hat, strands of gray hair hung to his shoulders. He wore a stained shirt and tan breeches cut off at the knees, and his skin was as weather-beaten as his boat. Flashing yellow teeth, he tipped his hat at Charlisse and smiled.

All around the docks, slaves were beginning their daily tasks. Charlisse's heart went out to them. How cruel slavery was.

Past the docks and up a hill the horse clopped onward. Upon arriving at the gravel courtyard of the governor's mansion, the reverend assisted Charlisse from the carriage, and arm in arm they walked the flower-trimmed path to the front door. The wind picked up, stirring the hem of Charlisse's gown before setting off a symphony in the wind chimes that hung from the front porch. Colorful parrots jumped from branch to branch in the palm trees that were planted in rows across the luxurious front lawn. Marble stairs extended like a giant fan, forming an elegant entrance to the cream-colored house.

Inside, they were escorted through a salon, down a long hallway, and through another door, which opened to a bright, spacious office where a man was sitting behind a massive oak desk. The servant announced their presence, and the governor looked up and smiled. Rising, he rounded his desk to greet them, a tall, corpulent man, exquisitely dressed, and wearing a heavy white periwig, which complimented his intelligent, gray eyes.

Charlisse examined the ostentatious surroundings. The furnishings were of carved oak and walnut. Tapestries and paintings, imported from the old world, lined the walls. Intricate maps hung on both sidewalls—one of the Caribbean, and the other of Europe—drawn with impeccable detail. The back wall consisted of shelves of books and glass cases filled with weapons. An Italian rug graced the hardwood floor, and two cordovan leather couches offered comfort to visitors.

She strode to the Caribbean map, noting the location of Port Royal, and glanced over the identified islands to the south, wondering which one, if any, was the wretched spot where she had been marooned.

"Governor, may I introduce Lady Charlisse Bristol." The reverend gestured toward her.

Charlisse swirled around.

"My pleasure, indeed." Governor Moodyford bowed with the graciousness of an English gentleman, but allowed his gaze to linger over Charlisse much longer than her comfort permitted.

The reverend cleared his throat, drawing Moodyford's attention. "We've come concerning Captain Edmund Merrick."

"Ah yes. I'd heard you were acquaintances of his." The governor leaned back on his desk and folded his arms over his prominent belly.

"It is my understanding you were acquainted with him, as well?" Thomas said.

"Yes," the governor snorted. "Some business dealings. . ."

"You refer to the letter of marque signed by both you and Merrick, giving him England's permission to raid upon Spanish vessels, and—"

"Yes, of course," the governor interrupted, waving a hand in the air. "But this is not why I had him arrested."

Thomas's jaw clenched. "We understand he has been accused of raiding British vessels, milord—"

"Yes, yes, quite disturbing. Merrick was a good man. We had an arrangement." He cast the reverend a sly glance.

"So I heard. He was to assist you with your *piracy* problem."

"Then you can imagine my bewilderment at his treachery." The governor folded his hands behind his back and paced in front of his desk.

"Begging your pardon, Governor, but we have come to inform you that these charges are false."

"Indeed?"

Charlisse's heart swelled in anticipation. She took a step forward.

"Yes, a conspiracy by those who hate Merrick," she said. "False evidence was planted on board his ship."

"Do you have proof of this?"

"Not yet, milord, but we have the word of his quartermaster, an honest, hardworking sailor."

The governor straightened his periwig and selected a cigar, then offered one to the reverend, who politely refused. Moodyford put a match to his cigar, took a few puffs, and stared off into the room. "Why should I take the word of one of his conspirators? Egad, he's a pirate on board his ship! Perhaps I should have him arrested, as well."

Alarm spiked through Charlisse reaching her heart with pounding fury. "You speak as though Merrick is already condemned," she blurted out, ignoring the reverend's cautioning glance.

The harsh look in the governor's eyes softened when his gaze shot to Charlisse. "I'm sorry to inform you, milady, that his trial was held this morning."

"And the outcome?" she pressed him.

The governor grunted and glanced at the reverend before opening the double veranda doors to a cobblestone courtyard outside.

With quivering legs, Charlisse followed the two men into the beautiful garden. She hardly noticed the magnificent rose bushes surrounding them or the gold- and silver-etched fountain in the center. All she could think about was why the governor hesitated in answering her question. Whatever the verdict of the trial, could he be reconsidering his stance?

"Reverend," he began, "milady." He nodded at Charlisse. "Captain Merrick stood out among the rest of his kind. He was not the usual greedy, villainous type you see in most pirates who call these waters their home. He carried himself as a gentleman. Then, when His Majesty, King Charles II, ordered me to arrest and hang all known pirates, Merrick offered his assistance." The governor took another puff from his cigar, stepped away from Charlisse and blew smoke into the air. A pungent aroma, both sweet and stinging swept over her.

"I assure you," he continued. "I would not have accepted these traitorous charges so ardently without a great deal of proof. But a great deal of proof is what I did receive when I sent my men to search his ship."

"False evidence," Charlisse added.

The governor lifted an eyebrow. "Perhaps," he continued, "but nevertheless, I must have proof, or there's nothing I can do. I know you wouldn't come here on Merrick's behalf if you didn't truly believe him innocent, but if I let him go without proof of such, it would give credence to every buccaneer in the Caribbean to attack British vessels at will. I must keep order among these ruffians, or all is lost." He looked at Charlisse. "I'm truly sorry."

Charlisse took a step toward the governor. "Pray tell, what is the judgment upon him, milord?"

A curious expression crossed the governor's face. "Who is this man to you, miss? You appear too fine a lady to be so upset over the death of one pirate."

"Death?" Charlisse's heart skipped a beat and then continued its furious pounding. The garden seemed to spin around her. If it weren't for the reverend taking her arm, she would certainly have swooned at the governor's feet. "Surely, you cannot put a man to death without reviewing all evidence in the case and speaking with all the people involved?"

"My chief justice has already done that, miss. I'm afraid the evidence against the captain is overwhelming. In addition, we have sworn testimonies of Merrick's own crew confirming his frequent attacks on British vessels."

"They are lying." Charlisse's blood grew hot. The reverend gave her hand a squeeze.

"Surely, you can see through these felonious allegations, Governor," the reverend protested. "You, being a man of great character, admitted noting a similar character in Merrick, as I sincerely hope you have in me. Isn't it obvious the captain has been a victim of the treachery of jealous and deceitful men?"

"Be that as it may." The governor shook his head. His eyes carried a look of regret, but the lines on his face drew taut. "I'm afraid that without proof clearing Merrick of the charges of piracy against England, I will be forced to hang him at Execution Dock come Friday."

Charlisse's breath caught in her throat. She staggered, and the reverend led her to a bench. She sat, holding her hand to her heart, so swelled with grief, it felt as though it would burst.

"My deepest apologies, miss, for having upset you," the governor said. "But I assure you, I have no personal rancor toward this pirate of yours. Surely you understand my position. Bring me the proof I require, and I will readdress this case without delay."

A servant arrived to escort them from the mansion. Charlisse clung dazedly to the reverend, feeling nauseated.

"We should have fought harder!" she cried, seated once again in the carriage. "Why didn't we say more? Why didn't we do more?" She turned toward the reverend, her eyes burning with emotion.

"I do not like to waste energy where nothing can be accomplished," Thomas replied calmly. "The governor is a stubborn man who has the difficult tasks of both maintaining order in this haven of ruffians and appeasing the king. To him, the life of one pirate is expendable if his death proves a lesson to all."

"I don't understand," she sobbed. "Why does the governor allow so many pirates to roam the streets of his city while he condemns to death a man who only assisted the British cause?"

The reverend snapped the reins, sending the horse into a trot. "If the governor captured or chased off all the brigands from Port Royal, he would be defenseless against the Spanish. He needs to only appear to be doing so for the sake of the king. That's why Merrick's offer to bring in the most vile pirates was an accord the governor could not forsake."

Charlisse dabbed her eyes with her handkerchief.

"Now, let's not give up hope, miss. God is still in control," the reverend added.

Charlisse turned to look at the passing scenery, no longer enjoying its delights, seeing only shapeless forms through the moisture that clouded her eyes. How could a loving God assign Merrick to such a hideous fate? It didn't make sense. Her newfound faith, so strong only an hour ago, was weakening by the minute.

Instead of heading back to the cottage, the reverend guided the carriage to the thick iron gates of Fort Charles. In her distress, Charlisse had forgotten that they had planned to see Merrick today. She quickly wiped her face and took a deep breath to calm her shattered nerves. She couldn't let him see her anguish—it would only cause him further pain.

The reverend squeezed her hand as he stopped the carriage. "Courage, my dear." He smiled. Nodding, she gathered her emotions and stuffed them behind a door of propriety.

When they approached Merrick's cell, Charlisse rushed up and grabbed the bars. He emerged from the shadows. His black hair hung to his shoulders in disarray. Four days of stubble shadowed his face and neck, and he smelled of mold and sweat. But all Charlisse wanted to do was break through the bars and run into his arms.

When he lifted his eyes to hers, a raging urgency burned in them. He flashed an angry look at the reverend. "I must get out of here, Thomas." His jaw clenched. He clutched the bars. "I cannot bear being locked up; you know that."

The reverend nodded. "I know." He stared at Merrick. "You must let go, son."

"Let go!" Merrick stormed. He turned and paced, tearing at his hair. "Let go of her?" He waved his hand toward Charlisse. "Let that villain, Edward, go free to continue his murderous rampage?" He cast an uneasy glance at Charlisse.

She stepped back from the bars, finger tangled in her hair, frightened at his sudden outburst. But how could she blame him? How could she expect him to maintain his calm, authoritative demeanor under such affliction?

"Give God the control," the reverend answered.

Merrick huffed and looked down, shaking his head. When he looked up once more, the anger had faded from his face. He let out a deep, ragged sigh.

"Quit playing with your hair and come here." He motioned to Charlisse.

Taking her hands in his, he kissed them. A playful smile danced across his lips. Alarm froze his expression when he noticed Charlisse's red-rimmed eyes. "What ails you, milady?"

She looked at him, unsure of what to say. "It's been a trying morning."

Merrick's lips drew into a straight line. He rubbed his chin. "How so? Name the rogue that has caused your tears, and I'll run him through."

Charlisse glanced at the reverend.

"They plan to hang you on Friday," he said simply.

Forgetting her resolve to hide her emotions, Charlisse burst into sobs.

Merrick reached up to wipe the tears from her cheek. "Is that all?"

"Merrick, this is serious." She glared at him. "How can you be so cavalier?"

"We went to see the governor today," the reverend said, stepping forward. "He insists there is nothing he can do without proof, and Sloane has come up empty so far."

Merrick sighed. "Thank you for trying, Thomas. I knew Kent and Edward would have covered their tracks well, and the governor is a strict man. I've dealt with him on many occasions." He faced Charlisse again. "It's going to be all right."

"I don't see how." Her eyes filled with tears again.

Merrick squeezed her shaking hands and enfolded them with his warm, steady ones. "I don't believe it is time for me to die." His glance swerved to the reverend. "I believe God still has more for me to do. But if I'm wrong and He takes me home, it's a far better place I'll be going to."

Charlisse searched his dark brown eyes, longing for that same assurance. "I cannot face that possibility. But if He intends to get you out of here, I wish He would tell us how. . ."

Merrick gave her one of his playful smiles. "Perhaps He will, if you will only listen."

"And a much better chance she'll have at that now." The reverend grinned, standing a bit taller.

Merrick glanced from him to Charlisse, a puzzled look on his face. Charlisse smiled at the reverend. Merrick crossed his arms over his chest and examined them both.

"What, pray tell, have you been doing with my beloved Charlisse, Thomas, while I've been locked in this prison?" The glimmer in his eyes betrayed the sternness in his voice. "There appears to be a glow about her, a sparkle in her smile." With raised eyebrows, he waited for an answer.

The reverend's face lit up. "Nothing but good things, I assure you." He looked at Charlisse. "Truth be known, Charlisse committed her life to Christ only last night."

Merrick's eyes locked on Charlisse's. She nodded. He held her hands while she relayed the whole story to him—the crow, the man in the light, and the incredible peace and love she'd felt in His presence. Merrick's smile spread wider and wider with each word she said, and Charlisse thought she saw a hint of moisture in his eyes.

"This is the grandest news I have ever heard," he said.

"No, it would have been much better if the reverend and I had come with news of your release."

He shook his head. "No, this is much more important."

Charlisse gave him a sideways glance.

" 'Tis true, milady. I prayed for this very thing just last night. In fact," he said, his gaze darting to the reverend, "the Lord may have been answering my prayer just as I was saying it."

She sighed, letting go of his hands and coiling a finger around a wayward strand of her hair. "I fail to understand why God allows you to remain imprisoned."

"Who can know the mind of God?" the reverend said. "His ways are not our ways, and His thoughts are not ours. It's not for us to understand, but to believe."

Charlisse's lips twisted in a pout. "Still, I cannot accept that He expects us to do nothing."

Merrick turned away, and Charlisse sensed despondency in his mannerism.

"No, but we've done all He has afforded us to do. Now it is in His hands," the reverend said.

Taking her face in his hands, Merrick placed a gentle kiss on her forehead and looked into her eyes. "Pray for me, Charlisse. Will you do that?"

"I'll try." She nodded, forcing a smile.

The guard motioned for them to go.

"I shall visit you every day," Charlisse whispered, swallowing hard.

Merrick's lips grazed her hand. She turned and allowed the reverend to escort her out before the tears that she had so bravely held back came gushing in a torrent.

Walking down the dark corridor, Charlisse vowed she would not sit by and do nothing while the man she loved was soon to be hanged.

Chapter 29
In Her Own Hands

Charlisse spent the rest of the day pacing the reverend's cottage while he attended to his duties at the church. Why didn't God do something? Her fears returned like vultures, pecking away at her withering faith and sending her hope adrift.

Sloane came by early in the evening to give his progress report. At the reverend's bidding, he stayed for dinner, and as all three sat dourly down to a meal of wild pork, mangoes, and corn, Sloane admitted in frustration he had nothing positive to report.

The reverend's news about Merrick's appointment at the gallows only increased the aged pirate's distress. Charlisse was sure she saw the weathered lines on his face deepen before her eyes.

"The audacity of that dawcock governor," he grunted. "After all the cap'n's done fer him." He threw his fork down and stood. "Beggin' yer pardon, miss."

"It's perfectly all right, Sloane. I feel the same way." It was the first time she had seen him lose his voracious appetite.

"I've a mind to scurry down to the Dead Reckonin', rip those two jackanapes to pieces, and feed their innards to the crocs, says I! Beggin' yer pardon again, m—"

Charlisse shot to her feet. "Are you saying that Edward and Kent are at the Dead Reckoning this very moment?"

"Aye, miss. I daresay they've bin there near e'er night drinkin' and laughin' 'bout what they done to Merrick."

"Now, Charlisse, there's nothing to be done about it," the reverend said.

Charlisse cast him a furtive glance of disapproval and marched to the window. "It angers me that they run about free while Merrick sits in a cell. Where is God's justice?"

"You can be sure that the Lord will have His justice, and these men will reap what they have sown." The reverend rose and began clearing away the uneaten food. "We must forgive our enemies."

"I cannot." Charlisse spat.

"God forgives us only to the extent we are willing to forgive those who have harmed us."

She fixed him with a cold eye, too angry to reply, too frustrated and overwhelmed to even think clearly. How could he be so calm when Merrick's life was in jeopardy?

Sloane straightened his headscarf and strapped on his baldric and pistols. "Maybe tonight is me lucky night," he remarked. "I best be out there seein' what I kin find out. Keep yer hopes up, miss." He smiled at Charlisse, nodded at the reverend, and gestured toward the door. Charlisse opened it for him.

"The rev's plan is to wait for the good Lord, God bless him fer it," he whispered, "but I've got a plan of me own." He winked at her. "So don't be worryin', miss. By the powers, the cap'n will not hang come Friday, not if I kin help it."

Charlisse smiled and planted a kiss on the sailor's cheek. He turned away, blushing, and sauntered down the path.

Excitement, coupled with a fearful apprehension, flowed through her. To break Merrick out of prison would be no small feat. People would get hurt, possibly killed, in the process. Merrick, if he survived, would be a fugitive, always on the run, always looking over his shoulder for the British authorities. What kind of life was that? Yet the alternative was unthinkable. She shivered, closing the door.

There had to be another way.

After a short while, Charlisse excused herself to her room. She would wait for the reverend to fall asleep. Even if no one else was doing anything—especially God—she was not without some recourse. She was the daughter of Edward the Terror after all. Perhaps she was the only one who could save Merrick and God was simply waiting for her to do something.

After donning her most modest dress and a voluminous gray cloak, she waited until she heard the familiar snores coming from the front room. Then she stole out into the cool night air.

It was close to midnight. The darkness enveloped her like a wicked shroud, frightening even the moon from showing its whole face. She glanced up at the arc that frowned at her from a tumultuous sky. Dark clouds abruptly absconded with any light it emitted. She wondered if it was an omen of bad things to come. Charlisse looked down again, feeling suddenly alone. A sudden wind whipped around her. The tangy scent of rain spiced the air. With each step she took, she felt her resolve weaken. Shady-looking characters appeared all around her; and the noise of revelry swelled—not pleasant sounds, but shouts and obscenities, hideous laughter, and the seductive calls of prostitutes cooing after their mates. An occasional musket shot sliced through the thick night air, and the clash of blades could be heard in the distance. A rumble of thunder echoed across the sky.

Pulling her cloak tightly around her, Charlisse crept onward, turning the final corner toward the Dead Reckoning. She had seen the tavern in the daylight as it slept off the night's debased inebriation. Even deep in slumber, it had appeared an unscrupulous, evil place. Thunder growled a warning across the sky. She took the final steps toward the entrance, unprepared for the vision of wickedness that appeared before her. With gaping black windows above and below, an open door from which poured its foul breath, and the cracked lines of grayed wood that made up its walls, the wicked tavern looked like the skull of a giant, laughing demon.

Male voices issued slurred, licentious comments in her direction as she walked by, head held high, unwilling to acknowledge them with her eyes. She felt her insides crumble with fear. *God, please protect me.*

The stairs splayed out from the open door like a tongue ready to receive its next victim. She hesitated. Scantily clad doxies, displaying their wares on the porch, examined her with interest. Hideous laughter and vulgar language poured from the windows. A man lay passed out on the porch. Another one staggered from the door, spilling rum over the sides of his mug. He grabbed one of the women and pulled her inside as if she were a piece of meat to be plucked off a shelf.

Charlisse froze. Her breath came in quick spurts. She felt as though she would faint on the spot, but thoughts of Merrick gave her renewed courage. Passing the remaining women with her chin thrust out, she entered the dark tavern.

Immediately the stench of sweat, rum, and vomit slapped her in the face. She lifted a handkerchief to her burning nose. The dirty tavern was packed wall-to-wall with the most scurrilous human vermin Charlisse could ever have envisioned. Filthy, unkempt men of all ages littered the room, drinking and shouting vulgarities at one another. Some were passed out on tables or chairs—one man's unconscious body lay in the middle of the room where he was continually stomped on by the unruly crowd.

A fight sounded from the back corner, and a mob gathered around to watch and cheer. Heated arguments abounded from every direction. Loud boastings and accusations were flung about like spurious flatteries at a courtly ball.

As her eyes grew accustomed to the gloom, Charlisse could see men entangled with women in compromising positions, and she averted her eyes. Her stomach flipped, and her dinner rose in her throat.

Sliding into the shadows behind the door, she stood, petrified, staring straight into the depths of hell.

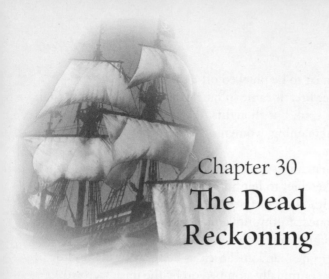

Chapter 30
The Dead Reckoning

Paralyzed with fear, Charlisse searched the crowd of men for any sign of Kent.

Thunder roared, shaking the lanterns that hung from the rafters. They swung back and forth, flinging monstrous shadows onto the walls. Lightning shot a brilliant blaze through the windows, momentarily distorting the figures within into hideous skeletons.

Something landed on her back. Chattering, it climbed onto her shoulder. Charlisse screamed and turned to see a pair of beady eyes staring at her. The little monkey scolded her before scampering down her arm, across a table, and onto the shoulder of a burly pirate, who looked up to see the cause of his pet's agitation. A sinister leer upturned his lips. He stood. Several men around him approached Charlisse. She was going to die. Squeezing her cloak more tightly around her neck, she tried to make herself invisible under its cover.

"What 'ave we got here?" one of the men said. "Come for a bit 'o fun, miss?"

Hands tugged at her, pulling her to the center of the room. An eerie hush fell over the tavern. A million thoughts of her immediate future flashed through her mind, and none of them were pleasant. Why had she been foolish enough to come here? *Where are you, Lord?*

Her cloak was torn from her, sending her into a spin and loosening her blond curls to cascade down her back. Her eyes searched the circle of men who surrounded her. Their licentious gazes scanned every inch of her body. She hugged herself and backed away.

The silence exploded into whoops and howls and lewd suggestions. Trembling, she closed her eyes and prayed. But no miraculous intervention came. A desperate fear clenched her heart so tight, she thought she would die and wished, in fact, that she would.

The pirate with the monkey on his shoulder came forward. "This might be me lucky night, after all, eh, mates?" He chuckled, exposing rotten yellow teeth. His scraggly, mud-brown hair hung in filthy strands to his shoulders. A rust-colored scar that ran from his forehead between his eyes and down his cheek gave him a mangled, frightening expression. He fingered Charlisse's hair, drew close to take a whiff, and grinned. His foul breath wafted over her.

"I believe we 'ave a real live lady on our hands, gents." He circled her, examining every inch with his shameless gaze. "Grown tired of your man at home, perhaps? Lookin' fer a real man?"

The monkey chattered, mimicking its owner. The men howled.

Charlisse turned to run. The pirate reached out for her arm before she even took a step. "Oh no, miss. Ye'll not be leavin' now." His strong fingers clamped down on her arm. She winced in pain.

"Now, where would our manners be, boys," he said, glancing at the other pirates, "if we was to let our guest go without being properly attended to?"

Again, sinister laughter filled the room and someone yelled, "I say we all take a turn showin' 'er our 'ospitality."

Grunts and hollers of agreement followed. Charlisse searched for any sign of a friend among the lust-filled eyes that continually raked over her. She found none. Not even the women were on her side. Several of them pulled on the pirates, trying to draw their attention back to the pleasures they offered.

"I'm here to see Edward the Terror," she said in a fit of courage.

"Edward the Terror? Now what would ye want with 'im when ye could have a man like me?"

The horde of men snickered.

Charlisse remained steadfast, determined not to allow the panic, that was squeezing its way through every nerve in her body, to show on her face. She had spent enough time in the company of pirates to know they fed on the powerless and the fainthearted. If she was going to be ravished—as seemed now unavoidable—then she would endure it with dignity, and not give them the pleasure they would derive from seeing her squirm.

Yet a faint glimmer of hope remained. If her father was here among these ruffians, and she could reveal her identity to him, then perhaps he would protect her. She knew he had conspired to put Merrick in prison. She knew he was a vicious beast, but what she didn't know—what nobody could know—was how he would react at the sight of his own daughter. Charlisse's hope that there was some decency left in him was what had brought her here in the first place to plead for the man she loved. She would not give up on that hope now.

She boldly returned the pirate's stare. Behind the haze of rum, his expression showed no mercy. He turned and jerked her with him toward the back of the tavern where Charlisse could see stairs that led upward. "Enough talk, let's give ye a try. I'll be a mite disappointed if ye aren't as good as ye be lookin'."

Charlisse struggled against his fierce grip. She pounded him with her other hand, but he dragged her along as if she were a paper doll. "Edward Terrance Bristol! Edward Bristol!" she shrieked. The pirates laughed and began chanting the chorus of an obscene song. Desperate, she sought a weapon from one of the tables. She clawed at the hilt of a wickedly curved knife, but its owner slapped her hand away and hooked his finger in the bodice of her dress. "Edward!" she screamed. A familiar face appeared in the crowd to her left—not a friendly face by any means, but one that brought her a twinge of hope.

Kent made his way through the crowd, followed by a large, gray-haired man who sported a captain's hat with boldly colored feathers.

"Yes, that's her," Kent said to the other man, who positioned himself directly in the first pirate's path.

The first pirate, his gaze fixed on the floor, barreled through the crowd until he slammed into the man. He looked up, annoyance written on his face. "Why, if it don't be Edward the Terror."

The two pirates stood staring at each other.

Charlisse felt her heart leap into her throat. *This man is my father.*

"Ye have to wait yer turn, mate. I saw 'er first." The first pirate grunted as he tried to push Edward aside.

"Sorry to disappoint ye, Flint," Edward said, a smirk planted on his lips. "But I believe the lady was asking for me."

Kent stepped forward beside his uncle and cast an insidious glance at Charlisse. A leer grew underneath his thin, polished mustache sending a shiver of disgust through her. Would she be rescued from the hands of one revolting pirate only to find herself at the mercy of another?

The room fell to a silence as all three men stood defiantly, hands resting on the hilts of their swords, ready for a fight.

Charlisse could not take her eyes from her father. Tall and burly, he carried himself with a haughty, commanding air. His clothes were of fine linen and silk, encompassed by a rich crimson damask waistcoat, and though covered with a layer of dust, they indicated a taste for style and unruffled urbanity. His weathered face was cracked and worn, but his crystal blue eyes were sparkling and alert. A bicorne hat with exotic feathers covered a mass of long gray hair that hung down his back. A matching beard that moved when he spoke framed his face. He did not once look in her direction.

Flint, who still had a firm grip on Charlisse's wrist, shook the monkey from his shoulder. The animal cackled as it scampered up into the rafters. He released Charlisse into the hands of another pirate.

Scowling, he approached Edward. "I'll not be givin' this delicate flower up to the likes of ye, Edward," he said, spitting, "or yer little dog here, waggin' his tail beside ye."

Kent took a step forward, but Edward held him back. "Well then, ye'll be meetin' yer grave a bit earlier than ye expected, ye thievin' barracuda, for the girl belongs to us."

Edward drew his cutlass, the blade reflecting the light from a lantern that hung above him. "And I'll kill every last one of ye that stands in me way!" He scanned the surrounding men with a gaze so ferocious, Charlisse had no doubt he could do exactly that.

A flicker of alarm flashed across Flint's eyes. He drew his sword in one swift move.

The room exploded into yells and curses as the two men clashed swords back and forth, sending the discordant clank of metal on metal echoing across the room. Rum was poured and bets were made, and in the chaos, Charlisse seemed to have been forgotten.

The pirate who held her turned to place a bet, and seizing the opportunity, Charlisse yanked her arm from his drunken grasp and slipped away through the crowd. She crept unnoticed through the throng of sweaty men, squeezing her way toward the front door, feeling their stench soak into her dress. *Oh, make me invisible, Lord,* she silently prayed. Hope surged within her with each unhindered step she took. The door was now within sight.

"Leaving so soon?" an all-too-familiar voice shattered her dream and halted her in her tracks.

She swerved. Kent grabbed her waist and lifted her off her feet. Smiling, he hoisted her back toward the center of the room. More in a fit of rage than in any hope to overpower him, she kicked and clawed at him, leaving red marks across his finely chiseled features.

He dropped her, raised a hand as if to slap her, but grabbed hold of her hair instead. He yanked it until she winced in pain. "Now, we are going to behave, aren't we?"

She looked up into his eyes—cold, lifeless stones, devoid of any trace of goodness—and nodded.

He let go of her hair and grabbed her arm just in time to pull her out of the way of the tumbling Flint. The pirate reeled backward, landing so hard on a table that it broke in two.

He shook his head, jumped to his feet, and flew back at Edward, plunging and slashing in a frenzied rush.

Charlisse glanced at her father, who parried each attack with fearless assurance. He returned the blows with much less effort than they were delivered, laughing as he fought. At one point, he stopped to take a drink from a bystander's mug, and the crowd howled.

Clearly outmatched, Flint scanned the crowd with terror. Sweat poured from his face. Charlisse almost felt sorry for him. Would her father take pity on him?

Charlisse struggled against Kent's firm grip, but to no avail. Casting her a look of annoyance, he heaved her in front of him, clamping her hands behind her. His heavy breath slithered down her neck like a snake.

The crowd of pirates continued to yowl, gulping rum from mugs, and spilling most of it down the fronts of their shirts.

Charlisse felt sick to her stomach. She watched her father continue his flagrant assault upon Flint. He did not know who she was. Perhaps her plan was not yet foiled. Surely he had a kind heart underneath that crusty exterior. Surely he was still the man her mother had loved.

Edward, a bored look on his face, landed a crushing blow against Flint's shaky cutlass, sending it spinning to the floor with a clank. Flint dropped to his knees, his breath coming in fast, hard bursts.

A hush fell over the men, broken only by the monkey's chattering from the rafters. Flint lifted his head and looked at Edward. Charlisse's father stood leaning on his sword, a smug grin on his face. He wasn't even breathing hard.

Flint's eyes became pools of pleading as he stared at his adversary. "Mercy?" he asked in a voice that said he knew there wouldn't be any.

The crowd began to chant. "Death. Death. Death. Death!" Kent joined in, thrusting his fist in the air.

Charlisse watched in horror as her father lifted his sword. Certainly, her father was bluffing. He would not kill an unarmed man begging for his life.

Edward the Terror plunged his sword into Flint's chest. Flint's last gaze was one of horror as he gasped, blood trickling from his lips.

Charlisse screamed.

The men cheered. Edward wrenched his bloody sword free, leaving Flint's lifeless body to drop to the sticky floor, eyes gaping at the ceiling. Her father knelt and wiped his blade on Flint's jacket before returning it to its scabbard. The crowd cheered, and the winners collected their bets. Edward looked up, and his gaze locked upon Charlisse. Every bone in her body instantly froze. He squinted his eyes, examining her. Confusion furrowed his brow. Lifting one hand, he beckoned her forward.

Charlisse took a step back, her eyes never leaving his. That was the last thing she remembered before everything went black.

Chapter 31
The *Hades'*
Revenge

The shriek of gulls and the lapping of waves against the hull of a ship woke Charlisse. A warm breeze caressed her face, carrying with it the smell of salt and fish. For a fleeting moment, she thought she was still aboard the *Redemption*, safe with Merrick, and the past week had been nothing but a bad dream.

She peeked from underneath heavy lashes, and the smile on her lips faded as unfamiliar surroundings came into view. She was in a ship's cabin, but it was not Merrick's. The bed was round and twice as large as his. Gone were the leather chairs, the big oak desk, the bookshelves, and the Persian rug. In their stead were a few rickety benches, a large table covered haphazardly with maps, and a glass-fronted cabinet filled with muskets, pistols, and knives. Scattered throughout the room were empty rum bottles and food-encrusted plates swarming with flies.

Charlisse's heart sank into an empty pit of despair. Scrambling to the oval window, she peered out and saw the harbor of Port Royal fading from view.

Dread seized her heart as memories from the night before played out in her mind—the hideous tavern, the sweaty, dirty pirates with their hands all over her, Kent and her father, the sword fight, and the cold-blooded murder of Flint. She could still picture the horrified look in his eyes as her father mercilessly ran him through with his sword and the disrespect Edward had shown by wiping his cutlass on the dead pirate's waistcoat.

She must have fainted, because she had no memory of how she came to be aboard her father's ship—for Edward the Terror's ship it must be. A week ago, she would have been elated at that prospect. But the man she had encountered last night—if indeed he was her father—sent shivers of terror coursing through every nerve.

The scuffing of boots and the muttering of voices filtered in from the hall. The wide door to the cabin burst open and in stomped Edward the Terror, reflecting every bit of his nickname.

He slammed the door and faced her with his hands on his hips and a menacing look in his cold eyes. "Welcome to the *Hades' Revenge*, miss," he said in a gruff voice.

Charlisse opened her mouth to respond, but fear squeezed the breath from her throat. She stood shivering in his presence.

"So ye're the little doll ole Merrick was playing with on that rotten piece of driftwood he calls a ship." He sauntered over to her.

Charlisse felt her insides clench.

"I daresay that mutinous jackal has much better taste than I would've expected." He perused her from head to toe as if he were a merchant examining his wares.

Determined not to appear weak, Charlisse met his gaze and held back the tears that threatened to fill her eyes. He must have been a handsome man at one time, but years of salt air, sun, and bad living had taken their toll on him. His gray hair, which had hung loose the night before, was braided down his back, and his beard had been shaved, leaving only stubble on his chin and neck. He was an intimidating man, not only in size—his mannerisms indicated a power and confidence not found in many men, except perhaps one other. But along with that power, Charlisse sensed a lack of restraint that frightened her beyond words.

He stared at her, as if trying to badger her into submission merely by the intensity of his gaze. Charlisse perceived intelligence behind his deep, crystal blue eyes.

"Hmm," he snorted as he turned and walked to the desk. He grabbed a bottle of rum, took a swig, and wiped his mouth on his sleeve. "What did ye want so badly with me that ye came a lookin' for me in such a scurrilous place as the Dead Reckonin'?"

Charlisse could feel the beating of her heart like war drums through every inch of her body, alerting every nerve to action. This man was her natural father. She had to keep telling herself that, because deep down inside, he was only a stranger to her, and even worse than a stranger, an enemy. She had so many things she longed to say to him, but all she could do was gasp and stutter in fear.

A trickle of perspiration made its way slowly down her back, and she fought a tremendous urge to run from the cabin and throw herself overboard—to end this encounter and her miserable life. *God, where are You? What should I do?*

"Speak up, girl!" Edward bellowed. "Answer me, or I'll get on with what I brought ye here for."

"I came to speak to you about Captain Merrick," she stammered, feeling her blood rush to her head. *And I'm your daughter!* Her insides screamed, but the declaration did not reach her voice. The image of a loving, kind father she had been carrying in her heart for so many years dissolved in the presence of the monster who stood before her now.

Edward chuckled and took another swig of rum. "And what of that worthless traitor?" He slammed down the bottle and squinted at her.

"They're to hang him on Friday." Charlisse heard the quiver in her voice. She felt her hands trembling, and she clasped them behind her back.

A slow grin overtook Edward's lips. "Aye, I heard that bit o' good news."

"But you can't let that happen!" Charlisse took a step forward. "You know he is innocent."

He stood, arms folded across his chest, a malicious grin on his face. Charlisse stepped back and looked down, unrestrained tears forming in her eyes. "Please. It isn't right." She felt her resolve weakening.

"Right or not, makes no difference to me. That ruthless mutineer will die, and he'll be gettin' what he deserves." His expression darkened. "No man steals a ship from Edward the Terror and lives to tell the tale!"

Charlisse lifted her head, allowing the tears to flow freely down her cheeks. "But he could have killed you, and he didn't. Can you not show the same mercy?"

In a flash, Edward jerked a knife from his belt and stabbed it into the table next to him.

Charlisse jumped.

"I'll not be hearin' another word 'bout *Captain* Merrick!" His face reddened and blue veins pulsed in his thick neck. "He'll hang come Friday, and they'll tar him an' string him up in a cage for the birds to feast on! In fact, I heard tell they might be hangin' him early. Today, if luck be on me side."

Charlisse retreated, horrified. The last speck of hope drained from her heart.

"My only regret is that I won't be there to see it." He stared at Charlisse, his gaze smoldering. A mocking grin played on his lips. "You're sweet on him, aren't you?"

Charlisse did not respond.

"All the ladies love Merrick," he said, then snickered. "But ye know why that is?" He approached her, unbuttoning his waistcoat.

Charlisse backed away, shaking her head.

"It's because they've not had the privilege of havin' Edward the Terror in their bed." His grin turned wicked as he tossed his waistcoat aside and unbuckled his belt.

A surge of terror swept over Charlisse. All of a sudden she was just a little girl again, alone in the dark rooms of her uncle's estate, helpless and frightened. But this was far worse. This was her father, not her uncle. This was the man who was supposed to protect her and love her and take care of her. Now here he was, leering over her with lust in his eyes—and intentions more evil by far.

"Kent says he had a go at ye, but Merrick stopped him." He dropped his belt, and cornered Charlisse near the bed, bathing her in his rum-laced breath. "He still wants ye, but I told him he'd have to wait his turn."

He seized her and tossed her onto the bed. Charlisse screamed and scrambled off the other side. He laughed and grabbed her, then fell on top of her, pinning her arms with his fierce grip. He smelled of sweat, smoke, and salty air. The weight of him nearly took the breath from her.

The hopelessness of her situation covered her like a death shroud. She was on a pirate ship in the middle of the Caribbean, and she was sure that unlike her time aboard the *Redemption*, there was no friend to be found on the *Hades' Revenge*. There would be no Merrick to dash in to her rescue, no one to hear her screams or to care if they did. Searching for her voice amidst the fright that strangled her throat, she parted her lips to speak.

His mouth came down on hers. She tossed her head violently, avoiding his kiss, trying to spit out the truth of who she was.

He lifted his head, his eyes burning with lust. "I haven't had a woman as lovely as ye in a long, long time." He paused, devouring her with his gaze.

"Not since Helena," Charlisse blurted, breathless.

Edward's expression instantly snapped from wanton desire to complete shock. He squinted. "Ye best be tellin' me where ye've heard that name," he demanded in a gruff voice.

"She was my mother."

Edward's eyes widened and a flicker of fear passed through them. He shot back from Charlisse and stood by the bed, gaping at her.

"I came here from London to find you," Charlisse said, sitting up and slowly backing away from him. "I'm Charlisse. Your daughter." She wiped the tears from her face, still trembling.

Edward turned away, retrieved his belt and coat, and threw them on a chair. He grabbed a bottle of rum and took a long drink. When he turned back around, he pointed at her angrily with the bottle. "What was your mother's full name?" he demanded.

"Helena Charlotte Bristol." Charlisse's voice cracked.

Edward plopped down in a chair and took another swig, spilling a splash on his shirt. His ruddy completion had turned ashen. One of his eyes began to twitch. "What do ye know of her?"

Charlisse hugged herself in an effort to stop her uncontrollable shaking. "Speak up, girl!" he bellowed.

"She was born in London to Richard James and Emma Louise Hemming," she stammered. "Her brother is Bishop Henry Hemming." Just saying her uncle's full name sent a shiver down Charlisse's spine.

Edward looked away.

Charlisse cautiously continued to spill random facts about her mother's childhood and upbringing, watching her father's reactions carefully. He never flinched, but she thought she saw a haze of sadness overshadow the hate in his eyes. She stopped, wondering if he was even listening.

He turned to her, the wicked glint in his eyes returning. "And what makes you think I'm your father?" he snapped.

"My mother told me you were." Desperate to remove herself from the bed, Charlisse stood, patting at the folds in her dress. Her legs wobbled beneath her, but she forced herself to remain upright.

Downing another swig of rum, Edward stood and swaggered toward her.

Charlisse backed against the bed frame. "In sixteen forty-five, my mother went on a voyage from London to the colony of Carolina to accompany her father on a business venture. I believe he was investing in a tobacco plantation. It was there that she met a handsome merchant sailor by the name of Edward Bristol." Her father stopped moving, his gaze darkening.

She continued, "Two months later, against the wishes of her father, they got married in secret. . . ."

Edward held up his hand. "Enough!" His harsh voice boomed through the room. The ship heaved, and he nearly toppled over. "How is it you came upon this information?" He scowled.

"I told you. She was my mother." Charlisse noticed her father's command of English had drastically improved.

"But you are not my daughter," he announced, fixing her with a cold eye. "The child died before it was born."

Charlisse felt a chill come over her. "What makes you say that?"

"Her brother sent me word of it." He slammed down the bottle, grabbed his belt and coat, and put them on. "The baby died in her womb." He turned his face away from her. She thought she saw a shudder run down his back.

"My uncle?"

"He also told me that trollop, Helena, wanted nothing more to do with me." He grunted. "That she had made a mistake in marrying someone so far beneath her." He strapped on his weapons and grabbed the bottle of rum again, swaying slightly. His eyes glistened with moisture.

"He lied to you. I am telling you the truth!"

Edward threw the bottle against the cabin wall. It exploded into a thousand shards, showering rum over the floor. Charlisse shrieked and jumped back. He marched toward her. "You, miss, are the liar and an imposter! Your intentions with this charade are lost on me, but mark my words, I will not succumb to your trickery!"

"What are you going to do with me?" She burst into sobs.

"Well, ye've ruined me mood for t'night, miss." An icy wall glazed over his eyes. "But I'll come back, ye can count on that, and when I do, daughter or not, I'll have ye as me own." He flung open the door, turned around, and added, "And when I'm tired o' ye, I'll pass ye 'round the crew for their pleasure, to be sure." He cast a wicked grin at her before he left, slamming the door.

Charlisse heard the harsh grate of a latch being dropped in place.

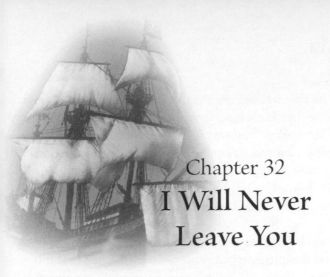

Chapter 32
I Will Never Leave You

Charlisse paced across her father's cabin. The constant barrage of curses streaming from the pirates on deck only added to her dismay. Perspiration dripped down her back and formed beads on her forehead and neck with the rising of the afternoon heat. Grabbing the edge of a sheet from the bed, she dabbed at the drops and slumped onto the hard mattress. She felt herself slipping into despair so deep and dark that she was sure she would never come out of it.

But what did it matter? According to Edward, Merrick was most likely already dead. The thought sent waves of agony coursing through her. Her eyes filled with tears. He was the only man she'd ever loved. And now the father she'd been hoping for her whole life had turned out to be a vicious monster who would probably toss her to the sharks at his first opportunity—either the ones in the sea or the ones on board this ship. *Does he believe I am his daughter? Does it even matter to him?* Yet hadn't she seen a flicker of emotion, a spark of recognition in his eyes when he looked at her, if only for a moment?

As she surrendered more and more to the despondency that dragged her down like quicksand, she wondered at the irony of how much more miserable her life had become since her encounter with God and her commitment to His Christ. Perhaps this was His way of telling her she just wasn't good enough for His kingdom, that she could never live up to His standards. Wasn't that what her uncle had been telling her all along? Maybe it was time she accepted the truth and quit wasting God's time on such a hopeless case.

How foolish she had been to believe the Creator of the universe could love someone like her—that He would have died just for her. What did she have to offer Him anyway? She was just a scared little girl with no special talents or value; *a seductress*, her uncle had called her, a woman who lured good men away from the path of righteousness.

She laid her head down, covered her face with a pillow, and sobbed. Without God, without Merrick, and without a father, what was there to live for?

Why prolong it? a sleek voice suggested. Darting up, she looked around the room only to realize the question had come from within her. Was it her conscience demanding retribution for all her transgressions? Or perhaps it was God, finally grown tired of her shortcomings and failings.

Yes, she thought, why prolong her life? She could see nothing but misery in her future. Even hope had forsaken her, to find a more worthy pupil. Scanning the cabin, her gaze landed on the cabinet full of weapons. It appeared locked, but after walking over to examine it, she swung the glass door open with ease. Grabbing a pistol and some powder, she prepared the weapon as she had seen the pirates do on board the *Redemption*. She could use it to shoot her father when he returned, but what good would that do? She would then be left at the mercy of his crew.

No, it would be much more gratifying to have her father return to find her lying in a pool of blood and realize she preferred death to spending any time in his company. The only misgiving she had was that she wouldn't be here to see his face when he came to ravish her.

Charlisse sat on the bed, fanned her dress out before her, and laid the hideous instrument on top of it. It would be easy to do. A quick shot to the head and she would exit this miserable life forever. Yet, was it right to take her own life? What if God had not abandoned her after all?

The loud snap of a sail taking on a full breeze startled her. She patted at the perspiration on her neck and tugged at the clinging fabric of her dress. Would she feel the shot penetrating her brain? Would God still welcome her into heaven? Or was she doomed to spend eternity in a far worse place than she could imagine, regretting her impending actions after all? As she mused over these things, a voice blared in her head. *Get on with it. End your wretched existence. There's nothing left for you here.*

She picked up the pistol. It was heavy and cold to the touch. She held it, staring at it. The thumping of her heart grew louder with each passing second. The ship creaked in its gentle heave through the sea, calling forth memories of Merrick and the *Redemption*. Tears rolled down her cheeks at the thought she would never see him again.

A loud "Caw" jolted her from her thoughts, and she looked up to see a crow sitting outside the oval window. In her daze, it took her a few minutes to realize it would be impossible for a crow to be this far out at sea. What was it doing here?

"Caw. Caw," the crow screeched, glaring at her with malevolent red eyes. It pecked at the window, trying to gain entrance. The longer Charlisse sat staring at it, the harder it pecked and the louder its cries became.

She remembered the crow at the reverend's cottage; the terrible sense of evil that swept through her room at its presence. A spike of terror penetrated her spine, sending shivers down her arms.

She released her grip on the weapon. It dropped to the bed, bouncing on her dress. The crow shrieked and flew at the window, hitting the glass pane with a thud. Charlisse bowed her head. "God, help me."

The shrieking and pounding ceased. When she lifted her head, the crow was gone. A breeze of cool air wafted over her—though the window remained shut. Closing her eyes, she allowed it to flow over her face and neck. After a few minutes, it faded away but left in its wake an overwhelming sense of love and peace.

Looking down at the vile pistol, she shook her head, wondering how she could have ever considered taking her own life. Was it possible God had rescued her again? Was it possible He had not abandoned her after all? "Oh, God, if You're still with me, what do I do now?"

She heard snickering from the hall, and the door crashed open. In stomped two brutish-looking pirates. Charlisse jumped, grabbed the gun still lying on the bed, and pointed it at them.

"Don't come any closer!" she commanded, her voice trembling as much as the gun.

The men glanced at each other and burst into laughter.

"Naw, miss, we won't be hurtin' ye none, not a pretty thing like you," one of them said. "We only come by on orders o' the cap'n to bring ye down to the hold an' lock ye up." They approached her, but Charlisse remained seated with the gun pointed straight at them.

"O' course, cap'n didn't say nothin' about not havin' a bit o' fun in the process," the other man added, leering at her. They chuckled.

Charlisse didn't know if she could actually shoot a man, but she was beginning to think it was time to find out. Of course, with only one shot, and a shipload of pirates, she realized how futile her attempt to defend herself would be. *God, help me.* Pointing the pistol at the larger of the two men, she closed her eyes and squeezed the trigger. The gun discharged, throwing her against the headboard. She heard a crash and then a dripping sound. Springing from the bed, she dropped the smoking gun to the floor with a loud clunk.

The two pirates stood aghast, their faces ashen. Behind them, shattered glass littered a shelf. Rum dripped from it onto the floor. Charlisse's ears rang from the loud crack of the pistol. A plume of smoke wafted upward, and the smell of gunpowder and rum burned her nose.

"The wench shot at us!" the large man cried. "By thunder, you coulda killed us!" The pirate's face reddened, and he spat onto the floor.

Charlisse backed up, incredulous at their outrage over her attempt to defend herself. These men who thought nothing of taking an innocent life were clearly mortified when she tried to preserve her own.

"And the cap'n's not goin' to be 'appy 'bout his rum, neither," the other one complained.

They rushed her, each one grabbing an arm, and yanked her toward the door, grumbling about getting her below into a more private setting. Charlisse screamed and kicked, but her struggle was as a futile as a mouse's efforts to free itself from the talons of a hawk. One of them lit a lantern, and they forced her downstairs to a cluttered deck where pirates slept in hammocks that swung with the movement of the ship. Down another level, and Charlisse caught a glimpse of the gun deck lined with rows of cannons perched atop wheeled gun carriages strapped with ropes. Like sleeping giants, they sat readied to be awakened by their master to fire their iron missiles on Edward's next victim.

With each step downward, the temperature climbed and the darkness grew thicker, and Charlisse's nose burned with the stench of mold and human waste. Rats scampered over the stairs, darting for hidden corners, running from the light. Terror pierced her heart and sent clenching waves of fear through her body.

She knew her only hope was in God—that He had not abandoned her, that He was still with her even though her faith had wavered. She prayed silently.

Finally, the pirates reached the bottom of the ship. They turned left, and Charlisse saw two iron-barred cells, both empty, one across from the other. A lantern swayed on a hook between them, casting gruesome shadows over the inside walls of the ship. Charlisse heard a hideous moan coming from the hull around them as the *Hades' Revenge* turned. The wood creaked in reply. She shuddered.

One of the pirates tossed her effortlessly into a cell and slammed and locked the iron gate behind him. Charlisse heard both pirates moaning as the thud of their steps faded up the stairs.

Shaking, she knelt on the dirty floor and prayed.

Merrick heard footsteps approaching and looked up. The familiar form of Reverend Thomas appeared in the dark hallway, followed closely by a guard. Merrick ran to the bars, straining for a glimpse of Charlisse in the dim lighting, but the look on Thomas's face told him she was not here.

Extending his arms beyond the iron rods, he clasped his friend's hand in greeting, but he sensed something was wrong. "Where is she?" Merrick asked.

The reverend looked at him, sadness emanating from his usually cheerful eyes.

"Where is she?" Merrick repeated, his tone demanding.

"She went out last night after I fell asleep," the reverend said, looking down. "I have not seen her since."

Merrick felt his insides crumble. He tried to speak, but the implication of the reverend's words constricted his throat.

"Sloane is out looking for her," Thomas added.

Merrick raked a hand through his hair and turned aside. "She's been gone all night and all day?" He'd heard the words, but his mind wouldn't believe them. Or was it his heart that wouldn't believe them? He clenched his fists.

"It's possible she went in search of her father—to try to negotiate your release."

"Edward the Terror?" Merrick clutched the bars, his knuckles turning white. "She went to see Edward the Terror? I ordered her not to!" He pushed off the bars and began to pace. "Why didn't you stop her? Why didn't you protect her?" He cast an accusing glance at the reverend.

Thomas sighed, a grimace marring his features. "I'm sorry, Merrick. I was asleep. I thought she was, too." He looked at the dirty stone floor again and shifted his hat in his hands. "I should have been more careful."

Merrick regretted his harsh accusations, but he was too mad right now to care about anyone but Charlisse. "Where is Edward now? Tell Sloane to find him. Perhaps he has Charlisse captive." His mind swirled with plans to rescue her, and he spat orders to Thomas as if he were one of his crew.

"Unfortunately, Edward weighed anchor and left Port Royal early this morning," the reverend admitted, his eyes moist. "Since we have been unable to locate Charlisse, I have to believe that he took her with him."

Merrick slammed his fists against the stone wall, leaving blood to mark the spot of his fury. "No!" he yelled, trying to collect his thoughts as well as his rage. He turned toward the reverend. "Do you know what he'll do to her?"

"We don't know how Edward will take the revelation that Charlisse is his daughter. Let us not assume the worst."

"Assume the worst! How can I not? The scoundrel himself told me what he would do with a beautiful daughter." He walked toward the reverend. "I should have killed him when I had the chance."

Thomas gazed at him, one eyebrow cocked.

"Don't look at me with those righteous, condemning eyes." Merrick swung away. "If I had killed him, Charlisse would be safe now."

"But she would hate you for it, and you would hate yourself for committing such an act."

Seizing the bars, Merrick shook them with a fury that sent the reverend back a step. "Get me out of here, Thomas." He looked at his friend, feeling pain reach his eyes.

The guard approached, and Thomas raised his hand.

"I feel as though I'm losing my sanity," Merrick whispered when the reverend returned his gaze.

"There's still a chance you won't hang," the reverend said, his eyes reflecting Merrick's suffering.

"Do you think that's what concerns me?" Merrick stomped toward the wall. "I have no fear of death. At least I will be free from this cage." He sighed and hung his head. "Charlisse depended on me to protect her, and I have disappointed her. Now her purity and her life are in grave danger." His faced the reverend. "What can I do in here, Thomas? Why has God taken my freedom from me? Why has He forsaken me?"

"Trust Him, Merrick. He is still in control."

"But I'm not anymore."

"Were you ever?"

Merrick grunted and offered the reverend a look of contempt.

"Give it to Him, Merrick," the reverend said.

"I don't know if I can." Merrick felt as though he were at sea being pummeled by a horrendous storm, unable to stop the monstrous waves from tearing his ship to shreds.

The guard cleared his throat and stepped forward.

Merrick leaned into the bars and pushed his hand through. He knew the reverend was doing his best to comfort him—to help him in the only way he knew. But Merrick didn't need a man of God right now. What he needed was a pirate, a rogue—a man who wasn't afraid to use his sword for a worthy cause.

The reverend clasped Merrick's outstretched hand. "I will pray for you. Don't lose your faith, son."

Merrick drew him close. "Tell Sloane to proceed," he whispered.

"With what?"

"He'll know what I mean," Merrick said. He dropped the reverend's hand, then turned and sought the shadows of his cell.

Chapter 33
Circle of Light

Well into the night, the lantern guttered, leaving Charlisse in a deep, thick darkness. The ship moved gracefully beneath her, sending a rush of water against the hull. If not for the hard wood under her feet, she could imagine herself floating endlessly through an empty void, a plane of existence halfway between death and her ultimate destination.

God was with her. She felt His presence in the cell and in her heart and knew He was still keeping a watchful eye upon her. Was He the father she had been searching for? She supposed time would tell whether He could be trusted, and whether He considered her worthy enough to be His daughter. The latter condition she doubted she could ever meet. If He truly was the awesome God she was beginning to realize He was, why would He want someone like her—someone who would only bring dishonor to His name?

She had finally found her earthly father. Not only was he not kind and loving, but he had also denied her birth and tossed her into a filthy prison with no regard for her safety. Though she could not ignore the pain in her heart from his rejection, she no longer hoped for his acceptance—or his love. He seemed nothing more than an angry, miserable man, whose only pleasure in life was invoking terror in everyone around him—especially those weaker than he. Her dreams of a father evaporated as the fading of the lantern light had, leaving her in the darkness once again.

Edward was not at all as her mother had described him. Could she have lied? Or was it the years of hardship and bitter disappointment that had changed him so drastically? And what was her uncle's part in this? How many lives had he ruined in his lust for control over everyone who crossed his path? Charlisse cringed at the remembrance of him and thanked the Lord she was no longer in his wicked grasp.

The gruesome moaning of the bulkheads grew louder sometime during the night as the tossing of the ship intensified. Charlisse felt queasy under the throws of the turbulent waters. Unable to see anything in the darkness, she heard the scampering of tiny feet. Rats, perhaps startled from their slumber by the increased movements of the ship, or worse yet, hunger. She stood, backing against the iron bars, afraid to breathe lest they find her. Soon, she felt their whiskers on her legs. Every time one of them nudged up against her feet, she kicked, tossing the hideous rodent through the air.

Charlisse clung to the rusty bars that held her captive. Hungry and tired, enveloped by a stench that would cause most women to swoon, and surrounded by rats and God knew what other slimy vermin, her resolve faltered.

"Where are you, God?" she cried, her voice echoing against the moldy hull. Was He still there? Or in her frenzied need, had she only imagined His presence? Voices in her head kept telling her, over and over, that she was a fool to believe in a loving God, that He was a figment of her deluded imagination, created in desperation to escape the horrors of her reality.

As she continued to cry out, renewed warmth flowed through her. A feeling—more like a knowing—of power and peace bubbled up inside her. Closing her eyes, she basked in it, refusing to give in to the voices of the enemy.

Some time later, the heat intensified, and Charlisse assumed that day had broken once again over the Caribbean, bringing with it its usual sweltering temperatures. Droplets formed on her face and neck, and her dress seemed permanently glued to her skin.

She heard footsteps on the stairs, and a faint light appeared to her right. Unsure whether to be relieved or frightened, she was seized by the latter as the devilishly charming Kent appeared with lantern in hand. Approaching the cell, he held the light up to her face and offered her a malicious grin.

"Ah, did they leave you here all alone in the dark?" His voice dripped with lecherous sarcasm. He glanced around. "Not a very charming place, either. . .and the smell, how awful for you." He pressed one hand to his nose.

Charlisse glared at him from the back of the cage. If she didn't know him, she would find him a handsome man—tall, muscular, impeccably dressed in satin and silver lace, dark curly hair, and enticing brown eyes. But that was only the outside of him. Inside he was pure evil. He alone was responsible for her predicament, and Merrick's. He had placed the false evidence aboard Merrick's ship and alerted the authorities. He had allied with her father to have Merrick arrested and finally, he had assisted in her kidnapping and imprisonment aboard this vile ship.

Charlisse sensed the darkness in his heart as he stood there leering at her, one side of his thin mustache lifting in a smirk. And to think he was her cousin. She shivered.

"What is it that you want, *cousin?*" Her voice quivered, but her gaze was direct.

"Ah, so you do believe you're Edward's daughter, eh?" He turned and hung the lantern on the hook between the cells. The tip of his rapier clanged against the iron bars. "It seems he believes it also, for the poor old fool has kept himself stupefied with rum since his encounter with you last night." His lips twisted in an insolent smile. "Nothing notable happened between you, I presume? No father-daughter reunion?"

"You uncivilized cad."

"Yes, quite so." He nodded, offering her a mocking bow. "At your service, cousin." He put one hand on the hilt of his rapier and the other on his hip, perusing her silently for several minutes. "That makes it much more interesting, don't you think?"

Charlisse didn't answer. She averted her eyes from his wicked gaze.

"Being related, I mean—makes the fruit even more forbidden, even more desirable." He paused, cocking his head. "Yes, I think we shall become the closest of relations." His eyebrows lifted.

Charlisse cast him a cold look from the corner of her eye.

"Come, come, my sweet. What have you got to lose? Surely you aren't waiting to be rescued again by the debonair Captain Merrick?" Kent paced in front of her cell. "Why, last I heard, he has an appointment at the gallows come Friday." He shook his head. "No, I don't think the illustrious captain will be able to get himself out of this one."

"And it's you who put him there with your lies and deceit," Charlisse spat, fury rising within her. God help her, she hated him. Even though she knew she shouldn't. She must love her enemies, the Lord said. Yet she felt nothing but loathing for this man. Holding her head high, her eyes burning with emotion, she added, "You'll never be half the man Merrick is."

Kent leaned into the bars, his brown eyes smoldering. "Why don't you try me and find out?"

Charlisse swerved away in disgust. A rat darted across the cell floor.

"I see you have company." Kent's tone turned lighthearted. Then with a curt wave he said, "Enough of this, I did not come down here to cause you any anguish, miss, nor to discuss the past."

"No? Well, you have accomplished both, and if you're quite done, you may leave."

"Not before you hear my proposition."

"There is nothing I could possibly want from you." Charlisse wrapped her arms around herself, feeling a wicked chill in Kent's presence even in the excruciating heat.

"I think you'll find me not quite the villainous scoundrel you think I am, miss. I do, after all, know how to treat a lady."

"I believe I had a taste of your chivalry on board the *Redemption*."

Kent looked down. "I hope you'll forgive me for that incident. I'm afraid I don't hold my rum very well."

Charlisse examined him. Could he truly be sorry for what he had done? When he looked up, a crooked smiled played on his lips, reaching his eyes with a strong cynicism. She turned away, and the silence lingered between them.

"It's terribly hot down here, don't you think?" he finally said with cool disdain, "and I tell you from experience, it grows worse as the day progresses. He folded his hands across his chest and sighed. "This is no place for a lady."

Charlisse's gaze veered to his, wondering what wickedness he was scheming.

"I could come in there and take you right now," he said, "but I won't. I'm going to wait until you've had enough, until the rat bites and the heat and the smell and the hunger become too much for you, and you beg me to rescue you." A faint smirk upturned his lips. "I have a comfortable room above where I assure you I will care for you properly—if you behave."

Charlisse sauntered out of the black shadows. "I would rather die a thousand deaths down here in the bilge and filth and be eaten alive by rats, than share one second alone with you." The smile fell from Kent's face. His jaw flexed with irritation, and his upper lip twitched. "We shall see, miss. You've not yet been down here a full day." He turned and retrieved the set of keys from a hook on the wall. "I'll come back in a few days and see how you're feeling then." He gracefully bowed and left.

Charlisse shuddered. She was thankful he had left the lantern. At least there would be light for a little while.

The day progressed, and with it, the torturous heat. Hunger clawed at her stomach, haunting her with memories of her time alone on the island. Did they intend to starve her to death? she wondered. Or was this just another form of pirate torture? Her legs burned in the effort to remain standing, but she didn't dare rest them and give the rats more flesh to chew. She prayed silently for strength as she hung drifting in and out of consciousness.

Sometime after midday, as best she could guess, Charlisse heard someone coming down the steps. A crotchety old sailor emerged from the stairway, the perfect epitome of a pirate from every fable and myth she had ever heard. Swarthy and muscular, he wore a white and red checkered shirt under a red waistcoat that was embroidered in black silk, baggy black breeches, red silk stockings, and heavy boots. His scraggly brown hair emerged from under a red scarf. A leather belt strapped over his shoulder held three brace of pistols. A long scar ran from his neck up to his right eye, where a patch hid whatever damage remained. By the scowl on his face and the fierce look in his eye, Charlisse could tell he was morose and had an ill disposition by nature.

He limped up to her cell, carrying a plate and cup in his hand, and despite his appearance, Charlisse's mouth began to water at the sight of food. A colorful parrot on his shoulder squawked when it saw her and began repeating, "Walk the plank. Walk the plank." She wondered if the creature was somehow foretelling her fate.

After searching for the keys to her cell—which Charlisse silently thanked Kent for taking—the pirate cursed and pushed the plate underneath the bars. Casting an angry look at her, he turned and limped away. The parrot on his shoulder continued its admonition over and over until she could hear him no longer.

Charlisse scrambled to the plate and grabbed the cup, downing the liquid in two huge gulps. The water was warm and had black specks floating in it, but she didn't care. It slid down her throat like spring water. The food, however, was a different matter. It was a gooey blob of brown-colored lumps that smelled as if it had been scraped from the bilge of the ship. She stuck her finger in the cold mass and held it up to her mouth, hoping it might taste better than it looked. Before she had even placed it on her lips, she nearly heaved up the water she had just drunk.

She slid the plate under the bars and into the corner, where she hoped its contents would satisfy the hungry rodents enough to leave her alone.

The lantern went out. A palpable darkness instantly surrounded her, trying with all its strength to penetrate her soul with its dismal tidings. The normal moaning of the wooden bulkheads and the creaking of hinges—at first terrifying sounds in the pitch black, like the weeping and gnashing of teeth one would expect to hear in hell—were now a familiar sound, reassuring her that she was still among the living and had not been transported to an eternity of dark loneliness.

Exhausted and dripping with perspiration, Charlisse hung onto the bars. The hours dragged on, bringing with them cooler evening temperatures, but unfortunately, also the rats, the pattering of whose feet she heard all about her. How long she could hold up against them, she didn't know. Would she topple to the floor, overcome with fatigue? Would her captors find nothing but a pile of half-eaten flesh come morning?

Hours went by and tears flowed freely down her cheeks as the hopelessness of her situation struck her like a cannonball. The carnivorous rodents constantly gnawed at her legs, tearing her stockings into shreds and biting her tender flesh. Soon she was unable to feel her feet as numbness began to migrate up her body.

"Oh, God," she cried out in desperation. "I know I deserve nothing more than this hideous fate for all I've done," she sobbed. "But I also know You have forgiven me and washed me clean with Your precious blood." She glanced upward, into the darkness. "Have mercy on Your daughter. Protect and deliver me. Give me Your strength, for I feel I have none left within me." She waited, but no answer came save the constant moaning of the ship mocking her for her foolishness.

Sometime during the long, agonizing span of the night, Charlisse felt her legs give way beneath her, and she collapsed in a heap to the damp floor. She could hear the rats gleefully scampering toward her, but she could not find the strength to get up. Her breath came in hurried and terrified spurts. She stared into the darkness, and a sudden panic surged through her at the thought that she would soon lose all consciousness and be entirely at their mercy.

A pinprick of light appeared by her feet. Curiously, she stared as it expanded and began to draw a line. Little beady eyes glowed beyond it, frozen in their advance, watching it with as much fascination as Charlisse. On and on it continued, weaving a luminous trail on the wooden floor. It rounded a curve and continued. She watched in awe as it ended up where it began, enclosing her in a circle.

The entire cell was illuminated by its radiance, and she could clearly see the rats waiting at its outer edges—dozens of them, vile and filthy creatures, staring at her with evil eyes and twitching noses. Three scuttled toward her, stopping at the light, sniffing, hesitating. Charlisse thought they would hop over it, but to her surprise, they spun around and rejoined the others. More came scampering over, and each one stopped abruptly at the light and turned back.

Tears of joy spilled down Charlisse's cheeks. Even as she stared at the shield of light, she found it hard to believe. Yet there it was, right before her eyes. "Thank You, Lord, thank You!" she exclaimed. "You are my fortress and my shield, thank You." She continued giving thanks for several minutes until finally, she curled up in a ball and fell asleep with the praises of God still on her lips and His light surrounding her.

In the early morning hours, as she was just regaining consciousness, her thoughts drifted to Merrick. Was he still alive? Or like her, was he still in his cell, dealing with rats and other vermin? She prayed that if he still lived, God was protecting him as He so miraculously was her. The similarity of their circumstances made her feel closer to Merrick. She had thought his love was the answer to the aching hole in her heart—that hole she had first thought could be filled only by her father—but now God had taken Merrick away from her, as well. She was alone again in this world—no father, no Merrick, yet God was still with her. Why would He stay, she wondered, when her faith was so weak and she had been nothing but a disappointment.

Around midday, in the peak of the heat, Charlisse heard the jingle of keys followed by the heavy step of boots on the stairs. She looked up from within her lighted circle and saw Kent, with lantern in hand and familiar smirk on his face. Charlisse waited for him to notice her miraculous shield, but when he turned to look at her, she detected nothing in his eyes to indicate he saw anything out of the ordinary. *He doesn't see it.* She grinned.

"Ah, do I perceive a smile on your face?" His dark eyes flashed with excitement. "Had your fill of this place? Ready to join me above, perhaps?" He shook the keys in front of her but stopped when she did not reply. He scrutinized her. "You must be hungry by now, and thirsty and tired of rats."

"I assure you, sir—" Charlisse's voice cracked from disuse but remained firm. "I am well cared for."

Kent's brow creased. "Indeed? And how can that be?"

"God takes care of me."

Kent's face couldn't have been more awestruck if she had broken through the bars and slapped it. He shook his head, regaining his composure. "Miss, I fear you are either delusional or have spent too much time with Merrick." He paused. "Or perhaps one is the cause of the other." Chuckling, he grabbed the bars. "I implore you, give up this insane pretense and accept my generous offer."

Kent's expression bordered on desperation, and Charlisse felt sorry for him. "If you are quite done, I need my rest."

"As you wish; I leave you here to die!" came his furious response. He swung around, grabbed the lantern, and stormed up the stairs.

The afternoon dragged on, and Charlisse, though very thankful for the freedom to lie down and rest, suffered from excruciating thirst. The surly old pirate returned with a plate of food, angry once again when he could not find entrance into her cell. After shoving the meager slop between the bars, he left without saying a word, although his parrot continued to make up for its master's silence. With one small gulp, Charlisse downed the dirty water, and then slid the plate of food to her furry cellmates.

Back inside the protective light, she lay down and tried to sleep. Every time fear snuck into her mind like a thief trying to steal her peace, she opened her eyes to see the circle of light and instantly felt comforted and protected. When the temperature cooled, she allowed the familiar swaying of the ship to rock her to sleep.

Sometime in the middle of the night, she awoke with a start to the loud thumping of someone coming down the stairs. The sound stopped abruptly for a few seconds, and Charlisse wondered if the person had changed his mind, but then it resumed. The shadow of a large man entered the room. She sat up. A twinge of fear ran down her spine. In the light of a bright lantern, Charlisse could make out the distorted face of her father.

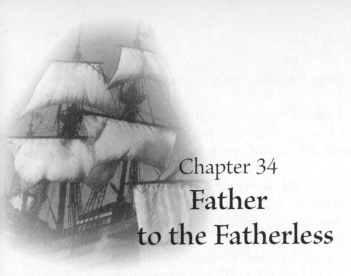

Chapter 34
Father
to the Fatherless

Edward the Terror staggered to the cell, searching for Charlisse in the darkness—the girl who had sent his life into a bilge pit for the past three days. The bars of the cage danced before him like snakes slithering down from a crossbeam. He held up the lantern and nearly toppled over. A belch erupted from his throat. He saw her, sitting toward the back of the cell, looking as innocent as her mother always had. *Trollop.* He wiped the sweat from his brow and tried to hang the lantern on its hook, but the blasted thing kept moving. Stumbling, he barreled into the bars and nearly lost his footing. "Can't those powder-brained apes keep the ship steady?" Finally, he got the lantern hooked in place and turned to face her.

Holding on to the iron bars to support his swaggering frame, he stared at her, trying to collect his fragmented thoughts. The lantern swayed back and forth in time with the creaking of the ship. A rat scampered across the cell into a dark corner. Edward watched it with interest, glad for the diversion, before returning his drunken gaze to Charlisse. She swirled like a mirage in his vision, like a dream from long ago—a vision of Helena.

He had not heard that name spoken in years, although both the name and the person who bore it haunted his dreams day and night. Not a day went by that she didn't invade his every thought, teasing him with memories of her beauty and love. Not a day went by that he didn't wonder what his life would have been like had she stayed with him—had she truly loved him.

Who was this girl who dared to speak the only name that could stir up such torturous feelings long since buried? It was a trick—one of Merrick's tricks, no doubt.

Helena. The sound of her name was still like a sweet song, an ancient song from a time long ago when Edward Bristol was a different man—when he had hopes and dreams and love in his life. But that man was dead now.

He focused his blurred vision on the girl in the cell. He let out a low curse. *She looks just like her. Why didn't I notice it before? The same sweet face, the flawless ivory skin, the long golden hair.* He shot her a fierce look and growled under his breath.

"What was your mother like?" He demanded gruffly.

Charlisse stood and crept toward him. "She was beautiful," she began softly, "with hair the same color as mine."

The ship lurched to the port side, and she nearly fell. Edward clung tightly to the bars to keep from stumbling backward. Stale rum rose in his throat. The ship spun around him, and he feared he would pass out. He didn't want to pass out. He wanted to look into the blue eyes of this girl who looked so much like Helena.

Three days in the rat-infested hold and she looked at him with tenderness, not anger, not hatred, as he'd expected. There was something else behind her gentle gaze—something that confused him.

"She was taller than me," she continued, "more elegant and graceful."

Edward listened, forcing his hazy thoughts to focus. Hearing about Helena resurrected a part of him that was long since dead, a part of him that had once known happiness. But along with the joy, the pain also rose, clambering from the ashes of his charred emotions to claw at what remained of his heart. Still, he bade Charlisse continue.

"She loved painting and music. She had the voice of an angel."

"Aye." Edward nodded. "She did, indeed." A smiled curved his lips, and with it, he felt all defiance and wickedness slowly dissolve, as if the two could not inhabit his being at the same time.

"She loved you, Edward."

That phrase, and the sincerity with which it was spoken, struck Edward like a rapier through his heart. His eyes grew moist, and he turned away. The words, like darts expertly aimed, reopened old wounds that had been cauterized, but had never healed. The pain, finally released from its prison, churned within him, eating at his soul. He scowled, forcing the agony back the only way he knew—with hatred.

"I'll not hear of that!" he stormed, and spat onto the floor. "She had no love for me. She loved only her silks and lace, her jewels and fancy food." He gave a curt wave into the air. "I was but a poor merchant sailor whom she cast tokens of her favor upon for her own amusement." He staggered in front of the cell and felt the heat rising up his neck.

"I hardly think marriage can be considered a *token of favor*," Charlisse whispered.

He shot her an angry gaze. "Even that had no true meaning for her," he bellowed. "Otherwise, she would have answered my letters."

Charlisse drew closer. "She did answer your letters, I assure you. At least the ones she received."

Edward snorted and flung his mass of hair behind him.

"She used to read me your letters when I was little—over and over again."

"Yes, I'm sure she had a great laugh at how foolish I was to believe she loved me. And the money I sent for her to come join me, the money I worked me arse off over a year for, where would that be?" He looked at Charlisse, raising a mocking brow and grabbing the bars to steady himself.

"I don't know, Father, all—"

"Don't call me that! I am not yer father!" His roar echoed off the planks and bounced around the ship like angry arrows. Drawing his cutlass, he pushed it between the iron bars, pointing it straight at Charlisse. She backed away, a look of horror on her face. "I'll carpse ye and tie yer body to the anchor and drag ye o'er the ocean floor if you call me that again, missy!"

When he saw Charlisse's wide, blue eyes and the fear that skipped across them, an unfamiliar emotion flooded through him—regret. He didn't know what to do with it. Withdrawing his weapon, he sheathed it with force. *What magic does this wench weave over me?*

He needed a drink. He wobbled over beyond the stairs. Finding a barrel, he cracked it open and, dipping his hands into it, brought the precious liquid to his mouth. Warm and sweet, it flowed through him, further numbing his senses and the pain in his heart. Wiping his mouth on his sleeve, he returned to the girl.

He stood in front of her cell, glaring at her. She would not come forward. He didn't blame her. An uncomfortable silence hung between them. He had no idea what else to say, but he could not pull himself away.

The sweet sound of her voice broke the silence. "My grandparents died shortly after Mother returned to London. I never knew them. My uncle, Bishop Hemming, became my mother's guardian."

The alcohol was having its intended affect on Edward's emotions. The tension in his shoulders released, and apathy extinguished the fire that had been lit on each nerve.

Charlisse crept from the shadows of the cell. "He was a vicious, cruel, and controlling man who used the power of the church to manipulate everyone around him."

"Why are you telling me thisss?" Edward slurred. "I have no interest in him."

"Because it was he who kept you and my mother apart," she explained, a pleading look in her eyes, "completely against her wishes and without her knowledge."

Edward fixed her with a cold eye, a troubled feeling brewing in his gut.

Charlisse's eyes glistened, and she stepped closer. "I assure you, she longed for you day and night. All she talked about was the day you would summon us to come live with you." She paused. A tear slid down her cheek. "My uncle lied to you about me. He lied to you about my mother's feelings toward you. And he confiscated all correspondence between the two of you until you both gave up hoping."

Edward shook his head. His mind was whirling in a thousand different directions, and he was having trouble getting it to land on any one spot. Yet something the girl said sparked a light in a very dark part of him. It was a light that seemed to dissipate the fog of confusion that had grown stale there for so many years. Her words made sense, but he wasn't sure he wanted them to. For so many years, he had wondered what happened to the incredible love he and Helena had shared. For so many years, he had not wanted to believe what her brother had told him. But years went by and the mind played tricks—he began to believe that he had been a fool. No woman like Helena could ever have loved him.

That was when the anger and bitterness had overtaken him, like an insidious disease that began in his heart and spread throughout his soul, devouring every good thing in its path. From then on, he had spiraled down into a life of depravity and wickedness, spewing out anger and hatred on everyone around him, hoping to rid himself of it. But the more he dispensed it, the more it grew inside him, becoming more and more powerful until it had made him the most feared and wicked pirate on the Caribbean—and the most miserable and empty.

If there was truth to her words, what good would it do him now? It would only make him more of a fool for abandoning Helena, leaving her to raise their child on her own. It would mean that all these years of hatred and evil had been for naught. He should throw the wench to the sharks before she burrowed any deeper into his heart. Yet he had to know more.

"How did she die?" he asked.

"She grew very sick with a fever one winter," Charlisse said, her voice quivering. "I sat at her bedside and watched her slowly dwindle away." Tears fell freely from her eyes. "In the end, I don't think she had the will to go on—even for me. I was only eight at the time." Charlisse slid down the iron bars and plopped in a heap on the floor.

Edward's heart sank, diving into the sludge of anguish that slithered in the darkest part of his soul. A desperate feeling of loss threatened to break his heart in two. Taking a deep breath, he searched for the rum's numbing effect that had dissipated and left him to feel such misery. Unable to find the liquor's soothing repose, he instead retrieved the stone wall of bitterness and hatred with which he had enclosed himself for years.

"Well, it makes no difference to me. It just be a silly story 'bout some frail woman who I 'ave no recollection of." He was Edward the Terror again—in control, vicious, and heartless. It felt good. He took a step to leave and almost fell. Turning, he gave her one last furtive glance before heading toward the stairs.

"Is that all?" Charlisse asked, rising and approaching the bars. "Are you going to leave me down here?"

Edward tottered away.

"Father!" Charlisse screamed. "Please don't leave me here."

"I told ye not to be callin' me that!" He turned and drew his pistol with much more swiftness and accuracy than he'd thought possible in his condition. He pointed it straight at her lovely head. The dark, ominous barrel shook in his hand. He could kill her right here and Helena's memory with her.

She did not flinch. Her eyes were wide and carried more sorrow than fear in their blue depths. He moved the gun back and forth, following her swaying figure. Moments passed. The ship creaked and moaned as if in protest of the impending disaster.

Then Helena appeared in the cell. She stood with arms outstretched, smiling. Edward closed his eyes. When he opened them, she was gone, but the product of her love for him remained.

Edward swore, lowered the gun, and left.

Sobbing, Charlisse crawled back to her circle and curled up in a ball, hugging herself. She wished her father had killed her. Why God allowed this endless torture, she could not fathom. As her tears rolled over the bridge of her nose and dropped onto the soggy wood beneath her, she gazed at the circle of light that protected her and realized God wanted her alive for some reason. For what purpose, she could not imagine. What did she have to offer Him? Yet in this dark, smelly, rat-infested prison, she could not deny she felt His presence. With these thoughts on her mind, she drifted to sleep.

It must be Friday. The realization pierced her heart like a sharp arrow as she slowly regained consciousness from her grief-stricken, fitful sleep. Had three nights passed in this horrifying cell, or only two? It seemed like a hundred to her aching body and frenzied mind. Weak from lack of food and water, she could hardly sit. It took every ounce of her strength to kneel within her circle and lift up a fervent prayer for Merrick. Today was the day of his appointed execution, and if he was still alive, God was the only one who could save him.

Chapter 35
Prison Break

His eyes watering, Merrick blinked under the brilliance of the sun. He had not been outside for a week, and as the Caribbean breeze caressed his face, he took in a deep breath of it, smiling. The salty air carried with it the lure of freedom, but the irons clamped around his wrists spoke otherwise. He was being led, along with two other prisoners, through a formation of well-armed British soldiers, toward a horse-drawn wagon. He was to be hung within the hour.

Regardless of the fate that loomed over him, he was elated to be out of that dark, damp cell. He loathed being locked up. It was only by the grace of God that he had not gone mad. Although it had been only a week, it seemed an eternity—an eternity in hell—as Merrick wrestled with the demon of self-reliance, battling against the realization that he couldn't save Charlisse, much less himself. For six days, he'd fought for the control he knew was only God's, until finally broken and weary, Merrick fell to his knees, released his clasp on the demon, and submitted himself to the Almighty.

Now, with the feel of the earth beneath his feet, the warmth of the sun on his cheeks, he felt at peace, knowing everything was in God's hands. He looked up and saw the swaying of the palm trees in the wind and heard the chatter of birds accompanying the distant, roaring surf.

The guards shoved him into the wagon. He stared at his fellow prisoners, who did not seem to be sharing his joy. One old fellow looked like nothing more than a poor beggar, who must have stolen from the wrong person to receive such a harsh punishment. The other, by his clothing and mannerisms, was a pirate, and Merrick gave him a quick smile.

"Ye are Cap'n Merrick, aren't ye?" the man asked.

Merrick nodded.

"I've heard of ye. By the powers, I ne'er thought to be seein' ye caught and forced to a pirate's death." He was a skinny young fellow with red hair and lively blue eyes. His fair skin had been sunburned so many times that it remained a hardened, rusty color, making him look much older than Merrick was sure he was.

"It was not a part of my immediate plans either, my friend." Merrick cast him a sly grin. "But we aren't at the gallows yet, now are we?"

The pirate, brow furrowed, examined Merrick's eyes with interest.

Merrick glanced at the soldiers. Four of them were mounted on horses and formed an armed escort around the prisoners. The other two sat in the front of the wagon. One now flicked the reins, sending the wobbly cart on its way.

The heat of the day rose as they passed through the main gate of the fort. The soldiers gave their formal salute to the men who stood guard. Rusty—as Merrick decided to call him—glanced at him with a look of understanding, mingled with respect. Whether it was because Merrick appeared to have no fear of death, or whether the young pirate hoped for a sudden rescue, Merrick did not know.

Passing over the crest of a hill, the wagon meandered down a narrow road. A strong, salty breeze carried in from the bay, wafting over them. Merrick looked up to see the sparkling turquoise waters of the sea he loved so much. Would he ever sail free over the crystal Caribbean again?

He had not heard from Sloane in two days. Had he been able to put his plan to action, or was this truly Merrick's appointed day to die? If it was, he was ready. He had already committed himself to God's perfect plan and timing, and he knew without a doubt where his spirit would go when it left his body. It would be a far better place than this—perhaps with even a thousand more beautiful oceans to sail.

Yet deep within him there was an intense yearning to stay, a feeling of unfinished business, and an excruciating sense of urgency to find Charlisse and rescue her from the evil clutches of Edward. Not an hour had gone by in his dark cell that he had not prayed for her, and not an hour went by that the Lord had not reassured him she was in His capable hands. Selfishly, he wanted to remain in this world a little while longer, just to be with her. But, he realized, the Lord might have plans for her—plans that did not include Merrick. He knew whatever those plans entailed, God would look after her now that she had turned her life over to Him.

They reached the bottom of a hill and made a sharp turn onto one of Port Royal's main streets. Crowds of merchants, privateers, and slaves parted to allow the procession through, while curious onlookers lined the dusty road. They stared at the three prisoners with varying degrees of pity and disgust.

A few pirates removed their hats and bowed. One of them yelled above the noise of the crowd, "Thar goes Cap'n Merrick, one o' the mightiest pirates e'er to grace our waters. I salute ye, Cap'n."

"Aye, aye," others shouted in agreement. Merrick acknowledged them with a nod.

"And I consider it a honor to be hung next to ye," Rusty said with all sincerity.

Merrick grinned at the compliment, then shook his head. "There's not much honor in hanging, mate, nor in dying. The honor is in what kind of life you've led."

"Aye." Rusty nodded. " 'Tis true."

They rode on in silence, listening to the *clip-clop* of the soldiers' horses and the rumbling of the wagon. Merrick looked down at the irons that bound his hands and yanked on them, longing to be free. Passing stores and pubs soon gave way to scattered houses and then to shrubs and greenery. The scenes slowly drifted by the wagon, like visions of an ever-changing horizon from a long sea voyage—a voyage that was soon to end in a deadly storm.

As they neared the final turn that would lead them to Execution Dock, Merrick heard the pounding of drums. Rusty began to sing a pirate's chant while the beggar, who had not uttered a sound until now, broke into sobs.

Merrick scanned the surroundings, alert for any unusual movement, every sense keen, and every nerve on edge. He said a silent prayer for the Lord's deliverance.

"I once went a sailing fer fun
With the fierce Cap'n pirate named Dunn.
We pillaged and plundered.
Oh my thunder,
Now I'm about to be hung."

Rusty continued his chant. They turned another corner. The gallows came in full view—a tall platform overlooking Kingston Bay where three nooses hung ominously over a crossbeam. The ropes swayed gently in the wind, passing idle moments before they would grab their victims' necks in torturous ecstasy. A burly man, dressed in black with a hood over his head, stood by them, the grim reaper waiting to escort the dead to the next world. Four British soldiers flanked the gallows. They were dressed in immaculate red and white uniforms with glittering gold buttons.

A noisy crowd of at least a hundred people had gathered to watch the spectacle, including women and children, and several pirate acquaintances of Merrick's—or *gentlemen of fortune,* as they preferred to be called—whom he assumed had come solely out of respect for one of their own.

Although still at a distance, Merrick quickly found the compassionate gaze of Reverend Thomas, who stood near the gallows, waiting to pray with the condemned. If Merrick was indeed going to die, he was glad to have his friend by his side.

Everything moved in slow motion. The scorching rays of the sun beat down upon them. Merrick felt a trickle of sweat slowly make its way down his back, taking every available detour around shoulder blade and spine in order to prolong its journey. A myriad of noises came to his ears—the horses clomping, the old man sobbing, the crowd yelling, Rusty chanting, and the foreboding, incessant beating of the execution drums.

To his left, down an incline, the crystal blue waters of Kingston Bay reflected the sunlight in sparkling clusters of radiance. Merrick squinted. Beyond the bay, the freedom of the Caribbean lay taunting him—beckoning him. Was the *Redemption* still in the harbor? He searched for it, but could not find it among the dozens of ships anchored at bay. Ah, for one last glimpse of his mighty vessel!

To his right, a thick layer of tropical vegetation grew untamed and, up ahead, a large tree spread its lush boughs over the trail. He would be glad for its relief from the merciless rays of the sun.

Merrick heard the chattering of a monkey. The wagon entered the shade of the tree, and instantly, a small, wiry creature dropped onto the shoulder of the man who drove it. The tiny animal wrapped its hands around the driver's eyes. The soldier screamed and furiously clawed the animal.

Several bulky, round objects that looked like cannon balls lit with fuses, flew at them from beyond the foliage. One landed in the wagon next to Merrick's boots. He quickly kicked it to the ground and barreled into his fellow prisoners, knocking them down.

The balls discharged with soft hissing sounds. Instead of exploding, they sprayed large plumes of white smoke that rapidly flooded the entire area with a cloud of dense fog.

Bone-chilling screams came from every direction. Merrick heard the soldiers' horses neighing and bucking and the scuffling of boots in the dirt. One of the soldiers issued orders in a panic-stricken voice. Merrick looked up, coughing. Curses and howls penetrated the thick vapor. He knew those war screams. It was his men. He stood, straining his eyes to see through the white haze, listening to the sounds of battle—thuds, shouts, and the clash of swords.

The smoke dissipated, and his crew came into view. One was clinging to a soldier on the back of a horse in an intense struggle to push him from the beast. Another was in a heated sword fight on the ground. Jackson had one man in a headlock, and two more of his crew had another soldier surrounded.

Merrick was about to jump down and join the fray when he heard the cock of a pistol. He turned to find a British soldier pointing the weapon at his chest.

"You aren't going anywhere, pirate," the man sneered, his dark eyes darting back and forth. "Tell your men to stop fighting, or I'll shoot you where you stand."

Merrick glared at the soldier. Only a few whiskers sprouted on his smooth chin. Droplets of sweat formed on his forehead. The gun shook in his hand. The young man shifted his eyes between Merrick and the ensuing battle. The sweat that had formed on his forehead dripped into his eyes. He blinked, and as he did Merrick twisted his shackles around the pistol and snapped the weapon from the soldier's hands. It landed in the wagon next to the beggar. Shock registered on the soldier's face. Before he could react, Merrick slammed his forehead onto the man's head and pushed him over the side of the wagon.

Rusty stood. "By thunder, that be 'ow to do it!"

Sloane jumped up into the cart. "Hey thar, Cap'n! We come to rescue ye!" A broad grin split his whiskery face.

Merrick chuckled. "And you're doing a fine job of it, my friend."

A pistol blasted behind him, and Merrick heard the thud of a body on the dirt. He swerved to see the old man, smoking weapon in hand, and followed his gaze to where a soldier lay wounded on the ground beside the wagon.

"He was going to shoot you," the beggar said with a Spanish accent. He dropped the gun in the wagon where he had found it.

Merrick nodded in thanks and looked to see how his other men were doing.

The soldier who had been battling for his horse was finally pushed from the beast's back and went tumbling down a slope. The other three soldiers were well subdued.

"Don't kill them," Merrick bellowed. "Just take their weapons and shove them down the hill."

The smoke had nearly cleared. Merrick heard commotion from Execution Dock. The crowds yelled. He looked up to see mounted soldiers galloping their way.

"Time to go, men," he shouted. Then lifting his shackled hands, he jumped awkwardly onto the back of a skittish horse.

Brighton bound the last soldier and pushed him down the slope. Sheathing his cutlass, he jumped onto a nearby steed and reined the fiery horse behind Merrick's. The other men doubled up on the remaining horses. Merrick gestured for Rusty to jump up behind him.

"Why, thank ye, thank ye. I knew ye was a good man, Cap'n," Rusty exclaimed.

"Take the old man." Merrick pointed to his fellow prisoner.

"But, Cap'n, we don't have time. He'll be slowin' us down," Sloane complained, his horse chomping at the bit.

Merrick glanced at the beggar. He was not pleading for his life as most people in his position would have done, rather he returned Merrick's gaze with staunch rectitude. "He comes with us," Merrick demanded.

Sloane nodded reluctantly and helped the aged man on behind him. The monkey slid down from the tree onto Sloane's shoulders. "Hold on!" Sloane yelled to the man, and turning to Merrick he shouted, "Follow me, Cap'n." He galloped off, spraying a dust cloud behind him.

Clumsily grabbing the reins, Merrick kicked his horse and sped after Sloane. The others dashed behind them. The crack of a musket rang through the air. Merrick felt the bullet pierce his skin and searing pain radiated through his body as he galloped around the corner.

Chapter 36
Kent's Prize

Time passed in a blur. Starving and dehydrated—still receiving only one cup of dirty water a day—Charlisse grew weak. She spent her days lying within her circle, drifting in and out of consciousness, praying that God would not abandon her.

Each afternoon, when it grew so unbearably hot that Charlisse felt as though she were being roasted alive, she sat and tried to pray. On one such afternoon, as soon as she had finished her petitions, the circle of divine, protective light vanished.

The sound of footsteps and the jingle of keys came to her ears, and she looked up to see Kent's arrogant smile flashing at her from the bottom of the stairs.

"I've reconsidered my prior outburst and ungentlemanly behavior and have come to show mercy on you and rescue you from this place," he said, fumbling with the keys. He found the right one and unlocked her cell.

Every nerve in Charlisse's body coiled in alarm. Her heart thumped wildly. She tried to stand, but could not. Instead, she scooted herself backward as far as she could into the dark cell. "Please, just leave me here," she pleaded.

Kent stepped inside and approached her. "Now that wouldn't be very chivalrous of me, would it?" he said, the corner of his mouth lifting his thin mustache.

He scooped her up in his arms without effort and carried her up the stairs and through the companionway. Charlisse did not have the strength to resist. Muttering something about her needing a bath, Kent kicked open the door to his tiny cabin, laid her on a cot, and left, locking her in behind him.

Charlisse scanned her new surroundings while gobbling down a tray of food she found on the table—real food, not the slop they had given her below. The cabin was so small it did not allow more than one step in any direction without hitting a wall. Besides the cot on which she sat, there was only one chair, a table, and a set of shelves built into the opposite wall. No weapons were in sight. A round window let in a shaft of sunlight, a ray of golden warmth that brightened Charlisse's soul after having been locked away in the darkness for so long.

There was commotion on deck. She heard the pirates scurrying about, yelling and cursing. Whatever it was, she was thankful it was occupying Kent's time.

After washing her face and neck with water from a small basin, she lay down to rest. She prayed to the Lord for protection before she fell into a riotous sleep filled with nightmares from her past.

When she awoke, it was dark in the tiny room save for a beam of moonlight that streamed in through the window. She had no way of knowing how late it was, but an eerie silence lurking through the ship set her nerves on edge. Could she have slept through the nightly drunken revelry? Creeping to the door, she turned the handle—still locked.

She heard the thudding of heavy boots in the hallway, followed by the clank of keys. Backing away, she sat on the bed. The door burst open and a man's bulky form entered. He stumbled across the floor, ran into the table, and cursed. After several attempts, he lit the lantern, and held it over his head, looking her way. Kent's leering smile gleamed like shark's teeth in the darkened room. Barely able to stand, he hooked the lantern above him and attempted to remove his baldric and sword. "I know you've been anxiously awaiting me, missss," he slurred. "Unfortunately, I've been indisposed." He fumbled with his brace of pistols and threw them into the corner, then staggered toward her. His rum-saturated breath wafted over her face.

He tried to unbutton his shirt as he swayed with the rocking of the ship. After several tries, he gave up and leaned over, flanking her with his arms. His eyes floated in a haze of lust. "Shall we?" He grabbed the front of her dress.

Oh, God, help me. Charlisse said a silent prayer and did the only thing she could think to do. Lifting her feet, she thrust them into Kent's stomach and pushed him. Arms flailing, he went barreling backward, scrambling to maintain his balance, eyes wide. His head slammed against the shelves before he hit the ground. A moan escaped his lips, then he was silent.

Charlisse trembled and stared at the fallen pirate, waiting for any movement or sign of life. Had she killed him? The ship creaked under the roll of a wave. Water crashing against the hull echoed through the room. The lantern swayed on its hook, casting eerie shadows over Kent. Still, he did not move. His muscular body lay motionless, like a sack of flour, taking up the whole floor of the tiny room.

Several minutes passed before Charlisse got up the courage to approach him. Terrified that he would jump at her, she tentatively knelt beside him and poked him with one finger. She shook him. Nothing. He was alive, however, for his chest rose and fell with each breath he took.

Charlisse began to shiver though it was not cold in the room. She clasped her arms around herself as she sat next to the still form of the man who had attempted to ravish her twice. Tears flowed down her cheeks. Kent looked peaceful in his sleep, but how long would it be before he gained consciousness and the angelic façade faded again into that of a monster?

She glanced at the door. His massive frame lay next to it. Standing, she yanked on the knob, but it would not budge. She tried pushing him out of the way, but after a week of being starved, her strength was spent.

Exasperated, she plopped down on the cot, out of breath and frustrated at her weakness. She stared at Kent, wishing with all her heart that Merrick were there. Tears pooled in her eyes at the thought that he was gone from this world—that she would not see him until the next. Desperately, she pleaded with God to take her life, for without Merrick, what reason did she have to live?

Hours passed while Charlisse waited for Kent to come out of his stupor. She thought of tying him up, but could find no rope. His weapons lay strewn in the corner where he had thrown them. Only once and very briefly did the thought of killing him cross her mind, but deep down, she knew it was wrong and doubted she had the stomach for it.

She picked up a pistol, remembering the time she had pulled one on

Merrick in his cabin, and smiled. Loading it, she laid it on the cot and returned to search for a knife. There was none, only his sword and three more pistols. Charlisse sat on the cot with the pistol in her lap and stared at the unconscious pirate, alert for any signs of movement. Well into the night she kept her vigil, but sometime before dawn, she dozed off.

Two strong hands grabbed her arms and shook her violently. Charlisse opened her eyes to find Kent's fierce gaze upon her. His curly hair surrounded his reddened face like a lion's mane. He was sober, he was awake, and he was livid. His breath smelled of stale rum. By his determined demeanor, she could tell he was finally going to take what he considered his. Frantically, she searched for the pistol, but her hands came up empty. Kent clawed at her dress.

A whistle blew and her father's voice bellowed from the deck. "Kent, come aloft!"

Kent held his hand over Charlisse's mouth, listening. Edward's thunderous voice echoed down the hallway again. For a minute, it seemed Kent contemplated disobedience. He shoved off her, frustration twisting his features, and grabbed the pistol from the cot. After pausing to tie back his hair, he gathered his other weapons and opened the door, turning to her with a look of fury. "I shall return, miss," he said before he left, locking her in the cabin once again.

Charlisse thanked God for yet another rescue and rolled over on the cot, releasing her tension with an outpouring of tears. She spent the rest of the day alone, without a drop of water or morsel of food. Yet she felt her health returning. She had been able to get some much-needed sleep, and the last meal she had eaten was more than enough to stimulate her waning strength.

Later in the afternoon, the wind picked up, and the sunlight was overshadowed with thick black clouds. The ship bucked under the mighty waves that rose with the approaching storm. Charlisse trembled at the memory of the last horrifying tempest that had cast her into the sea. Kent returned with water and salted meat in the early evening. By that time, the last thing Charlisse wanted was food in her unsettled stomach. For hours she had been tossed back and forth in the cabin like a stuffed doll with each roll and heave of the ship. The torrential rain pelted on the deck above her like grapeshot. Blast after blast of furious waves hit the window, and as the ship bolted and groaned under the force of the swells, it took all her strength to remain upright. Kent handed her a jug of water. A flash of lightning illuminated his face, twisting his already wicked expression.

"Are we to sink?" she asked, above the roar of the storm.

He smiled, and for a moment she thought she saw a trace of kindness in his eyes. "No, miss, it's highly unlikely," he answered, reaching his hand up to the wall to keep his balance. "I've seen much worse storms than this. And Edward is a good captain."

He took a step toward her.

"Are you the son of my father's brother or of his sister?" Charlisse blurted in an attempt to divert his thoughts.

Kent's brow darkened. "I am the unfortunate offspring of Edward's brother, James."

"Unfortunate? How so?" she pressed him, noting his aggrieved expression.

He looked at her, his mustache twitching above a surly mouth. His hand clenched the hilt of his cutlass. "My father is much like Uncle Edward—a hard man to please."

"Is he a pirate also?"

Kent chuckled. "My father would never so blatantly display the wickedness of his heart. No, he prefers an outward pretension of social grace and propriety and reserves his depraved demeanor for his family."

His gaze landed on her again, and she perceived a battle raging behind his eyes. She had obviously opened a deep wound, and the more his thoughts dwelt on it, the less they focused on her. She was playing a precarious game. "Was he cruel to you?"

"Cruel, ha!" Kent pulled his sword a few inches out of its scabbard and then thrust it back. He glanced toward the window where the rain and wind still pummeled the glass. His focus was distant, in another time and place. His eyebrows knit together and he touched his forehead. There was something about the way he stood that made him seem smaller in stature. "It was his purpose to prove his supremacy over me in all things. I grew to believe he sired me only for his own cruel pleasure and mawkish dalliance." A shudder crossed his shoulders, and he regained his haughty mien. "But I will prove myself to him yet." His gaze swerved back to her, and anger smoldered in his eyes. "For I shall soon become the most notorious pirate in these waters. My name will invoke terror wherever it is spoken, and I will have whichever lady I desire."

His harsh tone sent a chill of dread through Charlisse.

Thunder exploded outside the window with a boom that shook the ship as if roaring its agreement with his declaration.

Kent shook his head, turned to the door, and left Charlisse ate the meat and drank the water despite the objections of her stomach. She thought perhaps the food would soothe the turmoil that raged through her body, but it did not seem to help. In fact, as the storm outside the ship subsided, the storm within her only increased in violence.

By the time Kent returned, the torrent had passed, and the ship was in no further danger, but by the smile on his face, Charlisse realized she was not to be as fortunate. He was sober, and apparently, for the time being, unfettered in his obligations. He tossed his weaponry aside with ease and began unbuttoning his shirt.

Charlisse backed onto the cot, fighting a wave of nausea. Bare-chested, Kent approached with a determined look on his face. In a split second, he was on her, pinning her down. She screamed. He covered her mouth and tore at her dress as she thrashed beneath him.

He momentarily released his grasp in an attempt to disrobe her. She bolted upright, clutching her stomach.

"Please, I'm going to be sick," she pleaded with him, trying to move aside.

"No, you're not, wench, lie back down," he demanded, ripping the buttons from the top of her dress.

Charlisse's stomach lurched. She held her hand over her mouth.

Kent looked up, examining her.

She closed her eyes, trying to calm the heaving of her stomach.

Kent started to back away.

Charlisse opened her mouth and spewed vomit all over him.

Kent froze, staring at the slimy liquid that slid down his bare chest onto his breeches. He stood up with a look of disgust on his face. The angry determination of a few moments ago vanished, replaced by a livid repulsion and a squeamish pallor.

"You can't say I didn't give you fair warning," Charlisse said curtly, feeling much better.

With a violent backhand, Kent sent Charlisse reeling onto the cot. "You impertinent shrew!" His face had turned scarlet. Purple veins pulsed to near bursting in his forehead. He turned away, holding his hand to his mouth. Grabbing his shirt and weapons, he backed out the door, choking and gagging.

Charlisse sat and rubbed her stinging cheek. Despite her situation, she couldn't help but smile. The look on his face had been. . .indescribable.

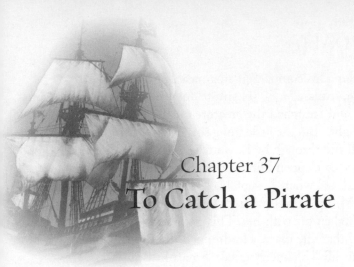

Chapter 37
To Catch a Pirate

Merrick once again stood at the helm of the *Redemption*. Bathed and clean-shaven, he wore a fresh suit of clothes, complete with his full array of weapons. Though he loathed the violence they sometimes brought, he had to admit he felt more in control with cutlass, knives, and pistols within easy reach. Did that mean he didn't trust God? He hoped not. For certainly today the Lord had proven His awesome powers of protection toward those He loved. And Merrick had no intention of entering another battle for control with the God of the Universe—one he was sure to lose.

He moved his right arm, stretching his shoulder, and winced. Miraculously, the pistol shot had gone clean through him, and Brighton had been able to patch up the wound before infection could set in. Merrick breathed in the fresh Caribbean night air as the ship glided quietly away from the coastline of Jamaica where she had been hidden just outside Kingston Harbor. After seven days of maddening confinement, he had thought he would never again feel the wind of freedom blowing across his face—that he would never again guide his mighty ship across the vast, unpredictable sea. Yet here he was. *Thank you, Father God.* He looked up toward the darkening sky, where innumerable stars were beginning to peek out from behind the curtain of dusk, and smiled at a loving God who had rescued him from certain death.

Sloane approached, carrying a cup of hot tea. The monkey sat calmly on his shoulder and grimaced at Merrick.

"I see you've made a new friend in my absence," Merrick said, taking the tea and offering his companion an amicable grin.

"Aye, Cap'n, 'twas a poor substitute for yer company, to be sure." He reached up and scratched the creature on the head, and the monkey chattered in delight. "But the little thing sort o' took to me after his master, Flint, got hisself run through by Edward."

"He belonged to Captain Flint, you say?" Merrick took a sip of his tea.

"Aye, he did, an' when I went back to the Dead Reckoning to be inquirin' about Miss Charlisse, that's when I found out Edward had killed Cap'n Flint an' taken off with her. This poor fellow here was still hidin' in the rafters of that vile place. He dropped onto me shoulder as if he'd known me all his life." Sloane grinned. "Smart littl' guy, too."

Merrick nodded "Yes, I can see that. He was quite useful today."

Was it just this morning that I was to be executed? Merrick thought. It seemed so long ago now. After evading the soldiers in a chase through the crowded streets of Port Royal, the old beggar, Rusty, Merrick, and his crewmen—the only ones loyal enough to risk their lives in his rescue—had hidden in the dense jungle until nightfall.

Merrick turned toward his friend. "If the good Lord had not used your courage and wits to rescue me, I'd be hanging from the dock right now with birds pecking at my flesh. I owe you my life."

The monkey jumped to Sloane's other shoulder and began picking through his hair. The pirate looked down, shuffling his feet. " 'Twas nothin', really, Cap'n. You'd o' done the same fer me. I knows that to be true."

Merrick nodded as Brighton and Rusty approached. "Cap'n, the old man has been fed and is resting below," Brighton said, "but he's anxious to be workin'."

"Tell him to regain his strength for now." Merrick wasn't sure what he would do with the vagrant, but he couldn't, in good conscience, have left him behind to hang.

"An' this one here." The doctor pointed to Rusty, who stood by with a gleeful look on his face. "He's healthy an' ready fer work."

"What is your skill, man?" Merrick asked.

"On me last ship, Cap'n, I was a helmsman."

"Well, it just so happens I'm short a helmsman," Merrick said, stepping away from the wheel. "I believe he and my ship's carpenter gave me up for dead and joined another ship while I was in prison. Isn't that so, Sloane?"

"Har, that be true, Cap'n."

Merrick gestured for Rusty to take his place at the wheel, which the red-haired pirate did with enthusiasm.

"Why, thank ye, sir," he said. "Now, where should I point 'er?"

Merrick scanned the dark waters of the Caribbean and jumped down to the main deck. Where, in this vast ocean, could Edward be? Memories of his time spent sailing under the blackguard passed through his mind, and he pulled from them snippets of information—Edward's favorite islands, his favorite hunting grounds. "Turn her three points off the bow, south by southeast!" he yelled over his shoulder. "Jackson," he bellowed, "unfurl the topsails and topgallants. I want us at full speed."

"Aye, aye, Captain." Jackson's eyes lingered a little longer than usual on Merrick's, and a hint of a smile touched his lips.

Merrick nodded. "I'm glad I'm back, too, Jackson."

Merrick leapt to the foredeck, listening for the familiar snap of the wind as it caught the sails. The *Redemption* jolted, then shot off, slicing a trail of white foam through the turbulent, dark waters.

The light from a half moon cast pearly glitter over the tumultuous sea. Somewhere out there Charlisse was held captive by one of the most vicious pirates ever to prowl these waters. He was also her father, and Merrick hoped that fact alone would prevent the insidious scoundrel from doing her any real harm. "Oh, Lord, help me to find her. Please protect her until I can," he whispered into the wind. The sea raged in a swirl of obscure uncertainty, like the emotions within him.

Sloane came up beside him. "Ye know the gov'nor will probably send a warship to hunt ye down."

"No doubt," Merrick replied, his lips curving with amusement. "I'd be disappointed in him if he didn't."

Sloane shook his head and chuckled. "Now that sounds like a bit o' fun, Cap'n, bein' on the run again, just like the ol' days, eh?" He looked at Merrick with a twinkle in his eye, and the monkey on his shoulder nodded and grinned.

Jackson approached. "Beggin' your pardon, Cap'n, but where might we be goin'?"

Merrick directed his gaze to the dark, passionate void into which they sailed. "To catch a pirate."

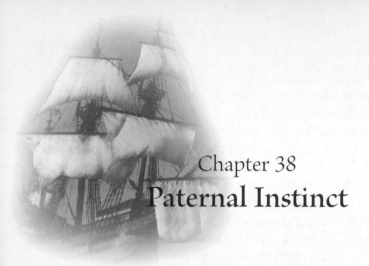

Chapter 38
Paternal Instinct

The thudding of boots and the clamor of voices startled Charlisse from her sleep. She heard the clank of keys, followed by the grating of a latch being lifted, then the door flew open, crashing against the wall. In walked her father, followed by another pirate—a boy of no more than thirteen years. When Edward saw Charlisse, a rush of scarlet suffused his already ruddy face. He grabbed her arm and dragged her from the room. At first, she thought he was returning her to her cell in the hold—the familiar tomb in which she had spent the past week. But instead of going down the stairs, he went up, hauling her behind him, pinching the blood from her arm under his strong grasp.

The sunlight struck her like a slap across the face. Tears seeped from her eyes under its intense glow. A million thoughts flew across her mind. Why was her father so angry? What did he intend to do with her? Maybe he was going to make her walk the plank with a cannonball tied to her feet, plunging her down to the dark void of Davy Jones's locker.

He dragged her across the deck and up the stairs to the forecastle and halted behind his nephew. Kent stood with his back to them, staring off the bow of the ship. His shoulders flinched, but he remained anchored in place.

"What be the meanin' o' this, Kent?" Edward bellowed.

Kent slowly turned around, glanced at Charlisse, and then faced Edward with a look of innocence. "Whatever do you mean, Captain?" He bowed politely.

Edward growled under his breath. "Ye know very well what I mean, ye insubordinate knave, and don't be thinkin' ye can play me fer a fool like ye did Merrick. I'll have none o' that aboard me ship, by thunder, or I'll have yer innards strung up on the yardarm for the birds to feast on!"

At that moment, Edward the Terror lived up to his nickname indeed. At least a head taller than Kent, his nephew's form was completely swallowed in his dark shadow. His long gray hair blew in the wind and spoke of a wisdom that came from experience rather than the feebleness of old age. He wore a captain's hat with a large ostrich plume that teased Kent as it fluttered in the breeze. His growing anger flowed down through his fingers to Charlisse's arm. She winced in pain.

"You did not have me permission to take her to yer quarters."

Kent lifted his chin and narrowed his eyes, but the slight twitch of his upper lip betrayed his fear. "When you left her below to die, I assumed—"

"Well, ye assumed incorrectly!" Edward roared.

Kent cocked an eyebrow. "I fail to understand why I cannot have her when it's obvious you want nothing to do with her. . .*Captain*."

"Because she's me daughter and that's the end of it." Edward glanced at Charlisse for the first time since he'd found her in Kent's cabin. His features softened, and he released his grasp.

She rubbed her arm. *Did he just call me his daughter?*

Edward swung his gaze back to Kent. "You're to keep yer hands off her, or there'll be hell to pay."

Tense silence stretched between the two men. They glared at each other, proud eyes shooting arrows of challenge between them. A sail snapped in the wind. Saltwater sprayed over the bow, showering them as the ship plunged through the sea. Neither man budged.

The pirates congregated on the main deck in anticipation of a fight. A strand of Kent's wavy hair came loose from his tie and blew across his cheek. He inched his hand to the hilt of his cutlass. Edward remained calm, undaunted by the impertinence of his nephew.

"Do not defy me, boy. Ye'll not live to regret it," her father said in a gruff voice that sent a shiver through Charlisse.

She took a tentative step back from the ensuing quarrel, her emotions whirling. She stared at Edward. Days ago, he'd spoken viciously about her mother, saying she'd only played with his affections for her own amusement.

Then he'd left Charlisse imprisoned in the hull to die. Now he stood ready to risk his life in order to defend her honor. Was it possible to hope there was more to this man than she had resigned herself to believe? Could he actually care for her—or was it only some masculine compulsion to defend his territory? Regardless of what his motives were, she would have to rely on Edward's sudden surge of parental protection and pray to God it sprang from fatherly love.

A brief wave of contrition flickered across Kent's eyes. He looked away momentarily, his rigid demeanor relaxing. But then, as if taken over by some demonic presence, he stretched his frame into an unyielding stance. He looked at Edward, his eyes blazing. "I grow weary of everyone and everything keeping me from this woman!" he growled through a clenched jaw.

"Sail ho!" a voice yelled from the crosstrees.

Edward shielded his eyes and scanned the horizon. "Where away, Perkins?" he called to the man aloft.

"Two points off the starboard bow!"

Edward glared back at his nephew. "Will ye be drawin' yer sword on me now? If so, be quick about it. I've got other business to attend to."

Kent rubbed the hilt of his cutlass and returned Edward's challenging stare. The sun's searing rays pelted over the ship, bouncing off the deck in sizzling waves. Kent flung a wayward strand of hair behind him. Sweat trickled down his neck. He bowed. "I am deeply offended you would think I would harm my own uncle."

Grunting, Edward dismissed him with a wave of his hand, and stomped down the stairs to the main deck.

Kent's face flared to the color of ripe plums as he studied Edward's retreating form. Then his shoulders slumped, and he looked out over the sea.

Charlisse backed against the foremast and followed the direction of the men's gazes. The slight shape of a ship appeared on the horizon.

When her father lowered the telescope, he growled something unintelligible and spat to the side. Marching closer to the rail, he held the glass to his eye again. Finally, he handed it back to the pirate who had brought it and sighed.

"Who is it, Cap'n?" the pirate asked.

"It's the *Redemption*."

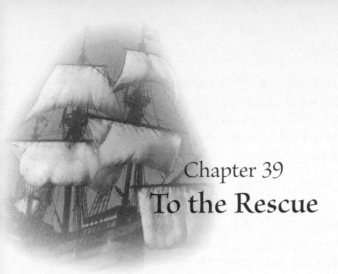

Chapter 39
To the Rescue

The *Redemption*. Charlisse's heart jumped at the sound of that mighty ship's name. She dashed to the railing to get a closer look, but saw only a brown blur on the horizon. *Oh, Lord, could it be Merrick?* Afraid to hope, she tried to quell the frantic beating of her heart.

Edward pushed off the railing and stomped across the deck, cursing and barking orders to his crew.

Kent turned to Charlisse. "Rest assured, miss, it is not him. Your precious Merrick is long dead, and his rancid remains are hanging in the town square at Port Royal for the mockery of the crowd and the feasting of the fowls." He grinned, gazing toward the ship. "I doubt you would find him so attractive now."

Charlisse fixed him with a cold stare. "I assure you, sir," she said, "I would prefer the company of his decaying corpse to you in your finest attire." She lifted her chin and moved farther down the railing.

"Brenton, take the lady to my cabin!" Edward shouted.

Charlisse turned to look at her father, who had already leapt to the foredeck, and was bellowing orders to the pirates climbing the ratlines. "Fa. . .Captain, please don't send me below," she called after him.

Edward swerved to face her.

She took a step toward him. "What if we are fired upon and the blast hits me?"

"No one dares fire on Edward the Terror." He approached the railing, grabbed the wood, and peered down at her. His harsh voice took on a milder tone. "Besides, I don't want ye in me way."

"I won't be in your way, I assure you." Charlisse offered him a pleading look as a stocky pirate grabbed her arm. "Please."

Edward stared at her with eyes that held a soft look, as if he actually cared about her. Shaking his head, he stepped from the railing and stiffened.

"Take 'er below. I've no time for her girlish whining," he ordered, turning away.

The pirate yanked her down the companionway. "No, Father, please let me stay!" she screamed, struggling to be free. "Please, Father." But he was already shouting orders to his crew.

Pulling her arm from the pirate's grasp, Charlisse tried to squeeze past him and make her way back up to the deck, but the man was as wide as a sail. Clumps of hair sprouted from the collar of his checkered shirt and grew in furry patches on his arms. Repulsed, she backed away. But he pursued her, forcing her down the stairs. Grunting, he thrust her into Edward's cabin and slammed the door.

Charlisse flew to the oval window. *Oh, Lord, have You indeed saved Merrick and sent him to my rescue?* It was far more than she could have hoped. But why? Was anything impossible for God? Hadn't He protected her time and time again? Still she doubted. Hanging her head, she asked forgiveness for her lack of faith and prayed that Merrick was indeed on board the ship that pursued them.

Edward the Terror stood with his hands on his hips, staring at the arrant intruder. It was rare that another pirate ship dared to approach the *Hades' Revenge*, let alone bear down on her at full speed. Could some cruel twist of fate have allowed Merrick to escape the hangman's noose? The thought set Edward's nerves on edge. Merrick was the only man who had ever bested him, both at sea and on land. For one brief moment, he considered fleeing from the fast-approaching ship—hoisting all sails and hoping his newly careened schooner could outrun the *Redemption*. But he had never run from a fight in his life, and he was determined not to start now.

Kent approached and stood by Edward's side, animosity igniting the air between them. Edward lifted the glass to his eye again, trying to identify the commander of the ship. The bowsprit of the *Redemption* nodded at him in recognition above cascades of white foam that spread out over the ship's bow as she sped through the water. Captain Merrick's colors could be plainly seen flying in the wind above the head of the mainmast.

Edward turned to Kent. "Turn 'er hard about. Beat to quarters."

Kent strode away, repeating the orders to the crew.

With straining cordage and creaking blocks, the ship swung around. "Furl the topsails and gallants," Edward ordered, and the men flung themselves into the shrouds and scrambled aloft.

The *Redemption* currently had the weather gauge. Edward must steer the *Hades' Revenge* on a southwesterly course in order to circle around her and end up on her windward quarter, where the advantage would be his.

Merrick stood on the foredeck of the *Redemption*, arms crossed over his chest, and watched the *Hades' Revenge* come closer into view. It had been no easy task to find Edward in the vast waters of the Caribbean, but he had two things on his side—the wisdom of God and familiarity with Edward's favorite hunting grounds. Even so, he had been surprised when the wicked ship suddenly appeared on his eastern horizon.

After almost a year of searching these treacherous waters for Edward the Terror, why had God allowed Merrick to find him now—now when Charlisse, the woman Merrick loved, was on board? Merrick's jaw clenched as he imagined what Edward—or Kent—might have done to her. His renewed fury toward Edward threatened to blast through the hull of his restraint, releasing a monstrous rage that would be appeased only by Edward's death.

Despite Edward's murderous atrocities at sea and his barbarous slaughter of the Arawak villagers, Merrick had vowed to God not to harm him, but to turn him over to the British authorities for justice to be served. But now, after Edward had nearly gotten Merrick hanged and had captured the woman he loved, Merrick feared, vow or no vow, he would not be able to stop himself from taking up his sword and thrashing Edward to pieces.

As Merrick stared at *Hades' Revenge*, the empty ache left in his heart by Charlisse's absence was beginning to find a hint of consolation at the thought that she was near. He prayed she was still alive. Surely God had not saved Merrick from hanging only to allow Charlisse to suffer a far worse death. Deep within his spirit, he knew she was alive.

Sloane came up beside him. "The *Hades' Revenge*. Now there's a worthy prize to be had fer sure, Cap'n."

"Yes, 'tis true, but my interests lie in a different treasure altogether." Merrick clasped the railing. He had regained the strength lost during his time in prison, and his muscles twitched in anticipation of a fight.

"Aye, that they do." Sloane chuckled. "An' who's to blame ye; who's to blame ye." The pirate rested his hand on the hilt of his cutlass, taking a deep breath of the sea air. "But I 'ave to say, Cap'n, 'tis good to be on the hunt again, even if it be fer Edward the Terror."

Merrick gave his friend a curious look. "Does he frighten you?"

"Me? Naw, Cap'n." Sloane gave him a sideways glance and scratched his gray beard. "But some of the men are a bit feared o' him, 'tis all."

"Are there any who cannot be trusted?"

Sloane looked out toward the *Hades' Revenge*. "Naw, Cap'n, they's all with ye, ye may lay to it. Leastways, there's not one o' them who would rather sail under Edward than ye—not willingly anyway."

Merrick had noticed the tension aboard the ship. It was more than the usual nervous excitement before a conquest. Edward had a reputation for cruelty, not only toward his victims, but toward other pirates who dared cross him. He gave no quarter to anyone who defied him. It was what had made him one of the most feared pirates in the Caribbean. But Merrick knew that those who ruled by fear and brutality often died by the same. Perhaps it was time for Edward to fall under the same vicious sword he'd been wielding.

Jackson came to stand beside Merrick. The *Hades' Revenge* began a slow turn toward the *Redemption*'s larboard side as the distance between the ships diminished.

Merrick chuckled. He knew Edward. The vile captain won more battles by outmaneuvering his opponent than by courage or firing skill. Merrick would never let him take the advantage that was already his. He ordered Jackson to put the helm down, keep close to the wind, and steer the *Redemption* on a course that would bring them upon Edward's quarter.

For the next hour, the two ships engaged in a dance of maneuvers. Edward, using his exquisite skill with sail and wind, attempted every sly move possible to gain the windward advantage over the *Redemption*. Merrick foresaw each advance and managed to keep the upper hand each time while slowly closing the gap between them.

"Turn her hard to starboard," Merrick yelled to Jackson. "Run out the guns, and on my order, put a warning volley over his bow." He glanced at Sloane. "Maybe he's in no mood for a fight." Merrick cocked an eyebrow at his friend as Jackson boomed orders behind him.

The old pirate chuckled. "I do think ye may be a mite disappointed in that, Cap'n."

Merrick grinned, grabbed the glass, and scanned his enemy. After several minutes, he made out Edward standing on the forecastle deck with glass held to his own eye. Merrick lowered the telescope. "By now Edward should have no doubt who his troublesome predator is. That ought to put a flutter in his belly, I should think," Merrick said, a smirk upturning his lips.

" 'Tis Merrick for sure. The audacity of that dawcock." Edward spat, heat radiating up his face. "I should've known it was him." Turning, he slammed into Kent. "And ye. Ye dare show yer face to me now when not twenty minutes ago ye near put me to challenge for both me and me daughter!"

"Let's put that behind us for now, shall we?" Kent offered him a slick, icy smile. "I'm still your first mate, Captain, and you'll need my expertise." Glancing toward the approaching ship, Kent's gaze turned troubled. "How could Merrick have escaped?"

"How should I know? You mutinous barracuda." Edward felt his boiling rage threatening to explode, whether at this loathsome carp standing before him or at the rapid approach of Merrick he didn't know. He moved his face to within inches of Kent's. "Methinks I won't be trustin' ye just now, or ever agin, for that matter." He felt veins pulsing in his neck. "So be gone with ye! Get yer deceivin' hideous face from me sight and—"

"Captain—"

"Quiet your insolent tongue, you arrogant son of a harlot. Off with ye this instant, or I'll do to ye what every inch of me yearns to do—hang ye up by yer toes on the crosstrees until yer fat head pops open!"

Kent's face blanched. The arrogance faded from his eyes. Offering Edward a short bow, he jumped down onto the main deck, and out of sight.

Edward followed him down the steps, calling for Hawkins to replace Kent as first mate. Just then Perkins, the boatswain, who had been in the crosstrees since dawn, shouted, "They're comin' hard about, Cap'n." Then he added, "Incoming!"

Two thunderous booms broke through the silent Caribbean breeze, one right after the other. Edward swung about, furious he'd allowed his anger with Kent to distract him. He marched up to the bow for a better look and saw two voluminous puffs of gray smoke hovering over the *Redemption*. The four-pounders sliced through the air so close he could feel the thrust of them as they zipped past his head. One splashed harmlessly into the sea beyond the port quarter, and the other shattered a section of the bulwark before joining its companion over the side.

Edward bellowed for Hawkins to turn her to larboard, ready the gun crew, and run out the starboard guns. They were warning shots, to be sure, but he would show them just what he thought of their warning.

"Merrick, that insolent English mongrel!"

The blasts from the *Redemption* sent Edward's pirates into a frenzy. They were not used to being fired upon—especially by a fellow pirate. Scrambling across the deck, they gathered arms for the battle ahead, grunting and cursing at the audacity of their enemy.

Dark clouds moved in and hovered over the battle scene like ominous spectators. The wind picked up, blowing Merrick's hair. He tied it behind him and donned his captain's hat. Thankful for the cooling breeze, he hoped it wasn't cool enough to calm the heightened temper of his opponent. If Edward had any weaknesses in battle, they were his pride and his temper. Often he let them both rule him when reason demanded otherwise.

It appeared from the activity aboard the *Hades' Revenge* that the warning shots had accomplished their intended purpose—to stir the tempers of Edward's crew. Now Merrick intended to further goad Edward into making a reckless mistake. Jackson approached. Merrick lowered his glass.

"Turn her to larboard, bearing our guns, loaded and ready," the captain ordered. "But keep three hundred yards' distance from her. Let's see if she'll take the bait."

Merrick lifted his glass again. Oh, for a glance of Charlisse, but she was nowhere in sight. He could only assume she was below, either locked in the hold, or in the captain's cabin. The thought of the latter made his skin crawl with possessive rage. He must be extremely careful not to damage the main body of the ship for fear of inadvertently blasting through an area where Charlisse might be hit.

The *Redemption* sailed teasingly across the starboard side of the *Hades' Revenge*—just within range of her guns, her sails flapping in a tempting display. As expected, Edward the Terror loosed a broadside upon her, spewing forth successive thunderous booms that bounced across the darkening clouds. The shots, however, blasted forth in impotence, landing just short of their target. Billowing smoke obscured the view between the two ships.

Merrick shouted orders to turn the helm hard over on a direct course for the *Hades' Revenge*. Judging both the distance and position of his enemy amidst the haze from the cannon blasts, he ordered a swift turn to larboard and loosed his starboard battery in the direction of Edward's main and foremast. Explosions filled the air, along with the sharp crack of splitting wood and the shrieks of wounded men. With spyglass to his eye, Merrick waited for a clear view, but when the veil of charred mist dissipated, two smoking, ebony holes glared at him from the hull of the *Hades' Revenge*.

"Jackson," Merrick stormed. "In God's name, I told you to position the guns above deck to the masts and sails!" He jumped to the main deck, as terror and fury battled for position in his heart. Lifting the glass again, he searched the deck for any sign of Charlisse.

Jackson's huge frame thudded across the deck. "Aye, Cap'n, that's what I told the master gunner. I dunno what happened."

Merrick scowled at him. "Go see to it, man. Tell them if they can't position the cannons accurately, I'll use them for shark bait and find someone else who can."

Returning his gaze to the *Hades' Revenge*, Merrick saw Edward scrambling over the deck, issuing orders. The other shots from the *Redemption* had shattered the foredeck railing and left the bowsprit hanging in a tangle of cordage athwart the ship's bow. The black fractures left by his round shots stood harmlessly above the waterline. Merrick was still searching for Charlisse when he noticed all sails hoisting and men flying up into the shrouds. The *Hades' Revenge* made a rapid turn, its sails gorging with wind.

It was heading straight toward him.

Slamming the glass shut, Merrick turned on his heels. "All hands, make sail. Turn her hard to starboard, Rusty. Jackson," he yelled, and the colossal dark man sprang up from the companionway. "Ready the larboard battery. Prepare the swivel guns."

"Aye, aye, Cap'n." Jackson bellowed orders that sent the crew of the *Redemption* swarming to their tasks.

Merrick gazed at the oncoming intruder as the *Redemption* swung about, her sails trapping the wind, sending her slicing a white trail through the blue waters on a collision course with the *Hades' Revenge*. He cursed himself for allowing his fear for Charlisse to distract him from his duties. After loosing his broadside cannons, he could have finished Edward off with a speedy turn and another battery of fire from his port side. Instead he had hesitated, and let Edward regroup and charge.

Sloane came and stood beside him.

"The audacity of that mongrel," Merrick said. "We have the wind in our favor, yet he barrels toward us at full speed."

"Har, he be a reckless varmint, that be true, Cap'n." Sloane scratched his beard and grabbed the hilt of his cutlass. "But that also may be the ruin of 'im, too."

A blaze of yellow light flashed from the bow of the *Hades' Revenge*, followed by a thunderous boom.

"All hands down!" Merrick bellowed, sending his crew to their bellies on the deck.

The blast struck the starboard bow of the ship, rupturing the timbers of the hull with a splintering explosion. The *Redemption* rocked and staggered.

Jumping to his feet, Merrick peered over the side at the damage. He had not counted on Edward having a four-pounder at his bow. He looked toward his enemy, now only yards away. "Lower top and main. Turn her hard to port." The mighty ship bungled with shifting sails and sharp rudder, creaking and moaning to make the spiked turn. Within minutes, she would be alongside the *Hades' Revenge*, presenting her larboard broadside.

In his efforts to avoid cannon fire from the *Redemption*, Edward forgot the chasers on her bow. As he played for a better position, he allowed the *Redemption* to close in on him. He realized this too late when he heard the guns blasting behind him and saw the shots rip holes though his mainsail.

Edward desperately tried to bring his ship about in order to bear her larboard guns upon the fast-approaching *Redemption*. With her mainsail damaged, the *Hades' Revenge* floundered in her turn and could not pick up enough speed for the maneuver. All the while, the *Redemption*'s demicannons swept across her deck with crippling fire.

Edward furiously answered her with fire from the chasers on his prow, but it was too late. The *Redemption*, at close quarters, followed up its attack with crossbar shots that cut and slashed mercilessly through the *Hades' Revenge*'s rigging. The ship labored clumsily, powerless to maneuver.

"Grapnels ready! Prepare to board," Merrick's booming commands echoed across the deck of the *Hades' Revenge*. A torrent of musket fire from the top yards of the *Redemption* scattered Edward's crew while Merrick's ship crashed alongside the crippled vessel.

Chapter 40
Bloody Pirates

The blast of cannons echoed through the ship in a thunderous boom and threatened to rip apart her timbers. When Charlisse looked out of her rattling window, gray smoke obscured her view. Her father's gruff bellowing sounded above, followed by the pounding of many boots. Minutes later, the air was aquiver with the roar of guns and the horrified screams of Edward's men. Face pressed against the window, Charlisse strained for a glimpse of the *Redemption*, but it remained out of sight.

Was it Merrick?

Another cannon roared in the distance and an explosion sent a tremor through the *Hades' Revenge*. Something crashed behind her, and she turned to see the door to the cabin had flown open. No one was there. As she approached it, she heard the loud snap of cracking wood. A deafening silence followed, only broken by the twang of snapping cords. Something smashed into the ship sending it reeling to port. Charlisse nearly lost her footing. Then everything erupted into a barrage of shouting and musket fire.

Charlisse crept to the deck of the *Hades' Revenge*. Grappling hooks struck, clawing the wood like giant birds of prey, leaving long splintered trenches in the deck. They locked onto the railing, and the ships smashed together with a jolt that sent a shudder throughout the ship.

Anxiety clenched at her heart as she scanned the huge ship that had rammed the *Hades' Revenge*. She noted Merrick's colors flying above the mainmast, but was he aboard? There stood Sloane and Jackson. Charlisse felt a jitter of excitement. Running her gaze across the mob of pirates, she felt hope give way again to desperation. Then she saw him. He leapt onto the bulwark of the *Redemption*, cutlass in hand, armed with pistols and boarding ax, ready to lead his men into battle. He looked her way and their gazes locked. A smile curved on his lips. He turned and shouted an order to his men. The crew of the *Redemption* scrambled over the railings.

Edward's men cursed at the oncoming intruders who were brandishing swords, knives, and muskets, thrusting them defiantly at his crew. Man met man in a clash of fury and hatred. Ducking behind the mainmast, Charlisse trembled. Pistol and musket shots cracked like whips through the air, spewing smoke and the bitter smell of gunpowder. Steel clanged against steel. Strained groans and frenzied curses bombarded her from all directions. The pirates battled without fear, their assaults vicious and relentless.

One of Edward's men, clutching his chest, fell to the deck near Charlisse. His pleading eyes searched hers, then a vacant stare sucked the life from them. She held her hand up to her mouth, suddenly queasy. Tears welled in her eyes. She heard a piercing screech from her right and turned to see a man with a sword protruding from his belly. His attacker withdrew it and kicked the man backward over the rail. Charlisse heard the hollow splash as his body fell into the sea.

Her gaze found Merrick. He thrashed, cutlass to cutlass, with one of Edward's men, moving swiftly as he parried his enemy's thrusts. Charlisse watched as the pirate's fierce determination faded into weariness. Merrick continued his merciless assault. The man's cutlass flew from his hand. Terror struck his face. Merrick smacked his head with the hilt of his cutlass. He crumpled to the deck.

A pistol shot exploded near Charlisse's head, ringing in her ears. She dropped, arms over her head. The sharp, bitter smell of blood filled her nose. When she looked up, Merrick was gone. Her gaze landed on her father who was battling one of Merrick's men up on the quarterdeck.

Searching the crowd, she saw Sloane in a fierce knife fight with a man much younger than he, and Sloane was getting the best of him.

Then she realized she was the cause of all this bloodshed. *Please, Lord, stop it now. Let no more blood be spilled on my account!* Tears slid down her cheeks.

A muscular arm grabbed her from behind in a savage hold that instantly sealed off her breath. A man's deep, scratchy voice flowed over her ears. She twisted to see who it was. The crotchety face of the red-scarfed pirate who had brought her food when she was imprisoned below leered at her.

"Yer not in a locked cage now, eh, missy?" She thought he was going to drag her down the stairs, but his grip tightened. She gasped for air, realizing he was going to kill her. He whispered something about women on ships bringing bad luck. Then Charlisse couldn't hear any more. Everything grew dark.

Merrick hunted for Edward, the cause of all this madness, while trying to keep an eye on Charlisse. Why didn't the silly girl go below, away from the battle? Though her clothes were tattered and she looked terribly thin, she was an angelic vision, and he thanked the Lord she appeared well.

He quickly disposed of his adversary and glanced toward her again. She was gone. He scanned the deck. Maybe she had finally come to her senses and gone below. A pirate charged him, grimacing through rotting teeth. Lifting his cutlass, Merrick met his blow, sending the man tumbling backward into the middle of another fight. A flash of golden hair caught the corner of Merrick's eye, and he glanced over to see Charlisse struggling in the grip of a brown-haired pirate.

Merrick charged toward her. A young, skinny man jumped in front of him and pointed a pistol at Merrick's head, grinning. Whipping out his boarding ax, Merrick launched it at the weapon, knocking it from the man's grasp. Then he barreled into him, pushing him aside. When he looked up the pirate had a tight grip on Charlisse's throat. The color had drained from her face. Merrick pummeled his way through the riotous crowd. The edge of a cutlass flew at his throat.

"If it don't be Cap'n Merrick," a squeaky voice said. Merrick turned to see a former shipmate of his.

"I don't have time for this right now, Hank." He pushed the cutlass away with one finger.

"Oh, I think ye do, ole friend." Hank turned his quid and spat, then grinned through blackened teeth. "I've a score to settle with ye."

Drawing his cutlass, Merrick met the traitor's challenge. Hilt to hilt, he forced him backward through the bloody fray. Wide-eyed, the man struggled to stay afoot, meeting each blow with quivering sword. Finally, Merrick backed him against the railing, knocked the cutlass from his grasp, and shoved him over the side. Panting, he watched the man plunge into the sea, then rise to the surface, gasping for air. "Now we're settled."

Merrick rushed to Charlisse. Wrenching the man's arms from her throat, Merrick landed a sharp blow across his jaw. The pirate folded to the deck.

Gasping, Charlisse opened her eyes.

"Milady." He bowed graciously.

She ran into his arms. "You're alive."

Relief flowed through Merrick's tense muscles. "Of course. How could I die with such pressing business at hand as the rescue of my fair maiden?" She felt soft in his embrace. He kissed her gently on the forehead. "Did they hurt you?"

"No." She smiled, her eyes shimmering. He saw love in their blue depths, and it set his heart aflame.

"Now get below," he ordered, nodding toward the stairs. Immediately a cutlass came at him. He lifted his own to ward off the blow and pushed the assailant back, away from Charlisse. Two more men advanced upon him. There was no time to see if she had obeyed his command.

In a flash of red hair, Rusty swung to his captain's aid. Within minutes, the two men prevailed against the attacking pirates, and Merrick clapped Rusty on the back, nodding in approval of his new friend's skill with a sword.

Looking up, Merrick spotted Edward on the quarterdeck. Rage suffocated his thoughts. He barreled toward his nemesis, flying up the stairs, cutlass in hand.

The captain had just killed two of Merrick's men, their bodies strewn at his feet. Sweat dripped from his face, and he bent to catch his breath. He looked up as Merrick approached. Fear—or perhaps remorse—flickered across his gaze.

"So it's come down to this, has it, Merrick?" he said, panting.

"By your choice." Merrick clutched his cutlass, waiting for Edward's first blow.

Edward poked his sword into the deck and leaned on it.

Merrick examined his ex-captain. His blue eyes were clear, no longer covered with a glaze of hatred and defiance. They searched Merrick's.

"So you're to kill me then?" Edward asked. "Captain Merrick, the great avenger of all evil."

"Not all evil," Merrick said, a wave of fury rising within him. "Only the murder of innocent people."

"Ah." A crooked grin spread across Edward's mouth. " 'Tis the Indian village you speak of."

Merrick lifted his cutlass, his heart aflame with rage. Yet Edward made no move. "Fight me!" Merrick yelled.

The derisive grin remained on Edward's lips as he stood staunchly in place. His gaze was full of sorrow. Confusion wrestled with Merrick's anger. He could slice Edward in half with one swing. Why didn't he defend himself?

Merrick's cutlass quivered in his clenched fist. Visions of the mutilated bodies of his friends flashed through his mind. He blinked, trying to push them away. He wanted to kill Edward. God help him, he knew it was wrong, but the urge consumed him.

Edward rolled his eyes and sighed. "What are ye waitin' for? Ye always were a yellow-bellied coward," he sneered.

Merrick gripped his cutlass, tightening his muscles. A flash of blond hair obscured his vision as Charlisse rushed in front of her father. "No, please don't!" she pleaded, holding up her hand to stay Merrick's advance. "Please don't kill him." Her eyes swelled with tears and her bottom lip quivered.

Fearing for her safety, Merrick dropped his sword and pulled her away from Edward. But Charlisse yanked her arm from his grasp and returned to her stance between the two men, glaring at them. "Hasn't there been enough killing?"

Edward's eyes widened and his mouth opened as he stared at his daughter. The rumble of thunder echoed in the distance, and the wind tossed both father's and daughter's hair. Pulling his sword from the deck, Edward returned it to its scabbard and sighed. "Perhaps she's right." He looked at Merrick.

Still gripping his cutlass, Merrick tried to release the fury that tore at his soul. "Will there ever be enough killing to suit you?"

Edward shifted his stance, his eyes squinting. "I believe I've had my fill." A glimmer of a smile lifted Edward's cracked lips. Charlisse turned to face him, and Merrick saw warmth in Edward's gaze as he looked at his daughter. Yet Merrick could not quell the grisly images of his butchered friends. The pain of his rage reached his fingertips as they clenched the hilt of his cutlass.

Charlisse swung around, her glistening eyes pleading with him. "People change. Forgive him as you have been forgiven."

Merrick's hatred melted under Charlisse's compassionate plea. Sheathing his cutlass, he nodded at Edward. There was a hint of moisture in Edward's eyes, and he turned aside just as three pirates plunged onto the deck from the ratlines above. Merrick drew his cutlass again and engaged one of them while the other two attacked Edward.

"Go below!" Merrick ordered Charlisse. Out of the corner of his eye, he saw her blond curls descending the quarterdeck stairs.

Charlisse fell onto the bed, trying to quell the shaking that had overtaken her body. She wanted to laugh. She wanted to cry. But no reaction came forth except the constant trembling that spread from her heart to each limb. She knelt to pray.

Boots scuffed the floorboards behind her. Swerving, she smiled, her heart filled with gratitude that Merrick had come for her.

Her eyes locked upon Kent's.

"Hello, my wayward blossom," he said with a sneer.

He wore a suit of black camlet with lace cascading from the sleeves. His dark curly hair was slicked back with a grease that reminded Charlisse of the oil of deceit that dripped from his lips every time he spoke.

"It seems our time together is always interrupted, my love." He shook his head, sauntering toward her. "And now it appears that indeed, as you had hoped, your beloved Merrick has come to rescue you." His gaze steady, he pulled a knife from his baldric.

His voice grew harsh. "Too bad it will be such a short-lived hope for the both of you."

Charlisse gasped and took a step back.

He approached her, his dark eyes flashing.

Glancing to her left, she grabbed the lantern from the table and threw it at him. He ducked and it crashed to the floor behind him, sending slivers of glass over the floorboards.

A wicked grin spread across his lips. Using both hands, she overturned a chair in front of him. He pushed it aside without effort and gave a humorless laugh. "Come now, my sweet. Quit playing games. You know how this upsets me."

She bolted for the door, skirting the table to avoid him, but he flung himself in her path, grabbed her arm, and twisted her around.

Holding the blade to her throat, Kent dragged her out the door and up the stairs. When he reached the deck, he strode defiantly through the skirmish to the leeward rail and backed against it. Charlisse struggled, and the sharp knife bit into her skin.

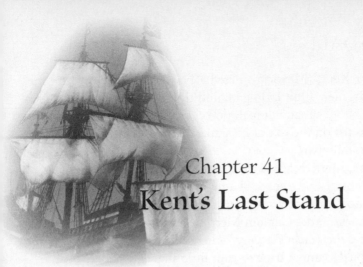

Chapter 41
Kent's Last Stand

Merrick heard a familiar voice calling for attention—a voice that sent a shiver down his spine. Kent. He looked up. Kent stood across the main deck, holding a knife to Charlisse's throat. Edward glanced up, too. Both men abandoned their opponents. Merrick jumped over the quarterdeck railing and landed with a thud on the deck while Edward rushed down the stairs, sword in hand.

"Hold up there, boys," Kent said, leaning over Charlisse, pressing the blade into her creamy skin. "I've got a bargain to make with you." He smiled, eyes flickering with excitement. Merrick and Edward stopped, brandishing their swords before them.

"What are ye up to, boy?" Edward stormed.

Merrick saw nothing but the tiny stream of blood that slid down Charlisse's neck. How could he have forgotten about Kent? He cursed himself silently as each nerve in his body lit like a fuse. The fighting faded around them as the ensuing challenge drew the pirate's gazes.

"Ah, I see I've gotten your attention." Kent's dark brows lifted in feigned innocence. As for you, my erstwhile captain," he said, looking at Edward, "you are in my debt, sir, for if I had not stopped this embarrassing display of a skirmish, which you might erroneously have called skilled combat, I fear you and your men would soon be dead." He sighed, feigning disappointment. "A tragedy for such a famed pirate as yourself."

Edward grunted and made an angry start toward Kent.

"Ah, ah, ah, I wouldn't be doing that."

"Let her go, Kent," Merrick ordered. "This is between you and me. Let's settle it like men. Quit hiding behind the skirt of a lady." Merrick's eyes met Charlisse's. Fear and desperation clouded their usual blue clarity. He clenched his fist on the hilt of his cutlass, resisting the urge to bolt at Kent and slice him in two.

"But you see, Merrick, this lovely lady has everything to do with it." Kent cocked his head, and a spark of amusement crossed his eyes. "She is, after all, the reason for your visit to our fair ship, is she not?" He paused. "This is my proposal. You, Captain Merrick, and your band of worthless ingrates will leave the *Hades' Revenge*." He nodded in the direction of the *Redemption*. "You'll scamper back to your little ship and sail far away."

"And why would I do that?" Merrick asked.

"Because, my dear captain, if you don't, I'll be forced to slice your fair lady's sweet neck." His keen eyes turned hard and cold.

Edward jumped at Kent's threat, but Merrick's firm arm held him back. Merrick had no doubt Kent was capable of carrying out his threat—if only from spite. "But if you kill her, what reason do I have not to cut you to pieces?"

"None, I suppose," Kent said. "But look around you, Captain—what have I got to lose? If I release her, you will win this battle, and I and this crew will find ourselves either dead or your prisoners. If I kill her, you will still win this battle. The only difference is, in one case she lives and the other she dies." His mustache twitched above an insolent grin. He tightened his arm across her chest and held her in place with the sharp point of his blade. "But if I threaten to kill her and you believe that I shall"—he waved his free hand through the air—"which I know you do, then you will retreat. The lady will live—just not with you." He buried his nose in her hair and took a deep breath, smiling. "She will learn to love me in time. And I assure you, I will give her cause to forget all about you."

Merrick glared at Kent, contemplating the ultimatum.

Edward, on the other hand, did not hold his temper so well. His face fumed red. Purple veins pulsed on his thick neck.

"Ye'll be doin' nothin' of the kind," Edward bellowed, his eyes black slits. "After Merrick and his men leave, I'm still the cap'n of this ship, and you'll not be touchin' me daughter!"

Merrick started, surprised by Edward's declaration.

Kent chuckled. "Oh, I forgot about you, Uncle." He smiled unpleasantly. "There'll be no problem there, for you will be on board the *Redemption* with your good friend here." He nodded toward Merrick. "And I'll be the new captain of the *Hades' Revenge*."

Edward charged Kent, cutlass in hand. "That's enough of this foolery, ye young half-wit. Unhand my daughter!"

Merrick—seeing the unleashed evil in Kent's eyes—tried to stop Edward, but he was too late.

Kent stumbled backward. Charlisse gasped and struggled as the knife dug deeper into her skin, releasing a wider stream of blood.

Merrick lunged forward, but stopped when he saw the deranged look in Kent's eyes.

Edward sheathed his sword and used both hands to pry the knife from Kent's grasp. Suddenly, his blue eyes widened. Shock registered on his features. Clutching his midsection, he staggered backward, his gaze shifting to Kent's with a look of painful bewilderment. He looked down, staring for a moment at the hilt protruding from his stomach. Pulling it from his gut, he examined the blade curiously, as if he could not fathom how it had gotten there. A red splotch blossomed on his waistcoat, expanding in a purple death march across the blue fabric. The bloody weapon fell from his hand and clanked to the deck. Edward stumbled, grabbed his midsection, and toppled, moaning.

Charlisse cried out, struggling to be free, but the sharp blade at her throat kept her tightly in Kent's grasp. Tears streamed down her checks.

Edward's crew shifted restlessly, grumbling. Yet not one made a move on Kent.

Kent's eyes held a frenzied look. He held the knife toward Merrick, tightening his grip on Charlisse with his other hand. "Sheath your cutlass. You and your crew will take your leave now," he commanded.

Merrick's eyes locked on Kent's, detecting the fear behind his insolent gaze. For a moment, Merrick said nothing, his mind racing. Out of the corner of his eye, he saw movement, but he did not avert his gaze from Kent's face.

Bowing politely, Merrick conceded. "As you wish." Then with a glance at Sloane, he nodded for his crew to proceed toward the *Redemption*.

Kent backed up farther against the railing, his lips twisting in a grin.

Merrick's crew shuffled begrudgingly toward their ship amidst a barrage of insults from Edward's men.

Charlisse's wide eyes locked on Merrick's. "Don't leave me here with him," she eked out in a scratchy voice.

Kent yanked her back, raising the knife under her chin. "Silence, you wench!"

Merrick froze, arresting every urge within him to pounce on Kent. Charlisse's head tilted upward to avoid the blade. A tear spilled from her right eye and slid into her hair. Her whole body trembled.

She tried to lower her head, but the point of the knife kept her in place. "Let him kill me. I'd rather be dead then be his mistress."

"I said, silence!" Kent pushed the blade and it pierced her skin. She choked.

Merrick clenched his fists over the hilt of his cutlass and glanced at Sloane. The pirate pointed up, then down, then covered his eyes with his hands.

"What are you doing, you crazy old man?" Kent yelled, pointing his knife at Sloane. "Stop that and be gone with you!"

Sloane shrugged and fell in line behind his shipmates.

The crew of the *Hades' Revenge* came forward, continuing to sling obscenities at the retreating pirates—willing, it seemed, to forget the attack on their captain and follow a new leader who promised immediate victory. Kent stood defiantly with knife outstretched, eyeing Merrick as he took his place behind Sloane.

As he passed Kent, Merrick stopped and stared into his eyes. Where there was life in Charlisse's, there was death in his, where there was love and joy and caring in hers, in his there was hate and selfishness—how completely different two members of the same family could be.

Droplets of sweat beaded on the young pirate's forehead. His knife quivered in his hand. He searched Merrick's eyes as if he knew his victory was not yet sure. "I told you to go. Now take your leave!" he bellowed.

Sloane cleared his throat. With fingers signaling into the wind, he nodded his head toward Kent.

"Are you daft, you insufferable fool?" Kent pointed his blade toward Sloane. "Stop that or I'll lance you to the keel and let the barnacles leech your old bones dry!"

With a slight chuckle, Sloane turned away.

Kent veered toward Merrick. "You, too—move, or I'll run you through!"

A soft chattering filled the air.

Merrick looked up.

Kent followed his gaze.

Sloane's monkey sprang down and covered Kent's eyes with two little hands. He stumbled backward. The blade cut deeper into Charlisse's flesh. She shrieked. Without releasing her, Kent tossed his body back and forth, trying to shake the creature's hold on his neck. His knife sliced through the air in front of him, daring anyone to come near.

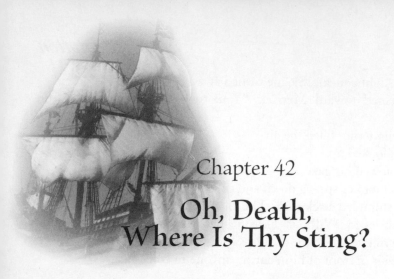

Chapter 42

Oh, Death, Where Is Thy Sting?

"To the battle, men!" Merrick yelled. His crew swarmed back over the bulwarks. The clank of sword and crack of pistol were accompanied by thunder bellowing across the sky.

Merrick charged Kent. With one hand, he wrenched the knife from Kent's grasp while he struck him in the jaw with the other, sending him flying onto the deck.

Charlisse rushed into Merrick's arms, sobbing.

He engulfed her in his embrace. "You're all right now," he said, still keeping an eye on Kent, who floundered on the deck.

Retrieving a handkerchief from his pocket, Merrick held it to Charlisse's neck, pressing it gently to stop the bleeding. To his relief, the wound did not appear too deep. He tied the cloth around the back of her neck and wiped the tears from her cheeks. Her liquid blue eyes reflected nothing but love and admiration. Holding her, he kissed her forehead and waited for her shuddering to cease when she gasped, jerked from his arms and ran to her father's side. Kneeling beside him, she squeezed his hand.

One eye opened. His face looked so pale against his blood-drenched waistcoat. He offered her a feeble smile.

"Father," Charlisse cried.

Turning, Merrick ordered his men to subdue the remainder of Edward's crew, and then had them bound, along with Kent, and locked up below. With Jackson's assistance, Merrick carried Edward to his cabin and summoned Brighton. Charlisse sat beside her father's bed while the doctor tended to his wound.

Leaning in the doorway of Edward's cabin, Merrick watched her. She never left her father's side, and he could not deny some surprise at the sentiment that seemed to exist between them. It was hard to imagine Edward the Terror capable of any depth of feeling toward anyone—even his own daughter. Yet Merrick had witnessed his defense of Charlisse at the risk of his own life, an action that could only have sprung from a father's love.

The sweet treasure of a girl who now held her father's hand so affectionately acted as though Edward had been a doting father all his life. What a heart of gold she had—capable of melting away the hard shell of corruption from every scoundrel who crossed her path. If it hadn't been for her intervention, Merrick feared he would have given in to his fury and killed Edward. Now he realized how wrong that would have been, for only God had the right to take a life. Once again, Merrick had tried to take control back from God—had tried to take matters into his own hands, as if the good Lord couldn't handle things Himself. From now on he determined to trust God, no matter what happened.

Merrick waited for some sign from Brighton on Edward's condition. After patching his cut as best he could, the doctor looked up and shook his head. Charlisse dropped to her father's shoulder and sobbed.

Merrick walked over, kissed her on the cheek, and gave her hand a squeeze. "I'll be on deck if you need me," he whispered. She nodded without looking up.

Charlisse reached for a handkerchief to dry her tears and glanced at her father. Edward peered at her through half-open lids. "Naw, don't be crying now, girl," he said with difficulty. "I'm not worth your tears."

Charlisse dipped a cloth into a basin of water and wiped the blood from his lips. "You are still my father."

Edward tried to laugh but managed only a cough of blood. "And a fine father I've been to you, to be sure," he sputtered.

"It doesn't matter now. I love you."

The pirate's eyes opened wide. He looked at Charlisse with a mixture of shock and sorrow. "You love *me*?" he grunted. "After I abandoned you as a babe, kidnapped you. . ." He coughed up more blood and took a labored breath. "Then threw you in the hold with barely anything to eat?"

"Now, shhh. . . You protected me from Kent. You stood up for me," Charlisse interjected. She dabbed at his head with the damp cloth.

He looked at her, his blue eyes moistening. "That was the only decent thing I done in my whole life." He gave her hand a squeeze. "That and marry your mother."

Charlisse smiled. Her eye filled with tears.

Edward cringed in pain. "You're the spittin' image of Helena."

"Did you love her?"

Edward turned away, closing his eyes. "With all my heart." There was a long silence. His breathing became labored. "If I could just make things up to you and your mother, I would."

Charlisse brushed the tears from her cheek, trying to remain strong.

He gazed at her. "I would do things so differently—so very differently," he gasped. "You have her sweetness, her forgiveness." He tried to smile.

Charlisse dabbed at the blood that dripped from his mouth.

"I've made such a mess of things," he whispered, "such a mess of my life."

A thought came to Charlisse, a gentle, silent urging. "Father," she began softly, "are you truly sorry for the things you've done?"

"I am now." He coughed. "Things become clear, I suppose, when you're so close to death. Oh, what a wicked man I have been, my girl!" He took a desperate gasp for air.

"It's not too late for you," she said with renewed hope and a sense of urgency. "All the horrid things you've done can be forgiven—and forgotten—just as if you'd never done them."

Edward cocked an eyebrow at her. "Naw, not for the likes of me."

"Father, the Son of God came to earth and paid the price for *all* of our wrongdoings. All we have to do is call on His name and repent. Will you, Father? Then you can have eternal life," she said, excitement stirring within her, "and see Mother again, too!"

Was it possible that after her father had spent years wallowing in the thick darkness of evil, his eyes could finally be opened to the truth? Was it too late, or could she penetrate the enemy's strongholds in his mind and shine God's love through the shroud of wickedness that had taken residence there? Then his death wouldn't be a good-bye. She would see him again in a far better place. *Oh, Lord, please open his heart.*

Edward looked at Charlisse. A glimmer of hope sparkled in his clouded eyes. "It's too late for me, girl. I've been far too evil." He struggled with each breath. His grasp on Charlisse's hand weakened.

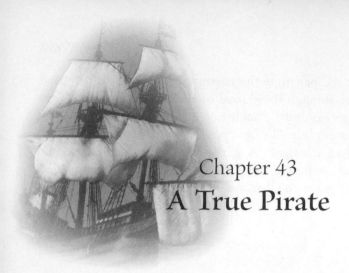

Chapter 43
A True Pirate

Charlisse watched as Edward's chest heaved. His blue eyes began to lose their glimmer. With one last minute of clarity, he looked at her and said, "I love you, my sweet Charlisse."

She squeezed his hand—a hand that was growing cold. The inescapable pull of eternity tugged on Edward's soul. Tears streamed down Charlisse's face as she watched the life slowly fade from his gaze. Finally, his grip on her hand loosened. He turned and looked straight up into the room, past her. His gaze remained there for a few brief seconds, and a trace of a smile appeared on his pale lips. He opened his mouth and softly uttered the words, "I see Him." He gasped. "Jesus, I repent." Then, with a groan and a sigh, he released his last breath, leaving this world.

Brighton prepared Edward's body for burial at sea. At twilight, as angry storm clouds gathered around the two ships, Captain Merrick, Charlisse, and a crowd of miscreant pirates stood around the wrapped form of Edward the Terror as it lay on the plank, ready to be slid into its watery grave.

Out of respect for Charlisse, Merrick had demanded his crew attend the ceremony. They stood, hats off, and maintained an attitude of polite decorum—more difficult for some than others. After all, none of them had kind feelings toward Edward. Most, in fact, had reason to hate him, but Merrick could plainly see from Charlisse's sorrow that there was more to his nemesis than he had known. According to her, the man may have been able to squeeze through the pearly gates at the last minute. He grimaced at the thought and prayed that should their paths cross in heaven, he would no longer have the desire to skewer Edward with a sword.

The wind picked up, and thunder echoed in the distance as Merrick read a long passage from his Bible. Finally, he concluded: "For whosoever shall call upon the name of the Lord shall be saved."

The plank was lifted, and Edward's body slid off into the churning waters. A flash of lightning lit up the western horizon as if in recognition of a soul slipping from time into eternity.

The men disbanded, and Charlisse fell into Merrick's arms. He held her for several minutes. A clap of thunder roared, shaking the ship.

"Let's get you to a cabin where you can rest," Merrick whispered in her ear. "The rain is coming, and you must be exhausted."

She looked up at him. "I love you, Merrick."

He had thought he would never hear those words from her lips. A burst of joy warmed his heart. Wiping hair from her face, he leaned down to kiss her.

A downpour of rain interrupted them, and Merrick lifted her in his arms and carried her to the *Redemption*.

While Merrick attended to business, Brighton properly bandaged Charlisse's neck, and Sloane brought her water and fresh clothes. Elated to be back aboard the *Redemption*, she kept assuring herself it was not a dream, that she wouldn't wake up to find herself still in the hold of the *Hades' Revenge*, or worse, in Kent's cabin. *Oh, Lord, that it would not be so, that you truly have answered my prayers.*

Then she remembered her father and realized she could never have dreamed a parting such as his. Although saddened by his death, she knew with certainty he had called on the name of Jesus. No one left this world with such a peaceful, happy look on their face unless they saw a vision of where they were going, or of the one who guided them there. Now, after all the lonely, miserable years apart, her father and mother were together again. Finally, the Lord had reunited them, and not her uncle, nor any force on earth, could pull them asunder.

Later in the evening, as the rain pounded on the deck above her,

Merrick joined Charlisse for dinner. They laughed and talked and basked in each other's presence, sharing everything that had happened to them since the last time they had seen each other—Merrick's daring escape from prison, Charlisse's kidnapping, her confinement in the hold, and her terrifying ordeal with Kent. Merrick sat on the edge of his chair, his eyes lit with excitement at the miraculous ways God had rescued her—especially the circle of light.

"We know we serve an all-powerful God," he said, shaking his head, "and with Him, nothing is impossible. Yet when He performs such astonishing feats, we still find ourselves baffled." He placed her hands in his. Bowing his head, he prayed aloud, thanking God for keeping Charlisse safe and for bringing them together again.

By midnight, the storm had passed through without harm, and Charlisse could hardly keep her eyes open. Desperately, she tried to stay awake, not wanting to miss a moment of her time with Merrick.

Sprawled on the leather chair next to the bed, he raked a hand through his hair and smiled. How many times had they sat just like this, talking? Yet before, Charlisse had been terrified of this rakish pirate and his seductive leer. Now she knew he would never hurt her.

He stood. "I've kept you up too long. You need your rest."

Charlisse shook her head. "I don't want you to leave."

He kissed a wayward tear that slid down her cheek. "I'm not going anywhere." He held out his hands. "See, touch me, I'm real."

Charlisse rushed into his arms. He lowered his head and placed his lips on hers, sending her world exploding into intoxicating flames. Melting into him, she abandoned herself to the hunger of his kiss. She felt the firm muscles underneath his shirt and the strength of his arms as they encircled her. He ran his fingers through her long golden curls, and then withdrew, leaving her breathless. He cupped her chin lovingly. "God willing, I'm never leaving you again." One side of his lips curved upward. "You've been braver than most men I know." He kissed her forehead, and sighed. "But if the Lord allows me the privilege, I will take care of you forever."

He stepped back, an expression of concern on his face. "You're shivering."

Charlisse looked away, feeling heat rise on her face.

"Are you ill?"

She shook her head, giving him a sideways glance. "'Tis your words, Captain, and. . .your touch. They seem to have a powerful effect on me."

Merrick chuckled—a deep, guttural laugh that warmed Charlisse's heart. He hugged her. "That is a good thing, my love, a very good thing."

He pushed her back, gesturing toward the bed. "Now get some rest." Grabbing his weapons, he headed toward the door.

"Where are you going?" Charlisse felt the familiar clench of dread around her heart.

Turning, he lifted a brow. "It wouldn't be prudent for me to stay here with you tonight."

"I don't understand."

"It was much easier to resist you when you shunned my advances, milady. Now I fear it would be impossible." His lips curved in a provocative grin.

Charlisse twisted a lock of hair between her fingers, unsure of her safety without Merrick close by. "What about your crew?"

"Believe me, I have no trouble resisting *them*." His eyes glinted with amusement.

Charlisse grabbed a pillow from the bed and threw it across the room, just missing Merrick as he ducked out of the way. "You cad, you know what I meant!"

Chuckling, Merrick opened the door. "I'll remain outside, milady. You will be safe," he said, offering her a wink before he closed the door behind him.

Charlisse leapt onto the bed. As tired as she was, she felt like dancing around the cabin. Just yesterday, she had feared for her virtue under the lecherous hands of Kent. Days before, she had faced rats and near starvation in the stench-filled, disease-ridden hold of the *Hades' Revenge*. And in each situation, God had protected her. Even so, she never could have dared to hope that she would be reunited with Merrick. Truly God was all powerful and all-loving, and He cared for His children as Reverend Thomas had said.

Falling back onto the bed, Charlisse gave thanks to the Lord for all His mercies and quickly fell asleep.

Warm rays of sun danced over Charlisse's closed lids, startling her from the deepest sleep she'd had in weeks. She sprang up, rubbing her eyes, and looked around. *Merrick's cabin*. She hadn't dreamt her rescue after all.

After splashing water onto her face and running a comb through her hair, she donned the dress Merrick had left for her, ran up the companionway stairs, and burst forth onto the main deck, silk and lace flowing behind her. Eyes turned her way, but only one pair of eyes interested her—the one that was watching her from the quarterdeck.

Merrick stood, telescope in hand, next to Jackson and another pirate she had not seen before. The captain's piercing gaze never left her as she bounced up the stairs and approached him.

His mouth curved in a sensuous smile. "Perhaps I should keep you hidden for fear I'll have to fight every rogue on board this ship before sundown."

She smiled, feeling the intense stare of the pirate next to Merrick— the one with the shock of red hair and a freckled face.

"My apologies," Merrick said. "Lady Charlisse Bristol, this is Rusty, our new helmsman." He nodded toward the man, who promptly bowed and said, "Nice to meet ye, miss, especially since ye're the cap'n's lady." He grinned, revealing a set of straight, pearly-white teeth.

"Rusty was in prison with me," Merrick added.

"Indeed," Charlisse said. "Then I am very glad to make your acquaintance, sir." She curtsied, and Rusty turned a shade of red to match his hair.

A monkey scampered down from the ratlines and jumped onto Charlisse's shoulder. She shrieked.

"Sorry, miss." Sloane jumped up the stairs. "I haven't quite got 'im trained."

Charlisse giggled and scratched the monkey's head. "It's perfectly all right. He's a charming little fellow, aren't you, little one?" The creature grinned and leaned against her cheek.

"I do think he likes ye, miss." Sloane chuckled. "He don't take to most people so quickly."

"I believe I've met this little guy before." Charlisse examined the monkey as he played with her hair. "At the Dead Reckoning." A shiver ran through her, stealing her smile, as she remembered the place.

Sloane nodded. "Aye, that's where I found 'im. He belonged to a pirate named Flint."

The horrifying vision of her father stabbing Flint through with his cutlass invaded her mind. Her father had been a brutal man, without any regard for life, but she knew now, deep down, that he was with his heavenly Father. All had been forgiven.

She turned, smiling at the little creature that was still perched on her shoulder. "And if memory serves me right, this is the little fellow who saved the day yesterday. Are you the same monkey who aided in Merrick's escape, as well?"

"Aye, that be true, miss. That he did." He grabbed the monkey from Charlisse's shoulder.

Merrick excused himself and strode to the railing, lifting the glass to his eye.

Charlisse sensed a change in his mood. "What's the matter?" She glanced from Merrick back to the three pirates who stood beside her.

Jackson finally answered. "Royce sighted a sail on the starboard horizon just under an hour ago, but she's not shown herself since."

A call from above confirmed their fears. "Sail ho! Cap'n, sail ho!"

Merrick looked up to the crow's nest. "Where away?"

"Nor'–nor'east, sir," came the quick reply.

Merrick lifted the glass once more, intently scanning the horizon. Sloane and Jackson joined him with Charlisse on their heels. Merrick sighed and handed the glass to Jackson, who took a quick look. He nodded at Merrick.

"What?" Charlisse asked, desperation cracking her voice. The gleeful mood from only a moment ago had dissipated into one that was earnest and grave.

Merrick looked into her eyes, anxiety furrowing his brow. Charlisse could tell his mind was racing in a thousand directions.

"That ship out there," Merrick said, nodding toward the horizon, "is a British warship. And she is at full sail, heading our way."

Charlisse's heart fell. She felt all her dreams, all the elation, of the past few hours slowly slipping away.

"You'll be hanged," she said in a tone of dazed resignation.

"That, milady, is not my intention." He turned and issued a series of swift orders, sending the three men by his side rushing off to do his bidding. He took Charlisse aside. Sorrow filled his eyes. It frightened her. Lifting her hand, he laid a gentle kiss upon it. "I'm sorry, Charlisse. I had hoped they would not find me so soon. I had hoped to settle you safely in the Americas until I could clear my name."

"We can still do that!" Charlisse pleaded. "We can outrun them."

"No, I would never put you in harm's way." He sighed, looking away. "You will go with Sloane on the *Hades' Revenge* and—"

"No, I will not! I won't leave you." Tears brimmed in her eyes. "Besides, my father's ship cannot sail."

"No, not very fast, but with a few quick repairs, it can make some progress."

She opened her mouth to protest, but he laid a finger over her lips. "Listen." He squeezed her hand. "Sloane will take you to an island where the ship can be repaired while I draw the British away. It is me they want."

She shook her head, trembling. He continued, "I will deal with the British authorities. I will clear my name, and I will return to get you." He lifted her chin and stared into her eyes.

"You said you'd never leave me again."

Merrick grabbed her shoulders. "I *will* return for you."

Reluctantly, she nodded, and he drew her into his arms. Charlisse could have stood forever in his strong embrace, but Sloane returned, and Merrick was forced to attend to his duties. Time was critical. The British warship was rapidly gaining on them.

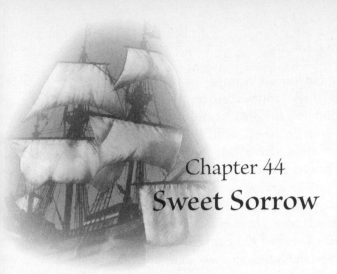

Chapter 44
Sweet Sorrow

Charlisse stood on the foredeck of the *Redemption*, holding back her tears. She watched Merrick as he and his men scrambled to make the *Hades' Revenge* seaworthy. They gathered the scattered pieces of the mizzenmast and mainsail and stored them below, and then hoisted the fore- and aft sails to ensure they could still hold enough wind to propel the ship. A dark hole, outlined in charred, splintered wood, stared from where one of Merrick's cannons had blasted through the hull, but since it was above the waterline, the pirates took little note of it.

When the preparations were done, Merrick selected twenty of his crew and made Sloane their captain. He gave them instructions on both course and conduct and put Charlisse under Sloane's care, warning the others that if she were harmed in any way, they would answer to him.

Charlisse watched Merrick's every move, memorizing the way he sauntered across the deck, his authoritative gestures, the flexing of his muscles beneath his shirt, the deep resonance of his voice. She didn't want to forget anything about him lest she never be graced to see him again. She tried to pray, but could not. Nothing made sense anymore. Through all her terrifying trials, God had protected her—had proven His faithfulness, and then brought Merrick back to her. Why would He take him away now? She had thought they would be together forever. She shook her head, and a tear escaped its lashed boundary and slid down her cheek. What cruel joke was God playing on her now? Just last night she had felt so assured of His love and care, but now she felt nothing but despair and loneliness.

Jackson's shaved head popped up from the hatch of the *Hades' Revenge*. Right behind him emerged Kent, his wavy, brown hair a chaotic mess. With a firm grip on Kent's arm, Jackson hauled him across the deck and over the bulwarks. The stylish pirate stumbled along, hands and feet shackled, head bowed. Merrick stood on the deck of the *Redemption* waiting his arrival. Kent looked up and sneered at Merrick, then his gaze landed on Charlisse up on the foredeck. A licentious grin spread on his lips. Even though he was bound in irons, Charlisse felt her blood run cold under his stare. Merrick shoved Kent along, following him until Jackson had dragged him down the companionway stairs and out of sight.

Charlisse drew a deep breath and looked out over the sea. The British ship loomed clearly against the blue horizon. Soon it would be within firing range. How would Merrick escape? Feeling his gaze upon her, she looked down. His eyes locked with hers. A look of love and understanding flowed from them. He held out his hand and bade her come.

It was time to leave.

Sloane and the others were already boarding her father's ship, getting ready to release the ropes that held the two vessels together. When she reached Merrick, he leaned down and kissed her gently, then gazed into her eyes and caressed her cheek with his thumb.

"Ye best be goin', Cap'n," Sloane shouted from the deck of the *Hades' Revenge*. He held out his hand to receive Charlisse.

Merrick assisted her over the railing. She didn't want to let go of his hand. Turning, she stared at him. His dark eyes moistened. A curve of a smile lifted the corner of his mouth. Charlisse saw strength behind his gaze and it comforted her. Giving her hand a squeeze, he released her into Sloane's waiting arms.

Clutching the railing of the *Hades' Revenge*, Charlisse watched as the grapnels were released and Merrick gave orders for every span of canvas on the *Redemption* to be unfurled. Anxious to catch the full wind and fill their hungry mouths, the loose stretches of fabric fluttered in the Caribbean breeze.

Fully armed for the forthcoming hostilities, Merrick stood near the main deck rail and issued commands to his crew. His loose, black hair darted in the breeze. He turned to look at Charlisse as the ships separated.

She felt her heart would burst with love for him and the wrenching pain of losing him again. Under his intense gaze, his affection seemed to close the gulf between their souls even as the gulf between their physical bodies widened.

The *Redemption* turned and caught the wind. The sails expanded to bursting, jolted the mighty ship, and sent it slicing a rapid course through the turquoise waters. She watched Merrick until she could see him no longer, and then she watched the ship itself until it was a speck on the horizon.

If Merrick stared at her long enough, took in every detail—the slight upturn of her nose, her dark lashes encircling ocean-blue eyes that reflected her sweet spirit, her long curls, glittering like gold in the sunlight, the soft, gentle curves of her body, the way she looked at him as if her heart was his alone—if he memorized every detail, then no matter how long they were apart, he could bring her image into his thoughts and find comfort there.

He hated leaving her. But to take her with him meant to endanger her life, and since God had trusted him with such a precious angel to protect, he intended to fulfill that responsibility—even if it cost him everything.

Not wanting to subject Charlisse to a life of piracy, nor to the constant fear of his being caught and hung, he had formulated a plan. The sudden appearance of the warship had altered that plan. He could not secure Charlisse in the Americas right away as he had hoped, but if his absence extended longer than two months he'd left specific instructions for Sloane to take her there. In the meantime, his efforts to procure his acquittal would have to be hastened.

That was one of the reasons he had brought Kent on board the *Redemption*. Not that he could get the traitorous cad to admit any foul play to the governor, but perhaps he would inadvertently disclose information pertaining to someone who would. He'd also wanted Kent as far from Charlisse as possible. The young pirate obviously had an unhealthy fixation with Miss Bristol, and although Merrick could certainly understand why, he suspected Kent's obsession had more to do with revenge and rivalry than with any affection for the girl herself.

The *Hades' Revenge* disappeared into the blue haze, and Merrick turned to the business at hand, trying to keep his mind off the exquisite girl he had left behind—the only girl in the world who had ever possessed his heart.

A thunderous roar split the calm morning air, bouncing across the white clouds. Merrick spun around to see a puff of black smoke spewing from the British ship. "All hands on deck! Beat to quarters!" he shouted, leaping to the quarterdeck. The round shot hit the *Redemption* with a shattering blast.

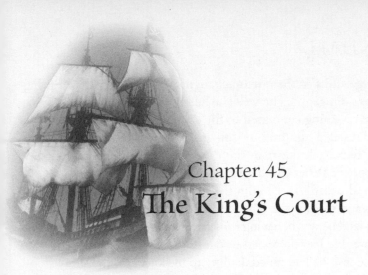

Chapter 45
The King's Court

Merrick shuffled into the courthouse, the chains on his bare ankles clanking over the marble floor. Hard iron rubbed against the rat bites on his feet with each step he took. Ahead of him, another prisoner staggered in, shoved forward by one of the two soldiers who had escorted them from the dungeons of Fort Charles.

The small but ominous hall of justice, situated just east of the governor's mansion, was thronged with spectators, inside and out. The room's tall stone pillars and white tile floors were only a mock imitation of the grandeur with which its predecessors in England were arrayed. At the far end, behind raised benches, sat seven men: Judge Baron Wilhelm, Governor Moodyford, the deputy governor, and four prominent men from Port Royal. Dressed in scarlet robes and thick white periwigs, they shifted uncomfortably in the stifling heat that permeated the building.

As the prisoners entered, the crowd erupted with howls and jeers, hurling insults at the captives. A crier yelled not once, but twice, to silence the unruly mob, and the second time with a threat of imprisonment. Finally the noise dulled to a murmur of hushed voices.

Merrick examined the prisoner who stumbled ahead of him, a pitiful-looking fellow who at one time must have been strong and virile, but now, after what Merrick guessed to have been many months in prison, was an emaciated shell of a man. He plodded forward, his head hung low, his ragged breeches revealing a multitude of festering sores.

Merrick silently thanked the Lord for the trial that was about to commence. Regardless of the outcome, anything was better than rotting away in the fort's dungeons. The week he had been incarcerated before his escape had been nothing compared to the six weeks he had just endured. Why had God rescued him from prison and reunited him with Charlisse only to throw him back down in the dungeon? Hadn't Merrick finally given up all control? What else did God want from him?

For days he'd paced his cell with the fury of a wild animal, pounding the stone walls and shaking the bars until he felt he was going mad. Then, one day, he realized he was behaving no differently from when he had been locked up before. He had professed to put his complete trust in God, but when put to the test, he had failed. Falling to his knees on the slimy stone floor, Merrick had repented and reaffirmed his faith in God's plan and his acceptance of whatever would come of it.

Afterward, with a much lighter heart and more peaceful spirit, the rest of his time behind bars—though certainly not pleasant—had been bearable. Reverend Thomas visited him nearly every day to offer encouragement and comfort. Without his friend, Merrick wasn't sure his faith would have remained so strong for all those long weeks. Also, the knowledge that Charlisse was safe and would be well cared for comforted Merrick a great deal. Some days he felt his heart would burst in anguish without her, but he knew it was up to the Lord whether they would ever be together again.

Merrick glanced up as they approached the judge's bench. Judge Baron Wilhelm's reputation preceded him. He was a vicious man, unsympathetic for the lot of the helpless and no lover of the truth. It was said he hated these yearly trips and despised the British outposts as uncultured havens of debauchery and lawlessness. He tolerated the assignment only to improve his position with the king's court and therefore expedited each case as quickly as possible. The only hope a prisoner had was that on the day of his trial, the judge would be in a favorable temperament.

That hope was quickly dissolved. The baron sat sifting through documents, his countenance sullen and angry. Sweat trickled down his swollen cheek. He reached periodically to scratch under his white, curled periwig. With a sigh, he looked up, annoyance tugging on his features. His face was pale from lack of sun, his folded neck was thick and flabby, and the dark bags under his eyes spoke of many a sleepless night. Merrick's heart almost went out to him until he bellowed the name of the first prisoner with such animosity it seemed he had already pronounced a death sentence.

The first prisoner stepped forward. The clerk of arraigns faced the crowd, and reading from a scrolled document, relayed the charges against him. . .something about thievery and impersonating an officer. Merrick wasn't paying attention, his gaze shifted between the faces of the judge and the prisoner. While the other judges remained attentive, Judge Wilhelm, head on one hand, gazed at the ceiling and sighed.

After the reading, the judge asked the man for his plea—guilty or not guilty. A long pause ensued, in which the man said nothing and the judge's countenance grew livid.

"What say you, man? I asked you a question. Are you guilty of these crimes or not?"

Still, not a sound was uttered—even from the crowd. The breeze rustling through the trees outside the hall and the squawking of sea birds flying over the nearby bay were the only noises that filtered through the room. Judge Wilhelm patted the sweat from his brow with his handkerchief and glanced at the prisoner with a look of arrogant disdain. He nodded for a nearby officer to approach the man.

"You will address this court when spoken to, sir, or I will have your tongue loosened by less amiable means," he bellowed.

The ragged man stood unmoving, shoulders hunched, head bowed, silent as the grave—either from brave defiance, which was to be commended, or an irreparable indifference, which could only be pitied.

At Judge Wilhelm's nod, the soldier drew his sword and struck the man hard across the back with the hilt, sending him toppling to the ground. The crowd gasped. Merrick flinched, aching to return the favor. The prisoner lay for several seconds before slowly rising to his feet. He lifted his head, opened his eyes, and stared with such solemn intensity into the droopy eyes of the judge that the man squirmed in his seat.

Still the prisoner said nothing, and Merrick found his respect for him growing as fast as his pity had before.

Judge Wilhelm regained his haughty composure and proclaimed in a loud voice, "I have no choice, therefore, but to find you guilty on all charges by your own unwillingness to voice any objections." He glared at the man, a sinister smile planted on his lips. "You shall be hanged by the neck until dead Friday hence, and may God have mercy on your soul."

The brave prisoner neither opened his mouth nor dropped his steady gaze from the judge's.

"Remove this man!" The judge waved his thick hand, heavy-laden with gems. Yet the prisoner continued to glare at him, his eyes ablaze as if casting a curse on him before they were closed forever. The magistrate squirmed in his seat and looked away until the soldiers escorted the man from the room.

Merrick nodded as the prisoner walked by and a flicker of emotion brightened the man's otherwise deadened eyes.

The harsh voice of the clerk of arraigns bade Edmund Merrick to raise his hand and this he did almost mechanically, stepping forward to the bench. A rustle of voices emanated from the hall behind him but soon quieted when the clerk began reciting the list of charges. On and on, the words echoed under the vaulted ceilings, making him a vicious traitor against the most glorious and magnificent King Charles the Second, his natural God-appointed Lord. The charges claimed that by following the wicked intent of his heart, without fear of God or the slightest respect for humanity, he had failed to remain loyal and obedient to the articles of privateering he had signed under the auspices of said Lord.

Merrick could not resist a slight smirk as the tirade continued, now listing more specific crimes such as brawling, drunkenness, rape, villainous thievery, lewdness, the attacking and looting of British merchant vessels, and finally, the attack upon the British warship HMS *Intrepid*.

"I hope we will find you more vocal than the last prisoner," the judge said.

"Oh, I assure you, your lordship, I have never been accused of not being so."

Laughter spread through the crowd, and some of the ladies in the gallery called his name. Merrick turned to acknowledge them. His eyes fell upon those of Reverend Thomas, who stood in the middle of the room. His calm demeanor and gentle smile brought a welcome comfort.

Judge Wilhelm, with annoyance etching his features, looked at Merrick. "I see you have gathered quite a following. But I assure you, your popularity is about to end."

Merrick bowed, smiling.

"Do you find this amusing?" the judge said. His jaw flexed in irritation.

"No, your lordship. I find nothing amusing about this mockery of a trial."

The judge's eyes narrowed, and his jowls flapped with the shaking of his finger. "How dare you address the court in this manner! I am Judge Baron Wilhelm, commissioned personally by King Charles the Second, to be judge and jury at these proceedings. The king himself has great confidence in my intelligent opinion, good sense, and keen discernment in criminal matters, and," he added, leaning forward, his eyes twitching with anger, "I'll not have the likes of you, a common thief and murderer, disgracing the court with your vulgar words."

"Then am I to assume by your own admission that I am already condemned as thief and murderer without so much as a word of defense on my behalf?" Merrick's lips curved in sarcasm.

The judge's face reddened. He grunted. "We will hear your case, and I assure you the truth will be found out, as it always is in my court." He shuffled papers on the bench and called for the first witness, Commodore Henry Norsten of the HMS *Intrepid*.

The commodore marched forward, dressed impeccably, his red coat trimmed with gold buttons down the front and on the sleeves. He wore a collar of white lace, cream-colored stockings, black boots, and a rapier, which hung menacingly at his side. Under his commodore's hat was a neatly curled periwig. He gave Merrick a look of disdain before turning to face the judge.

His story was a simple one. He had been given orders to pursue and capture Captain Merrick, who had recently escaped from the prison at Fort Charles, and bring him back to face charges of piracy. After spotting the rogue pirate ship and signaling quite clearly for Captain Merrick to put the helm down and lie to, the *pirate*—he spoke the word with contempt as he nodded in Merrick's direction—dared to fire a round shot at the HMS *Intrepid.* He said the last phrase as if he were still shocked by the audacity of the action.

"What say you to that, rogue?" The judge gave him an icy smile.

"I would say that he relayed the incident most accurately, your lordship," Merrick said.

Judge Wilhelm's eyebrows shot up, and the other judges murmured amongst themselves. "So you are admitting to firing on a British warship?" he asked, his brow furrowed.

"That I am, your lordship."

Looking at his compatriots and accepting their nods of agreement, the baron shrugged. "Then I daresay there is no more to be said in this case. The villain has confessed."

A low grumble erupted in the crowd.

The judge opened his pale lips to pronounce sentence. Merrick's voice rang across the room. "I said I fired on the HMS *Intrepid*, indeed I did, but 'twas only a warning shot. I did not hit her."

"That you are a poor shot makes no difference to this court." The judge chuckled in a haughty tone.

"If I had wanted to hit her, your lordship, she would be at the bottom of the Caribbean."

A ripple of laughter crossed the galleries but was immediately silenced by the stern voice of the crier.

Judge Wilhelm's face contorted, his lips twisting in fury. He patted his moist forehead, shooting a hard gaze at Merrick.

"It was my intent to warn the ship," Merrick continued calmly, "but when I saw she would not relent, I raised my white flag and surrendered willingly, without another blast from my cannon." Merrick nodded toward the commodore, who still stood next to him. "Inquire of the commodore, if you like."

The judge looked at the British commander. "It is as he says," the officer admitted, reluctance edging his voice.

"I have never fired upon a British ship with intent to harm, your lordship," Merrick offered.

Judge Wilhelm glanced down at the papers on his bench. Sweat formed in beads on his forehead. He adjusted his periwig. For a moment, Merrick thought the aged reptile had found a small spot in his embittered, cold heart where a speck of justice survived, but his hopes were crushed when the judge looked up.

"Nevertheless, there are the other charges to account for," Judge Wilhelm said sharply, his demeanor changing instantly from uneasiness to hardened resolution. "The merchandise from a sunken British vessel was found on board your ship, I believe?"

He looked at Moodyford, who nodded and added, "Yes, several articles, including the ship's bell with HMS *Challenger* engraved on it."

"They were placed on my ship without my knowledge," Merrick intervened.

"Silence, you scoundrel!" the judge's voice boomed, his face livid. "You will speak only when spoken to." Composing himself, he turned to Moodyford. "How did you come by this information?"

"His first mate, a man named Kent, informed me of Captain Merrick's traitorous activities. I sent men straight away to the *Redemption* to ascertain the situation."

The judge nodded. He looked at Merrick, his eyes simmering pools of hatred. "What say you to that, *pirate*? And don't waste the court's time with more vain subterfuge."

"Master Kent betrayed me, your lordship. He placed those articles on board my ship. My crew—Jackson, Brighton, Royce, to name a few—will testify on my behalf."

"Come now, sir, are these your only witnesses? *Pirates?*" The judge laughed, and the other men on the bench joined him.

Merrick lifted a mocking brow. "You took the word of a pirate to condemn me."

The crowd burst into a clamor of protests that could not be quieted even after several attempts by the crier. Judge Wilhelm scowled down at the unruly mob. Pointing a finger in their direction, he threatened them with imprisonment, and one by one, their voices stilled.

"Was there ever such a devilish impudent villain as this?" His voice raged across the hall. "It is truly a wonder to me that your neck has survived the noose this long."

A deep voice reverberated from the back of the hall. "And a wonder to me, sir, that you have survived in the king's court as judge for equally as long."

Gasps burst from the crowd and all heads turned. The judge looked up, outrage and shock imprinted on his face.

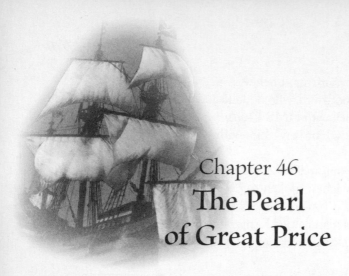

Chapter 46
The Pearl
of Great Price

Charlisse sat on the sandy beach admiring the Creator's artwork as He splashed oranges, reds, pinks, and yellows across the horizon in an exquisite masterpiece of light and color. Each sunset was more magnificent than the one before. She could not remember it being quite so beautiful when she had been marooned on this same island nearly four months ago, but perhaps it was because she now believed in a loving God, and everywhere she looked, there were glimpses of His radiance.

Each evening she sat in the same spot watching the sun go down, praising her Father in heaven and lifting Merrick into His safe hands. Yet each evening the same fears crept into her heart, testing her faith to the breaking point. Would she ever see Merrick again? She was beginning to have her doubts. He had told Sloane to wait only two months before taking her to the Americas, and that time was coming to a close.

A cool breeze wafted in from the sea, lifting her errant curls. Pulling her knees to her chest, she wrapped her arms around them and watched the final rays of the sun disappear. Bit by bit, the luminous colors faded to gray as the encroaching night pushed them back—unwilling to give up its appointed time to reign.

She sighed, watching the bubbling foam atop the waves as they spread out on shore. This was the very beach she had crawled up on five months ago, battered and beaten, both outside and in, a little girl, lost and afraid, running from life—running from God. But the Almighty had rescued her in every way possible. Now she felt like a new person—like her life had begun afresh.

She lacked only one thing—Merrick. Her heart cried out for him. For weeks after she had watched him sail away to confront the British frigate, she'd cried out to God, pleading with Him to bring Merrick back to her. When no answer had come, she had shuffled around the island for days in a frustrated depression, unable to speak to anyone—especially God.

One night, after an endless day of weeping and self-pity, Charlisse had plopped onto the beach, exhausted, and lain down on the sand. As she reclined, too tired to move and too despondent to care, the rising tide brought the gentle touch of a wave to caress her face. She opened her eyes to find a battered gray shell lying before her, its halves parted at the center. She sat up and pried it open, slicing a finger on the sharp edges of its mouth. Inside, a white pearl glimmered atop a throne of slimy gray flesh. Charlisse plucked it from its home, remembering a story from the Bible about a pearl of great price and a man who had sold everything he owned to buy it. At that instant, a lazy moon ascended from the horizon and showered its light onto the pearl. A soft voice echoed within her, telling her she was the pearl the story spoke of and Christ was the One who had given everything to possess her. He was the only one who could truly fill the emptiness in her soul. He was the only one who would never leave her, who loved her beyond measure. No man—not even Merrick—could ever do that.

In the days that followed, an incredible peace flooded over her as she allowed God to fill her with His love and take His rightful place as her one, true Father. No longer plowing around the island in a cloud of gloom, she started helping the pirates search for food. They taught her to fish and showed her which plants were edible and which ones to avoid. She even helped Sloane teach his monkey—which he'd named Solomon —to climb palm trees and shake coconuts loose from their top branches.

Soon, however, they would be leaving, for the repairs on the *Hades' Revenge* were nearly done, and Merrick's two months were almost spent. Sloane said he would take her to the Americas, to the colony of Carolina. Merrick had instructed him to settle her there on a small estate using the treasure the captain had accumulated over the years. She felt uneasy at the thought of starting over in a strange place, not knowing a soul, but she knew God would be with her and His plan was best.

Yet she still missed Merrick. The worst part was not knowing what had happened to him. Even with assurances from Sloane that he would seek Merrick after settling her, she feared for his safety. She prayed God would protect him and not allow him to rot away in prison or end his life at the end of a rope like a common criminal. Most of all, she prayed they could be together, but she knew she would have to accept God's will.

As each day went by with no sign of her pirate captain, her heart sank lower and lower. She hoped she would have the faith and strength to go on without him.

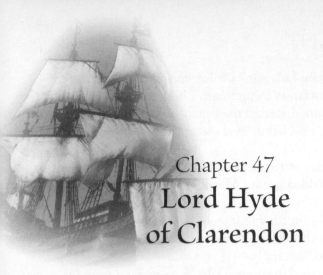

Chapter 47
Lord Hyde
of Clarendon

Merrick glanced over his shoulder at the intruder, feeling his heart clench and the blood drain from his face at the sight of him. In walked the large, imposing man in a royal suit of black camlet, edged in silver lace. His tall, thick boots made an ominous thud as they crossed the hall of justice. A gold-encrusted sword hung at his side, his hand resting idly on the hilt. He proceeded, scanning the judge's bench with dark, handsome eyes and an austere expression. Under his wide-brimmed hat, from which a large purple plume extended, his thick graying hair was pulled back in cavalier style. Two men in similar exquisite dress followed close behind him.

He marched gracefully toward the front bench, a wave of gasps flowing in his wake. Merrick turned forward again. Judge Wilhelm stared aghast at the man, momentarily silenced.

The man halted abruptly beside Merrick. He turned briefly and winked at the captain. Merrick gave him a puzzled look. Finally the judge, regaining his composure, demanded, "Who, pray tell, are you, sir? And how dare you interrupt these proceedings."

The man smiled briefly, but his eyes held a steady, authoritative gaze. "Lord Edward Hyde, first Earl of Clarendon, at your service." He bowed. The room exploded in a multitude of astonished exclamations.

The judge's eyes widened, and his complexion blanched to a sallow hue. Merrick thought it possible the poor man would faint on the spot. The other judges whispered among themselves.

"He's the king's chief advisor," a voice whispered behind Merrick.

"Also a personal relation by marriage, I hear," a man added.

Judge Wilhelm stood, circled the bench, and came to bow before the Earl, placing a kiss on his hand. "A thousand pardons, my lord, I did not know it was you."

Lord Hyde quickly retrieved his hand. "Then you also did not know that this man," he nodded toward Merrick, "this *pirate* as you call him—this rogue—is my son."

Gasps, followed by the rumble of muted voices, sprang from the mob—some laughed, others cheered, some shouted obscenities at the judge.

Lord Hyde turned toward his son and smiled.

Judge Wilhelm gaped in stunned silence, unmoving from his spot.

"What on earth are you doing here, Father?"

His father's unexpected intrusion was just as much a shock to him as it was to the judge. After all, he had not spoken to him for over five years, and the years before that were filled with nothing but quarrels and rebellion.

"Isn't it obvious?" his father replied, one brow lifted. "I have come to save you." He nonchalantly brushed some dirt from his elegant coat. "I cannot have the son of Edward Hyde being hung like a common pirate, can I?"

The crier silenced the crowd at the command of Governor Moodyford, who had left his place on the bench and rushed over to meet the earl, excitement glittering in his eyes. He stood behind Judge Wilhelm, waiting his turn, but the judge remained unmoving, his quivering jaw hanging agape.

Finally, the judge found his voice. "This man is your son?"

Lord Hyde faced the judge again. "Yes, as I have said, and"—he reached within his doublet, withdrawing papers—"I have the honor of informing you, as is proclaimed in these documents signed by King Charles the Second himself"—he handed them to Judge Wilhelm—"that the king has been informed of Captain Merrick's great feats of courage and fortitude in the pursuit and capture of several Spanish vessels in the West Indies, thereby doing a great service to the crown. Henceforth, any current charges of piracy will be dropped and his immediate release procured."

Cheers burst from the crowd, and the judge, pale and sweating, glanced quickly through the documents. With shaking hands, he handed the royal parchments to the other judges for their perusal. Then, bowing graciously to Lord Hyde, he nodded to the crier to dismiss the court and turned to take his leave.

Merrick whispered in his father's ear, and the earl's voice echoed across the hall before the judge could slither out through the side door. "Lord Wilhelm, a word, if you please." When the judge returned, ashen-faced, Lord Hyde brought up the matter of the prisoner who had been tried prior to Merrick. He insisted the man be given a fair trial with proper witnesses and informed the ill-fated judge that he intended to assign one of the king's own judicial aides to co-preside over each trial to ensure that justice was served in the future.

The crowd dispersed, and Lord Hyde graciously talked to the governor and deputy governor of Jamaica before turning back to his son.

Merrick stood before his father, not knowing what to expect.

"Faith, you do look like a pirate!" the earl exclaimed.

A familiar feeling of diffidence resurrected from Merrick's childhood and pressed down on his shoulders. He looked down at his slovenly appearance—his wild hair hanging loose, his dirty, torn clothes—and he felt like a little boy again, caught playing in the mud.

Chuckling, his father placed his hands on Merrick's shoulders and squeezed them. "And you've grown into quite a man, too."

Merrick stared at the man before him, remembering only the tyrant who had offered him insults and orders, never love or praise, remembering a childhood of never doing well enough, never being enough, to please him. But this man seemed different. Something had softened in him.

"I suppose I should thank you for what you've done, but I daresay I don't understand why or how," Merrick finally spoke.

"As to the why, well, you're my son," his father replied with a gleam in his eye. "As to the how..." He looked up as Reverend Thomas approached. "I believe this is the man to answer that."

The reverend bowed to the earl. Merrick soon discovered that his friend had sent a post to his father as soon as Merrick had been imprisoned the second time—informing him of the dire situation in which his son had found himself. Also included in the letter was a copy of the Letters of

Privateering that Merrick had signed and a list of his accomplishments on the Spanish main in the name of England.

Merrick shook Thomas's hand and embraced him. "Once again, you have saved my life."

" 'Twas nothing," the reverend said. He held Merrick back and looked at him with the affection of a father. "But now I must take my leave. There is another pressing matter requiring my attention." He put on his hat and nodded to the earl, who bowed graciously in return.

"Always saving the world," Merrick said.

"One soul at a time." Thomas grinned with a wink. Then turning, he left.

After Merrick's chains were removed, father and son sauntered out of the courthouse. Lord Hyde put his arm around his son. "We have a bit of catching up to do, do we not?" A grin caught the edge of his mouth.

Merrick, still a bit puzzled over the change in his father, nodded.

"Now, what's this I hear about a lady?" His father leaned toward him, a sly smile curling his lips. "Lady Charlisse Bristol, I believe?"

A tiny crab skittered across the sand by Charlisse's feet, reminding her of her first night on this island so long ago. She stood, sighing. It was almost dark, and Sloane would be worried if she didn't return to camp soon. Wiping the sand from her shabby dress, she headed toward the jungle at the edge of the beach. Their camp was located on an inlet on the other side of a small patch of forest—the same sandy shore where she had stumbled into Merrick's camp, half starved and delirious with fever. She smiled, remembering how petrified she'd been when she'd heard his deep voice and looked up to see his immense frame towering over her.

Charlisse stumbled through the tangled vegetation, tripped over a rock in the darkness, and regretted delaying her return. Her heart and mind were full of wonderful memories of Merrick, and though they caused an endless ache in her soul, she refused to chase them from her thoughts. He was a part of her now and always would be.

Blazing firelight from the camp lit the remaining way, and she quickened her pace. As she approached the edge of the forest, a deep voice echoed through the trees, "Alas, what rare beauty hides beneath this ragged disguise?" Excitement coursed through her.

Charlisse whirled around. Merrick leaned casually against a tree, the features of his handsome face, along with the curve of his smile, illuminated by the firelight in the distance. She froze, afraid to move, lest the vision disappear.

"Forgot about me already?" he asked.

She rushed into his arms and nearly knocked him over. Burying her face in his doublet, she wept tears of joy.

"I must admit, I didn't think my presence would make you quite so sad," he said in a teasing tone, embracing her.

Stepping back, Charlisse looked up at him. She touched his face, ran her fingers through his hair, then squeezed the muscles of his arms. "You're real."

"That I am, milady." He wiped the tears from her face.

"It's been so long." Charlisse's voice quivered. "I thought I'd never see you again."

"I told you I'd come back for you, didn't I?" He leaned down and kissed her. She returned his kiss with all the passion and longing that had been building up for so long, enjoying the spicy taste of him, his salty smell, the scratch of his stubble on her cheek. At first his touch was tender. Then pressing her against him, he kissed her like a man consumed by a desperate hunger.

Breathless, Merrick pushed her away from him and gazed into her eyes. "You captivate me, milady. I fear I am lost to your charms forever."

Charlisse smiled. "And I yours, milord."

Merrick took her hand in his. "I've come to take you back to Port Royal."

A spike of fear sped through her. "But the British are looking for you."

He shook his head. "Not anymore. I've been acquitted." He brushed a wayward curl from her face.

"But how—"

"It's a long story," he interrupted, "meant for another time. But right now I have something to ask you. . . ." He gave her a solemn look, but the slight curve of his lips betrayed him.

Charlisse waited, her heart bubbling with joy. It didn't matter what he wanted. He was alive and he was here. She gazed at him and for the first time noticed his elegant apparel. He wore a black velvet doublet lined down the front with buttonholes edged in silver and a silk shirt open at the neck. Breeches of black taffeta clung to his muscled legs. The pants were tucked inside leather boots that reached his knees. His unruly hair had been combed and tied behind his neck. He seemed apprehensive—*or was it nervous?*—a most uncommon condition for a fearless pirate.

Pulling a cord from around his neck, he broke it and slid something off into his hand. He knelt on the sandy soil of the forest floor and looked up at Charlisse. Her confusion gave way to ecstasy when he opened his hand, revealing a diamond-encrusted gold band that sparkled in the firelight.

"Lady Charlisse Bristol, will you do me the honor of becoming my wife?"

Charlisse's hand flew to her mouth. Elation flared in her heart. "You want to marry me?" she asked, unable to believe her ears and wanting so desperately to hear him say it again.

Merrick nodded. "With all my heart."

Charlisse glanced from his loving, hopeful eyes to the glittering ring in his hand, savoring the precious moment, storing it deep in her mind, where it began to soothe the wounds from her childhood.

"Don't leave my pirate heart adrift at sea." Merrick's dark eyes twinkled. "What is your answer, milady?"

Charlisse smiled. "My answer is yes." She giggled. "Yes!"

Merrick stood and slipped the exquisite ring on her finger. "It was my mother's," he said, taking her in his arms.

"I shall cherish it forever," Charlisse whispered.

"As I shall cherish you." Merrick held her in silence for several moments then whispered in her ear, "Reverend Thomas is ready to marry us as soon as we return. And my father awaits us also."

"Your father?" She looked up at him.

"Yes, another long story." He grinned.

Charlisse gazed into his dark eyes. He was alive. He was here, and he loved her. Soon, she would be his wife. How the Lord had blessed her! They had been through so much in the past months. But through it all, God had been faithful. It really was true that all things worked together for good for those who loved God and were called according to His purpose.

His lips met hers again. Charlisse felt all her fears drift away as she yielded to his touch. She could have stayed all night in his arms, hidden within the tropical maze, but the worried voice of Sloane soon thundered through the trees. Hand in hand, the two lovers emerged from the dark web of tangled forest and burst into the camp, much to the old pirate's delight.

In the morning, aboard the *Redemption*, Merrick stood behind Charlisse on the foredeck, his strong arms wrapped around her. The mighty ship rose and plunged a steady course through the tumultuous azure waters, heading straight into the most glorious sunrise Charlisse had ever witnessed. It was the dawn of a new day—the dawn of a new life. With God at the helm of her ship and Merrick by her side, she saw nothing but blue skies and glorious adventures ahead.

Holding her close, Merrick nibbled on her neck, his warm breath caressing her. "I love you, Charlisse," he said in a deep voice that sent warm waves radiating through her.

She turned her head and smiled. He pressed his lips upon hers. As the *Redemption* gently rolled through the Caribbean waters, Charlisse finally understood the meaning of the mighty ship's name. Standing in the warm, protective arms of the man she loved, blessed and cared for above all her expectations by the God of the universe, she thanked the Lord, her new heavenly Father, for the redemption of her soul, the redemption of her life, and the redemption of her heart.

ABOUT THE AUTHOR

M. L. TYNDALL

MaryLu Tyndall spent her early years basking on the balmy shores of South Florida, where she grew to love the sea and the tropics. After attending Oral Roberts University in Tulsa, Oklahoma, she moved to California and graduated from San Jose State with a degree in math. During the next fifteen years, she worked for a software company, got married, and started a family. She also began pursing a writing career, and her love of history sent her delving into the past through books and movies, in search of fascinating stories and heroic characters. MaryLu now writes full-time and currently lives in California with her husband, six children, and three cats. For more information on MaryLu and her upcoming releases, please visit www.mltyndall.com